WITH
PREJUDICE

WITH PREJUDICE

ROBIN PEGUERO

GRAND CENTRAL
PUBLISHING

New York   Boston

Grand Central Publishing
Hachette Book Group
1290 Avenue of the Americas, New York, NY 10104
grandcentralpublishing.com
twitter.com/grandcentralpub

First Edition: May 2022

Grand Central Publishing is a division of Hachette Book Group, Inc. The Grand Central Publishing name and logo is a trademark of Hachette Book Group, Inc.

The publisher is not responsible for websites (or their content) that are not owned by the publisher.

The Hachette Speakers Bureau provides a wide range of authors for speaking events. To find out more, go to www.hachettespeakersbureau.com or call (866) 376-6591.

Library of Congress Cataloging-in-Publication Data
Names: Peguero, Robin, author.
Title: With prejudice / Robin Peguero.
Description: First edition. | New York : Grand Central Publishing, 2022.
Identifiers: LCCN 2021041294 | ISBN 9781538706282 (hardcover) | ISBN 9781538706305 (ebook)
Subjects: LCGFT: Thrillers (Fiction) | Legal fiction (Literature)
Classification: LCC PS3616.E3534 W58 2022 | DDC 813/.6--dc23/eng /20211222
LC record available at https://lccn.loc.gov/2021041294

ISBNs: 9781538706282 (hardcover), 9781538706305 (ebook)

Printed in the United States of America

LSC-C

Printing 1, 2022

For Kris,
my protector from birth,
and all of my reasons,
who loves and supports me—
without prejudice.

00 | GETTING TO SEVEN

The five men and two women of the jury sat in silence. The air-conditioning rattled and hummed, blowing frigid air their way. Juror number eight hugged herself. The soundtrack from the city below—wailing sirens, honking horns, and screeching tires—floated in past a closed window. Juror number one added to the cacophony by rapping his fingers against the top of the oblong, mahogany table that swallowed the space with its grandeur. Carved into its side, within eyesight of only juror number sixteen, were the words "Set me free." He fingered the grooves with his thumb.

"What do you do?" juror number one asked juror number three. The speaker was white, in his fifties, and portly. He smiled broadly and nodded compulsively as others spoke, whether he agreed with them or not.

"I'm a tax collector," said number three. The responder was black, of the same age, but heavier in build. He sat with his arms resting on the rolls of fat collecting at his stomach. He wore tiny glasses that all but disappeared on the enormity of his round face.

"Wow," said number one with a chortle. "You're hated as much as defense attorneys."

Number three raised his eyebrows.

"Or, depending on your politics, as much as prosecutors."

Number one cut his laughter short. Discomfort flashed noticeably in his eyes. But he smiled through it and bobbed his head in polite agreement.

The strangers eventually ran out of meaningless things to say. The sound of the long hand on the outdated clock on the wall rifled through the air, a click every minute. The seconds between—at first, a breezy sixty—grew longer as time and patience wore thin.

"We all know he's guilty."

The declaration came from juror number six, loud enough to carry to all of the room's occupants. A significant number of them shuffled uneasily in their seats.

"The judge instructed us not to talk about the case yet," number three shot back.

Defensively, number six looked down at her rose-painted fingernails. "I'm just trying to save us time. Get us home at a reasonable hour. If we can get a feel for where we're at now, we can shorten our deliberation."

Juror number eight extended her right hand to number six—shoulders now sagging, chest deflated—and laid it over her forearm. The fingers were chilled, but the gesture was warm. Number eight had a daughter of similar age.

"She was just trying to help," number eight said, tight-lipped, her eyes locked with the girl's. "It wouldn't hurt to get an early count."

Juror number seventeen cleared his throat. He was a lawyer, a fact he had mentioned several times. His conspicuous cough redirected their attention. He answered with self-effacing diligence. "Before we begin deliberations in earnest, the judge will ask us to elect a foreperson. We can just do that now and save time that way."

No one dared make eye contact with him again, lest he take it as an indication that he ought to nominate himself. Instead, most eyes moved to number one: the oldest, a man, and a *white*, old man at that. Even the progressives in the room tapped into muscle memory, turning instinctively for leadership to the one who most looked the part.

Number one smiled, acknowledging the vote of confidence. But his grin soon faded as anxiety took root.

"I don't know," he stammered.

He looked to the side. "How about my friend over here?" he said, placing a plump hand on the shoulder of number three. "He's awfully professional."

Number three's eyes softened behind their spectacles. The compliment was both surprising and flattering.

"And I think it would *look* better."

The sharp but fleeting pain of a microaggression sliced through the black man like lightning. His heart rate accelerated, his breathing came short and staccato, and the hairs on his arms stood at attention. But seconds later, his vitals returned to stasis. He said nothing. It was forgotten.

A wave of nods surged down the table. By murmured assent, number three became the black face of the jury.

Earl Thomas bought his first car at age twenty-eight. It was foreign. Its black steel gleamed in the South Florida sun. That was by design. Earl washed it just about every day. He had kept his focus trained in high school, his nose buried in boring books filled with technobabble in college, and his head down thereafter as he inconspicuously ascended the ladder at his nondescript job working for nondescript bosses. All for that car. He loved that car. It was his status symbol.

Ten thousand miles later, he kept it pristine. It looked just like new.

Officer Lance Hollister noticed.

He flipped on the blues and reds, triggering their accompanying wail. Unsurprising to Earl, but nonetheless startling. The routine was frequent enough that he ought to have grown used to it. But he never did. The same physiological response of the heart, lungs, and nerves in a fritz seized him. It made him seem nervous, and therefore suspicious, which in turn escalated his nerves and aura of suspicion.

Officer Hollister lingered in his car. A favorite song of his was a minute from ending on the radio. He was pre-filling tickets: one for no seat belt, the other for a malfunctioning taillight. He had initiated this streetside confrontation, but he, too, felt tightness in his chest, his overworked vital organs reeling with adrenaline.

The slow walk to the suspect's window—punctuated by the deliberate beat of boot on asphalt—marked a tense countdown. The early seconds of the interaction set the tone. Earl had no way of knowing which side of the heavy hand of the law would greet him: the rough, calloused back hand or the smooth, soft palm. Officer Hollister was similarly at an informational deficit. He spent the walk, and indeed the whole of his working day, wondering if he was marching to his death.

Officer Hollister fingered his gun compulsively. Earl caught sight of the tic in his side-view mirror.

"Do you know why I pulled you over?"

The question was not condescending. It was strategic. An answer might include crimes unknown to the patrolman. *I'm sorry, Officer. I know my license is suspended.* Or, *There's only a baggie of weed in the center console. Nothing more.* Better yet, the officer gets to quote the admission in his report as a so-called spontaneous statement. Merely delete mention of the opening inquiry. No Miranda rights necessary; admissible at trial.

Earl had a caustic answer at the ready, one he was prepared but failed to bury deep in his belly: "Not an earthly clue, sir." The words discharged from his lips with unexpected defiance. Even as his grip trembled on the steering wheel, Earl's voice took on a steely resolve.

Officer Hollister whipped back as if physically struck. He grew visibly annoyed.

"Get out of the car, *son*."

Earl sneered, sucking at his teeth in disbelief. Noisily, he unfastened his belt, flipped up the lock, and swung open his car door. The imposition was aggravating, but not more than being called "son." At twenty-five and fresh-faced, Officer Hollister was three years his junior and looked it.

"Up against the car."

Earl turned grudgingly in a half circle, laying the side of his face and the front of his pressed suit against hot metal. Officer Hollister dug his elbow painfully into his upper back.

"Spread your legs."

Earl obeyed. Methodically, the officer patted him down, sliding his hands haltingly along the outline of his body. Passersby in cars and on foot slowed down to peer at the suspect—all white faces and rapt, wide eyes. *I wonder what that man did.* His eyes locked with theirs. It was humiliating.

Turning up nothing, the officer flipped him by the shoulder, bringing their faces inches apart.

"You don't have any weapons or drugs in your car, do you?"

Ever so slightly, subtle enough to go unperceived, the defeated man shook his head in the wind.

"You'd have no problem letting me search, then?"

Earl found his voice.

"Are you asking for my consent?"

"Are you *making* me ask for your consent?"

With a tight, pained smile, Earl relented. "No."

He watched from the curb as the officer rifled through his car. He snapped open the glove compartment. He popped open the trunk. He had Earl input the combination to his briefcase—09, 11, 47—to find nothing but papers with equations and numbers scrawled on them. Satisfied, or perhaps ultimately not, the officer culminated the affair forty-eight minutes after it began by handing Earl the two previously filled tickets.

"False alarm," Officer Hollister explained. "But inconvenience is a small price to pay for safety. You understand."

Earl's silence was intentional. He inspected the two citations.

"Have a good evening, *son*."

Officer Hollister walked away, past Earl's car and halfway to his own, but the suspect's final quip cut him short, midstride. Earl had finished reading his tickets.

"What's wrong with my taillight?"

The officer gritted his teeth. His muscles tensed. He turned and walked back. Upon reaching the trunk of Earl's car, he paused, drew his baton from his belt, and—in one swift, forceful motion—slammed its black body into the light. It shrieked as it shattered. Red glass rained down onto the pavement.

"It's busted," Officer Hollister said, then left.

Earl recounted the experience to his wife later that day with verve and indignation. She waited until he was done to respond.

"It's always cat and mouse with these white folk. A modern game of master and slave."

Earl said nothing. He purposely didn't correct her. He didn't tell her that Officer Hollister was black.

Mr. Earl Thomas, the foreperson, tore a blank sheet of paper into sevenths.

"We'll gauge the temperature of the room, but it'll have to be by secret ballot, so none of us are influenced one way or the other," he directed. "Write guilty or not guilty, fold once over, and hand it back."

Solemnly, they jotted down another man's fate. Mr. Thomas collected the slips of paper and tallied the vote, sans pomp or circumstance. Five guilty. Two not.

"Well," juror number one sang, making eye contact with both Mr. Thomas and juror number eleven. "We have our work cut out for us, don't we?"

He had directed his words to the panel's two black jurors.

Number eleven openly sighed, eyes rolled to the ceiling. Mr. Thomas smiled emptily.

Number one had been only half right. Mr. Thomas had, in fact, been a guilty vote. It was juror number seventeen, the white lawyer, who represented the second not guilty.

"One of us is the alternate," number seventeen volunteered. "There can't be an odd number of us. When it's actually time to deliberate, they'll cut one of us loose."

When Mr. Thomas next spoke, the deep bass of his voice commanded the room's attention. "I'm a numbers guy," Mr. Thomas began. "For now, it's seven. We get to seven, we go home. Let's get to work."

01 | THE STATE WEARS HEELS

Sandy Grunwald is always in a hurry. It's pure affect. She finds that men take her more seriously that way.

"A made man always has somewhere to be," the most important man in her life once told her. "Have somewhere to be, Sandy."

Rumor has it the Honorable Jack Grunwald, ferociously protective of his only daughter, instilled this idiosyncrasy in her merely so that prospective suitors could not—literally—keep up. True to form, at twenty-nine, Sandy remains conspicuously single, singularly wed to her work as a prosecutor.

She bolts down the slick sidewalk made wet by a seconds-long sun shower, leaving an intern struggling to keep up with her and the trail of words she slings over her shoulder.

Sandy speaks in a perennial hurry, too. This quirk, conversely, has not paid professional dividends. In meetings, she has often sprinted through brilliant proposals to little fanfare from her colleagues, only to hear those same ideas immediately parroted back by slow-speaking, faux-contemplative male counterparts to a roaring reception.

"I won't apologize for having thoughts and expressions that

aren't tempered by the general malaise that seems to afflict the male sex," she complains, but never too loudly, and only to other women.

On this day—the day the man she sought to condemn to prison for life met the six arbiters of that decision—she doesn't seek the company of women. At least, not too many of them.

"Women are liberal. Women have sympathy, compassion, *feelings*—all virtues in the real world that are of absolutely no use to us in the gallows of that jury room," she instructs. "Men have no heart. You want your father on that panel. Better yet, you want your grandfather. The older, the better. You want to see gray."

Her breathless protégé scribbles away—capitalizing and then circling the word *gray* five times over—as she avoids bumping shoulders with the slow-moving crowd in Sandy's wake.

"But what of the sexual assault charge? Won't we want women for that?" the girl offers.

Sandy sneers. As a novice prosecutor, Sandy had once ecstatically chosen a jury of all women to sit in judgment of a college freshman who had held down a girl against her will and ejaculated on her back. The six girls returned a verdict of not guilty. Her insides had wilted at having to call and tell the victim—who had broken down in violent sobs on the stand—that the jury had simply disbelieved her. Her howling on the other end of the line sounded like that of an injured animal. *Never again*, she told herself. At least one man would serve on every one of her juries.

Cocooned in the company of women, the jurors had felt safe reprimanding a girl who had naively invited her attacker into her dorm room in the first place. All it would have taken was one man, she was convinced, to have made an off-color remark, and the women would have rallied together, reminded of the injustices of womanhood.

"OK. So we remove women," the intern concludes.

Sandy whips around, leaning down and into the girl with stern eyes and a hushed voice.

"Absolutely not. That's illegal," she reproaches, peering around for eavesdroppers. "We listen to their words. What they say. We strike jurors based on that. Make sense?"

The girl nods, the doublespeak unresolved in her mind.

Sandy reengages her power stride, flashing her badge and waltzing past security at the attorneys' entrance to the court-house. The intern wrestles with her purse and fumbles with producing her own, less glamorous identification. Sandy keeps talking.

"You'll see how the defense will jump up and down and holler every time we propose to strike a black juror. 'Batson! Batson!' they'll yell. Some of my colleagues get offended. 'I'm not racist!' they whine. I don't get offended. I always tell them, 'You *are* racist. We're all racist. There are very real, entrenched structural disadvantages that African Americans face in our society.' I'm a good Democrat. I know the deal.

"But the Batson challenges are disingenuous, and I'll tell you why. For one, African Americans are far more conservative when it comes to criminal justice than they're given credit for. Christian judgment goes a long, long way. As a Jew, I wouldn't know.

"And secondly, I am not striking jurors *because* they're black. If a black panelist admits he does not believe a word any officer says, because he has undergone a lifetime of traffic stops for Driving While Black—and God knows that happens *all the time*—then I am striking him because he has plainly conceded to automatically disbelieving most, if not all, of my witnesses. A white man says the same, and he's off. Conversely, a black man says he loves law enforcement, and he's on. The true test of racist jury picking is if I were to strike a pro-State juror who is black. Now *that* would be a violation!"

Her scribe is catching only every other word. The girl crudely boils down her mentor's speechifying to six words: *Christian black = good. Angry black = bad.*

Sandy sweeps open the courtroom door. High ceilings, painted stained-glass panels, and cold air greet them. She takes a seat at the table farthest from the empty jury box.

"Honestly, I could tell you the jury verdict from the moment the six of them are selected—before any evidence is presented, before any testimony. I'd only need to ask one question: 'Who did you vote for in the last election?' Except for maybe gun cases, acquaintance rape, or crimes against gay or trans victims, you just don't want progressives like me on the jury. You want Republicans. In the end, it's all tribal. For the next couple of hours, the defense attorney and I will ask them every question *but* that, all the while trying to figure out that one answer."

Sandy has her hands and nose in her trial box, sifting through reams of paper, lecturing still.

"The jury is a crew of misfits. The scraps that neither side particularly wanted, those who end up saying nothing of importance or intelligence over the course of several hours of questioning. You don't pick a jury. You're left with a jury. If you're too informed—you know, actually read about the world around you, pick up the newspaper now and again—then you might know too much. The court itself kicks you off. If you're too opinionated—you know, actually have given thought to the prudence of this country's drug policies or formed a well-reasoned conviction against the death penalty—then you might think for yourself too much. It's a race to the bottom, and it's unfortunate."

She takes a breath to force a smile at opposing counsel as they enter, and reengages her pupil at a lower volume. The intern leans in as she furiously takes notes.

"This is how you play the game: I'll find those who are just a wee bit biased in favor of the State, and then pressure them into sounding impartial. Not with the hopes of getting them on the jury. But, if a prosecutor can make a juror predisposed to lean her way *sound* fair, she makes the defense use one of their limited no-questions-asked vetoes on him, instead of getting that juror automatically kicked off for cause. It's a game of burning your opponents' vetoes before having to use up all your own."

A panel of fifty prospective jurors enters the courtroom.

"All rise."

Sandy spends the next fifteen minutes while the judge acclimates the hostile crowd to their new formal surroundings memorizing fifty surnames and assigning faces to them. *Beal. Beal, Jaramillo. Beal, Jaramillo, Miller. Beal, Jaramillo, Miller, Gonzalez-Rincon. Beal, Jaramillo, Miller, Gonzalez-Rincon, Sierra.* It's a small gesture, addressing them by their names without having to look down at her list. But it reveals an invaluable tell of their reaction to her dogged preparedness. Keep those whose expressions betray flashes of admiration. Strike those who seem put off by the extra effort, those who might find her hard-nosed bravura symptomatic of a woman trying too hard, who might call her a "bitch" under their breaths. The second-smartest girl in class is almost always universally preferred to the first.

Hours later, a jury is sworn. The intern has run out of paper on her notepad.

"Do you feel good about this jury?" she asks.

"I do, but you never know in Miami. They will let a man walk for the most incredulous of reasons."

"But these jurors seem particularly fair, don't they?"

"Fair? What's fair? We pretend the chosen six are blank slates, but we all have biases. Theirs were just harder to ferret out. You can drop in another random six from ten years ago, and it wouldn't make a difference. The forces at play are the same.

"One thing I do know: Although the heavy lifting is about to begin, the most consequential part of our work is already over. The evidence will shift those six minds very little. The verdict is more or less written in stone. Take the Rodney King beatings. Those were recorded! And yet the very same images meant two very different things for different people. Take climate change. The facts don't matter. All that matters are the lenses with which people view those facts. And that isn't shaped here in the courtroom. That was shaped long ago, over the course of a lifetime of experiences. We don't know exactly what it will be, and those six might not know it yet, either. But the fate of this defendant is—as of today—already decided."

"Isn't that awful?"

"Horrifying."

Sandy follows an oak tree of a man—tall and wide, with roots for legs—across a yard of wild, untended grass and up to the door of a shack obscured in the brush. Lead Detective Samuel Sterling is dressed inappropriately in slacks, long sleeves, and a tie. The soles of his Italian-leather, size-fourteen shoes sink into the muck as his giant hand slaps at his sweaty neck, trapping and killing a pest. Sam played Division I college football, but he couldn't go pro, and chose instead a career in law enforcement, given his size and stature. The former lineman was far more sensitive, pensive, and analytical than his colleagues, so he rose in the ranks precipitously. He noisily pulls a pair of latex gloves over his hands and offers the same to Sandy.

"They're triple XL. Sorry."

Sandy is more sensibly dressed for the late-night excursion. Her hair is pulled back into a tail and set off by a headband.

She wears sneakers, running tights, and no makeup. She adds baggy, blue, sterile gloves to the ensemble.

Sam sweeps aside the caution tape shaped into an X on the door.

The two step into the black. Sam gropes the air until he catches a dangling metal chain, which he pulls. A bulb flickers on, sending a cascade of yellow to the far stretches of that one room. The air is heavy. It still smells of must—that common, lived-in, stale but not necessarily foul odor that pervades the quarters of bachelors. It's wood all over, floor to wall to ceiling, interrupted by a single diminutive window facing west. No irksome sunrise for late mornings in.

Sandy shuts her eyes as she crosses the threshold. Her heart drums in her chest.

"In a dim, dingy room—out in a farm in Homestead, Florida, where the defendant lives a hermetic—"

"Ten-dollar word," Sam warns. Sandy nods.

"In a dim, dingy room—out in a farm in Homestead, Florida, where the defendant lives a lonely, shut-off life; where no one could hear her scream—that man, sitting right there before you, abducted, raped, and killed a young woman."

Sandy places her body up against the doorway, head against the post.

"Grab my wrists."

Sam cocks his head to the left and squints in hesitation.

"Don't question my preparation, Sterling. You did your job. Now help me do mine. Grab my wrists."

Standing opposite the small prosecutor, he wraps his hands around her slight arms, so thin his fingers fold over themselves.

"He slammed her—*hard*—against the doorframe as he forced her inside," she intones. Her eyes shoot open. "We know that because that's where we found her hair. Isn't that right, Sterling?"

The large man nods, but the question was largely rhetorical. Sandy knows exactly where every piece of evidence was found over two years ago.

"Two strands of her long, brown hair got caught on a doornail. A DNA analyst—who knows exactly zero about the facts of this case or the people involved—will tell you with a remarkable degree of scientific certainty that that hair belonged to the victim. He will testify that the odds of it belonging to anyone else are one in nine octillion. There are only seven billion people on planet Earth. Melina *was* in that room. She didn't leave alive.

"Without letting go of my arms, take me to the table," she commands. Her breath begins to quicken. Panic floods her irises. The slightest tremor accosts her mouth. It unnerves Sam. Nonetheless, gingerly and mutely, he leads her the few feet to a wooden table—four legs, coarse surface, benches flanking its sides. She kicks the nearest bench over and away, tossing herself supine on the table's face.

"He threw her on top of a cold, hard table in that room. He pinned her down. He climbed her. She fought to get free—to no avail.

"Put your weight on me."

"No," Sam finally objects.

He has long been forewarned of Ms. Grunwald's intensity. It draws high praise and high criticism. He has, over the course of their professional relationship, largely acquiesced to her requests, however left field. This is the first he openly flouts.

Resistance is short-lived.

"Detective, just keep me from moving. If I'm to be her advocate, I need to feel what she felt."

He grunts in disapproval but does the bare minimum to hold her in place, pressing his knees lightly against her shins and arresting her shoulders with open palms. Sandy flails, shocked at

15

how little effort on his part paralyzes her completely. Claustrophobia sets in. Her adrenaline spikes, even as exhaustion takes hold and sweat coats her temples. She relents her struggle.

"We know he ejaculated. A stain on that table is tested. It's semen. It's *his* semen. And there is a box of condoms in his room. Sealed, unopened. The exact thirty-six that come from the manufacturer."

"You want to highlight that?"

"I need to prove it's nonconsensual."

"Plenty of consensual sex is done without condoms."

"These two didn't know each other. If this is a supposed one-night stand, no girl is consenting without a condom. Not anymore. Not nowadays. These aren't kids—they're in their late twenties.

"Onto the bed."

In a half circle, Sam swings her to the opposite end of the room, tossing her onto springs that groan beneath her weight.

"It's while she's on his bed that he resolved to kill her. She had rejected his advances earlier in the night. She was now a living, breathing eyewitness to his sexual assault. As she sat up and contemplated making a run for the door, he tightened his grip on a blunt object. He wound it up. He brought it down with brute force against her head."

"Not a drop of her blood found in any inch of this room," Sam counters.

"That's why the bed is brilliant. Sheets can be burned. He scooped her out of there cleanly by undoing his thick bedding and wrapping her in it, like a cocoon. His bed was found stripped of its sheets. It's still bare to this day. The bed he sleeps in. Not even a pillow. Nothing but lumpy, hard mattress."

Sandy pops out of bed and charges out of the shack, leaping onto damp soil. Sam follows.

"He carries her limp body, bundled in his sheets, out to the bed of his truck."

"A small man carrying dead weight," Sam challenges again.

"He's around her same height, yes, but he's stockier, heavier. Plus, his adrenaline is pumping now. It strengthens him. He feels invincible, all-powerful. He thinks he's about to get away with murder. He drives her into the city to dispose of her."

"Forty miles. A body covered just by sheets—out in the open in his truck, visible to the public . . ." Sam pretends to sneer.

"It's late at night. Although this is Miami, the city is asleep," she answers, walking up and staring down—or rather, up at—the towering man.

" . . . And he takes her *into* the city. When there are miles and miles of Everglades nearby—of dark, deep marsh where alligators would undoubtedly do most of the work of swallowing up his crime."

"He's not familiar with the swamp. In crisis, man seeks out the known. He went down his everyday route. He was aware of all the back roads. He went to where the dead bodies go."

Sam smiles, shining white enamel in the darkness.

"You're ready, counselor. How confident are you in every detail of that chronology?"

Sandy shrugs.

"I am confident that that man killed her. Everything else is high-level conjecture. The State can't afford not to have a ready-made answer to every question—especially in a case as circumstantial as this one. I am a storyteller, if nothing else. Stories can't have gaps."

"The other side will have a story, too."

"The best we mere humans can do, after the fact, is come up with competing stories, and ask six strangers to decide which of the two sounds more or less right. The exact, uncontroverted truth—with a capital *T*—is for God now."

*   *   *

Sandy is there—body wrapped in his arms, face buried in his shoulder, his hot breath in her ear—but she isn't there. She oscillates between nascent pleasure and preoccupation. Her frustrated grunts sound identical in either state. Her partner moves for the both of them, exerting himself with strenuous, workmanlike efficiency. The romp is more pragmatic than passionate. The strain of withholding begins to manifest itself in his tortured breathing.

"You can finish, baby," she advises.

"You're not..."

"Not tonight."

She's sure. Sandy's words never leave room for the slightest doubt. She speaks facts into existence.

He complies. Within seconds, he is done. He wilts on top of her. She flips on the lamp. He turns over, stands, cleans up, and dresses himself with his back to her. She pulls the covers up over her naked body.

"Is it the trial?" he asks. She nods, but he can only see the walls and his own shadow. Now wearing pants, but no shirt, he stalks over to her side of the bed and sits down, close to her.

"It was meant to relax you. You know, decompress."

"Yes. Thank you. But I thrive on stress. And it's the night before. It isn't going away."

His eyes dart down in contemplation. It's as if he's summoning his nerve.

"May we kiss?"

"You want to kiss?" she asks, staggered.

He takes her non-reply in the affirmative. He places his lips softly on top of hers—so lightly she can barely feel them—before ardently tugging hers apart with his. He speeds up, and then slows inhumanly down, massaging the back of her head with his hands as they kiss. The shifts in speed come and go abruptly. She feels a swell and a tickle in her chest. The affection is loving—not lustful. It overwhelms her.

"That's enough," she says breathlessly, pulling away.

He springs to his feet, letting loose the unremitted sigh of a deflating balloon. He turns away from her, hands on his closely shaved head, before picking up his glasses and, newly bespectacled, lashing out.

"What are we doing, Sandy? What even *is* this?"

"If it's my stress you're trying to reduce, that question isn't helping."

"Is it your father?"

"Is *what* my father?"

"All of *this*. You letting me inside of you, but not kiss you," he charges crudely. "Is it your father? And that I'm black?"

Her smile is wide and mocking.

"You're not black. You're Dominican."

"It's the same thing."

Domenico Santos is tall, lean, and mostly silent. He's partial, instead, to emoting with his smoldering brown eyes. He saves his words for his stories. He's a print journalist. The martyrdom of parlaying a (meager) living from a dying medium matches his personal victimhood complex. Everything he does in life, he does with melodrama. He moves with romance.

Dom doesn't crack at her quip. He lets his eyes express the gravity of the moment. A short, caustic laugh erupts from her belly.

"You're not kidding," she observes. "You're way off. My father would have loved it if I brought home a black boyfriend— even better, if I married one. His proudest moment in life was voting for Barack Obama. He would have featured our beautiful, mixed children at the front and center of every one of his campaign ads. *No*, the memory of my dead father is not keeping me from you, Dom."

"Then it's you. Or it's me."

"It's definitely *me*," she mutters somberly, running her fingers through her hair.

"Don't do that, Sandy. Don't do the whole 'I'm broken, something is wrong with me' song and dance. Nothing is wrong with you. You're strong. You're deliberate. Nothing you do is by accident. It all has a purpose. You know exactly why you keep me at a distance. It's well plotted and predetermined. You just won't tell me."

She swallows hard, trying but failing to clear the lump in her throat.

"I can be two things at once, you know. I'm not immune to vulnerability. Everyone expects me to be one-dimensional. As if a woman is allowed only to be either levelheaded or an uncertain, emotional mess. But I'm human, and, just like you, I'm both."

He drops to his knees, collecting her hands in his.

"I like you, Sandy. I *might* even love you..."

"Exactly the equivocation every girl wants to hear."

"...if only you'd let me. It's been long enough. Let me in or finally, blessedly, do away with me."

"What is it you want? To go steady or something?"

"Don't patronize me."

"Well, honestly. Do you want some sort of public proclamation? And now? Let everyone know that enterprising *Herald* reporter Dom Santos is sleeping with one of the subjects of his investigation?"

"I'll take myself off of it. I've told you, I don't care about this case!"

"And you very well know that I do!"

He stands and scoffs.

"I know. I know. You get a conviction in such a high-profile case, with all of the media circus watching, and in a few years, you get to be state attorney or governor or president—whatever it is you're trying to be."

"Now, *you* don't patronize *me*."

He avoids her cold stare. Her eyes had begun to shine with hurt. Nothing is more important to her than her ambition—no one, either. Both she and Dom are well aware of that hierarchy. It had merely remained unspoken.

"I have no intention of holding you back," he nearly whispers, turning away. "I'd just like to be there—beside you, behind you—when you accomplish all that I know you will. I'm not an impediment to that."

She nods, but he can't see it.

"I'm going to give you space during this trial. Put me out of your mind. Do your job. I'll do mine. And after it's over, I'll ask you again. And we'll come to a resolution—one way or another."

It sounds like a breakup. Regret stings her heart.

Her phone rings. It's late. She looks over at its lit-up face. It reads simply: Sterling. She rushes to answer it. No greeting.

"What's wrong?"

"I'm not sure how the forensic analyst missed it. The defendant must have been hiding it well. We didn't know he was that savvy with computers."

"Missed *what*?"

Dom hears the alarm in her voice. He lays a comforting hand on her leg.

"The analyst ran another check of the defendant's laptop in anticipation of trial. I don't know the terminology. They were behind a firewall or something. Lots and lots of gay pornography—videos, photos, deleted cookies and links. Just men. Absolutely no women."

"Shit, Sterling."

"Do we need to tell the defense about this?"

"We tell the defense *everything*, always," Sandy rebukes.

Once she's off the phone, quiet pervades between her and Dom. He had overheard it all.

"Just give me a few hours before you print this," she pleads. "I need to alert defense and the judge tonight before it gets out."

He doesn't answer, in part because the request offends his journalistic ethics. But both of them know he will oblige. Nothing is more important to him than Sandy—not even his ambition.

"How bad is this?" he manages to ask.

"Murder is all about motive. On the eve of trial, the State has just lost theirs."

02 | TWO MEN TALK

Jordan Whipple douses his hands in antiseptic before pulling open the jailhouse door. He moves through the lobby and past the metal detectors as he always does, in his perpetual strut, like he has all the time in the world. He chats up the correctional officers as he goes, but only the women and only the black ones. He's a whirlwind of flirty "*sweet peas*," "*honeybuns*," and "*sugars*," feigning a Southern accent as he festoons the greetings on fawning passersby—even though he's from the Midwest. It brings these older black women fleeting delight, but it isn't serious. As he freely mentions in mixed company: "I'm just *not* attracted to African American girls."

The thirty-one-year-old assistant public defender is exactly six feet tall, with parted and gelled light brown hair, alabaster skin, and cerulean eyes. He wears his suit jackets far too tight, meant to highlight prominent glory muscles swelling underneath. Opposing counsel leer at and taunt him out of earshot: "Has '*Bis and Tris*' made it to court this morning?" Jordan overheard the nickname once. He thought it was a compliment.

Jordan studied at a good law school that was not an Ivy League. The average person recognizes the name and is impressed, but Jordan always notes that all of the Ivies rebuffed him. It's a chip he carries on his overdeveloped shoulders. He blames affirmative action. "If a poor, black kid with lower test scores and worse grades gets *my* spot as recompense for slavery that happened—not to him, not by me, and a long, long time ago—well, then so be it," he grudgingly concedes. Academics were not his priority in college, however. He spent most of his time in extracurricular activity: social chair of the College Republicans; goalie on the lacrosse team; member of the Asian American Christian Fellowship, which historically had a sizeable share of white, male attendees cruising for Asian women; and pledge master at his fraternity.

On this day, his soft, brown loafers land noiselessly on the tile floor. The clink of his wedding ring as he idiosyncratically raps it against surfaces resounds through the cavernous halls.

It's early morning and still dark outside. Jordan has already fit in a macronutrient-heavy breakfast, a ninety-minute workout, and a segment of a morning talk show. It dealt with condominium associations in Brooklyn that hold doggie interviews before admitting their owners as tenants and the instructors who charge top dollar to train those pooches to pass. It was an alliterative eight minutes.

"Your client is still sleeping."

"Bring me over to him. I want this beaming, handsome face to be the first thing he sees when he wakes."

Jordan is walked to the human cages. Men in orange are stacked, one on top of the other, behind peeling gray bars. The large windows opposite them face the east, so they have less than half an hour of night—and sleep—left. The accused is alone in a corner, appendages spilled ungracefully on a mattress with no sheets. Beside him, on the floor, the sheets have been balled up and discarded.

"Gabriel! It's showtime."

Gabriel and six others stir and look up. It doesn't take much. Sleep in jail is a persistent light haze. The others lie still as Gabriel gets up and drowsily makes his bed.

"They make you sleep without sheets?" Jordan asks.

"No. I like it this way. Since I was a boy."

Together, escorted by a guard, the men walk silently to an interview room, the shortest of the three in the middle at an unremarkable five foot seven, handcuffed. Once inside, security bolts the door. They sit. Nothing stands between the alleged murderer and his attorney but a wooden table and a button on the wall that illuminates a red light indicating an emergency. It takes the guards an average of four minutes to respond once it's lit.

Jordan breaks into a grin. Gabriel does not.

"This is good, Gabe. This is very good," Jordan nearly sings. Gabriel has never authorized him to use the nickname. "But I will say, bro, you should have told me. There should be no secrets between us. Your life is an open book to me and only me. I've always told you, I need to know everything—*everything*—except for one thing: Did you do it?"

"I didn't."

Jordan raises his hands in protest and interjects loudly over him.

"No, no, no. I don't care about that. I don't want to know that. *That* limits me. *That* doesn't matter. Whether you're *innocent* or not is inconsequential to me. You are *not guilty*, you understand? They're different," he chastises. "But you're accused of raping and killing a—Lord forgive me— quite hot piece of ass, and you neglect to tell me that you're gay?"

Gabriel has a subtle, physiological response to the word. A twitch overruns his left eye.

"I'm not."

25

Jordan lingers in a pregnant pause and chuckles to himself curiously. After collecting himself, he leans over, sympathy in his eyes but condescension in his whisper.

"It doesn't matter to me, buddy. I'm a libertarian. Live and let live, right? How you choose to go about your life is no one's business but yours," he says, before leaning in even closer. "In fact, you'll find some pretty fucked-up shit in my browser history, too. I wouldn't want my wife seeing any of that. Nothing gay, of course. I find the thought of two men together nauseating. I literally couldn't stomach it."

Jordan taps the palm-end of his ring finger on the tabletop, providing a brassy countdown of the seconds Gabriel fails to react, in any capacity, to his optimism. He folds his hands together as if in prayer.

"Do you understand what I'm saying, Gabe? You won't find that sort of stuff on my computer because—as a straight man— not only do I have no curiosity whatsoever, I find it repulsive. No offense," he semi-apologizes, hands wide in the air. "But police found a prodigious amount of the stuff on yours. I'll now have to spend most of my morning looking at it, in fact. That *means* something about you. Something good, in this context. You know what they didn't find? No search terms like 'how to dispose of a body?' or any sadomasochism directed at women. This is *golden* for our defense."

Gabriel finally stirs. Frenzy seizes his brown eyes.

"I don't want anyone to know about it."

Jordan shakes his head slowly, lips pursed, as if the statement is incomprehensible. But he softens—relaxing the muscles in his face, sitting back in his chair, eyes now shaded with concern.

Jordan lays his ringed hand on top of Gabriel's. Alarm strikes Gabriel at the male touch. Heat rises to his face. He doesn't move, although it feels like fire on his skin. Jordan is an affectionate man for someone who intentionally projects so much masculinity. He suspects the move might assist Gabriel in acknowledging his latent attractions.

"Let's make a deal," he offers, smiling impishly. "Outside that courtroom, you can be anyone you want to be. But inside those four walls...Think of it as a performance. How many suits do you own, Gabe?"

"None."

"That's right. But every day of this trial, what will you wear? Suits. Because we're attempting to convey a certain image to the jury. I'm a nice guy. I don't hate anyone. And I certainly respect the hell out of law enforcement officers. But that's not the role I'll be playing. I'm going to be a massive jerk. I'm going to paint every single one of those cops as lying, lazy, corrupt, and potentially racist motherfuckers. Because I get to be with my family at the end of the day and continue being the cop-loving, good-hearted patriot that I am—free and unrestricted in the privacy of my own home.

"That's what I want for you, Gabe. I want you to go home. But for me to succeed at that, you need to let me perform. You must let the show go on. In that courtroom, you will be the outest, proudest gay man any of those people has ever seen. Do you understand that? *That* is how I save your life."

Jordan stands at a lectern just feet away from his opponents when he does battle. They do not face or talk to one another, although they will often speak about one another as if they're not in the same room. When Jordan gets animated, he presses down on the sides of the podium, rocking back and forth on his soles, the muscles in his arms tense and taut. His voice booms and ricochets against the wall, assuming a nasal, high-pitched tenor when he's particularly riled up. Sandy is not as animated. She is cognizant of not appearing shrill, as so-called mouthy women are often labeled. She is a pillar of steadfast restraint.

"Your Honor," Jordan begins, "we are not asking you to delay the trial or declare a mistrial—although this late discovery is a serious prosecutorial violation, and I find it suspect that we found out about it, literally, in the early morning on the very eve of trial. We ask merely to be allowed to use this newly discovered evidence as a matter critical to my client's defense."

"What about that, counsel?" the judge asks, swinging her eyes to the other end of the courtroom like a pendulum. "This *is* very late discovery. You know the drill. I have to assess three things: Was the delay inadvertent or willful? Is the late material trivial or substantial? Lastly, has the defense been prejudiced in its preparation for trial without this information?"

"It certainly isn't willful," Sandy replies. "The defendant himself hid this material—and hid it well—in the recesses of his computer. It was discovered only because forensic analysts ran a precautionary, routine scan in anticipation of trial. The material turned up, fortuitously, now but never before—no one was intentionally keeping it secret. No one but the defendant, of course.

"And it certainly isn't prejudicial to the defendant. If Mr. Whipple believes his client's sexual orientation is material in this case, he had the better part of two years to ask him about it. The defendant knew the material was there. The defendant knows what's in his mind and what's in his heart. If anyone stymied Mr. Whipple from developing a defense around his client's sexual impulses, it's the defendant—and no one else.

"Ultimately, the third question of whether this is substantial or trivial relates to whether it ought to be admissible in this trial. The State argues it should not. The defense has every opportunity—as it should—to cross-examine the forensic analyst about what was *not* found on that computer. No search terms that indicate consciousness of guilt. No depictions of violence against women on his server. That's fine. But to allow *affirmative* testimony of the graphic material found on his computer is not only irrelevant, it's salacious, and it's distracting."

There is a rustling in the crowd. It is the first some of them have learned of the nature of the uncovered evidence, notwithstanding an early morning *Herald* story written by Dom Santos. With a stony glance at the overflowing gallery, the judge cuts short the murmurs.

"*Irrelevant?*" Jordan sneers into his microphone. "My client is charged with the sexual assault of a *woman*. The fact that he is exclusively attracted to men is supremely relevant. His body simply cannot respond that way to a woman. Per my client, it never has."

"Rape is not about sex," says Sandy, nearly spitting the statement out, as if dislodging it from her throat left a rancid taste in her mouth. "It's not about sexual attraction. It's about power. For the defense to claim that a gay man cannot rape a woman is absurd."

"Not impossible—*fine*. But less likely," Jordan remarks as he begins to rock. "And that's the standard, Your Honor. It appears the State has forgotten that it's a very low standard indeed. Does the evidence move the needle—in *any way*, no matter how small—toward or away from guilt? If it does, then that evidence is relevant and, therefore, admissible. This information is exculpatory, no matter how you slice it. How do we know that? We know that because, up until last night, the State's theory of the case was that a loner, outcast kid was romantically rejected—viscerally and embarrassingly—by a pretty girl, so he rapes and kills her. This discovery eviscerates the supposed motive for the killing."

"Firstly, the State has never divulged its theory of the case to defense—nor are we obligated to do so. We have not even presented our opening statements to the jury yet. So I would appreciate it if the defense would allow the State to speak for itself and not impute—"

Jordan cuts her off.

"The local news outlets are calling him the Love-Spurned Slayer. Come on!"

A few spectators groan at the moniker. Sandy takes a beat after the interruption to temper her reaction.

"I do not control what the media writes and the narrative it promulgates," she answers, instinctively looking over at the first row of the gallery where the journalists are penned, including Dom, scribbling madly in his notebook. "Secondly, Mr. Whipple continues to advance the very outdated notion that sexual urges fuel rape. And, if anything, the secret homosexual impulses of his client dovetail well with the theory that a man trying so hard to fit in and appear heterosexual might fly off the handle at yet another rejection from a world that so cruelly makes him shameful of his sexuality. His apparent attraction to men and the sexual assault of a traditionally attractive woman are not inconsonant."

"But that's argument, Ms. Grunwald," the judge intervenes. "You have every right to argue that to the jury. Just as Mr. Whipple has every right to argue the opposite: that his client has no interest in women, and therefore he had no interest in bringing the victim back to his place, no interest in having sexual contact with her of any sort—coerced or otherwise—and no reason to murder her. Is he not correct that his client's potential homosexuality is—however slightly—relevant, at the very least to the sexual battery charges the State has levied? And, if so, how do I legally exclude evidence that is—however slightly—exculpatory without risking a successful appeal, should he be convicted?"

It's a good question. Sandy knows it's a losing battle. She pauses.

"I do concede that that is the proper standard, Your Honor. Does it move the needle toward or away from guilt in any way? And I cannot in good faith argue that the evidence has zero probative value. But that probative value *must* outweigh its prejudicial effect. The evidence is not without prejudice. You can exclude it on that account. Its introduction would devolve into a trial within a trial over the secondary and minor question of how exclusively gay the defendant truly is. So videos of sex between men have been found on his hard drive. Does that somehow exclude the possibility that the defendant is bisexual? Am I now allowed to call potential ex-girlfriends or any woman with whom he has had any sexual intimacy in his life? Am I permitted to call to the stand any friends or acquaintances who have seen him turn his head at a woman passing by or made a comment indicating sexual interest in women? Where does all of this stop?"

Sandy has found a lifeline. She can't help but smile.

"Answer that question for me, Mr. Whipple," the judge says, eyebrows arched. "What would any of that have to do with the price of tea in China?"

The gallery explodes in laughter. The bailiff sternly shushes the crowd as Jordan's palms dig into his podium.

"Because the State itself is questioning the authenticity of my client's homosexuality. Asserting, without proof—as it is wont to do—that perhaps he is bisexual. Or that perhaps he can physically respond to a woman, adverse sexuality notwithstanding. I can tell you, Your Honor, my client cannot force arousal on himself with a woman any more than I can force it on myself with a man."

This time, Sandy intercedes.

"As much as you are clearly dying to inform us of your sexual proclivities, Mr. Whipple, they aren't relevant here."

Laughter again erupts behind them. His face teems with red.

"Quiet, everyone! And do not speak directly to each other, counsel," the judge rebukes. "Go on, Mr. Whipple."

When he next speaks, the bravado has been stripped from his tone. There is a sentimentality, genuine emotion, that takes Sandy aback.

"It has brought my client great pain and shame that he has never been able to respond to a woman the way his religion tells him he should. This has been a lifelong struggle for him. If he could be with women, he would. He would want nothing more in life. But since he was a boy, he knew that that was just not ever going to be possible. In the end, a gay man who cannot enjoy sex with women stands accused of sexually preying on a woman. It's a sad, sad irony. And it would be tragic if the one thing that has been used as a sword against him all of his life is now taken from him when it could be used as a shield to save it."

Peace grips the courtroom. The judge takes in the poignancy of his words.

"I'm ready to rule," the judge finally responds, softly. "I open myself up to criticism that I am splitting the baby—and engaging in lazy judging—but I do believe the law dictates the following result. I am allowing testimony regarding the gay pornography found on the defendant's computer. Much of it is contemporaneous to the time of the murder, down to the very weeks and—it's my understanding—up to the day leading up to the victim's death. That makes it quite probative of the defendant's sexual interests at the time the State is claiming he sexually assaulted the victim to the point of climax. The evidence does not point to mere digital penetration or other forms of sexual assault that do not require male arousal. His semen was found on that table. He has every right, in a trial where his life-long liberty is at stake, to use evidence that arguably supports his lack of sexual interest in women.

"But that's it. I am not interested in presiding over a trial within a trial about the defendant's sexuality. If the defendant testifies, of course, he has every right to share with the jury that he did not make a pass at the victim that night and why—as a gay man—he never would. But, otherwise, we will focus on the events of that night, and the sexual experiences of either the victim or the defendant *before* that night are immaterial."

"All rise."

As the judge exits, the crowd stands and disperses. Sandy organizes her papers and files at the prosecutors' table. Jordan stalks over to her.

"Good argument, Sandy."

"Thanks. You, too."

"How does it make you feel that you're about to spend day after day pummeling a poor closeted gay kid in order to earn a conviction?" he asks, equal parts joke and accusation.

"The same way, I assume, you'll feel about portraying a poor dead girl as a reckless, drunk whore who brought this all on herself," Sandy snaps back, no hint of jocularity. "I know public defenders like to claim the moral high ground, but at the end of this, no one emerges with clean hands. You will malign witnesses and impugn credibility in ways that you know, deep down, are dishonest and unfair. You perpetuate and bolster the system the same as I do—just on a different side. I don't judge you for it. It's your job. But don't consider yourself somehow above it."

Jordan profusely blinks his disagreement. He leans in, as if he's about to share a secret with her.

"That's where you're wrong, Sandy," he whispers, conviction in his eyes. "You're the one trying to condemn a man to a cage for the rest of his life. Don't forget that. You can't bring the victim back from the dead. The only life left to save is his, and I'm the one doing it. I proudly claim the moral high ground."

03 | ME, OR YOUR LYING EYES

After a morning calendar call that featured a loose chicken flying from wall to wall in the courtroom, a sovereign citizen who spoke in third person, and a mystic in all white who placed a hex on his lawyer, the judge takes a shot of cortadito and ushers in the jury. Having tended to its business, the People's Republic of Miami is now ready to try the murder case against Gabriel Soto.

"State: Call your witness."

"The State calls Lisa Murrow to the stand."

The five-foot-two woman briskly walks the length of the courtroom. Her sandals clap against the soles of her feet. The bracelets circling her wrist rattle. She pulls on her purse, bringing it closer to her as she passes the jury box, as if she were walking the streets of a disreputable neighborhood. She doesn't turn to face them. She merely plops down in her seat, crosses one leg over the other—wildly shaking her elevated foot—and waits, lips pursed.

"How *darling*," Sandy mutters before approaching the lectern facing her witness.

The clerk asks her to raise her bejeweled right hand.

"Do you swear to tell the truth, the whole truth, and nothing but the truth?"

"So help me *God!*" she bellows. A few spectators snicker.

"Good afternoon, Ms. Murrow." No reciprocation. Just a straight-lined smile. "Where do you live currently?"

"Jersey."

"And what do you do for a living?"

"Hair."

"I'd like to direct your attention to the evening of November 13, two years ago. Where were you living at that time?"

"South Miami."

"Do you remember that night?"

"Yes."

"Where were you just before midnight?"

"At a bar. The Saloon off of U.S. 1."

Sandy's intern, eyes wide, jots a question down in her note-pad for later: *How OLD is she?*

"Let me ask you right off the bat: Were you drunk?"

"Two vodka sodas. In maybe four or five hours. That's it."

"It's been two years, Ms. Murrow. How can you be sure how many drinks you had that night?"

"South Beach."

"I'm sorry?"

"The diet? You heard of it? I was strictly following the South Beach Diet at the time. Phase one. I was disciplined. Vodka, club soda, lime. Two of 'em. That's it."

"And do you wear glasses for your eyesight?"

"None. Perfect twenty-twenty."

"I'm showing you what's already been admitted into evidence as State's Five. I'm handing you that photograph. Have you ever seen the person it depicts before?"

"Yes, that night. At the bar."

"Had you ever seen her before that?"

"No."

"Let me be clear: You do not know the woman in this picture, the victim in this case?"

"I don't."

"You only saw her this once?"

"Yes."

"On the very night she went missing?"

"Objection! Personal knowledge. Speculation. Hearsay," Jordan rattles off.

"Sustained. Don't answer that, ma'am," the judge orders.

"Ms. Murrow," Sandy begins again, "how is it you remember seeing this girl at a bar on an uneventful Friday night two years ago?"

"Because she was very pretty. All of the guys that night apparently thought so, too. But mostly because I remember that *he* was bothering her."

She lifts her pointer finger—long acrylic hot-pink nail attached—and motions to the defendant. Faint chatter and nervous movement overcome the gallery.

"Alright. Let's talk about that, Ms. Murrow. Where were you when you saw the victim being bothered, as you put it?"

"Outside. I was taking a smoke break. I had floated out to the farthest corner of the bar, down to the sidewalk. She was there, too. And so was he. But at the other corner of the bar. They were talking."

"Could you hear what they were saying?"

"No. I was too far. And the music was too loud. But I could tell it wasn't a pleasant conversation."

"Why do you say that?"

"She looked agitated. She was turning her back to him. Her hands were in the air. He wouldn't leave. He followed her a bit. Stood very close to her. Too close. She seemed uneasy. I don't think he appreciated that reaction."

"Objection! Speculation."

"Sustained. That last remark is stricken. Members of the jury, you are to disregard it."

"Ms. Murrow, how long did this carry on?"

"I don't know. A minute or two? Not long."

"Then, how is it you remember it?"

"Because I remember almost intervening. It was that bad. There was a knot in my stomach. Women just know. We've all been there before. When a guy just won't take a hint. It bothered me."

"You said *almost* intervene. Why didn't you?"

"Because as soon as I found the nerve, she was gone. She had reentered the bar."

"Without him?"

"Without him."

"Ms. Murrow, did you ever see this woman interact with that man before or after this argument? As far as you could tell, were they together?"

"Ha! Fat chance."

The audience and jurors roar. The lawyers and judge all suppress a smile.

"Why do you say that?"

"Girls like that don't go for guys like him. She had her pick of the litter."

"Objection! Nonresponsive," Jordan interjects.

"I'll rephrase the question, Your Honor," Sandy answers before the judge can make a ruling. "You had occasion to watch either that girl or that guy at earlier points in the night, is that correct?"

"Yes."

"Did you ever *see* them together other than those one or two minutes?"

"No."

"Do you see that man—the man who was standing too close to the victim, who you say wouldn't leave her alone, the one with whom the victim seemed annoyed and agitated—do you see that man in the courtroom today?"

"I do."

"Can you point him out and identify him by an article of clothing he's wearing?"

"He's obviously the one between the two defense attorneys," she remarks condescendingly. It earns her more laughter.

"Ma'am, if you would please point him out and identify what he's wearing."

"He's right there," she says, dramatically leaning out of her seat and shoving her finger aggressively in Gabriel's direction. "Wearing the pink tie and that ill-fitting suit."

Sandy pauses, blinks profusely, and stares down at her notes before continuing. "Do you remember speaking to police about what you saw?"

"Many times. Over and over again. I opened my big mouth, and now no one will leave me alone."

Sandy smiles through her frustration. "Do you remember telling police that the man bothering the victim that night was black?"

Sandy is compelled to bring it up first before defense has the opportunity. All noise flees the room. Not a breath is taken in the interim—seemingly stretched into eternity—between the attorney's question and the woman's answer.

"I do. Yes."

"Looking at him today, you don't think the defendant is black, do you?"

"No. He's very clearly a Mexican or a Latino."

Sandy noticeably winces. Gabriel is of Cuban descent. The conflation of Latino groups in South Florida—particularly that of a Cuban and anything else, really—is sacrilege. She sweeps past it as you would an errant bone in your fish or a problematic passage in the Bible.

"Well, are you sure that this man sitting here is the same one you saw that night?"

"One hundred percent."

"How can you be so sure when you first thought he was black?"

"It's the same face. I saw the curly hair. I saw the skin tone. It was dark. I guessed his race. And I got it wrong. But it was him. I'm sure of it."

"Thank you, Ms. Murrow. No further questions."

"Cross-examination," the judge declares.

Jordan saunters to the lectern deliberately. He buttons up his blazer, clenches his muscles, flashes a smile at the jury, and goes to work.

"Ms. Murrow, you're forty-eight years old?"

"Yes."

"You're unmarried?"

"Yes."

"And The Saloon—that's famously a college bar?"

"I don't know what that means. It sells alcohol. That's all I need to know about a place."

"Well, it sits right across from the university campus, right?"

"I suppose so. Yes."

"And—being there for four or five hours—you had an opportunity to look around at the clientele that night?"

"Sure."

"And they were young, right? College-aged?"

"Objection! Relevance."

"Overruled. It's cross-examination. I'll give Mr. Whipple leeway. You can answer that, Ms. Murrow."

"Younger than me, if that's what you're getting at. Yes."

"Well, even my client and the deceased—both in their late

twenties at the time—were older than most of the kids in that bar, correct?"

"I didn't know them. How would I know their ages?"

"Fair enough. You didn't know that—or their correct races, it appears?"

"Objection! Argumentative."

"I'll withdraw," Jordan concedes, before moving on. It was a question to be posed for effect but left unanswered. "And you went there alone?"

"I did."

"You sat yourself at the bar?"

"Yes."

"And you say you had only two drinks, right?"

"Right."

"Because of the South Beach Diet?"

"Yes. Didn't I already answer all of these questions?"

"I'll ask the questions, if that's alright, Ms. Murrow," he chides her charmingly. "You even told us you were still in phase one of the diet?"

"Yes."

"But phase one dictates absolutely no alcohol."

"So?"

"So, you were not so 'disciplined,' as you called it earlier?"

"It was a Friday night. I was treating myself."

"On a Friday night, for five hours at a college bar, you were surely treating yourself to far more than two drinks, weren't you?"

"I already told you: Two. No more. No less."

"Well, you certainly didn't pay for those drinks, did you?"

"Probably not."

"Because you were there—a single woman, all alone, sitting at the bar—to get men to buy you those drinks, right?"

"Nothing wrong with that."

"College-aged men?"

"Objection!" Sandy fails at hiding the contempt in her voice.

"On what grounds?" the judge asks.

Sandy's mouth opens, but nothing rational comes out. "This is inappropriate, Your Honor."

"That's not a legal objection, State," the judge notes, "but for other reasons, the objection is sustained. Move on, counselor."

"The deceased—she was alone, too, for most of the night?"

"Yes."

"No boyfriend that you could tell?"

"No."

"No girlfriends that you could tell?"

"No."

"There, just like you—a single woman, all alone, sitting at the bar—to chat up men?"

"Objection! Speculation."

"Sustained. I told you to move on from this line of questioning, defense."

"Yes, Your Honor," he says, feigning apology. "You mentioned that all the guys at the bar apparently found her pretty. Why do you say that?"

"She was getting a lot of attention from them."

"And she was giving them lots of attention back, wasn't she?"

"Objection! Rape shield."

But Ms. Murrow answers anyway: "Yes, she was."

"To *lots* of guys, right?" Jordan sneaks in there.

"Your Honor, objection!" Sandy insists.

"Sustained. Ms. Murrow, you are not to answer when an objection is pending. Mr. Whipple—you know better. You wait until I make a ruling to ask another question. The objection is sustained. The jury is to disregard the witness's last answer and counsel's last two questions. Now, not another word on this, defense. Do you understand me?"

"Yes," he answers meekly. She had reproached him in front of the jury, but it had been worth it. Zealous defending was all about treading right up to the line—and, every so often, only just crossing it.

Sandy's intern leans into an attorney sitting beside her and whispers.

"Why don't we ask for a mistrial?"

"The State doesn't ask for mistrials," he tells her. "Double jeopardy attaches. We don't get a do-over. We bite the bullet. That's why defense attorneys push the limits. There's no consequence."

"Ms. Murrow, you testified on direct examination that you didn't think girls like the deceased go for guys like my client, right?"

"Well, look at him."

Anxious mirth spills out from the audience like catharsis. Jordan, wasting no time, pounces.

"You mean she wouldn't go for a gay man like my client?"

"Objection!"

"Overruled."

"Counsel, your client's not gay," Ms. Murrow replies, smiling wryly.

Jordan is flummoxed. He doesn't know exactly how or why the witness is claiming to know so definitively. In cross-examination, you only ask questions to which you already know the answers. You don't invite surprises. Jordan fails to utter another word for fear of inducing harmful testimony.

After long consideration, he treads lightly: "To be clear, you don't know my client? You have no idea what he is?"

"I saw the way he was looking at her. Like I said, we women know it when we see it. He was interested. He's not gay."

He nearly cut her off. "You say it was dark when you saw a couple arguing outside?"

"I didn't say a couple."

"Alright. It was dark when you saw two people arguing outside?"

"Yes."

"And you say they were far from you?"

"I wouldn't say *far*."

"But you did. Just a few minutes ago."

"I don't think so."

"Well, you were too far to hear their words, correct?"

"I couldn't hear them."

"It was a yes-or-no question, Ms. Murrow. You were too far to hear their words—yes or no?"

"Yes."

"But close enough to notice that the man bothering the deceased was black?"

"I've already addressed this. I saw curly hair, so I assumed he was black."

"You can see my client's hair as he sits there, right?"

"Of course."

"Wouldn't you consider those loose curls atop his head?"

"I don't know what you mean by that."

Jordan presses down on the podium, so firmly the color flees his hands, and he begins to rock. He is giddy with excitement. He thinks he's got her number.

"Ms. Murrow, you took an oath to tell the truth today?"

"I did."

"So help you God, as you yourself said, correct?"

"Yes."

"And you told the men and women of this jury that you do hair for a living. Are you trying to tell me *and* them—in the same breath—that you have no idea what I mean when I say 'loose curls'?"

Ms. Murrow's cheeks go red. She stammers in response, unsuccessful at completing a full thought.

"You've cut and styled African American hair before, haven't you?"

"Yes."

"And you've cut and styled Caucasian curly hair before, yes?"

"Not men's often, no."

"That's not my question, Ms. Murrow. Listen to my question. You have before dealt in a professional capacity with a white person who has naturally curly hair?"

"Yes."

"So you are aware of the difference between the two?"

"It depends. There can be a difference. Yes."

"You know what it means for curls to be tight, for them to be kinky, don't you?"

"Yes."

"And looking at my client's hair, you would not—fairly, professionally, and honestly, recalling the oath you took today—consider it to be curly of the kinky or tight kind?"

"No."

"That's because my client is unequivocally *not* a black man, wouldn't you say?"

"Yes."

"Thank you, Ms. Murrow. That wasn't hard now, was it?"

Sandy flies from her seat to make the objection, but the judge beats her to it.

"Sustained. Refrain from making extraneous commentary, Mr. Whipple."

He nods, peering over at the jury to wink slyly.

"Now, isn't it true, Ms. Murrow, that police didn't find you? You went out of your way to find police?"

"I didn't go out of my way. I called them."

"Because you wanted to tell them what you had seen, right?"

"I thought it was my duty. I regret that now."

"And you called them weeks after it happened?"

"I didn't call until I heard on the news that the girl was dead. Why would I call them earlier than that? I didn't see anything but an argument."

"You called them once you heard the case was on the news, right?"

"That's what I just said."

"Once you already knew that this was a big case in the media?"

She gives him a puzzled, perturbed look and a shrug.

"I need an answer."

"No, I didn't know—nor did I care—that it was a 'big case in the media,' as you put it."

"You called knowing that police already had a suspect: my client?"

"No. I don't think so. I don't know if I saw that in the news."

"In fact, you continued thinking that the man you saw that night was black for weeks, up until you saw a picture of the guy police suspected—my client—and that's when you switched your story?"

"No. Like I said, I always knew it was him. When I saw a picture, I recognized him immediately. I was just wrong about his race."

"You live in New Jersey now, right?"

"Yes."

"So you traveled over a thousand miles to be here today."

"Unfortunately."

"The government paid for your flight, didn't it?"

"I wasn't spending a damn cent."

"And the government has put you up in a hotel, hasn't it?"

"Yes."

"It's paying for everything, right?"

"Not my losses taking off from work. I lose money every hour I'm away. Who's going to pay me for that? Will you, fancy-pants defense lawyer?"

Jordan, this time, leads the courtroom in laughter.

"That's over my pay grade, Ms. Murrow," he answers. "One last question: That first week you came forward, you spoke to the media, didn't you?"

"They tracked me down. I was just answering questions."

"You were just answering questions—for three different news stations and two local newspapers, right?"

"I didn't keep count."

"Too many to keep count, huh?"

She doesn't answer. It isn't necessary.

"No further questions, Your Honor."

"Redirect," the judge notifies Sandy.

"Yes, briefly, Your Honor," she answers. "Ms. Murrow, are you getting paid anything to testify here today?"

She sneers loudly: "No."

"In fact, do you even want to be here today?"

"No."

"Why are you here?"

"Because you threatened to arrest me."

Sandy closes her eyes as she waits for the crowd's reaction to dwindle. She needs the pause to maintain a level head.

"You were made aware that you were subpoenaed to be here?"

"Right."

"And that it is illegal to refuse a legal subpoena?"

"Yes."

"And that one possible consequence of disobeying a court order, like a subpoena, is jail?"

"Yes."

"Safe to say, if you had your way, you would not be here today?"

"Absolutely not."

"In fact, you testified on cross that you sort of regret becoming involved?"

"Yes."

"And you're of course aware that if you changed your story—such as to say you no longer remembered what happened two years ago—you would have likely successfully gotten out of having to testify here today?"

Ms. Murrow mulls it over, lending the impression that this is quite possibly the first time such a tactic has crossed her mind. Sandy briefly panics under her veneer of serenity. Nevertheless, the witness answers in the affirmative.

"Yet you are saying the same things you said two years ago—that you saw this man bothering the deceased on the night of her disappearance. Why? Why not lie and be done with this?"

For the first time, earnest reflection seizes Ms. Murrow's voice. There is a tremble in it, foreign to the listeners who have come to expect a certain brashness to her affect.

"Because it's the truth. And that girl who died, she deserves the truth. I don't know what happened to her. I'm not telling you anything more than what I saw. I saw a pushy guy and a girl wanting to get away. I should have intervened that night. I didn't. That was my duty, and I didn't. This is my duty now, too. I won't make the mistake of failing her again."

Sandy had more questions to ask, but she let the poignancy of the moment linger instead. When you elicit a powerful answer, you sit. So she did.

"No further questions."

"State: Call your next witness."

"The State calls Humberto Rivas to the stand." That declaration came from Sandy's co-counsel, Nathan Parker—a balding, soft-spoken, and bespectacled man of considerable height and girth who was a few years junior to her in the office. She had relegated to him what she anticipated would be a minor witness. It was the most amount of control the notoriously domineering prosecutor felt comfortable ceding.

Nate walked as if he had cushions adhered to the bottom of his shoes. It lent him a certain grace uncommon to men of his stature. But he droned in monotone, and he appeared perpetually lost, which engendered a strong nurturing impulse from even the least sensitive of his peers. His type of weird pulled others closer. Most people were nonetheless surprised by the sight of a wedding band and even more shocked by his stunningly attractive wife.

When Sandy selected Nate as her second chair, the office rumor mill tried its best to make sense of the unconventional choice. She had overlooked other hotshot rising stars for a man who had likely reached the summit of his career.

"He's a sympathetic character. You immediately feel for him," was Sandy's official line. "They have an awkward but potentially lovable nerd on their side. We need ours."

Colleagues had instead settled on more superficial reasoning.

"She couldn't stand to have her shine dulled by a competing spotlight. Nate Parker won't upstage her. He'll put them to sleep, and she gets to snap them out of it."

Mr. Rivas strides into court looking every bit the ranch hand: sun-kissed bronze, leathered skin; immaculately white vaquero hat, which he slips off to reveal slicked-back graying hair; a curly mustache obscuring a stiff upper lip; and noisy boots muffled by dulled, aged carpet.

"He'll need the services of the interpreter," Nate alerts the judge.

A short, squat woman emerges from the sidelines, assists Mr. Rivas in taking his oath, and follows him to the witness stand.

"I'll remind you, members of the jury, that even if some of you are fluent Spanish speakers, resist the urge to translate the witness's testimony yourselves," the judge instructs. "You are to accept the translator's version of the testimony as true and accurate."

The admonition falls on deaf ears. Spanish-speaking jurors will instinctively assess his words first, before they're converted to English, and silently criticize the interpreter's language choices. Anglo listeners hear only the slow, deliberate, near singsong cadence of his voice, followed by the filtered translation stripped of the emotion and tone needed to judge credibility. It will have to do.

"Good afternoon, Mr. Rivas," Nate begins.

"Good afternoon," the witness's echo repeats.

"Where do you live?"

"Homestead."

"And what do you do for a living?"

"I work on a farm. I pick fruits and vegetables. I'm the foreman."

"Where exactly do you work as a foreman?"

"Orwell's Berry Farm."

Nate walks over to a blown-up map that he sets up on an easel.

"I'm showing you what's already been admitted into evidence as State's Eight. Does this depict the property lines for Orwell's Berry Farm?"

"Yes."

"Do you live on the property?"

"Yes."

"Whereabouts?"

"In a shack, over here." He points west.

"And this cabin on the outskirts—is it within the property line?"

"Yes."

"Who lived there?"

"A young man."

"Do you see that young man who was a neighbor of yours in the courtroom here today?"

"Yes."

"Can you point him out and identify him by an article of clothing?"

"He's wearing a suit."

"May the record reflect that the witness has identified the defendant. Mr. Rivas, would you say Orwell's Berry Farm is a secluded area?"

"Yes."

"There's not a lot of traffic passing by?"

"No. There's just one road to get in and out."

"And how long do you have to travel on that road to reach a main thoroughfare?"

"Several miles. Ten. Fifteen."

"Are you aware of the defendant's living arrangement with the farm?"

"The owner has always rented out the room. He rents it out cheap. It's a long commute into the city. Small square footage. Bedroom, kitchen—it's all one room."

"What kind of people rent this room?"

"Objection! Speculation. Personal knowledge."

"Overruled. Answer only if you know, Mr. Rivas."

"What are they called? Young, hip people. Artists. Kids who think it's cool to live like that. Off the grid."

"Well, what about loners?"

Mr. Rivas laughs.

"It's in the middle of nowhere. You certainly need to appreciate being alone."

"Well, what about this defendant in particular? Did you know him well?"

"No."

"But you had interacted with him?"

"Very briefly over the course of the few years he lived there."

"And you live and work close enough to see and observe him and his home?"

"Sure."

"Lots of parties?"

"No."

"Lots of women over?"

"No."

Nate pauses, contemplating an ad-lib inquiry.

"Lots of men over, for that matter?"

"No. Neither."

"Not a lot of company or friends, is that fair to say?"

"More than fair. I have never seen him with another person. I have never seen him have company. I have never seen another car parked in front. That's in the three years he lived there. Zero."

"How would you describe him personally?"

"Doesn't really maintain eye contact. Shy guy. Doesn't say much. Quiet."

"Same for his cabin? Relatively quiet?"

"Yes."

"Was there ever a time you heard noise coming from his cabin?"

"Yes. Two years ago. A night in November."

"Did you come to eventually learn that it was the same night the victim in this case went missing?"

"Yes. That's what police told me."

"Does November 13 sound about right?"

"Right."

"What did you hear that night?"

"It was very early in the morning. Maybe four in the morning. I was preparing to begin my day. We begin very early. I was seated outside of my shack, on the porch, drinking coffee. I heard screaming coming from his cabin. Distinct yells."

"Let's talk about those yells. Yelling like arguing, or screams?"

"Screams. It raised the hair on my arms."

"How many screams did you hear?"

"It's hard to say. Hard to say when one ended and another began. But I'd say only a few. Maybe two or three. Because as soon as it caught my attention, it stopped. And because it wasn't sustained, I let it go. I put it out of my mind."

"Could you tell the gender of the screaming person?"

"Female. It sounded like a woman."

"Did you look over at the cabin?"

"I did. I just stared at it for a while. Trying to see if I could spot anything off. But I didn't see anything."

"Could you tell if the lights were on?"

"I think so."

"Thank you, Mr. Rivas. No further questions."

"Cross-examination."

Jordan doesn't stand right away. He whispers in his client's ear—nonsense—and gives his arm a squeeze. He then doodles on his notepad—more nonsense—shows it to the defendant, and finally, painstakingly, approaches the lectern.

"It's the Jordan Whipple show," Sandy whispers to Nate. "Stay attentive. Object to his theatrics. Mess with his rhythm."

"You don't pick fruit or vegetables before sunrise, do you?" starts Jordan.

"I begin preparing for the day before the sun rises."

"Thank you, Mr. Rivas, for offering that tidbit, but try to answer my question. I'll ask it again. You don't pick fruit or vegetables before sunrise, do you?"

"No."

"And sunrise after daylight savings doesn't happen at four a.m., does it?"

"No."

"It doesn't happen at five a.m., does it?"

"No."

"It doesn't really happen at six a.m., does it?"

"Around there."

"On November 13, two years ago, sunrise happened at exactly 6:39 a.m., right?"

"If you say so."

"That's a whole two-and-a-half hours after you were up, on your porch, drinking coffee?"

"I don't know the exact time. It was around four in the morning."

"None of your men had arrived for the day, had they?"

"No."

"It was just you, by yourself, awake, on your porch, staring at this young man's home?"

"I didn't look over until I heard the screams."

"Screams that you didn't report to anyone?"

"I eventually told police."

"But not that night, right?"

"No."

"You didn't dial 911?"

"No."

Sandy's hand shoots over to Nate's notepad, writing down questions—sideways and on the margins—for his redirect.

"You didn't run over to check on this screaming woman yourself?"

"No."

"Even though you heard her screaming so frighteningly that it raised the hair on your arms?"

"It didn't last long. And I was still waking up."

"You worried that you were maybe hearing things?"

"Right."

"That maybe you dreamt it?"

"Sure."

"And so you were convinced that you hadn't really heard anything at all?"

"I wasn't sure."

"And yet, you're here, two years later, sure of yourself now?"

"I'm just telling you what I heard."

"What you think you heard?"

"That's all I can do. Be truthful."

"And what you *think* you heard was a woman?"

"Right."

"But in your statement to police, you didn't mention a gender?"

"They didn't ask."

"And what made it sound like a woman exactly?"

"The voice was female."

"OK. You tell me what that means to you."

"I don't know. It's hard to describe."

"Try it for me."

"It was high-pitched."

"So, you'd agree with me, women generally have high-pitched voices?"

"Yes."

"And men generally have low-pitched voices?"

"Yes."

"But some women have low-pitched voices, isn't that right?"

"I suppose."

"And some men have high-pitched voices, right?"

"OK."

"And you've never heard my client yell before?"

"No."

"In fact, you have no idea how my client sounds when he yells?"

"I don't."

"And would you agree with me that women yell for all sorts of reasons?"

"I'm sorry?"

"A woman can yell for reasons other than expressing fear?"

"Like what?"

"Like screams of passion. Women can yell, for example, in the middle of passionate consensual sex?"

Mr. Rivas laughs nervously.

Sandy leans into Nate: "Is the kid gay or not? What's exactly the defense theory here?"

"I didn't hear a woman moaning that night, counsel."

"And I'm sure you've heard a few of those in your day, am I right?"

Jordan is all pearly whites. The gallery is all laughs. The men in the jury respond positively; the women do not. Sandy rolls her eyes. Nate shakes his head disapprovingly.

"Move on, Mr. Whipple," the judge reprimands.

"Mr. Rivas, ultimately you cannot tell us with perfect certainty whether the screams you heard were female or male, or whether you actually heard anything at all?"

"I am certain only of what I believe I heard at the time. I believe I heard a woman screaming. That's what I thought at the time. That's what I'm saying here today."

"You characterized my client as a quiet guy?"

"Yes."

"But you two were barely acquaintances, right?"

"Sure."

"You didn't do more than exchange pleasantries?"

"Right."

"And, in fact, you don't speak any English?"

"I don't."

"And my client prefers to speak in English?"

"I don't know."

"Let me ask it in a different way. You have no idea whether my client even speaks Spanish?"

"I know he's Latino."

"That doesn't mean he speaks Spanish?"

"I think we've spoken in Spanish before. As you say, I don't speak any English."

"So you have no idea whether my client came off as quiet to you because perhaps he feels uncomfortable speaking Spanish or maybe he just didn't like you or want to engage in anything more than just 'hi' and 'bye' with you?"

"Objection! Form." Nate shoots up from his seat. Sandy had elbowed him in the ribs.

"I'll withdraw. Mr. Rivas, you weren't born in this country, were you?"

"No."

"You were born in Mexico?"

"Yes."

"And you are not here legally, is that right?"

"Objection! Relevance."

"What are you getting at, Mr. Whipple?" the judge asks.

"Bias, Your Honor. I'm getting there."

"Get there quickly. Overruled."

"You are here illegally, right, Mr. Rivas?"

The interpreter has now twice translated the same question. Mr. Rivas has heard it, but he hesitates. A sadness sweeps over his hooded eyes.

"Yes."

"But you are now in the process of applying for a U visa?"

"I think that's what it's called."

Sandy taps the point of her pen on the paper, calling Nate's attention to a question she had written. He waves her off, trying to listen.

"And U visas, for the members of the jury who are unaware, are reserved for victims and witnesses of a crime who assist in the prosecution of that crime?"

"Something like that. I'm not a lawyer."

"So you're benefiting personally from your testimony today?"

"I haven't been granted any legal status as of now."

"I take it you don't want to be deported?"

"No."

"You have American citizen children who live here, right?"

"Yes."

"You don't want to be separated from them?"

"No."

"You would do anything to avoid being separated from them?"

"I wouldn't lie under oath."

"Because that's a crime?"

"Because it's a crime."

"But you came to this country without papers even though *that* was a crime, didn't you?"

Begrudgingly, Mr. Rivas nods his head.

"You have to say it aloud so that the record can pick it up. Is that a yes?"

"Yes."

"No further questions." Jordan races to his seat, adrenaline sending him reeling.

"Redirect."

"Thank you, Your Honor," Nate says methodically, slowing the pace with his drawl and ambling up to the lectern. If Jordan was a firecracker, Nate was the cold water that extinguished the sizzle. Nate has intentionally left behind his notepad—and Sandy's questions—without a glance. She clenches her teeth nervously as seconds pass in awkward silence. Nate is hardly moving, staring blankly at his witness. The judge nearly prompts him to begin, but he speaks abruptly before she can.

"How long have you lived and worked in this country?"

"Twenty-seven years."

"All of those years—working with your hands?"

"Yes."

"Long hours in the sun?"

"Yes."

"And for some of that time, for only minimum wage, I imagine?"

"Right."

"You pay taxes?"

"Objection! Improper bolstering."

Nate's tone doesn't change, but the speed with which he counters takes his audience by surprise.

"Defense has gone on and on impugning this man's character, intimating that coming to this country to provide a better life for him and his family lessens his credibility—all under the guise of eliciting bias. We should be given the opportunity to briefly respond as to why none of that is the case."

The judge nods admiringly, even as she rules against him.

"You've made your point, Mr. Parker. Move on. Sustained."

"Explain to the jury your relationship with law enforcement as an undocumented person."

"I obey the laws. I work hard. But it's scary to report what we see and hear to police. Many in my community do not do it, because it attracts attention to us."

"Anything that attracts attention to you raises your risk of deportation, is that fair to say?"

"Yes."

"Safe to say this two-year ordeal—reporting to the police what you heard and coming here to testify today—has attracted attention to you?"

"Yes."

"Is that why, in part, you hesitated in calling the police?"

"Yes."

"And is that why you have a lot more to lose by coming here and telling the truth than you stand to gain?"

"That's how I saw it. That's how I still see it. I'd rather not put myself out like this."

"And let's talk about what defense asserted you'd stand to gain. Isn't it true that the status you've applied for allows you to remain in the country during the pendency of this trial?"

"I think so. Like I told the gentleman, I'm not a lawyer."

"And isn't it true that the U visa counsel was talking about does not apply to witnesses? It only applies to victims. You're not the victim in this case?"

"No."

"Is it your understanding that whatever the outcome of this case, you won't be guaranteed legal status in this country?"

"That's what I'm told. I am still very much at risk of being deported."

"And yet, here you are, coming out of the shadows to testify. Why?"

"Unlike what the gentleman said, I care about the laws. I care about obeying this country's laws. This is my country now. I was told to be here, so I came. I was told to tell the truth, so I did. It's my duty. It's what's right."

"Thank you, Mr. Rivas." Nate turns to sit, halts, and swivels around with uncharacteristic alacrity. "And I, for one, hope you get to stay in this country, sir. We can stand to have more citizens like you."

Jordan doesn't dare object. Nate exudes such earnestness, such do-gooder sentiment, that it would be akin to objecting to a Boy Scout. That it doesn't come from a firebrand but from a mouse in a blazer shields what the judge would otherwise deem improper. He takes soft steps back to counsel's table as his words linger in the air.

Sandy emphatically crosses out the unused questions she had written for him and, instead, pens three words.

Good job, counselor.

*   *   *

The jurors sat stone faced, slumped in their chairs. Feet shuffled. Hands fidgeted. Sighs and yawns ran on intermittent loop.

Juror number eight dozed off. A statement by juror number eleven freed number eight from drowsy purgatory.

"People lie through their teeth, man."

After a stretch of silence so deep, the words were just short of comprehensible.

"What was that?" Mr. Thomas asked.

"People lie."

Juror number six sat up in her seat.

"You're talking about the eyewitness?" she asked, her tone skeptical.

He crossed his arms in reply.

"Oh, you mean the *independent* eyewitness? The one with no bias whatsoever? The one who doesn't know the defendant or the victim? The one who swore an oath to tell the truth before God? That one?" juror number one inquired, his smile never faltering and his pale cheeks reddening in equal parts vehemence and embarrassment. His passion caught his peers off guard.

Number eleven shook his head, staring at the wall.

"She lied."

"Don't just keep repeating that," number six pled. "Explain. *Why* would she lie?"

"For attention. To feel important. To feel useful," he answered. "I'm not saying she made the whole thing up. She ain't got no dog in this fight, I agree. I'm saying she made up the details. She filled in the holes. She saw what she wanted to see."

His words hung in the air, thick as molasses. No one was maintaining eye contact. Juror number seventeen, incorrectly reading the room, brazenly dove in.

"Well, there is such a thing as cross-racial identification bias—"

An audible moan rippled down the line.

"—and confirmation bias," he finished weakly, buried under a chorus of protests.

"For Chrissake, why does it always have to be about race?" number one asked.

"Because I can't shed my blackness, sir. It can't be left at home. It has no days off. Race—at least *mines*—is ever present. Yours is invisible," number eleven said.

"Let's not make this about ourselves, gentlemen," Mr. Thomas warned.

"Well, that's who she identified, right? A black man. Pretty generic. Always the default. Hey, maybe it was *me* she saw?"

Juror number sixteen snorted and snickered, his laughter staccato like the clucking of a chicken. Number six, sitting directly beside him, pivoted in her seat to catch sight of the young man. It was the first noise he had made in hours.

"The woman saw what she saw. That's it," number one proclaimed.

"She saw what she *thought* she saw."

"Well, it's clear you've made up your mind based on God knows what: your gut, a *feeling*, counsel's hippy-dippy psycho-liberalism. It don't mean we have to go along with it."

Number eleven flipped open his spiral notepad. Its plastic cover slapped the tabletop. On its first page, he had sketched a street, complete with light posts, clusters of trees, and angular lines for perspective.

"This is the street she was at. These light posts are few and far—maybe half a block in between. The radius their light gives off is no more than five, maybe ten feet. The rest of the street is all darkness, even in twilight. The shrubs on the patio are tall. We watched her walk up to the witness stand: She's short.

Her view was obstructed and dim. She saw what she wanted to see."

Number one swallowed hard.

"What are you—some kind of city planner?"

"No. Just a mailman who has walked that route, down that very street, hundreds of times, by pure coincidence. Including in the winter, when darkness comes early. There ain't high visibility there, partner."

Mr. Thomas smiled to himself. "That's certainly more than a gut feeling. We ought to pay it some mind."

"I don't think we're supposed to consider anything external to the evidence," number one muttered.

"She was *so* certain, though," number six said.

"That was going to be my point," number seventeen, esquire, again intervened. "You see something. You form an opinion. And, afterward, you interpret every new fact according to that opinion. You bolster your own sense of certainty. Mix in the emotion of the moment, and you've got a false identification. She's clearly an emotional woman—we can all see that. That's got to mess with your recall."

"That's not right, actually."

The voice—feminine but weathered, faintly accented, and measured—was new. It was not captive to the emotion of the voices that preceded it.

Mr. Thomas had been hoping to hear it.

"What's not right, Doctor?" he asked.

Juror number eight flitted her eyes upward at him. She was surprised that he had remembered her profession from jury selection.

"Emotional events are easier to recall, not less. Particularly strong, negative emotions. I see it with trauma patients all the time. Strong recall. Down to the positioning of a shadow on the wall. The same part of the brain is stimulated during emotional

63

stress as during memory retention. Looking at a scan, you can't really tell the difference."

Silent nodding spread with increasing fervor through her audience.

"That's what *I* was saying. She saw what she saw," number one huffed.

Juror number eight stared at her hands, at the wrinkled skin draping her metacarpals—spotted, vascular, and ringless—and stopped herself from laughing at her male echo.

Laura Hurtado had an affinity for lists. As a young girl, at the direction of her doting father, she'd alphabetize and memorize series of words as study aids: capitals for geography tests, vocabulary for spelling bees, and the Latin names of her favorite dinosaurs just for fun. She had impeccable recollection. It was handy in medical school. Her classmates called her Encyclopedia Brown—a nod to her chocolate-brown hair and eyes, the earth-tone color of her preferred scrubs, and the morbid mnemonic song she had invented to learn the bones of the body, befitting a crime caper.

"You'd *kill* at a murder mystery party," a friend once noted.

She left school and her yearlong residency with two new honorifics—Dr. and Mrs.—and a hyphenate. Dr. Richard Perez had slick black hair, burning green eyes, a fanatical devotion to fitness, and an intensity that fueled his disarming humor, precision at the operating table, and volcanic temper. He and Laura shared in common neurosurgery and two sets of immigrant parents who fled Communist regimes (hers Nicaragua; his Cuba) for America.

"I don't like how gringos shorten Richard to Dick. That doesn't communicate great things about the man attached to it," he once lamented. "But Rich: That's a nickname—and a fate—I can get behind."

"Aren't you humorous?" She rolled her eyes.

"It *is* my favorite bone."

After thirteen years and two children together—their eldest, Rich (full name), and a much younger daughter, Diana—they divorced. She kept her hybrid last name, mostly for the sake of the children.

She didn't often deal with the humerus in her specialization. It came up one evening while she was washing dishes. The water sent cool, welcoming shudders over the skin of her carpals, metacarpals, phalanges, lower ulna, and radius, and muffled the voices down the hall. The voices, one considerably deeper than the other, carried with them the imprint of panic.

The hairs on her arms stood at attention, independent of the chill from the water. The human body recognized the melody of danger, lyrics unnecessary. She left the faucet running. She scrubbed harder.

The voices sniped at each other, a pair of nipping rattlesnakes that came within inches but never kissed. And then, a cacophony of sound: a heavy weight against the wall, a collapsing shelf. A shrieking teakettle sounded the alarm. An anxious cup hurtled out of Laura's hands and clinked against the metal sink. She shut off the stream and squelched the neurotic pot's antics.

Quiet abounded. It stung.

She watched the hall leading to the rest of her home, back pressed painfully against the waist-high sink counter, as if she wished to disappear into it. A single light sent warm orange onto the walls and carpet of the hall. A shadow, wide and tall, dwindled as it approached. Out of it appeared a woman, her daughter-in-law, Hannah. Like a movie abruptly unmuted, sound rejoined the universe. She was crying.

Laura careened into action. She dragged a chair from the kitchen table as its hind legs howled in protest. She methodically filled a Ziploc bag with three handfuls of cubed ice from the freezer and resealed it. The sobbing woman orbited for a few aimless feet—hands in her pulled-back hair, tongue tasting the iron that fled her busted lip.

Laura directed her to sit, leading her by the unaffected scapula. She went to work, reading nonverbal cues to follow the injuries. The patient's hand flew to the back of her head, in search of something. Laura peered under her hair, found blood and a lump, and applied the makeshift cold compress. She dabbed at her lip that glistened with saliva and blood.

She held her arm in place. Hannah grimaced at the touch. The pain sprung from the humerus. Laura said nothing. Her counterpart did all the talking.

"I can't, Laura. I can't go on. No more. I think it's broken. I think he broke it. I can't move it. It hurts so much."

Laura undid the top buttons of Hannah's blouse, disrobing her of one side to inspect a fledgling bruise: burst capillaries, the reddened and raised mark of large fingers coiled around a thin arm, the purple bar where a wedding band seared into skin. She removed her blouse, leaving her in a tank top underneath, and converted the outer layer into a sling.

"I need to call the police," Hannah said. "Right now. I need to call the police."

Hannah shot up from her seat and rocketed over to the landline hanging on the wall. In a single bound, Laura closed the distance between them. Before Hannah could lay her palm on the handset, Laura did first, pinning it against its holder. Hannah's mouth trembled. Tears collected in her eyes. The two women stared at each other bleakly. But Laura's grip, unlike her spirit, did not let up.

"I'll drive you to the hospital."

As they left, her teenage daughter, Diana, descended from her room upstairs—one earbud of her headphones popped in, the other dangling freely by her sternum—and silently drank in the scene. Laura watched as confusion in the girl's eyes converted to recognition and, ultimately, familiarity. Laura cast an encouraging smile in her direction. She did not receive one back.

Seated shoulder to shoulder in the waiting room, Laura penned the paperwork for the patient, leaving blank what she could not—or would not—answer. A nurse approached and crouched down, clipboard and completed form in hand.

"Hannah Perez?"

Hannah nodded.

"You left what happened blank. Can you briefly tell me so the doctor knows what to expect?"

Laura had not turned. Her steely eyes remained fixed in front of her.

"A shelf fell. The books on it landed on me," Hannah responded tightly.

All passive. No actor. No agent.

Laura waited in the lobby as Hannah disappeared into a room to await examination. Two revolutions of the wall clock passed before Officer Alexander Kimbie pulled Laura aside.

"May I ask you a few questions, ma'am?"

"Of course."

Officer Kimbie was young, short, and burly. He had light, vacant eyes and patches of stray hair sprouting from his chin and above his lip. Dressed in his uniform—gun strapped to his side and warm-climate shorts several inches too short—he looked like a high school jock playing a role on Halloween. He chewed gum, smacking his lips loudly in between halting, unpredictable bursts of speech that swept past natural pauses. It did little to assure his listeners that he possessed much intellectual heft.

"Were you present, ma'am, when your daughter-in-law was injured?"

"Yes. Well, no. I was down the hall."

"So you didn't see what happened, ma'am?"

"No."

"Did you hear anything?"

Laura paused. His chewing filled the intermission.

"Only a loud thud. What sounded like the shelf falling."

"You didn't hear anything else, ma'am?"

"Do you mind not calling me ma'am, Officer? I just don't prefer it."

He blinked heavily in response. She could see now that he was much older in spirit and more sophisticated than he initially appeared. Being underestimated was his greatest asset.

"You didn't hear anything else, ma'am?" he repeated.

"No. Nothing else."

Out of his shirt pocket, he produced a pen and pad. He leafed through it, ostensibly reading notes, but it was all for show. The pages were blank.

"Who was your daughter-in-law with at the time?"

"I don't know."

"Well, who was home?"

"I can't say. I arrived not long before."

The young officer perked his head up and furrowed his brow, a newly stoked fire in his eyes.

"Where was your son?"

"I'm not sure."

"Well, was his car parked in the driveway when you arrived?"

Laura scrutinized her hands before replying, performing, as if lost in thought.

"Uh, I think so. Yeah. Probably."

"I'm going to need you to make intelligent inferences for me, ma'am, alright?"

Laura physically recoiled, propelled backward by the force of his derision.

"May I have your badge number, Officer?"

He sighed. He had previously worked retail. In a different context, and just two years earlier, she would have been asking to speak to his manager. And he would have feigned remorse. No longer. He had the gun; he had the badge.

"Call the station. Kimbie: K-I-M-B-I-E. Is that all you can tell me about what happened?"

"Pretty much. Yes."

"And it would be consistent with the statement Hannah would give me?"

"I imagine so."

He lingered tens of seconds longer, dawdling wordlessly. Laura nearly walked away, full stop, but she could not compel her feet to make the bold move. He scribbled on his pad and stalked away after a valediction she could barely hear.

He had written down just two words as his notes.

She lied.

On the drive home, drugged and bandaged, Hannah was quiet. Laura continually gazed into the rearview mirror, expecting to see an inconspicuously dimmed police cruiser trailing her, but one never appeared. Hannah spoke just once.

"He learned it from watching his dad. You stayed too long. I won't make the same mistake."

Once home, Laura poured herself a whiskey, neat, before collapsing onto the sofa. She held the sweet, tart intoxicant against her gums like mouthwash for so long they began to break and bleed fibrous tissue.

Her son poked his head out from around a corner meekly, just as he had as a boy ginning up the proper contrition for a recent misdeed. The rest of him followed, and he skulked over to sit beside his mother. Dr. Rich Perez was an amplified version of his father: taller, handsomer, and, on the whole, angrier, but also more affectionate. When junior lashed out, he paired it soon after with effusive recompense: hugs, wet

69

kisses, declarations of love, and gifts, very expensive gifts. You wouldn't even find his eyes straying toward an attractive woman for two weeks after a thumping. He was, technically speaking, the perfect man in that refractory period, and then only. Senior had never bothered with such theatrics.

"I'm sorry, Mamá, for bringing my personal family issues into your home. It's tacky, and it's low-class. It should remain behind closed doors, between husband and wife."

Her reaction was no reaction. He filled the awkwardness with sound.

"She didn't tell anyone that *I* did this to her, did she?" he asked.

Laura shook her head faintly, mostly because she was trembling.

"She holds it over me, you know. It's sick. She would ruin me. And she loves the idea. Me losing everything: My practice. My kids."

Her hands sat politely on her lap.

"It's just that she has a way of getting under my skin like no one else. She makes my blood boil. I love her far too much, and she knows this. She pushes me on purpose."

"And Nicole?"

Her voice punctured like a dagger, swiftly but sharply.

His brush-up with his college sweetheart Nicole had been expunged from his record long before medical schools could scrutinize it.

"Mamá, Nicole was different."

He left it at that and scooted over, so that his knee brushed up against hers. He laid a solid palm on her scapula, leaned in, and whispered.

"You know it's different in this country, Mom. Women don't respect their husbands. It's untraditional. It's disruptive. You have to let a man be a man. Not emasculate him in his own home. He will find a way to feel strong if you won't let him feel it in normal ways."

At this, Laura swiveled to stare into the face of her child. His candid self-prognosis had stunned her. It was both absurd and awfully self-aware, bordering on parody. The look she gave him must have expressed this. He shrank under her ultraviolet stare.

"I'm not a bad man, am I, Mom?"

The question nicked her heart. An irregular beat besieged the organ, like a hand had enveloped it and squeezed. The pain was fleeting but stole her breath. His eyes shook, threatening to let loose a torrent of hurt. It was his turn to tremble. Laura didn't see a man. She saw a boy, a vulnerable boy, and the love of her life. A tiny gasp escaped her lips.

He crumpled onto her lap and cried. Her caress of his hair was barely volitional.

"I can't live without her. I won't live without her. I'd rather us both be dead than apart. That can't be bad, can it? A love that powerful?"

Laura was moving, but she was outside of her own body. She felt hair and tears and skin—and nothing at all. Her memory fled. Before long, it was morning, she was still on the couch, and she hadn't a clue how she had gotten there.

Dr. Laura Hurtado-Perez, juror number eight, looked up from her hands at the six other jurors watching her. The attention unsettled her. She preferred to hang back, not lead.

"You believe her?" juror number six asked. The young woman was easily suggestible. Not long ago she had committed herself to guilt. The equivocation from others had softened that conviction. But it was clear she felt an unspoken kinship with Dr. Hurtado-Perez. She held her opinion in high regard.

"I do," she answered, breathlessly. "It's hard for witnesses to come forward. It's a drain on their time. It's emotionally crippling, particularly during cross-examination. It's scary to accuse someone, anyone, of a crime. To potentially help condemn a man, a scary man, a violent man, a *bad* man, as you look him square in the eye. I, for one, can't help but find her brave."

Number six smiled at her.

Dr. Hurtado-Perez felt a hollow twinge in her beating heart.

04 | BYE-BYE, BABY

Domenico Santos usually drinks his coffee brimming with milk and sugar. Not this morning. He orders a steaming dark roast, black, an early morning jolt after a sleepless night and, perhaps, preemptive self-punishment. His mustachioed server brings it to him in an oversized white ceramic cup and saucer. It takes his two hands wrapped around its circumference to bring the cup to his lips. The bitterness smarts his rear taste buds; the heat sears the roof of his mouth.

Malcolm Mora arrives in what has become his public-eye attire: a black T-shirt with an image of a smiling, raven-haired girl superimposed on it, worn above a pair of thin khakis and brown leather boots and below windswept hair down to his eyes and thick-rimmed spectacles. He sits across from Dom and, without greeting, spills the contents of his hands—a dozen photographs—onto the round bistro table that separates them.

"These are the ones I was talking about," he begins, hands spreading and sorting through the pile. He wears a silver ring around his thumb, an eccentricity he has donned since adolescence. "The ones that really capture her spirit. Birthday parties and school dances—she was homecoming queen, you know?

Just a widely beloved, social, and garrulous girl. But a popular girl with heart. Not cliquish. Not mean."

Dom picks up a photo that long predated digital technology, so it's jaundiced, blurry, and out of focus. The girl at its center is clear—young, attractive in low-cut glittery blue—and the man beside her, her date, is suited, strapping, and winsome. It's the solitary figure off to the right and out of focus—diminutive, pale, and pockmarked by acne—that catches Dom's eye.

"Where was your date?" Dom inquires, flapping the photo in his fingers.

Malcolm pauses and blinks in a flurry of noticeable agitation.

"I didn't bring one," he intones. "But my sister made sure I wasn't alone. We rode in the limo together. She had me sit at the table with her and her date. She invited me up to dance every so often. She was kind and generous in that way."

Dom fingers another image. This one is even older, featuring a cake decorated half in blue, half in pink, surrounded by beaming female faces—Malcolm's sister at the center—and just one little boy, caught bawling hysterically.

"You're crying in this one," Dom says.

"Yes, well, that was our joint fifth birthday party," he recalls. "No one showed up for me. I was distraught, naturally. But Mel always had so many friends. It more than made up for it. From then on, she made it a point to celebrate our birthday together—no matter the age or the distance between us. She always included me."

Dom smiles and nods politely. He opens the laptop set in front of him. The glare of its light mercifully bounces off the lenses over his eyes, masking them from Malcolm's view. His fingers shake as he begins to pound heavily on the keyboard.

"It sounds like a very special relationship you two had: close and loving. So I can't imagine the feeling of loss, even now, two years later."

Malcolm's eyes narrow in response. He suspects this is courteous prattle, a preamble to graver, darker fare.

"Do you have any comment on the allegations that your relationship with your sister might have been inappropriate?"

Dom doesn't look up from his screen. He feels the burn of Malcolm's glare, but he focuses on the cursor blinking on his word processor. As soon as his subject speaks, Dom fastidiously transcribes.

"I thought this was for the *Herald*, not some trash tabloid," he fires back.

"Malcolm, the defense has made it a critical piece of its theory. It's been elevated from the tawdry rumor mill to the courtroom. I *have* to ask you about it."

"And I thought the story you were writing this time would focus on Mel. Put a human face on the person who actually lost her life in all of this. The coverage out there revolves exclusively around *him*—the animal who killed her. You told me this would be different. That's how you sold it to me."

"My story *is* about Melina," Dom insists. "And her family—*you*—are pivotal to that. I can't tell the story of Melina's life without you in it. And I can't ignore, without comment, what the defense is claiming. It's bullshit. I know that, Malcolm. But I need to hear it from you. I need to print the denial."

Dom should not have said that. He should not have divulged an opinion, however insincere and meant solely to placate the man. But he feared Malcolm might walk away if he didn't cajole him in some manner.

Malcolm bares his teeth and speaks next through a clenched jaw.

"We were twins, Mr. Santos. Others simply cannot understand that bond. We spent all of our lives together—spent even our prelife together, attached and sharing a single womb. I recognized her heartbeat. She was the most important person in my life, and she felt the same about me."

He swallows back emotion.

"My sister was a *gorgeous* woman, and yes, she had a healthy and robust sex life. But it did not include the indecent behavior the defense is claiming."

"What about yours?" Dom asks warily. Malcolm leans back in his chair and smiles.

"I haven't had as much success. But I have had girlfriends. Nothing out of the ordinary."

"Were you in love with Melina?"

"Romantically? Absolutely not."

Eyes downcast, Dom lowers his voice to slightly above a whisper for his final question.

"Did you have anything at all to do with her disappearance and death?"

In the silent seconds that proceed, Dom has to look up to make sure Malcolm is still there. Not even his breath is making a sound, but tears collect in the corners of his eyes. Dom's throat swells with shame. He sees a lost man before him.

Dom first stepped into *Miami Herald* headquarters as a twenty-year-old intern in the fall semester of his junior year. He was overdressed. Among the journalists crammed in cubicles clothed in jeans or wrinkled slacks, unbuttoned and untucked plaids, and soft footwear, the baby-faced aspiring newspaperman stood out in trousers, buttoned-up long sleeves, squeaky shoes, and a bow tie.

On that Tuesday, he walked into the office of his editor—a stout black woman of middle age spreading chicken salad on a cracker in the early morning—and received his first assignment.

"Go to this address. Knock on the door. The family there lost their young son a few hours ago. A tow truck ran him over, left him pinned beneath its tires, and dragged his body down the block. Get a quote from them."

Dom said nothing, but his dark brown eyes betrayed his shock. His supervisor smiled toothily.

He now suspects it was meant to serve as a cold, hard lesson in journalistic ethos. That, and no paid staffer wished to descend into *that* kind of neighborhood to pry intimate words from grieving parents for a story running in the back pages of the local section. Send the kid.

Dom put the dozen miles on his leased car, pulling up to an unassuming home sitting beneath gray clouds and in front of pronounced tire marks and dried blood trailing north on hot asphalt. The siren calls and yellow tape and radio feeds of the police had long gone with the rising sun. Dom stepped into marshy grass—unbuttoning his sweaty shirt, rolling up his sleeves, and tossing his tie in the car behind him—and skulked up to the door.

One knock. Two knocks. And a head finally poked out of a darkened sliver of an opening: ashen complexion, puffy eyes. Dom stuttered.

"I'm so—so—so—sorry to bother you, sir. I'm a reporter for the *Miami Herald*—"

"No comment."

The door slammed shut, the punctuation mark to his brief statement.

Dom stared at wood inches from his face for a full minute before returning to his car. He pulled out a clunky cell phone from his pocket and dialed the office before daring to drive off.

The directive was clear: "Go back. Knock again. Ask again."

Dom's stomach clenched into a fist. He felt for the first time the unique blend of mortification, dread, spiked adrenaline, shame, and shot nerves that comes from pursuing a reluctant source. He considered driving off, conjuring up a tale of a second failed attempt. Or simply driving home, never to return to print media again. But he did neither. Relief came only in trying again. He would spend his whole career trying to discern if that feeling—which never did permanently go away—was appealing or not, whether it was adventure or aversion.

He sped up to the door and knocked again. The same man answered.

This time, Dom spoke not a word in English, only Spanish.

"I'm sorry, sir. It's just that my bosses won't let me leave without a word from you. I'm so sorry for your loss. Will you do me the favor, sir—just a few words? And I will leave you to grieve. It would help me so very much."

Dom knew the power of relatability. Minutes before, he was just a black boy. But now, the light-skinned Hispanic man at the door might see a part of himself—or of his perished son—in him. It was a well-worn tactic on Dom's part. He would often code-switch, particularly at department stores and restaurants in Spanish-speaking enclaves, as a means to garner attention he would otherwise be denied. The recipient was usually surprised.

"I didn't know you were Latino," they would say, as if that mattered.

Dom had to bite his tongue—every time—from replying: "What country are you from without black people?" There wasn't a single Latin American country like that. Or, if he knew his interlocutor was Cuban: "You *do* know that the majority of your country right now looks like me and not you?"

He would smile instead and silently accept the short-lived privilege afforded him by the colonizer's tongue.

When it really mattered—in the dead of night, on a vacant seat on a bus or train, and strolling down an unlit street—his countrymen always found a way to see his blackness, regardless of what language it was cloaked in.

The man acquiesced. His voice quivered.

"We are devastated to have lost our son. Write that."

That was enough for Dom. He had gotten his quote. He was simultaneously elated and nauseous on the ride back. He planned to personally submit it to his editor. By the time he returned, however, a larger story had gripped the newsroom and the nation, and his work went unused.

Malcolm's tears spill from his eyes.

"You're a bloodsucking leech, you know that? How is it you do what you do?"

Dom doesn't usually defend the profession, particularly not to hostile sources who care not at all in this emotional moment about the nobility of the fourth estate. But he feels compelled to do so, perhaps more to convince himself than anyone else.

"I am in the business of seeking out truth. It can topple the powerful and the corrupt. It can lend a voice to the abused and forgotten. It's important work."

"That's all well and good, but what public interest is served in dragging a violently raped and murdered young woman— and her family—through the mud? What exact power structure is being held to account here? Whose vulnerable voice is being amplified? Other than whoring yourself out to sell more papers for your corporate benefactors, where is the honor in what you're doing?"

Dom cannot answer. Malcolm doesn't wait for one anyway.

"Go to hell."

His chair screeches and falls back from the force with which he rises and leaves. A few patrons turn to stare at Dom. He ignores them.

Dom plugs headphones into his laptop and double-clicks on a video file, tapping wildly at the volume button until the voice of the narrator resounds loudly, the same voice that had just cursed at him before departing. The shot features Malcolm, yet again wearing his sister's face on his chest, walking down a street alongside a search party with signs and near acres of undeveloped land and thick, untouched greenery—a place ripe for hiding a body. A microphone from a newscaster is shoved in the man's face as he speaks. It's a video the defense plans on introducing to the jury.

"We are here for Mel. We all love Mel. We miss Mel. And we will find Mel," he says. "My mother is a shell of herself. I am beside myself with grief. But we just have to keep moving. Keep walking. Keep looking. In honor of Mel. In her memory. She deserves a proper burial. And whoever did this to her is a monster and will pay."

The clip captured only the seventh day following her disappearance. Police had not yet ruled it a homicide. They had no reason to do so. She was merely missing. He was the first person—from investigators to family members to the media— to suggest that his sister was dead, weeks before it was officially corroborated.

Rocky Sandoval doesn't look the same anymore. He is just as tall and sturdy, but his belly now pokes out over his belt like a pouty, distended bottom lip. The hair atop his head— and the youthful light in his eyes—have fled him. Green and blue ink cover his forearms, and he wears a dense beard with flecks of red and white in an otherwise dark mane. He is freshly in his thirties, but he looks several years older and not like a contemporary of the beautiful dead girl he used to date.

As he takes respite in the shade from the punishing heat, clad in his reflective vest and boots, Rocky gulps down paper cup after cup of water dwarfed in his massive paw. Dom holds up the photograph of prom to compare the men, separated by twelve years. The water Rocky drinks seems to enter his body only to be secreted from his brow seconds later.

"My break's just fifteen minutes," he warns. "And I have to take a massive shit. So what's left is all the time you get."

Dom laughs halfheartedly, but Rocky doesn't. Dom hides his smile behind a cough.

"Thank you for speaking with me. How long did you and Melina date?"

"Five years, on and off. We were high school sweethearts and sort of together the year after her graduation, before we drifted apart. But we always stayed in contact. Our families remained friendly."

"Can you tell me about your impressions of Malcolm?"

Rocky smiles. Perfect teeth. It brightens his face, revealing glimpses of his former good looks.

"You want to know if they were fucking?"

Dom's face heats to the point that the blood underneath begins to itch his skin. He abstains from replying out of fear of trampling on an answer—and no words are able to pass through his tightened chest anyhow.

"I can tell you for sure that Mel would *never*," he spits out, hawking saliva onto the ground as if to clear the repulsive notion from his system. "She was close to him. She defended him. But she wasn't into anything gross. Certainly no incest shit. It's silly to say, but he wouldn't even be her type. She had a number of flings with guys who were more like the jock type. She was sexually free. What would she call herself again? A feminist. I think she used it as an excuse to be a slut. That's why we were on and off again. She cheated on me all the time. But she was a sweet girl. She just needed constant attention from men to fill the hole in her heart from when her daddy passed away—that's all."

Dom presses his pen furiously into his notepad, recording every word.

"Besides," Rocky continues, "we all were pretty sure Mal was a homo."

Dom looks up. "What makes you say that?"

"He was sensitive. He wore his hair long. Liked to wear jewelry. Stuff like that. He got the shit kicked out of him all the time. Mel came to his rescue. That didn't help—having a girl fight your battles for you. I tried once to give him some advice. He didn't have any brothers growing up. I told him to find the biggest of his bullies, ball his fist, and land one square between the eyes—out in the courtyard during lunch, in front of everyone. He would get his ass kicked afterward, no doubt, but he would have earned some respect. They would have left him alone after that. But he started shaking and nearly crying from just my suggestion. So I stopped trying to help."

Malcolm saw the boys congregated at the end of the hall. He heard their whispers and hushed laughs, caught their darting eyes. He felt pinpricks on his skin. His neurological response suspected danger. But he kept walking toward them. He had lost the free will to make a course correction. He knew what lay in waiting but could do nothing to avoid it.

The present and the future sped up to meet one another. The middle was inconspicuously cut out. He was suddenly on the ground. He had seen the leg extended out before him, but his mind blacked out the trip and fall—a form of self-preservation. He came to with searing pain shooting through his jaw that had just met with hard floor.

"Freak down!"

A boy held him supine, legs straddling the sides of him and seated down on his chest. Malcolm flailed.

"Isn't this how you like it?" the boy taunted.

"Be careful. He might get hard," one of the others warned.

The stench of the boy—pubescent body odor and hot breath—made Malcolm gag. Panic sent him reeling. He felt suffocated. It was psychosomatic. His passageways were clear of everything but stifling humiliation. His lungs were inundated by shame. He began to convulse, an attempt to ward off his predator. It was strategy, not injury. The boy shot up and off of him in one bound.

"You broke him."

The boy slapped the speaker across the chest, a symphony conductor desperate to choke off the mockery. He was now all nausea and speechless worry.

A frenzied girl arrived. She shoved the boy, newly contrite, with both hands. His sneakers skidded and squeaked against the tile floor.

"What's wrong with you?" Mel exclaimed. "Preparing for a future at the state penitentiary? You have idiot and future criminal written all over you."

The boy opened his mouth but formed no words. The gaggle behind him turned their sneers on him.

Mel raced to the floor, where her brother was now sitting up. She was an avalanche of caresses and concern. He tore himself away from her.

"Stop, Mel. Just stop."

He struggled to his feet. She stepped back, a flicker of hurt coloring her eyes.

"I can take care of myself. Just leave me alone."

"Go see the nurse," she said as he stormed off, back turned to the scene and his sister.

Rocky peers at his watch, more for effect than utility, its face muddied beyond discernibility by red earth. Dom picks up on the tell, hurrying his speech before his interview came to an unceremonious end.

"So those rumors about the two of them, they're recent? Only nasty gossip invented after her death?"

Rocky hesitates, literally sucking on the insides of his cheek, chewing on his words, contemplating whether to expel them. His eyes shoot to the ground as he relents.

"No. They've been around awhile," he grumbles. "Since they were teens. They were sometimes weird with each other. They would kiss on the lips. Even as adults. No tongue or anything like that. But full on the lips. Others noticed. That's probably where it all started. But the whole family did that. Their mother is a hippie. All of it was innocent.

"And Mal, he asked for it, being the nutjob that he is. He deserved it. But Mel, she was just *too* perfect. She had it all. Jealous people wanted to bust her chops. Find one thing wrong with her. Fucking your brother was just sexy and silly and awful enough to be that one thing. She didn't deserve it. Not then, and especially not now.

"That last year, when we weren't doing that hot as a couple, she checked in on me all the time. She would hear something horrible in the news—something across the world—and *still*, she'd call, asking if I was OK. She just cared so much, about everything, about everyone."

Rocky's phone vibrated on the nightstand. He groaned, rolling over in his tangled sheets to see the name on the screen, an anachronism by that point—Baby. He rushed to answer it.

"Hello."

The voice on the line merely breathed. Rocky reveled in hearing the sweet sound. He did not violate the silence.

Finally, a woman, *his* woman: "Are you alright?"

"Yes. Still sleeping."

"On a Tuesday?"

Rocky cleared his throat without response. She had gone off

to college. He had not. She spent her mornings in class. He spent his mornings sleeping in. He tried—and failed—to not let it bother him.

"You're at school?"

"No."

"What is it, honey?"

"I wanted to see that you're alright."

Rocky scoffed playfully.

"What happened in Indonesia today?"

"Turn on the news."

Rocky looks forlorn, lost in memory. It's all he has left of her, and it shows. The strain of loss wrinkles the corners of his eyes. It adds years to what is mere seconds.

"You've seen the accused?"

Clouds darken his eyes. Rage replaces regret. He nods the slightest of nods in reply.

"Any way she went to that shack of his voluntarily? That she slept with him of her own free will?"

"No." It is definitive. "She was sweet but shallow. She didn't pity-fuck anyone. The creep killed her."

One hand encloses the cup and strangles it, crumpling it into a ball before it's tossed in the trash.

"Time's up."

He reemerges into the blinding sun, saying no more.

BY DOMENICO SANTOS
Staff Writer

CORAL GABLES—Marta Mora sits on the edge of the neatly made bed of her late daughter, not an inch of it—or the room where it rests—touched since her girl was killed over two years ago. Her clothes still lie in an uneven pile on a vanity stool opposite a large mirror. A half-full glass of dusty water is still set on the nightstand, with a half-ring of her cherry lipstick coating the edge. A brush of hers still has loose hair clinging to it. Posters of famous art and musical bands from the '90s still adorn her pink walls. The room somehow appears both presently lived in and like an abandoned moment of a slice in time.

On the night before she is set to testify in the murder trial of the man accused of murdering her daughter, Ms. Mora, 45, sits among her daughter's things and ruminates.

"It's hard when there's no body. It's hard when nothing but air fills her coffin," Mora says. "You can't quite put her things away. There's always a feeling—an impossible, but nagging feeling—that she might return. That she might come back. You know, traditionally in Hispanic culture, children do not leave the home until they marry, no matter how late in age that may be. Mel never did get the chance to marry, so I guess she—um, her things will remain here, like this, forever. My baby gets to be here with me forever."

Melina Mora had lived in her parents' home up until her untimely death at age 27. Her room captures that motley evolution from child to adult, mixing remnants belonging to a little girl (rows of stuffed animals), teenager (school trophies and tiaras), and woman (a bookcase shelf with handles of liquor). In stark relief to the clutter of that room stood the bed: pristinely made in what her mother says was a compulsive early-morning ritual.

That level of refinement amid chaos, friends and family say, sums up Melina well.

"She was grace under fire," recalls longtime friend Catalina Rosenberg.

That fire began to burn, people close to Melina say, when tragedy struck early in her life. Melvin Mora, her father, died when Melina was only eleven years old after taking a spill on a walk home, hitting and concussing his head, falling asleep in his bed, and failing to wake up the next morning, according to police reports. The medical examiner, Leon Musgrave—the very same one who would end up analyzing the remains of his daughter nearly twenty years later—found that Mr. Mora had a blood alcohol level of .18 several hours after the accident. He was 27 years old.

Melina grew even closer to her twin brother, Malcolm Mora, in reaction to their father's sudden death.

"M and M were inseparable," Ms. Mora recalls. "That's what I called them: M and M, like the candy. Even as they started hanging out with different crowds, Mel always looked after her brother. That was Mel. Loyal to a fault, but what a beautiful quality to have, no?"

Ms. Mora is an optimist by nature. She consistently wears a readymade smile, sometimes through unshed tears. She keeps her hair long, nearly down to her waist, and allows it to gray naturally. She avoids chemicals, dyes, and synthetics of all kinds, she says. When she leaves a room, she tells every single person left behind, separately, to *"Go in beauty."* She is a tactile person, stroking the shoulders and arms of acquaintances and strangers in greeting, including the author of this story.

"I can read energies that way," she offers, before adding: "I don't think Mel had that same ability. She, unfortunately, trusted everyone. She could never tell apart those who wanted to harm her, who wanted to use *her, from those who wanted to be near her for the right reasons."*

Interviews with over 10 friends and family members of Melina revealed a girl popular by dint of her good looks and sweet disposition, but one who harbored a wild streak.

"Everyone loved her because she was beautiful but not self-absorbed. That's not to say she was clueless about her beauty. She was meticulously put-together—everywhere she went. It was intentional," Ms. Rosenberg says. "It's just that she was nice about it. She had the friendly personality to back it up. Plus, she was a fairly smart girl. She had it all, really."

Melina won the title of homecoming queen her senior year. She was in the top 10 percent of her graduating class. Her high school sweetheart played for the football team. She earned her bachelor's degree at Florida International University in psychology. She went on to work in human resources at a large marketing firm, receiving steady promotions and earning positive reviews as she worked her way up.

Some peers bristle at a portrait of Melina's life that is too perfect in hindsight.

"The dead are always treated as saints—but she was certainly no saint," said a former classmate able to corroborate a close relationship with Melina but who wished to remain anonymous in order to speak candidly without fear of reprisal. "She liked to drink heavily. It always worried us because of her dad. She liked to party and stay out late at night. She loved male attention. It started in high school, but she kept it up through adulthood."

Rocky Sandoval, Melina's ex-boyfriend, on and off

again for five years in their teens, confirms that Melina sought comfort and security by engaging in frequent one-off romantic flings.

Said a longtime coworker of the victim's who also wished to remain anonymous in order to speak frankly: "It honestly didn't surprise me to learn that she had been hurt by a man she met at a bar. She should have been safer. That it was this *guy did surprise me. Not her type at all."*

Gabriel Soto, 30, is charged with the premeditated murder and sexual battery of Melina Mora. His lawyers say that police prematurely settled on Mr. Soto as the prime suspect and closed their investigation before adequately following other leads. Despite a pretrial ruling largely excluding testimony about the victim's sexual history—known popularly as the Rape Shield Rule— defense attorneys for Mr. Soto have argued that the victim's supposed penchant for going home with strangers should have impelled investigators to find those men and rule them out as suspects.

*"You will hear that Melina Mora often went home with strangers. But you will hear that police did nothing—*nothing—*to follow up with those other men. Who are they? What are their alibis? You won't know. Because police don't know either," defense attorney Jordan Whipple told the jury in his opening statement earlier this week. "Once they decided it was Gabriel who did this, they shut their eyes and ears to any and all evidence that pointed to someone else. And you will hear plenty of evidence in this trial that points to someone else."*

Defense attorneys plan on supplying the jury with a few alternative names. Mr. Sandoval is one of those. Police failed to interview Mr. Sandoval in the several months after investigators ruled Melina's death a homicide. By the time police arrested Mr. Soto, they had yet to have one conversation with Mr. Sandoval, although the victim's cell phone records show that Melina called Mr. Sandoval on the night of her disappearance. The time of that call approximately coincides with the hours prosecutors say Mr. Soto lured Melina to his home in Homestead and raped and killed her.

But, police sources say, records show that Mr. Sandoval did not pick up that phone call from Melina, and Mr. Sandoval otherwise has a solid alibi. He was not in town but across the country visiting family the week of her disappearance.

"Rocky is a red herring. The defendant is just throwing everything at the wall to see what sticks. His lawyers know—as does anyone who has ever spoken to Rocky— that he had absolutely nothing to do with harming this girl who he still seems to very much love," says a source within the Miami-Dade Police Department, speaking on the condition of anonymity in order to publicly comment on the details of an investigation.

Another name on the lips of defense attorneys— heavily mentioned in their opening statement—is that of the deceased's twin brother Malcolm.

"Melina had many friends, but very few close friends. Friends came and went. But her love for Malcolm never faltered," says a third source who knew both Melina and Malcolm, but requested anonymity to speak freely about their relationship. "She was a touchy person, just like her mom. The siblings would kiss on the lips. I've seen them hold hands. I found it odd but harmless. Other people made it nasty."

Defense attorneys for Mr. Soto blame police for

refusing to investigate Malcolm as a possible suspect. They claim that he has never supplied a proper alibi for his whereabouts on the night in question—he was at his apartment, alone, he says—and police never secured a search warrant for his residence. The blunt object that killed Melina, likely a bat per the theory of the prosecution, has never been found. The defense has also insinuated that Malcolm had an unhealthy affection for his twin sister, a rumor that plagued the two long before her death.

Not one friend or family member took seriously the notion that the twins had anything other than a close sibling relationship.

"Wherever he was, he would fly across the country just to spend his birthday with her," says Ms. Rosenberg. "I don't think he missed one. She wouldn't have it any other way."

So far, Melina—the human face behind the tragedy—has not drawn much attention in her own murder trial. The prosecution hopes to change that by calling her mother to the stand first thing this morning.

Dom's hard shoes squeak as he passes through the metal detector. Its siren wails. On the other side of a glass screen, Sandy fast-tracks through the attorney entrance in gender-performing stilts that pound on stained tile. Her hair is pinned up for relief from the stifling heat, but not for long. Her hair is always down in front of the jury, because men like their women with long hair, and it helps cover the blotchiness that seizes the fair skin of her neck in moments of acute stress.

A mentor of hers within the office—a fierce pit bull of a middle-aged woman with a barbed exterior who routinely lies to juries about having children to appear maternal—once derided a particularly hip pair of her shoes as insufficiently feminine.

"Scrap those hooves," the senior trial counsel growled at her. "You'll look like a bull dyke."

Sandy tossed those shoes in the trash that evening. But not without first donating a hefty amount to the Human Rights Campaign to ease her liberal conscience.

Dom freezes in place, staring at his former lover. To him, she's absolutely gorgeous with her hair up.

The guard's words cut through his daze.

"Sir! The shoes. Take them off."

Dom falters awkwardly before tearing off his shoes, pulling on them forcefully to wedge them off without loosening the laces. Sandy overhears the commotion and halts. Dom walks through the detectors in socks and, again, its sensors clamor. The line of people behind him erupts in a smattering of impatient hollering. Dom pats his pockets and lifts his shirt in search of the culprit.

"Your belt, sir!" the guard shouts.

Sandy intervenes, moving forward in a swift, graceful bound and placing a reassuring hand on the guard's shoulder.

"It's fine, Mark. He's with me."

Like elastic, the tensity in Mark's body relaxes at her touch, deflating him. Dom gathers his belongings, struggling to put on his shoes as he tries to keep up with Sandy.

The two are side by side but wordless. Sandy breaks first.

"I read that hit job you published this morning."

"It's not a hit job."

"And yet, it remarkably parrots everything the defense is claiming."

He grabs her by the arm and diverts their course into an empty corridor. Their eyes are more level than usual, given her heels, and hers smolder into his at the indignity of his action.

"It was a fair piece. It fleshed out the counterpoints to every defense claim. I'm just doing my job. I'm not being disloyal to you."

"Don't make this about us," she begs, eyes rolling to the back of her head. "This is strictly about that ham-fisted story of yours. Four anonymous sources. Really? I see you couldn't find anyone to attach their real names to that garbage. It's embarrassing, Dom."

"I've heard you, Sandy. I've heard you in moments with your guard down express every one of the concerns my piece raises. These are legitimate doubts and threats to your case. Everyone knows Malcolm is a weirdo. Everyone knows police ignored other leads. I'm just vocalizing what other people are already saying."

"You're helping a murderer get off."

"How? What does it matter what the court of public opinion says? All that matters is what those six jurors say—and you've got him dead to rights in that courtroom."

"They're not sequestered, Dom. They go home, and they watch, and they read. They're not supposed to do that, but it's nearly impossible to avoid. And on the morning I'm putting the victim's mother on the stand—at this emotional crescendo that's supposed to be about Melina—you print the accusation that her children were sleeping with one another. That *filth* will be on those jurors' minds."

"They haven't read it!"

"You don't know that!"

Peering around to ensure no ears and eyes are eavesdropping, he leans close and—woozy from the excitement that it brings—has the breath and words sucked right out of him. Instead, his eyes linger on her lips and he soaks in her scent. His lungs tighten, and air passes through in tortured, noisy bursts. His grip on her arm softens and melts into a caress.

He whispers: "Would it turn you on if I told you that I missed you?"

She laughs, patronizingly.

"It's been a week," she notes. "No. That wouldn't do it for me. It's . . . *you're* . . . far too sappy."

Undeterred, he keeps his proximity and, baring his teeth in a snarl, fastens his grasp onto her buttock, pinching so hard that it hurts. This time, it's Sandy who has the wind knocked out of her. Her head snaps back onto the wall, but she barely feels it.

"Better?" he asks.

"Warmer," she answers breathlessly.

Faint alternative music played in the bar dimly lit with a purple hue, on the night Sandy, a green misdemeanor prosecutor, met Dom, a reporter newly on the crime beat, over beers. Hers was a hoppy India pale ale; his was a lager. A colleague of hers—a loud but endearing braggart whose childish name, Skippy, matched his ebullient personality—had brought Dom to an after-work happy hour. Eager to avoid cross talk of prosecution, she pulled up onto the barstool beside him, away from the crowds of lawyers steeped in navel-gazing.

"Who shortens Domenico to Dom? It should be Nico," she teased. She was bold and strong at first blush, like her beer preference. "Are you Italian or something?"

He laughed. "No. I think my mom's just a bit of an Italophile."

"Now, Santos—*that* name I like. It's the name of the president on my favorite TV show."

"You're interested in politics?"

"Something like that. I myself plan on running for president of the United States one day."

She said it facetiously, but Dom believed it. Humor reveals more than it obscures, he found.

"Well, I plan on writing for the *New Yorker* one day."

"The writing's a tad flowery and overindulgent for my taste."

"I once had a professor—who nonetheless gave me an A, by the way—criticize my writing as too melodramatic for her department. Too melodramatic for academia. Too melodramatic for journalism. Where can a man of letters just indulge in vanity projects that feature lyrical prose, overly complicated sentence structure, and ornate, high-minded vocabulary?" he wondered. "The *New Yorker*'s all I've come up with."

"How about fiction? Write a novel."

"No one will buy it," he lamented. "Nobody speaks that way. Nobody wants to read anything above a certain grade level. Nobody wants to think that hard."

"Give the literate public more credit than that."

The hour ended, coworkers departed, but the two remained entrenched in conversation. The night grew long. A sharp switch in song drew him to his feet. A Latin song, a merengue, blared through the speakers after hours of slow-tempo rock. It was very Miami, marking the point of the night when even hipster bars prepared for drunken carousing. No one was dancing, but he propositioned her.

"You just want an excuse to touch me," she accused.

She was right. It was his go-to move. Get a girl dancing. Pull her near. A kiss—or an attempt at one—won't be far off. And he *was* a good dancer.

Sandy agreed. Spectators gawked at the solitary couple on the makeshift dance floor. The contrast of their colors drew attention, even in the dark, from those who found it unfortunate and those who found it refreshing, a problematic form of diversity fetishism. Sandy had previously fallen into the latter category.

"Is it wrong of me, but I automatically like a white guy a trillion times more if I find out he's dating a black girl? Like, good for you," she once shared with her woman friends of color. It didn't sit well with them, but they couldn't exactly verbalize why.

Dom fumbled his hand placement at first, searching momentarily for the right level before settling several inches above the waist. She protested.

"Cold," she announced.

He ratcheted up, misreading her direction.

"Colder," she quipped.

He grinned and slid down to her hip.

"Warmer."

He flashed her a sideways look. Her eyes were rife with challenge. The alcohol fueled his courage. He widened his palm and shifted it down to her buttocks. She massaged the curls at his nape. His hand stayed put for the rest of the dance.

The loud voices of passersby send Dom's hand off Sandy as if fleeing a burning surface. He turns away from her, collecting himself.

"I don't know that Ms. Mora can handle testifying about her daughter," he suggests once he settles down.

"You spend a few afternoons with her and now you can diagnose what she can and cannot handle?" she snaps. He winces at the lashing. She casts her eyes down in shame. "That's the point, Dom."

"The point is to put her through the emotional wringer?"

"That's right. I want to make her cry. I want her to go through a full breakdown. I want the jury to see her heart breaking before them. I want it to hurt," she insists.

Dom appears both quizzical and horrified. Sandy softens.

"I want to win. My job is to win. For Melina, above everyone else," she says. "In the short term, her mother will hate it. But in the long term, she'll thank me. When I successfully lock up her daughter's killer, she'll thank me. I can't be weak. I need to be as brutal as he was when he murdered her. I need to be as unfeeling."

He nods. Clouds still darken his expression, but understanding pokes through. He knows intimately what it means to shut off your humanity in pursuit of an allegedly nobler cause.

She bridges the space between them, extending her hand to his arm.

"When this is over, I'll go back to thawing out all of the feeling: self-doubt, disgust, empathy, vulnerability, *love*." His eyes snap upward at her at the mention. She has never before used the word. She reassures him with her gaze that her word choice was intentional. "But not until my job is over. Not until he is punished."

Minutes later, they take their respective places onstage, and the show goes on.

"Good morning, ladies and gentlemen of the jury," the judge begins. "I'll ask you, again—as I do every morning—have you obeyed my order not to discuss the case with anyone, including among yourselves, and not to engage in any media surrounding the case? Left every conversation in which this case is brought up? Put down any story that you immediately recognize to be about this case? Turned off the TV upon the very mention of anything familiar to this case?"

The members nod in silent assent.

"Great. State: Call your next witness."

"The State calls Marta Mora to the stand."

As the bailiff escorts Ms. Mora through the courtroom, jurors lean forward to closely inspect the woman. She looks so much like her daughter that it's the closest they'll get to imagining the living, breathing version of the deceased. She acknowledges the jury with a smile, looking into the eyes of every one, and, only briefly, sweeps her gaze past the defendant—panic noticeably seizing her senses—before settling on the prosecutor. Gabriel is unreactive.

"Good morning, Ms. Mora."

"Good morning."

"What do you do for a living?"

"I do real estate, specializing in the Coral Gables area."

"Are you married?"

"Widowed."

"When did your husband pass away?"

"Almost twenty years ago, when the kids were only eleven."

"How many children do you have?"

"How many? Well..." she struggles, eyes aflutter. Sandy purposefully does not clarify, to highlight the discomfort in speaking about her daughter in the past tense. Ms. Mora finally settles on the most painful tense. "I *had* two. My twin boy and girl: Malcolm and Melina. Mal is still with us."

"And what happened to Melina?"

"She was killed."

Jordan twitches in his chair, nearly springing forward to object, but he thinks better of it. It is too late, and the reward of it being sustained—highly likely—too small anyway. Mom has no expert, personal knowledge that her daughter's death is a homicide, but she is a civilian speaking colloquially, so he lets it slide.

"Tell me about Melina."

This, Jordan will not let slide.

"I'm going to object to relevance."

It is technically strictly irrelevant, and it's almost nakedly meant to appeal to juror sympathy, but judges allow some leeway in the background exposition of the major players in the case. This judge is no different.

"It's one question, Mr. Whipple. For now, I will overrule. But just one question, Ms. Grunwald."

"You may answer the question," Sandy instructs. "Tell the members of the jury about who Melina was."

"She was a beautiful person—inside and out. Very loving. Very friendly. Very trusting. She saw the best in people. Hard-working. Smart. She was well-liked. Beloved, really. I miss her every day."

Her lip shakes, but it is glued into a smile nonetheless.

"Talk about the last time you saw Melina—the night of November 13, two years ago."

"She left for the night. She got all gussied up, as usual. Hair, makeup—the whole nine. She really knew how to do all of that to perfection. It was an art. It was Friday. She was going out. She took her phone with her; I know that. She gave me a kiss goodbye. She was a good girl; she never left without saying goodbye first. I'm sure I told her how gorgeous she looked. I *always* told her that. It never felt repetitive. It was like I was stunned silent every day I saw her—for twenty-seven years. And then, she left. That was the last time I saw my baby."

Her voice cracks at that last line.

"Do you know exactly where she was heading?"

"No. She was an adult. I knew she was going out for the night, but not exactly where."

"Did she leave with anyone else?"

"No."

"Did she tell you she was meeting anyone else?"

"No."

"Ms. Mora, I'm going to ask you to look at the man seated at the center of that table, the defendant in this case. Can you do that for me?"

Tears glisten in her eyes but do not fall. Not a muscle in her face moves, stretched into a forced grin, as her vacant eyes look not at Sandy but seemingly through her. She does not answer for what feels like a full minute. Sandy worries she might refuse to turn to him at all. But she quietly nods, and ever so slowly, pivots her head methodically to the man standing accused of murdering her daughter.

Sandy lets the moment linger.

As if she were staring at the sun, Ms. Mora—failing to blink even once—trembles as she gazes into the browns of his irises. She wants to pull away but cannot.

Gabriel is a blank slate. His attorney has counseled him to remain so. Feigning compassion can backfire and read as regret. Any attempt at charm, like a smile, can come off cold and creepy. Better to remain neutral at the risk of coming across as inhuman. But Jordan is surprised at how well Gabriel emotes nothing, as if he were not even present. It sends a chill down his spine. He pretends he's just cold, wrapping himself in his arms for show.

"Do you recognize that man at all?"

"No!" She nearly yells the word. It breaks the spell. She can look away. And she does, but not without those pent-up tears silently freeing themselves down the length of her face.

"Had you ever before seen him with Melina?"

"No."

"They certainly weren't dating?"

"Objection! Speculation."

"To her knowledge, Your Honor," Sandy defends.

"If you know, ma'am, you may answer the question," the judge rules.

Ms. Mora snorts, in what has now become a common reaction at the suggestion that the defendant and the victim were at all romantically linked.

"No. I have met every single one of Melina's boyfriends. She and I were close. She brought them home. Every single one. I have never in my life seen that man before. He and Melina were not dating."

"Have you met someone by the name of Rocky Sandoval?"

"Yes, of course," she answers, physically relaxing at the mention. "Rocky was the one who got away. He loved my daughter. She loved him. He has known the family for a long time, and I've known his for a long time: good people. He has been there for us in this rough time, since Melina's death."

"Was Melina spending time with Rocky around the time of her disappearance?"

"No, unfortunately. They had long called it quits. We saw him every now and again, during the holidays. And I know Mel would call to check in with him sometimes. But they were not spending time together, no."

"I want to get back to that night, November 13. When did you start suspecting that something was amiss?"

"Not until the following afternoon. I didn't think anything of not hearing from her that night. She would often spend the night at a girlfriend's house or at—" She censors herself abruptly. Her face turns maroon. "I wasn't expecting a call from her that same night. But when I didn't get one by the afternoon of the next day, I became worried. She was very good about calling."

"But you didn't call police that next afternoon or even that next night. You waited until the following morning. Why?"

"I don't know. I had always heard you're not supposed to report a missing person until twenty-four hours later. That they won't take you seriously until at least twenty-four hours later. I didn't want to be *that* mother." Her chest rises and falls rhythmically with her overwrought heart. As she speaks, it sounds as if she's simultaneously gasping for air. The smile previously plastered on her face like a china doll has evaporated, replaced by a mouth agape in search of more oxygen. She is careening into an emotional wall. "I was wrong. I regret that now. I should have called as soon as I felt it in my gut. Maybe I could have saved her! Maybe she would still be alive if I had!"

She buries her head in her hands. Her body quakes as she conceals her shame. Sandy waits until she reemerges, reddened and sniffling.

"How did her brother, Malcolm, react to her disappearance?"

"Overcome with grief. They were close. He felt the loss physically in his bones. He was quite depressed."

"Ms. Mora, did you at some point receive the call every mother hopes to never get?"

"Yes," she whispers, so low she may have just mimed it without producing a sound.

It is time.

Sandy saunters over to the clerk, picks up a photo, and shows it to defense counsel.

"I am showing defense counsel what's already been admitted into evidence, by stipulation, as State's Thirty," she announces for the record.

Jordan is flummoxed. He pops up from his seat.

"I object!"

"To what, Your Honor?" Sandy interjects. "It's already in evidence."

"May we come sidebar?"

The judge relents. She waves them forward as she plays a noise scrambler designed to mask their conversation at the bench. The two sides approach, as the jury sits excluded from the exchange.

"Your Honor, there is no proper reason for counsel to show this witness this picture," Jordan explains, hopped up on adrenaline. "No reason but to dislodge an emotional response from her and inflame the passions of the jury. That is not allowed."

"We have to prove legal ID. Prove that a person died, beyond a reasonable doubt. In a case without a full body intact, this picture is the best we can do," Sandy counters.

"They have DNA analysts for that. They have a medical examiner for that."

"Counsel cannot dictate how I present my case. If I have to prove something beyond a reasonable doubt, I have the responsibility to prove it as solidly as I can, with as much testimony as I can."

"There's simply no way this civilian can identify anything from this picture. That defies credulity."

"And counsel will have the opportunity to cross-examine Ms. Mora as to whatever she can identify. But he can't micromanage her answer before she gives it. She's under oath. She determines what she's able to identify and what she can't."

"Then, I'll stipulate to legal ID."

"The State won't accept that stipulation."

The judge raises a finger, squelching the back-and-forth to which she has so patiently listened.

Her Honor speaks: "Let me look at the picture."

She inspects it closely before turning her eyes to Sandy, eyebrow arched in disbelief.

"You're asking her to identify her daughter from this?"

Sandy begins to reply, but halts. The judge reserves a cloying smile for her, impressed with her gall, but she ultimately sides against the defense nonetheless.

"The State is free to ask what it wants to ask, and the witness is free to answer however she chooses to answer. Defense has the opportunity on cross-examination to attack what very well may defy credulity, as you say."

The attorneys step back, and the judge clarifies for the record, for the jury, her ruling.

"That objection is overruled. Ms. Grunwald, you may proceed."

She walks the photograph over to the projector, magnifying the image on a TV screen for the courtroom to see.

"Is this all that's left of your daughter?"

A photograph depicting a smattering of nondescript bones sits on that projector. Nothing can be made out of them. Not even a human shape, as there are too few and they are too haphazardly laid out to indicate anything. Sandy can hardly get out her question. As soon as the image makes it to the screen, and Ms. Mora turns her head to peek at it, she erupts. She devolves into full-fledged sobs.

"My baby! My baby!"

Her moans reverberate throughout the courtroom, guttural at first, before fading into high-pitched wails. There is uncomfortable shifting in seats, but no sound. The air is heavy. It weighs down the heads of spectators. It's physically difficult to keep them up. Her cries last for minutes, without interruption. Sandy hears sniffles behind her in the gallery and even within the jury box.

She doesn't wait for a clear answer. The exercise was never meant to have her seriously identify anything anyway.

"No further questions."

Sandy sits as the blubbering continues. She feels no joy.

Gabriel is staid. The jurors oscillate between watching him and a mother in vocal mourning.

Jordan has pages of cross-examination prepared. His partner lays a hand on his shoulder to preempt his rising.

"You can't do this right now," she warns. "You can call her up again later, if needed. But no good will come from this right now."

Sullen, lips in a tight line, stretched so thin they are white under the strain, he rises only to say: "Nothing from the defense."

05 | FEVER DREAM

Joseph Cole dug into earth with fattened fingers, parsing black soil that clung to his white skin. It was damp, cool, and pliable to the touch. He pawed at the ground, uncovering a concave valley just deep enough for the leafy green whose roots he interred. After parting and then marrying the newly disparate sides, he patted at the land repeatedly, erasing any trace of his human intervention. He stood from his crouch and returned to the sidewalk, where he had left his shoes and crew socks, because the sole of no shoe touched his well-manicured lawn and garden. His bare feet hopped on scorching concrete as he raced to slip on protection.

The neighbors across the street interrupted the dance.

"Good morning, Joe," the father called out, his wife and young child beside him.

"Howdy."

Joe waved shortly, before tensing his body in an unnaturally straight-spine salute, hand at his eyebrow and elbow out. He maintained that position, eyeline clear in front of him, so that the unfocused trio blurred into the foreground. It kept him from discerning the awkward smile his neighbor flashed him, before nodding in strained acknowledgment and walking his family hurriedly indoors. Only when the door shut behind them did Joe finally stand at ease.

His neighbor had served in the military. Joe had not.

He wiped his sullied hands on the lap of his jean shorts, spat out the saliva collecting in his mouth, and turned in an about-face toward his home. A towering American flag hoisted above his front door flapped thunderously in the wind as he entered.

He strode into his kitchen and up to the sink. At the table sat his wife and two daughters.

"Chase and Becca from across the street returned with an Oriental."

"*Joey!*" his wife responded in horror.

"What, Syd? I can't say that word now?" he asked, feigning puzzlement. "He served in the Gulf War. Not Vietnam. So, where'd he pick up that fetish? It's like he has this compulsion to save the world or something."

"Maybe his equipment doesn't work. Ever thought that's why he and his wife adopt?" Sydney asked.

Joe huffed pensively to himself, smirking. He much preferred that theory.

"I have nothing against diversity," he continued. "I'm thrilled to add a little color to the neighborhood. Didn't I say that about the Franklins moving in down the street? That it was about damn time a chocolate swirl was added to what has been plain vanilla for generations?"

"You made a point of saying it to their faces. And just as *colorfully* as that. It was embarrassing, Joey."

He dismissed the criticism with a tsk.

"I wanted them to know I was one of the good ones. How would they ever know if I didn't tell them?"

"The good ones don't need to say it."

He shook his head in polite disagreement.

"I'm glad Chase brought home an *Asian*," he remarked, stressing the new imposition on his lexical freedom. "Only thing is that the little genius will give the girls a run for their money, academically. There goes their shot at valedictorian one day."

Sydney sighed, rising from her seat and leaving her children to continue their coloring as she neared him at the sink. He had removed his wedding band, laid it on the countertop as he washed the grime from his hands, and then washed the charm itself, precariously over the drain.

"If you just take it off before you garden, you can skip this step and save it from potentially falling into that abyss," she cautioned as she rubbed his upper back in concentric circles.

"A married man keeps his ring on in public at all times. It never comes off. You know that."

She nodded. They kissed. She returned to the children.

One evening, weeks later, Joe stopped short on the walkway up to his front door. Twilight had cast its obscuring pall over suburbia, so he stared long and hard at the spot in his lawn that had drawn his stunned attention. He strained the muscles in his eyes, causing a twitch in the nerves now protruding from his skin, creating phantom lightning that sieged his vision. Sucking in his breath—to both still his heightened pulse and contract his paunchy stomach—he squatted down and extended his fingers to investigate. Two fresh footprints had depressed the height of his uniformly cut grass and kicked up clumps of dirt in their wake.

On any other, lesser, uncultivated lawn, the transgression would not have been as visible.

"Missing something?" said a booming voice that cut through his trance.

It was Chase. Tall, fit, deep-voiced, and self-assured—if potentially sterile—Chase from across the street.

"What, sir?"

"I just asked if you were missing something, too. You seemed to be looking. And we lost a package earlier this week. Company said they delivered it, but we never received it."

Joe leapt to his feet in a bound and shook his head no several times. He added no words.

After a while: "OK." With that, Chase turned to reenter his home.

"Thank you for your service!" Joe blurted to his neighbor's back as it nearly disappeared behind the doorframe.

Chase half turned and gave him a nod, or what could be loosely interpreted as a nod, and a smile, or what could be loosely interpreted as a smile—"Good night, Joe"—and shut his door behind him.

Mumbling under his breath, Joe retreated to his sanctuary. Inside, he nearly ran right into his wife.

"What's wrong, Joey?"

"The lawn. It's been compromised."

"Huh?"

"Someone stepped on it, Sydney! There are two gaping depressions on my perfect lawn."

"Oh, Joey. Maybe the girls got carried away during playtime. I'll talk to them. They know better."

He shook his head vigorously.

"No. No. No. No," he rattled off. "Too big. It was a male foot. A man's or maybe an adolescent boy's. But not the girls'."

Her mouth fell open. He fumed for a beat, and then stalked off.

"Did you see my workout videos out there?"

He drew to a halt.

"What are you talking about?"

"My VHS workout videos. I bought them from the Home Shopping Network. Were they out there? I was expecting them today."

The next morning, he crawled out of bed early and returned with a store-bought apple pie.

"Unpack this, and make it look homemade," he told Sydney.

"Why?"

"Because that's what I'm telling the Franklins. That you baked it."

Skeptically, but dutifully, she unwrapped the pie and transferred it over to one of her sheet pans.

"Why are you bringing the Franklins a pie?"

"As an offering," he began. "And to see if I can spy any fresh mud caked on their teenage boy's shoes."

"Joey!"

"What? It won't take much. They insist on that God-awful request that visitors discard their shoes and leave them at the foyer like their floors are made of Italian marble or something."

"It's very nice hardwood, Joey."

"That don't make them better than us," he scoffed. "I'll take a quick peek at Tyrone's Air Jordans, and I'll be out of there."

"His name is Timothy."

"That's what I said: Timothy."

"I don't like this, Joey. I don't like why you've gone off and just assumed it was Tim to begin with. I don't like the look of it."

"Get off your high horse, Syd. *That* has nothing to do with nothing. The Franklins and their boy just so happen to be the latest addition to the neighborhood. And these disappearing packages are a new phenomenon."

"That's not quite true. Chase's kid is newer."

"The Asian?" he shot back, mulling the prospect over momentarily. "Naw. Nope. Don't think so. That don't make any sense."

He left and, exactly six minutes later, he was back, defeated.

"That quick?"

"They didn't invite me inside. I couldn't get a good look at anything."

Joe didn't often get invited inside homes.

Joe's next move was surveillance. He hired men to install a camera directed at the walkway and the surrounding greenery. He had them hide the equipment in a floral arrangement that hung overhead.

"What's the point of that? Won't making it visible and obvious prevent the theft outright?" Sydney asked.

"The purpose isn't deterrence. It's capture."

He placed a decoy box on his lawn. It contained only index cards, retail value of a couple dollars. But it was just the right size: big enough to potentially contain valuables, small enough to remain portable and easy to swipe.

Technology didn't allow for contemporaneous viewing of the footage. So he waited. He directed his family to leave the box untouched. It sat there for days. But on the day it disappeared, he barricaded himself in his room and reviewed hours of video. The quality was poor. When the figure appeared within frame, Joe sprung out of his chair. No shot of his face. He wore a hoodie in the desert heat and kept his eyes down to the ground. But after his silhouette came into focus, his hand reached down to pick up the box, and seconds later, he was gone.

On his desktop computer that night, Joe designed a flyer. In the morning, he made a trip to the office supply store, made hundreds of copies, and by afternoon, he was taping them onto light posts throughout the neighborhood. He knocked on a few doors belonging to the neighbors he knew best. Chase was, of course, paid a personal visit.

"I'm starting a neighborhood watch committee," Joe told him. "Binoculars, walkie-talkies, armbands—the whole nine. Get a handle on this crime wave that's sprung up."

"Armbands? Isn't that a little gestapo?"

"Ges—what?"

"You know, Nazi. SS. Heil Hitler. That sort of thing."

"Oh, no. Not at all. We don't have any Jews in this neighborhood."

"Joe, I'm Jewish."

"Really? But you're so . . . tall. You definitely don't look it."

Chase involuntarily rolled his eyes and sighed audibly.

"Don't you think this is something better left to police?"

"We need to protect our own turf, where we lay our heads. Protect our children. Not outsource the security of our homes. We're men, aren't we? The first meeting is this Saturday. You don't have anything on Saturdays, do you, Chase?"

"I'll see you later, Joe."

That first meeting was sparsely attended. Lou was a silver-haired biker with arms bare in the Arizona sun and combat boots covering sweaty feet. He had no discernible politics—the greened tattoos covering his white skin featured incoherent symbols spanning Buddhist China, astrology, nihilism, and Irish dissidence. Lou famously attended community events solely for the free swag, food, and refreshments, but Joe, for whom money was tight after purchasing the surveillance system, had sprung only for a pitcher of terrible lemonade that made sensitive gums bleed. Todd wore a conspicuous ponytail, thick-rimmed glasses, khaki pants, and a mustache the same color as his skin. He was known for exactly two things: having a more-than-passing resemblance to serial killer Jeffrey Dahmer and spending his weekends serving as the local Peeping Tom. His interest in neighborhood watch was strictly prurient.

Harris rounded out the quartet of disaffected white men, and he was the most ideologically aligned to Joe and his pursuits. Harris was conservative, clean-cut, and average in every way imaginable. He attended church on Sundays, had strictly missionary-style sex with his wife on a biweekly basis, drank a single beer and smoked a single cigarette every night at dinner, and—most relevantly—stored a stockpile of firearms and ammunition in his attic. The inaugural watch party turned into a Second Amendment convention rather quickly.

"What will you do once you catch one of these people? Ask them politely to sit on the curb until the police arrive? These gangs of kids are super-predators nowadays, barely human at all," Harris proselytized. "The only language they speak is violence. Weapons—not words—will bring them to heel."

Joe was enraptured. Lou and Todd not so much.

"Guns make me nervous," Lou offered sheepishly.

"But look at you," Joe remarked. Lou took offense.

"I am a pacifist, dude," he scoffed. "These tats are all about love."

The meeting spilled over, sans the pervert and the hippie, into Harris's attic only a block away from the community center room Joe had rented for the hour. He presented Joe with gun after gun, disassembling and assembling in a reflexive, elegant choreography of his hands as he bore into the minute and technical detail that set each one apart from the others.

"It's almost sexual," Joe murmured impulsively, without a hint of irony, as he fingered a particularly long barrel.

"It's intoxicating," Harris agreed. His wife, in fact, had come to expect rare unscheduled romps after particularly prolonged sessions of him playing with his lethal toys.

"There isn't much in a man's life that doesn't necessarily, in some way, connect back to his penis," she was fond of saying. She could have easily labeled herself a Freudian, had she known who Freud was or read anything whatsoever.

"Would you like me to sell you one?"

"Today? Right now? Is that legal?"

"Yes."

It was.

Joe made two purchases—one openly, one in secret—that rattled Sydney in the subsequent weeks. The first grated on her because of the expense. He parked his newly bought golf cart in the driveway one afternoon, beaming and soaking in self-satisfaction. He had provided her no advance warning. Sydney did not regularly yell, but she reserved her highest octaves for that occasion.

"What is this even for? You don't golf!"

"The neighborhood watch, honey. I can't make good time patrolling the block on foot."

"God forbid you exercise," she charged, under her breath. "How can we afford this?"

"I'm in charge of the finances, Syd. Leave it to me," he said evasively. Joe had developed a habit of taking out several relatively small loans with the community bank whenever he made impulse purchases, leaving him with varied interest rates across numerous accounts that he failed to properly track and for which he consequently faced steep late fees.

"Please, Joey, don't borrow against our future—and the girls' future!"

"I'm making sure we even have a future. The money'll be no good if we're dead after a burglary gone wrong."

After work, in the waning luminosity of dusk, he rode for hours in his motorized cart, armed with a bullhorn. With a tight smile, a stiff wave, and sunglasses shielding his eyes, he wordlessly acknowledged residents as he swept by with the stoic self-grandeur of a reluctant hero. He received quiet disdain or stifled laughter in response. He reported what he deemed to be suspicious activity to police, racing home to get to a phone and provide what by then had become outdated and useless information. They had come to recognize his line with nascent caller ID technology, and relied on the same patient, even-toned dispatcher, Rosa, to field his calls. But mostly he shooed playing children off the street or shouted at and failingly pursued cars speeding past the posted limit.

He sometimes stopped by Harris's house and invited him to sit shotgun in his makeshift patrol car.

Sydney inadvertently discovered her husband's second purchase stowed away in his underwear drawer. Although she laundered nearly all of the clothing worn by her family, she refused to touch his underwear because the sight of skid marks made her gag. It was the one article Joe had to deal with on his own. That drawer became, as a result, his prime hiding space for any unmentionables, and Sydney knew it. Every so often, she would feel around inside—but not look—and, on that day, she felt cool metal, not the glossy pages of a magazine like she usually uncovered.

The scream that lurched up from her diaphragm and out her throat was bloodcurdling. It was more terror than anger that greeted her husband when he came home later that night.

"Why is there a gun in my home?"

"It's for protection, Syd. Self-defense only, I promise."

"From what? From who?" Hot tears began to fall from her widened eyes. Her voice quaked and her body trembled. The physiological response was so stark that it alarmed him. "Is it loaded?"

"It won't work without bullets. Seconds in delay can mean the difference between life and death."

A prolonged shriek escaped from her mouth.

"The girls! They're old enough to reach inside. Have you given this no thought? Are you blinded by this *obsession* of yours?"

"Calm down, honey. I'm a man. Shielding my family from harm is my job, not an obsession."

"A man? You're a buffoon!" she exclaimed.

He opened his mouth but only stammers exited it. She

had never been so defiant. His face burned from how red it became.

"You don't go out in the streets with it, do you? On your silly rides playing pretend sheriff with your idiot friend? Loaded and everything?"

Confirmation was unnecessary. She backed away slowly, eyes glued to him but looking past.

"Don't look at me like that."

"*You're* the threat."

"Don't say that. Once I catch him, I'll stop. I just can't let him get away."

"Pray you find him first."

"Before what?"

"Before *I* finally find the courage to get away myself."

Joe misinterpreted her warning and, in the coming days, redoubled his efforts to find the culprit. He set up a stakeout in his living room: seated in his favorite chair, angled perfectly to peer out of the window and onto his lawn, shrouded in shadows, gun in his waistband, television volume up but screen unwatched as he maintained a visual lock on the package—this time large—that he intentionally left out as bait.

Days passed, and yet, there it sat. Joe ate his meals in the same watchful position. He ran to the bathroom and eliminated in haste. He nodded off, day and night, as restlessness kicked in. He was bleary-eyed and minutes from surrender when a figure appeared in the early evening of the third day. His heart rammed up against his ribs, bruising itself. Stunned, his brain received, on notable delay, the signals it was sent from his overwrought eyes. In fact, he watched nearly the entire theft—the blackened figure approach; crouch; hug and lift the relatively light box; and walk away—before registering a reaction at all.

But once he sprung into gear, it was like one fluid, wild motion: up from his seat, over to the door, and outside. He garbled his admonition to the fleeing perp: It approximated words but could mostly be understood as a guttural growl from the belly of a man apoplectic with rage. His yell and the noisy opening of his front door caused the suspect to turn around, toss the box over and out of his arms, and run.

"Stop! Thief! Stop!"

Joe gave chase. His body was not in sprinting shape. But it had a way of rising to the occasion when adrenaline, survival instinct, bravado, and the right moment combined. He flew, carried by the wind of his own making, legs taking bounds in excess of their length. It defied physics. It still wouldn't have been enough, had the boy not curiously turned to gauge whether he was still being pursued and how many steps remained from being caught.

The boy tripped and fell, chin scraping against asphalt as his body lay prostrate.

Joe climbed on top, giddy with excitement. He flipped him over to finally glimpse the face of menace. He was black, and he was familiar. The incident might have deescalated if the boy had not bled so profusely. The gash on his chin was wide and awash in red. The liquid, so bright and warm, bathed Joe's hands. It kicked up something primal and unhinged in him.

Grabbing the boy by the sides of his head, Joe positioned his thumbs so that one penetrated his eye. He slammed him against the jagged road repeatedly, methodically, waiting a beat before crashing him again into the earth so hard there was splatter. New blood—this time darkened by dirt and gravel—spilled onto the canvas. The boy begged for respite that did not come until he lost consciousness and Joe lost his nerve.

Joe lifted himself, his head and hands convulsing, and walked—as if in a trance—onto the sidewalk toward his home. The sound of the approaching sirens seemed impossibly distant because his ears had plugged with the rushing of his own blood. He heard only a peaceful, quiet night before chaos descended.

At home, he stood mute as his wife—who he could not hear—yelled questions as she stood with him over the sink, scrubbing away at his stained skin. She removed the gun, untouched in his waistband, and returned it to its hiding place.

The law arrived at his doorstep in flashing lights.

At the station, he had to strip himself and his pockets of all items, including his ring. He hesitated—*"it never comes off"*—but he ultimately complied. Caked in between it and his skin was dried blood that scratched him as he twisted it off.

He asked police only one question: "Is Timothy pressing charges?"

They asked him back: "For what? Are you?"

Sydney had not accompanied him. And she was not there, nor were the girls, when he eventually got home. He found only his gun as a paperweight and a handwritten note on the kitchen counter waiting for him.

Felons cannot serve on juries. None of this appears in Joe's history.

Mr. Joseph Cole, juror number one, fiddled with his ring as he sat in silence, twisting it in circles around his finger. Mr. Thomas noticed.

"Wife at home?" he asked his neighbor, cutting through the stillness with forced small talk.

Mr. Cole grinned but didn't reply. He was no longer married, and not by his choice. Nevertheless, it never came off.

In their makeshift war room, Sandy, Nate, and the intern stew.

"I like the middle-aged white man," Sandy says.

"Don't we always?" Nate asks.

She chuckles. "Generally, yes. But I've watched him. He

watches me like a father watches his daughter. He looks horrified by the whole thing. He's on our side."

"I'm not sure about his rapport with the other jurors. He sits off by himself every day," Nate says.

"Is that important?" the intern asks.

"The modern jury is a social experiment at its core," explains Sandy, who's prone to soliloquies. "Who you like, who you don't like—all of it plays a role. They must reach a unanimous verdict, and if there are holdouts, if you yourself are a holdout, who are you going to ultimately side with? Someone you like, who you've spent the past week chatting with, eating lunch with, sharing about your life and your family? Or the social outcast you found suspicious right from the start?"

"At least he appears to hate Jordan," notes Nate. "Never smiles when '*Bis and Tris*' is up at the podium."

"Not true for his female counterparts, unfortunately," Sandy says.

"The preppy black man can pull him in," Nate says, nodding to himself. "He's serious, sober, stoic. He pays great attention to everything. They're different, of course, but I think they have more in common than they'd be willing to acknowledge. He'll bridge the divide."

A pair of prosecutors enters the room.

"How goes the trial?" Skippy Rodriguez asks.

"Fine, so far. Still setting the table. Haven't gotten to the meat and potatoes yet," the first chair answers.

"So tense. Massage?" Rodriguez offers, grinning.

"Don't touch me, Skippy."

"I was asking my boy Nate," he jokes. "Don't flatter yourself, Sands."

Skippy notoriously toes up to the line of sexual harassment but never faces any consequences because he is so well-liked. No matter how progressive the office, a strain of conservatism is subconsciously present in any prosecuting agency. It's endemic to an institution whose central aim is jailing people. That means it lags behind the general culture in matters of political correctness, so that the instances of a man openly commenting on a woman's body or using a derogatory term for a gay individual, for example, were several years away from going extinct. Skippy thrived in that shrinking gray area, right on the margins of offense. He is a proud and vocal Democrat, too, so his tolerant politics shield him from reproach. He is Dom's good friend, knowing full well the on-again, off-again dynamics of Sandy's relationship with him, but Skippy isn't fluent in shame.

His off-color remarks inject levity into what could otherwise be a dark, depressing, and disheartening profession.

"We trade in tragedy," Sandy tells friends. "It's joyless. You win sometimes, but no one ever really wins. The victims are still victimized. The defendants are now condemned. Their families are torn apart. The witnesses are reluctant, or worse combative, and they're out time, money, and energy. Everyone hates or merely tolerates you. You do what's right because it's just, but not because it makes anyone all that much happier. And once it's over, you move on to the next tragedy."

The man who enters beside Skippy is his antithesis. Osniel Borges is short, accented, and a devout Catholic. His eyes widen in shock at the facts of his cases—he cannot comprehend a world motivated by sex, indolence, and greed. He himself is not compelled to act by any one of those three. Or, rather, he abstains from alcohol to avoid the influence of the three. His wife, ironically, is quite busty—perhaps unjustly seen as incongruent with his conservatism—a feature all notice but no one has the courage to vocalize but Skippy. He often uses his hands to crudely mime exaggerated breasts on his body while standing directly behind, and out of the eyeline of, Osniel—to equal parts laughs and sneers, often divided along gender lines.

"Is it really irony if no one says it?" he muses.

Osniel's naivete inspires in him harsher judgment, not less. His plea offers to defendants are known as some of the most exacting in the office.

On this day, Osniel is uncharacteristically empathetic: "The kid goes away for life if he's found guilty?"

Sandy winces at Osniel's use of "kid." She finds that her traditionally hard-nosed, conservative colleagues are only able to summon sympathy for the accused when they look like them or face accusations that might reasonably one day ensnare them, like sexual assault. An alarm, however faint, goes off in the mind of every man hearing accusations of criminal conduct between the sheets, warning: *It could be you.* The defendant in this case is in his thirties. Where was Osniel's bleeding heart when, only a week earlier, he secured a conviction and thirty-year sentence for an actual kid of nineteen who robbed a lightly crowded convenience store?

"He's an animal," Osniel snarled at the time.

He was also black.

As if intending to prove Sandy's private judgment, Osniel leans in closer and alters his voice to a more muted tone.

"I just went out to the scene of a homicide, and I felt so bad for the shooter. He'll be facing a lot of time. Seemed to be a road-rage incident. And I look into his car—left abandoned in the middle of the street—you know, to see what I can find in plain view. And his phone is tossed onto his seat, and it's lit up. The background pictures are these two little girls, you know, *blonde.* Just beautiful children. And your heart goes out to that family that will likely lose their daddy for a long time."

Sandy shifts uncomfortably in her seat. The sentiment itself does not irk her; in fact, she agrees with it. It's important to her—whatever the outcome of her cases—that she never lose sight of the fact that the defendant is a person himself, with innocent loved ones who will suffer by his being sent away and caged. But that small detail—their *blondeness*—reveals his real sympathies. And he hasn't even noticed it.

The room goes dead silent in response. Sandy considers making it a teachable moment but chooses to overlook it instead. As Skippy and Osniel depart, Nate shoots a knowing glance at Sandy. At least she was not alone.

"The black juror will be our saving grace, Sandy," he says, returning to their previous conversation. "He'll bridge the divide."

Two lamps cast a cozy, yellow pall over his living room as his wife entered, singing off-key with a round single-layer cake on her flattened palms. A chorus of voices joined at staggered intervals. Earl Thomas sat on his couch, flashing a mouthful of whites and slugging his half-empty beer. The shadows of lit candles danced on his face. A little girl, dark-haired and not blonde, climbed up his knee. She joined him in blowing out the tiny fires, darkening their brown faces.

"How old are you now?" sang one disembodied voice.

"Over the hill!" another answered.

"On top of the hill!" Earl corrected.

The crowd cheered.

Upbeat music began playing. Hands slid furniture into the room's corners for dancing. The smoke from the candles tickled Earl's nose. He laid a hand on the small of his wife's back and pulled in close.

"I'm heading to the gas station on the corner," he advised.

She wrinkled her nose.

"For smokes? I thought you quit."

"For gas. And lotto numbers. And snacks." He paused. "And cigs—yes. Just today. As a treat."

She sighed. He chugged the remainder of his beer and laid

out an open palm. She placed in it the car keys. He bent down to kiss the top of the girl's head at his hip, and he was off.

He rode with his windows down. Gray skies were on the verge of opening. The intermittent drops that fell sideways onto his face were cooling in otherwise flaring temperatures. He placed one hand on the top of the wheel, and he slung the other arm outside his window, hanging it halfway down his car. He drove at a leisurely pace.

He pulled up to the left of the pump, headlights flush with the levers, and parked. Inside the convenience store, he grabbed a bag of chips and candy and asked the clerk for a pack of cigarettes and a lottery ticket.

As the ticket printed loudly, the clerk furrowed his brow.

"Is that today's date?"

"My birthdate. I always play those numbers today."

He chuckled. "Well, good luck, and happy birthday."

Earl emerged with a slender cylinder in his mouth, which he met with fire. He puffed, staring at his car and realizing he had forgotten to buy gas.

"Shit," he muttered to himself.

Before he could act, a car screeched onto the tarmac, pulling in front of Earl's car and then reversing to within an inch of his bumper.

"Whoa!" Earl impulsively yelled.

The woman exited her car, slammed the door shut, unscrewed her gas cap, stretched the pump from the dispenser directly beside Earl's car, stuck it in her tank, and sauntered over to the store.

"What are you doing?" he asked, intercepting her. "My car's right there."

The moment before she spoke felt unnaturally long as his mind processed the detail it was receiving: eyes of crystal blue; the way she pulled her purse into herself as he neared; the smack of her lips as she chewed gum; her hands and neck overdressed in jewelry; her sight flitting on him for mere seconds before shooting elsewhere, as if—unlike him—she had captured all she needed to know about him instantaneously.

He remembered thinking she was pretty—and hating himself for that.

What she said next was both astonishing and inevitable.

"Don't get close to me, nigger."

He shrank at first. He was a wilting flower. Tears sprang to his eyes. That reaction was short-lived. Next he shook with rage. Just as quickly as he had pulled back, he drew closer, straightening his spine and growing several feet taller. His arm shot out, but only to float aimlessly as he quickly reconsidered the reflex. She diverted her beeline to the store, creating more space between them, and walked past him.

Weakly, softly: "That was my spot."

For a minute, he floundered. He felt limbless, possessed by the strongest urge to act but lacking the tools to do so. He contemplated following her inside but had no plan for what came next. His eyes swept the scene and settled on the police car parked just steps away.

Anger fueled his walk to the squad car; he was a spectator now, detached from his own body.

The officer had been leaning on the side of his car, but the intensity of Earl's march brought him tensely to his feet. An alarm inside him had been tripped. Earl spoke, but he had no idea what he was saying: A string of words, coherent or not, flowed from his id.

"Sir, have you been drinking?"

"I've had a single beer."

"Don't wave that cigarette in my face, sir. Put it out."

He let the burning stick fall to the ground. The officer watched its descent, perturbed.

Earl was still reeling when he caught sight of the woman exiting the store. He turned his back to the officer. The woman, wide-eyed, saw his rapid approach. The officer called into his radio for backup.

"That man assaulted me! He's harassing me!" she yelled.

"You bigot!" Earl shot back. "Get away from my car."

He felt hands on him from behind. He pushed them away.

"Do not move a step closer, sir."

"I'm just walking to my car," he offered.

"Stop right there. Do not walk anywhere. That's an order."

Earl turned around, hands up in a plea. He began to assess the threat. It wasn't from her.

"I'm just going home, Officer. I'm leaving now. Forget it. It's no big deal," he said, retreating backward.

"I told you to stop moving. Put your hands behind your back."

"No, Officer. I'm just leaving. I'll go home. It's right around the corner."

The officer lunged forward, grabbing him by the collar. Earl tried to turn and run to his driver's-side door, as if only could he reach it, would he be safe, but the man's boot driven into his shin sent him collapsing. Once he was prostrate, the officer's full weight kept him pinned, his knee resting sharply on Earl's back.

"I'll just go home. Let me go home."

"Not tonight you won't. You're under arrest."

"For what? I'm the one who asked for your help."

"Resisting an officer."

He watched from that position—flat on the earth—as his aggressor rushed to her car and drove away. She never turned to face the commotion erupting behind her.

All of his fury had drained from him by then. So had any sadness. He was left only with shame. There was no room for anything else.

06 | THE JUDGMENTS OF SAMUEL

On game day, Detective Samuel Sterling is calm. He sits on a bench outside of the courtroom: palms on his lap, binder wedged underneath his arm, soles of his feet flat against tile, and legs out in front of him, parallel to one another, knees high and unshaking. Hours pass, and he doesn't move or say anything. He runs plays in his mind. Numbers swirl in his head. He will direct every answer to the jury. He will make eye contact. He will smile. He won't fight when antagonized. He will readily concede when he doesn't know or doesn't remember something. He will exude confidence but not arrogance. He won't smack his lips or sigh. He will be a gentle giant.

His mother instilled in him this peace as a young boy. In Little League, before play began, she would take him aside. She would pull out her Bible from her purse. She would flip to a preselected passage: always uplifting, never fire and brimstone. She would read. They would pray. She would place her hand over his heart as she spoke. It would pacify his rattled nerves.

"Repeat after me," she instructed. "Sterling is golden."

He would. He didn't have the nerve to tell her that sterling was silver. It didn't matter. He was her golden child. He was her singular pride. And, with her by his side, he was golden. Always.

He is called to the stand, abruptly and without warning. He feels the phantom pressure of a comforting hand against his chest. He walks inside, careful to smile, careful to nod and acknowledge the seven seated in the box. He doesn't smile at or even acknowledge Sandy. He doesn't want to show overt familiarity or trust with the prosecution. He is not a partisan. He is without vendetta. He is a straitlaced, antiseptic, cold, and buttoned-up investigator who goes wherever the evidence leads him: Guilt or innocence, it makes no difference to him. And it just so happens, with no thumb on the scale whatsoever, the facts led him to Mr. Soto as the culprit. He is there to share his findings. Not judge. Not condemn.

She begins her questioning. He allows her to fade away. It's what she wants. To ignore her. He looks to the jury. He is talking directly to them. They are all that matters.

"Good afternoon," he greets them, before giving his first answer.

After eliciting his law enforcement credentials, Sandy gets his size out of the way. The jurors will be distracted by it through-out his testimony if she does not.

"You're a big man, Detective. What did you do before joining the force?"

"I played football. College ball at a solid, national program. I was a defensive end. Played in a few bowls. Tried to go pro. Participated in a couple of scouting combines, even. But it didn't work out."

"Why not?"

"I had a few nagging injuries. But the truth was: I wasn't quite good enough. I can say that now."

The self-effacement draws smiles from the spectators.

"Did that experience help you in what you do today?"

"Yes, actually. You have to think clearly under pressure. Make snap decisions that are thoughtful and measured. But most of all, it exposed me to many different types of people. It helps me relate. It gave me perspective. If you can see life through the eyes of your witnesses, through the eyes of your suspects, you can better piece together what happened."

Anthony Giordano was a newly signed and heavily courted recruit with a rocket of an arm who was still seventeen and months shy of high school graduation. His single mom drove hundreds of miles, having never flown in a plane, and dropped him off on campus—with a public avalanche of loud kisses on his face—for the week of wining and dining that recruits at top programs enjoyed. Sam, in his junior year, noticed three things that week about "Big Toe Tony," the tall, lanky kid whose large shoe size matched those of his much bigger teammates: He did not partake in the drinking, drugging, and women that were generously foisted on him and his fellow recruits as a sign of goodwill; he never took off his baseball cap; and he wore, always, a gold Christian cross around his neck. The combination ingratiated him to Sam.

"That your favorite cap or something?" Sam asked.

Tony's face reddened.

"I just need a haircut badly. I'm wolfing under here."

"Say no more. I'll take you to my barber."

Sam drove Tony several miles away, to the outskirts of that college town. As they neared their stop, he pulled into a neighborhood off the highway that made Tony's eyes widen. The sidewalks were lined with trash, and the streets were crowded with people who had pulled up lawn chairs onto the curb, were huddled in groups in the middle of the roadway, and peered suspiciously at Sam in his midsize sedan as he navigated around it all. He parked in the tiny lot of the barbershop, opposite a panel of long windows.

"This is it?" Tony squealed.

"They give the best fades," Sam assured him. "All the boys go here."

That wasn't exactly true. All of the team's *black* boys went there.

Sam entered to a reception of hooting and soul handshakes: *slap*, *grip*, and *lock*. He greeted everyone personally, by name, and echoed back a detail of their lives he had learned on his last visit. He participated in the group talk, but not too much. Mostly, he listened. He didn't alter his speech; he spoke as he always did. When a popular song hit the boom box, he rapped along with the rest of the shop, remembering to censor the n-word, remaining mute at its mention even as his black counterparts sang it freely, and continued on without missing a beat.

Tony didn't say or do much himself, but not out of discomfort. He was awestruck. He had never seen anything like it.

After their cuts, in the car, Tony was nearly breathless.

"That was amazing."

Sam refrained from remarks that made his outreach appear effortless. It was a talent, undoubtedly, but it wasn't without work. A different man—a self-congratulatory, Pollyanna, and saccharine soul—might have called it easy: We're all human. Our similarities far surpass our differences. Just be yourself. The Golden Rule and other such platitudes. But he groused at that lazy worldview. If empathy came altogether naturally, then a failure of it was equally natural and inevitable. It required intention.

In a way, original sin wasn't fatalistic. It was aspirational. His mother taught him that.

"Being a good person takes work, Sterling," she would say.

"We are a fallen people, prone to selfishness and cruelty. Man uses his supposed good nature to excuse and justify a lack of trying. The moment it feels easy, the moment it feels like second nature: Question and reevaluate your actions. I bet you'll find that they aren't all that nice and that you can do better."

He had once as a young man inadvertently revealed this philosophy on a first date with a young woman.

"How are you such a nice guy?" she had gushed.

"I work at it. I try hard. Every day."

Her joy evaporated. Perhaps it was too serious a reply for flirty banter. Perhaps she was too shallow to appreciate his sincerity or vulnerability. But mostly she just didn't want a nice guy who had to try. She wanted one who didn't have to.

Not so for Tony.

Platonic male relationships aren't spoken about in a certain way, but had social convention not prevented it from being put in such blunt terms, Tony could have pointed to that night, that moment—after watching him work the room—as the moment he fell in love with Sam. It might have said more about Tony than it ever did about Sam, but if Sam could see himself in *them*, he thought, this towering man of power and self-assurance could surely also see himself in him: a green, gangly, small-town boy.

Sandy grips the lectern, inconspicuously turning the page of her notes.

"Did you make an arrest right away in this case?"

"No, ma'am."

"Why not?"

"The victim was a missing person for a time. Several weeks, in fact. We had not confirmed her death."

She steps away from the podium—and from her list of prepared questions—and opens her hands in an inviting gesture, as if she were about to go off script. But she isn't. It's her signature move when she's seeking to neutralize a counterargument to her case. It's part of the choreography.

"Does that mean you were sitting on your hands, doing nothing that whole time?"

He chuckles.

"No, ma'am. My work began on day one. We were, of course, leading search parties and engaging the community to provide us with any leads. But, in a less public manner, I was interviewing family and friends. Retracing her last known steps. I am a homicide detective. I treated this as a potential homicide from jump."

"You said you interviewed family. Did that include Malcolm Mora?"

"Of course. He's the victim's twin brother. It was my under-standing early on that they were close. That they spoke all of the time. I interviewed him the very first night I was assigned the case."

"Detective, did you treat him as a suspect?" She pauses after each word for emphasis.

"I treat everyone I meet with suspicion. That's my job. Was he in handcuffs? No. There is no crime at that point. He has rights, just like Mr. Soto has rights. It was a consensual inter-view. Malcolm wanted to speak with me. He wanted to help me. He wanted his sister found. Now, I was *kind* to him. I won't say I wasn't. He was distraught and emotional, like any brother would be. But, for one, I am kind to everyone I interview, in-cluding suspects, including defendants. That isn't good nature; it's strategy. People tell you more when you're friendly. And, secondly, even though I am nice, I never let my guard down. I am always analyzing what is being presented to me."

"And how did Malcolm present? That first night, and in the following days when Melina was still missing?"

"Open. Cooperative. Involved. If he had anything to hide, if he were looking to avoid scrutiny, he wasn't doing a good job of it. He was always at the station. He was calling every day. He was leading searches. He was engaging with the media. He assisted me enormously. He did everything I asked."

"Did you search his apartment? Break down his door?"

"No, ma'am."

"Why not?"

"As I mentioned, everyone has rights. I cannot violate the Constitution, even when the charge I am investigating is murder, perhaps especially when the charge is murder. I would have to get a warrant to search his apartment. And, for that, I would need probable cause to believe evidence of a crime was located inside of it. I didn't have probable cause that a crime had even occurred, let alone that something specific—something I could name—was inside this man's private residence."

"But you could have asked him? Gotten his consent to search?"

"Sure. And I could have asked to search his car. And his locker at the gym. And his desk at work. And not just his but those of every person within Melina's orbit. But that's not practical. And that isn't my job. My job is to follow *leads*. Not to turn over *every* stone, but to turn over the smart stones. To make intelligent inferences from the evidence. Time is finite, and it's critical in those first few days. Nothing in my numerous interactions with Mr. Mora ever led me down that road."

"Had you been inside of Malcolm's apartment?"

The detective's eyes light up, and he emits a sigh in relief, pleased she had reminded him of it.

"Right. Yes, that's another thing. I had been there several times. I had met with him there early on to discuss the process moving forward. It's where I told him that his sister's remains—if you can call them that, what little we found—had turned up.

I wanted to share the sad news with him in person, so I showed up unannounced. He let me in without an issue. I never saw anything inside that looked off."

"Were you so focused on Mr. Soto those first weeks that it blinded you to anything suspicious Mr. Mora might have done or said?"

"I didn't even know who Mr. Soto was at the time. It wasn't until those few bones were found that I even first heard his name."

"What about Rocky Sandoval? Had you heard his name?"

The detective grits his teeth. It's his only tell that the terrain ahead—his justification for an alleged overlooked lead—might not be as smooth.

"Yes, ma'am."

"Who is he?"

"He was an ex-boyfriend of Melina's, her high school sweetheart. They had been on-again, off-again for several years but most recently apart for the years leading up to her death."

"Did you interview him?"

"No, ma'am."

"Why not?"

"Well, he wasn't around that first week. That's because he wasn't even around the night of her disappearance. I came to learn that he was out of—"

"Objection! Hearsay," interjects Jordan.

"Sustained."

"Without telling me the substance of what you were told," Sandy counsels, "did you come to learn where Mr. Sandoval was on the night Melina disappeared?"

"Yes, ma'am."

"And how did that news affect your investigation?"

"It ruled him out as a potential suspect."

"I'm showing you what's already been admitted, by stipulation of the parties, into evidence as State's Forty-Two and Forty-Three. What are these?"

He flips through the pages she hands him and pretends to scan them, but he's already aware of what they are without close inspection.

"They're the victim's cell phone and bank records. With the assistance of your office, Ms. Grunwald, we subpoenaed them while Melina was still a missing person to see if she was still using her phone or bank cards. We hoped it would give us a lead to her location or, if it ended up being a homicide, who might be involved."

"Was there any activity—on her phone or bank cards—after the night of her disappearance?"

"No, ma'am. None."

"What did that tell you about the kind of homicide case this might end up being?"

"That it was unlikely to be a botched robbery. You'd expect some sort of charge or cash withdrawal if the motivation were money."

"Have her phone or wallet ever been found to this day?"

"They have not."

"At the time you received these records, did you have any idea that the victim had been last seen at The Saloon?"

"No. We had not heard from Ms. Murrow yet, and the victim's mother did not know exactly where Melina had gone that night."

"But given what you know now, surely you would expect to see a charge from The Saloon on her statement from that night?"

"Not necessarily. Young ladies don't always pay for their own drinks."

"So, what *was* the last charge on her bank card?"

"She paid for a cab around the time she was last seen by

her mother leaving home. The statement won't tell us where she was picked up from or where she went, but we know the amount charged: twenty-two dollars and seventeen cents."

"Do you know the distance from her house to The Saloon?"

"Yes; it's about six miles."

"And did you have an opportunity to investigate the average charge for a taxi in that area?"

"Yes; it's a little over three dollars a mile with a starting base rate of a little under three dollars."

"Is that total—the twenty-two dollars and seventeen cents—consistent with a trip from her home to The Saloon?"

"By my calculations, yes."

"What about the phone records? To whom did she make her last call?"

"She made an outgoing call to the number belonging to Mr. Sandoval."

"When?"

"Long after the cab ride. Early in the morning and into the next day. I believe the exact time is 3:21 a.m. They never spoke. The call is zero seconds long. Not even a voicemail left."

"What investigatory value does that call have in your mind? Isn't it significant at all that Mr. Sandoval is the last contact for a murder victim on the night she was allegedly killed?"

"It's significant, but not in the way one might think," he lectures. "If anything, it corroborates that the victim and Mr. Sandoval weren't together that night. Why call him on the phone if they were? He also didn't pick up the call. So it's unlikely they met up afterward. They exchanged no texts. Her records additionally show that the two did not speak at all that month or in the months leading up to that night. They were in sparing contact, over the phone at least. Whatever was happening to her that night, she opted to call a close but old friend, out of the blue, and after months of not speaking."

"Would that be usual for a murder that was domestic in nature, involving former lovers like Mr. Sandoval and Ms. Mora?"

"The few calls? The little interaction? No, that would not be common."

When Sam turned fifteen and earned his learner's permit, he drove his mother everywhere. She had eagerly awaited the day. She wanted to roll her window down, lay her head back, kick her feet up onto the dashboard, pump up the volume on the radio, and sing. It embarrassed him, particularly as he sometimes picked up friends who snickered in the back seat, but he never whined about it. He suffered in silence.

"It's nice to have a man of the house now," she remarked. "It means that, every now and again, I get the pampering every woman deserves."

He, too, saw it as a rite of passage to manhood. That summer, he boasted a growth spurt of several inches, began shaving, and touched a girl under her skirt for the first time. The limited license was just the manifestation of his already burgeoning virility. He felt the intoxicating power of maleness.

"Do women feel that?" he remembered asking his mother. "I pull my shoulders back. I deepen my voice. And I feel invincible. Untouchable. I feel strong."

It was a Sunday night. He was driving. She was reclined in her usual lackadaisical position. It had become ritual. Fifteen minutes before the neighborhood ice cream parlor closed, he drove her down the back roads for a frozen nightcap. She insisted they were most generous with their scoops at that time. She ordered mint chocolate chip on a cone. He ordered vanilla in a cup. They were on their way back, licking at their treats before they melted in the Miami heat.

Her face darkened at his observation.

"Oh, we feel it from you all, too," she responded. The boy

meant women as subjects, not objects; as actors, not targets, but she flipped his intention on its head. "It's why if we're the only woman in a room of men, a primal, primitive part of us feels fear. It's why we don't feel complete security walking down a street or an alley. Every single one of us, Sterling. Not necessarily because of the physical gap between men and women. But because of that feeling you describe—that *perception* of difference, in power, in stature—that fuels male behavior, good and bad.

"Be mindful of that, Sterling. Have a soft touch. Not just with women. With men. With everyone. And especially you. You will be physically imposing. You'll command more power than any man needs. Allow most of it to go unused. You won't need it."

He choked up on the steering wheel, his hands at ten and two.

"Why do you say that?"

"Say what?"

"Especially me? You always say that. That I'll be a big man."

"It's in your genes, honey."

"Grandpa's not a big man. I've already surpassed him in height."

Stillness.

"Where's my dad, Mom?"

Jordan waits for Sandy to sit before rising and stalking—on the balls of his feet—up to the lectern. It is performative: Conservatives on the jury will extol his chivalry at making way for a woman, and liberals won't notice or care one way or another.

"Cross-examination."

"Marta Mora reported her daughter missing to police more or less thirty-six hours after she was last seen, is that right, Detective?"

"Good afternoon, sir," says Detective Sterling instead, pleasantly yet pointedly.

A mixture of laughter and nervous whoops spills out of the crowd, including within the jury. Jordan reddens. His voice in reply is as sweet as honey, but his face tells another story.

"Where are my manners? Good afternoon, Detective. Nice to see you again. Is it true that police didn't get involved until thirty-six hours after the deceased was last seen?"

"Yes, sir."

"And you spoke with Malcolm Mora that night?"

"Yes, sir."

"And he was free to go home that night?"

"Yes, sir."

"And every night after that?"

"Yes, sir."

"You didn't walk into his apartment for the first time until several days later?"

"I can't recall exactly, but yes, it'd have to be days later."

"And when you did, you didn't search the place?"

"No, sir."

"I take it you didn't go into his bedroom?"

"No, sir."

"And the weapon allegedly used in this case, it was never recovered?"

"That's right, sir."

"And you testified on direct that Mr. Mora called you nearly every day?"

"Yes, sir."

"That he was very much interested in the progress of the investigation?"

"Yes, he was interested in finding his sister."

"Well, let me ask you about that. Isn't it true Mr. Mora resigned, fairly quickly, to the idea that his sister was dead?"

"No, I would not say that. He participated in searches for weeks."

"He certainly asked you whether police had any suspects?"

"Yes, I believe he did."

"And he asked you that *weeks* before she was confirmed dead?"

"Yes, sir."

"He certainly expressed to you his early opinion that foul play was involved in her disappearance?"

"He did."

"And you would agree, he spoke about her—the chances of finding her—differently than, say, his mother did?"

Detective Sterling mulls his answer. Sandy perks up in her chair.

"He was the more realistic of the two, I will agree to that. Ms. Mora clung to her optimism, as any mother would, even as the days and weeks piled on."

"That's a good word. Mr. Mora was more *pessimistic* about his sister's survival?"

"Yes, sir."

"And he sought nearly daily updates on the homicide investigation?"

"I wanted to keep the family informed. He was the liaison, of sorts. So I spoke to him."

"But he called you more than you called him, is that fair?"

"Yes, sir."

"And it was daily? Even if you had nothing new to report?"

"Yes."

"And, in fact, after your department confirmed the victim's death, he became obsessed with knowing about the murder weapon?"

"Certainly not. He did not become *obsessed*."

"He certainly asked you whether police had found a murder weapon?"

"I believe so, yes."

"And he did so several times?"

"A handful of times."

"Mr. Mora and his sister were very close?"

"Yes, sir."

"So close they developed somewhat of an indecent reputation for—"

"Objection! Hearsay, and improper character evidence."

"Sustained."

"It's reputation evidence, Your Honor," Jordan argues.

"Not without a proper foundation, it's not," the judge
blusters.

Jordan huffs and tries again.

"Did you not, Detective, as part of your investigation, look
into the *closeness* of the twins' relationship?"

"I don't know what that means," Detective Sterling chides.
"Did I look into the *closeness* of their relationship? No, I did
not. That's not my job."

"It's your job to collect and digest information, is it not?"

"Yes, sir."

"And it's your job to make—what did you call it—'intelligent
inferences' from that information?"

"Yes, sir."

"And those intelligent inferences on the part of a lead detective help shape and direct the investigation?"

"Yes, sir."

"So, it sounds like you ignored information that you received regarding the twins' closeness when making intelligent
inferences about your investigation?"

"I didn't ignore anything. I analyze everything. It wasn't
relevant to nor did it affect my investigation."

"And it's your decision—and yours alone—as to what is
relevant to *your* investigation?"

"I work in consultation with others."

"But you're the lead detective? You have the ultimate say over who gets arrested and who doesn't? The buck stops with you?"

"Objection! Form. Is counsel going to let the witness answer before spouting off another question?"

Sandy's nerves have begun to fray. It's unlike Sandy to speak out of turn, so the judge doesn't reprimand her, but her eyes involuntarily widen.

"One question at a time, counsel," Her Honor softly orders.

"Detective, most homicides are committed by someone the victim knows, right?"

"Yes, sir."

"In fact, most are domestic—that is, they occur between romantic partners or family members?"

"I don't know the statistics. Some are. Many are."

"You never officially considered Mr. Mora a suspect in the murder of his sister?"

"No, I did not."

"You never considered anyone other than my client a suspect in this murder, isn't that right?"

"That's right."

"And *you* made that decision, correct?"

"Correct, sir."

"You never officially considered Mr. Sandoval, who you spoke about on direct, as a suspect in this murder?"

"I did not."

"You didn't even first speak with him until *months* after the victim had disappeared?"

"Yes, sir."

"That was well after my client was already arrested and charged with this crime?"

"Yes, sir."

"And you had known for *months* by that point that Mr. Sandoval's number was the last to appear on the victim's cell phone records?"

"Yes, sir."

"You testified you also knew the whereabouts of Mr. Sandoval on the night the victim was last seen?"

"I did."

"But he hadn't told you that himself?"

"Right."

"You heard it from other people?"

"Yes, sir."

"Melina was known to go home with strangers?"

Sandy stands, anticipating an objection, but sits back down. Jordan is right on the line of slut shaming, a violation of the Rape Shield laws, but he has not quite crossed it.

"I understand she was a single woman that, at times, spent evenings with men she had met, and spent time with, earlier that same night."

"So, strangers?"

"That's your word. Not mine."

"Anyone track down any of those strangers? Interview them? Officially consider them suspects?"

"You mean other than your client?"

The detective's eyes sparkle mischievously.

"I do, Detective."

"Then, no."

"And you have no idea exactly when Melina was killed, do you?"

"No, sir."

"You only know when she was last seen alive?"

"Right."

"You made the decision to charge my client with both premeditated murder *and* sexual battery?"

141

"I make a decision to arrest. It's the prosecutor's office that decides which charges to move forward with, if any at all."

"Alright, well, you arrested my client, in part, for sexual battery?"

"Yes, based on the forensic evidence available."

"But you did that long before an analyst that works for *your* department found copious amounts of gay pornography on my client's personal laptop?"

The detective clears his throat.

"Yes."

"Care to reevaluate your decision in light of this newfound evidence?"

"Objection! Argumentative, and invading the province of the jury."

"Overruled."

"You may answer, Detective," Jordan coaxes.

"No, I would not." Sandy grins. She finds the simplicity of the answer masterful. Better not to get bogged down in a debate.

"Gabriel's homosexuality doesn't give you any pause, Detective?" he tries again, incredulously.

The switch in moniker is momentarily jarring, not only for the witness but for everyone following along. The judge bristles. Calling defendants by their first names is frowned upon, but she lets it go without comment.

"I don't know anything about your client's sexual orientation. Does the fact that gay pornography was found on a laptop in his home give me pause that he raped the victim before killing her? No. Given all of the evidence, it does not, sir."

"What about disgust?"

"Excuse me?"

"You had to watch clip after clip of my client's pornography collection, didn't you?"

"I had to watch some of it, yes."

"And, by the way, not one woman appeared in any of those films or images, isn't that right?"

The detective smiles against his better judgment.

"Not exactly. For purposes of the plot, some female actors did appear."

Folks laugh. Jordan does, too.

"Allow me to rephrase: No naked women, is that right?"

"None appeared for the purposes of sex, counsel, no. They exclusively featured men."

"And my question is: Do you resent that? Having to watch men having sex in order to condemn my client to prison for the rest of his life?"

"Objection!"

"Come sidebar, counsel," the judge requests. The two sets of attorneys approach out of earshot of the jury. "Where are you going with this?"

"I'm exploring bias," Jordan responds. "My defense is that the police rushed to judgment in arresting Mr. Soto for this crime, particularly the sexual battery charge. My client is gay. If the lead detective in this case has any feelings of anti-gay bias, I am entitled to expose it."

"He's on a fishing expedition," Sandy counters. "By his own line of questioning, counsel has established that any indication that the defendant is anything other than heterosexual is an extremely recent phenomenon. Mr. Whipple has no good-faith basis to suggest that this man is in any way biased against gay people *and* that it affected his decision to arrest him over two years ago."

"Then, Ms. Grunwald, the detective is free to say that for himself," the judge decides. "You have a very, very short leash, Mr. Whipple. Do not ask him what he personally thinks of gay sex. That isn't proper or relevant. Ask him if he is biased against gay people. One question, and then you move on and are stuck with his answer. That's it."

The attorneys return to their places. The courtroom sits in silence as Jordan carefully phrases his one stab at it.

"Detective, have you—in your many years on the force or in your personal life—ever hurled a derogatory term for a gay person at someone, anyone?"

Nothing strips the shame out of a man like a locker room. It's the Garden of Eden before a taste of the apple. Boys disrobe to the skin, mid-conversation, legs spread, inches away from one another. They squat on toilets, stall doors open; urinate freely in shared showers; expel gas near the eyes, noses, and mouths of others.

None of it done modestly. None of it discreet. It's bullhorned, advertised, broadcast. The tension of it all is, indeed, diffused the more attention is called to it. Secrecy invites ridicule. It regains its perversion when hidden.

But Henry Finnegan was a sensitive soul. That was apparent to all—in the way he moved, the way he spoke. A freshman kicker, he stood shorter and scrawnier than his teammates. Whatever the reason, before and after a long day's practice, he grabbed a corner and—back turned, eyes down—changed his clothes at a breakneck pace. He never showered in the locker room, choosing instead to walk home to his apartment in fresh clothes laid over sweat and musk.

The boys noticed.

"Maybe Finn's just got a small dick."

"We can test that theory."

Sam, within arm's reach of Finn, caught the mischief through the corner of his eye as he undressed. As soon as Finn's drawers dropped, a flurry of hands snatched them, his clean pair, and the rest of his clothes laid neatly on the bench. One of those hands belonged to Tony. Finn flipped around, revealing his nakedness and the flood of horror on his pale face. The room erupted in a smattering of applause, laughter, and noisy curiosity.

Finn would have suffered commentary, but also swift understanding, had his privates, as speculated, turned out small. Even better, if big, they would have engendered kinder teasing. But all could now see he was perfectly average in every way.

That invited the greatest mockery.

"Give them back," Finn protested weakly, hands flying down to shield himself.

"Come and get them!"

His clothes were dangled from across the room. Retrieving them would require a strut down a makeshift catwalk surrounded by hollering brutes. He shook his head ever so slightly.

Jeers besieged the mob. One in particular cut through the clamor.

"Don't be a fag, Finn."

It wasn't clear from whom it came, but one perceptive participant turned to the team's ever-steady captain, who had been watching quietly.

"Sterling! What do you say?"

Silence befell the room, but for the slapping of bare chests— the boys' signal to each other to hush and pay attention. Sam, in contemplation, swept his eyes toward Tony. Sam's convictions carried weight: with him, with all of them.

"I say, don't be a fag, Finn," he boomed authoritatively, slapping the naked boy's back in a halfhearted attempt at levity.

Cheers followed, unanimous but for one. The lone dissenter, Finn, took his walk of shame.

"Detective, have you—in your many years on the force or in your personal life—ever hurled a derogatory term for a gay person at someone, anyone?"

145

Detective Sterling is unequivocal at the question. This, he does not pause to contemplate.

"No," he lies curtly. He happens to know that Finn is today married to a woman and father to six children, as if that mattered.

Jordan grimaces as if pained by the denial, but he proceeds.

"Weeks after the deceased was last seen, bones purportedly belonging to Ms. Mora were found, right?"

"At the defendant's workplace, yes."

Jordan is thrown off rhythm by Sterling's barbed addition.

"Well, he works at a morgue, right?"

"Yes, sir."

"That houses hundreds of dead bodies?"

"I have no idea how many."

"And has hundreds of employees?"

"I am not aware."

"And police were led there by an anonymous tip?"

"Yes, sir."

"You still have no idea who this anonymous tipster is?"

"No, sir."

"This jury won't get to hear from him, will they?"

"I imagine not."

"They won't get to assess his credibility?"

"I don't know."

"You know about him only because he filled out an employee comment card?"

"We believe so."

"And that's when you first focused like a laser on my client, right?"

"No. We interviewed the employees with access to that area. That's how Mr. Soto's name continually came up. It wasn't until we searched his home, after a judge-authorized warrant, that we found the victim's hair, and it became clear that the defendant was the guy we were looking for."

"We'll get there, Detective," Jordan snaps. "So you interviewed employees—all of whom had access to the area where those bones were found—and none of them fessed up to being the one who threw my client under the bus?"

"I don't understand the question, sir."

"I'll repeat it: This anonymous tipster is one of those employees you interviewed?"

"I don't know that to be true."

"And that means one of those employees *lied* to you about tipping off authorities?"

"I don't know that."

"And yet, it isn't *that* person—a known liar—who sits behind that table, accused of murder, it's my client?"

"Because it's your client who killed Melina Mora." It shot out from his lips like a cannon—deadweight lead, crashing with a thud on the courtroom floor.

"That's for the jury to decide, Detective," Jordan responds, beaming at having gotten a rise out of the even-keeled man. "The same night of your employee interviews, as you've said, you asked a judge to let you search Mr. Soto's home, correct?"

"Yes, sir."

"He wasn't allowed to go back into his home until that warrant was executed, right?"

"By that time, twenty-seven days had passed since the victim's disappearance. He had plenty of time to do whatever he needed inside of his home."

"Listen to the question, Detective: He had no opportunity, between when police descended upon his place of work and the search of his home, to return to his place and manipulate or hide anything?"

"No, sir. The place was sealed off until a warrant was secured."

"And how many men went in that first time?"

"I don't recall."

"Ballpark for me. More than three?"

"Yes, sir."

"More than five?"

"No, not that many."

"So, between three and five people searched what—you would agree—are very, very small quarters?"

"Yes. It's a small single bedroom."

"And the search party included a crime scene technician?"

"Yes, sir."

"A crime scene technician is trained to find and lift fingerprints?"

"Yes, sir."

"Trained to take swabs for DNA?"

"Yes, sir."

"And DNA can be found in bodily fluids like blood, semen, even sweat?"

"I'm no expert, but that's my understanding."

"And yet, after scouring the place, no weapon was found, is that right?"

"That's right."

"No fingerprints from the victim?"

"Right."

"No blood from the victim?"

"Right."

"No DNA from the victim?"

"We found her hair."

"But not on that *first* search, right, Detective?"

"That's right."

"And your team searched a second time?"

"We conducted a more thorough review."

"And, *still*, you found nothing that placed the victim in that room?"

"We found her hair on our third search of the room."

"You said 'we,' but that isn't fair, is it, Detective? *You* found the two hairs that purportedly belonged to Ms. Mora?"

"There were others in the room with me. I alerted them immediately in the moment."

"But *you*—yourself—are the individual who actually first stumbled across them?"

"Yes, sir."

"After several other people had stripped the room of its contents, turned it upside down, and found *nothing*?"

"It's hair clinging to a doornail. It's hard to find."

"You had—by that point, I'm sure, three weeks into your investigation—spent some time in the victim's bedroom?"

"Yes, sir."

"Where she used to lay her head to sleep? Where she used to brush her hair?"

"Yes, but I hadn't been there in some time. Weeks, probably. We toured her room those first few days to get some clues as to her whereabouts."

"And it just so happens that the lead detective—who had already decided that my client was the culprit, who had access to the victim's pillow, her hairbrush—finds the only evidence placing her in Mr. Soto's room after a team of professionals found nothing in their first two searches?"

"Objection! Asked and answered, and form."

"Sustained."

"I didn't plant a thing, if that's what you're suggesting, sir," the detective answers anyway, disregarding the judge's ruling. "I would never frame an innocent man."

"But what about a man you've convinced yourself is guilty?"

"Absolutely not, sir. No case is worth my honor, my integrity, my word."

"You spoke with Mr. Soto's neighbor, Mr. Rivas, during one of these searches?"

"Yes. It had to be that first night we searched the premises."

"You spoke to him through an interpreter, right, because you don't speak Spanish?"

"I have learned a fair amount of Spanish throughout the years. I spoke with him myself to get the broad strokes of what he knew. I returned later that night with a translator to go into greater detail."

"And he was somehow able to remember something he overheard twenty-seven days earlier in the minutes after waking?"

"It had stuck out in his mind, yes, because Mr. Soto never had any guests over."

"But he hadn't reported it to police before then?"

"No, sir."

"And, at some point later, Ms. Lisa Murrow reported to police an encounter she had allegedly witnessed between a man and Ms. Mora on the night of her disappearance?"

"Yes, sir. She saw a news report about Ms. Mora having disappeared and recognized her."

"But she first described that man with her as black to police?"

"She was correct as to the rest of her description—hair, build, height, age—but yes, she first reported his race as black. And that was only in her initial call to police. That was the only time she specifically called him black."

"And Mr. Soto had been formally arrested by that point?"

"After the medical examiner conducted his autopsy of the remains—and the hair came back as conclusively belonging to Ms. Mora—yes, he was arrested."

"And that arrest was reported in the news media?"

"Yes, sir."

"This included widely publicizing his mug shot?"

"I'm not sure. Some did, probably. But I can't say for sure."

"Local news channels even dubbed him the Love-Spurned Slayer. You heard of that, right?"

"I did."

"And it was only *after* all of these reports that Ms. Murrow changed her mind about the race of the suspect?"

"No, that's not right. We showed her a photographic lineup. She immediately identified the defendant. Said she was one hundred percent sure. We reminded her that her very first report described him as black. That came as a shock to her. She did not remember saying that. Nonetheless, she reiterated that her identification was correct. That she was mistaken that first time she called him black."

"As the lead detective in this case, you make judgments, is that right?"

"I go only where the evidence leads me."

"But you make choices in the interest of time and resources, right? You can't turn over every stone, as you say, so you have to make judgments as to what qualifies as a smart stone and what's a dead end?"

"Yes, sir."

"So, you would agree with me, a lead detective should have good judgment?"

"Yes, sir."

"My client, he's Hispanic, right?"

"Yes, sir."

"Have you ever in your life expressed personal disdain for the Hispanic community?"

"Absolutely not."

Jordan walks back to the defense table. Leisurely, he picks up his leather designer briefcase, places it softly on the tabletop, unbuckles the strap, pulls out a thin manila folder, returns the briefcase to its spot on the floor, strolls past the lectern, stops right at the jury box, flips the folder open—so wide and low, nearly at his navel, so that the front row of jurors can easily peek over and see its contents—and reads quietly to himself. Sandy's stomach flips.

"It's your personal judgment, is it not, that, quote, illegal spics should be deported from this country?"

Sandy shoots up from her chair so fast it is knocked back and her head reels with wooziness. Jordan is clearly reading from something he has never shown the prosecution.

"Objection! This is a *Richardson* violation."

"Sidebar. Now." The judge is seething. The lawyers congregate.

"Your Honor, I have never seen whatever counsel has in that folder."

"Have you shown the State what's in that folder, Mr. Whipple?" the judge asks.

"No, Your Honor. It's for impeachment purposes. I have no obligation to turn over impeachment materials. I intend to introduce it only if the witness lies."

"That may be *technically* true, counsel, but why not show your counterpart?"

"In full candor to the court, I didn't want her to coach her witness beforehand. I wanted an honest reaction from him."

"That's trial by ambush, Your Honor, and that is not allowed," Sandy stammers, her voice rising.

"Whisper, counsel," the judge rebukes.

"I still have no idea what *it* is," she tries again, in a hushed but cross tone. "It should not go unnoticed that Mr. Whipple appears to be purposefully leaving the folder wide open so that the jury can read its contents before it is formally admitted. It's difficult for me to argue its admissibility—for impeachment purposes or otherwise—if I haven't even seen it."

"Well, show it to us, counsel!" the judge demands.

Jordan hands the judge the folder. She reads the single sheet to herself. Her eyebrow lifts in surprise. Once done, she wordlessly hands it to Sandy. She takes three full minutes to inspect the words on the page. She maintains a veneer of calm.

She uses only the first minute to read; she indulges herself with the other two to craft an argument.

"First, Your Honor, this line of questioning is irrelevant and prejudicial. The defendant is not an illegal immigrant, and the detective's political beliefs—whether we agree with them or not—have no bearing on Mr. Soto's guilt or innocence. Defense is wielding them purely in an effort to sow *personal* dislike of the witness with the jury. Secondly, the detective has not said anything contradictory in order for any of this to serve as impeachment. Nothing written here is at all inconsistent with his belief that he holds no disdain for the Hispanic community, as counsel put it, writ large. Third, impeachment material is not admissible if it pertains to a collateral issue. This is not central at all to the case. Fourth, counsel hasn't even laid a proper foundation. These statements aren't authenticated. We have no idea if they can be properly attributed to the detective."

The judge swings her attention to Jordan with a glance.

"If these were naked political beliefs, that would be one thing, Your Honor. But these statements are colored by racist language. Mr. Soto is Hispanic. I am allowed to attack the biases of witnesses, including racism. On the homophobia front, I did not have impeachable material. Your Honor was right. I was stuck with his denial. But as to racism, I have proof that the detective is lying about his sentiments toward Hispanic people. I am allowed to confront him about that lie."

The judge shakes her head in melancholy. She is clearly repelled by what she's read.

"Ms. Grunwald is right that you haven't laid the foundation. Do that first, counsel. She is also right that he has not lied to this point. They are not yet admissible. But *you* are right, Mr. Whipple, that you can ask about it. Bias is central to your defense. Ask your questions. Don't beat around the bush. Be direct. See what he says."

"And if he lies?" Jordan probes.

"We'll cross that bridge when we get there."

He begins to turn and leave, but Sandy isn't budging.

"Your Honor," says Sandy, bewildered. "I strongly object to all of this. It sets a horrible precedent. The words of every witness—however old, however tangential—can now be thrown in their faces years later as a means of distracting the jury from the task at hand. Had the detective directed a racial slur at Mr. Soto, yes, of course, his attorney would have every right to question him about it. But this has nothing to do with Mr. Soto, and everything to do with simply making the detective look like a bad guy. He is not on trial here."

"I have made my decision, Ms. Grunwald. It's my job to protect this record on appeal. If you secure a conviction in this case, and it gets overturned because I handicapped counsel's defense, we have to do this all over again. I am not, as of now, admitting the statements. I agree with you there. But I am not going to limit his cross-examination. Pick your battles, State. This isn't worth the risk. Now, stand back."

Jordan returns to his spot. He collects himself. He draws forward.

"You have before posted messages online under the name sterling_is_golden, is that right, Detective?"

Detective Sterling flashes Sandy a look. She casts her eyes downward. He writhes briefly in his chair, awaiting the objection. But it never comes.

"Yes, sir."

"And in those messages, you expressed your views that illegal Hispanic immigrants—who you called spics—should be deported from this country?"

He furrows his brow.

"Honestly," he begins, lingering on the word painfully long, "I can't recall exactly what was said. It's been some time."

Sandy reanimates, holding out hope that the tempest will pass. The detective cannot be impeached if he doesn't recall the statement. Poor memory wouldn't be a lie. He has stumbled on an out.

But Jordan deftly shifts tactics.

"Don't you think taking a look at those comments would refresh your memory?"

The detective has backed himself into a no-win situation. He cannot credibly reject reviewing the copy as a refresher. But being handed the sheet—and reading it quietly in front of the jury—is just as good for the defense as introducing it outright. Maybe even better, as the imagination can always conjure up worse than what is plainly true.

"Sure. I'll look at it."

Jordan walks over to the witness stand. Over and behind the detective's shoulder, he lays the sheet in front and—for pure effect—points a finger at the offending word, although the detective can read for himself what amounts to a few short lines on a page.

Blinds drawn against a midmorning sun, sitting in underwear before the blue glow of his desktop computer, Sam wiped away dried tears with the back of one hand and frantically typed with the other. His inner thoughts materialized on-screen beneath two other posts:

by thelastgr8marine (5,875 posts)
11 Sept. 2001, 10:31 a.m.
these arab fuckers declare war on american soil ...we da-
port and bomb Mohamad into the sand ...its the only way

by DocKirby (1,763 posts)
11 Sept. 2001, 10:33 a.m.
The border with Mexico is porous. Drugs, terrorists, brownies flowing in. You close the border, you protect Americans. It's that simple.

by sterling_is_golden (1 post)
11 Sept. 2001, 10:34 a.m.
Romans 13. Deport criminal illegal spics, too.

Detective Sterling's mouth forms a tight, straight line. His eyes dawdle on the sheet. He has to nod tersely before Jordan finally withdraws it from his sight. Back at the podium, he repeats the inquiry so unhurriedly that each syllable counts the seconds down to the detective's answer.

"You have before expressed publicly the view that illegal, your word, 'spics' ought to be deported from this country?"

"Yes."

Jordan lets it sit in the dense air seconds long before sitting himself.

"Redirect."

Sandy does not immediately rise. Her limbs feel frozen to her seat. When she finally does move, she saunters to the podium in slow motion. She takes a sustained gulp of her water. The microphones pick up the thrumming of her heart. Her voice, when it flees her, is surprisingly steady.

"Detective Sterling, are you married?"

He looks lost, but the resolve in her speech enlivens him somewhat. He leans forward to speak into the microphone. He is afraid his first words will be too low, crushed under the weight of his embarrassment.

"I am."

He appears as puzzled by the question as some watching from the gallery.

"Where's your wife from?"

"Objection!"

"This is rehabilitation, Your Honor. I promise you the answer is relevant."

Sandy speaks so authoritatively while still visibly shell-shocked that the judge's ruling follows almost as reflexive mercy.

"Overruled."

"What country is your wife from, Detective?"

"Guatemala, ma'am."

"Was she born there?"

"Yes, ma'am."

"And when did she immigrate to this country?"

"As a teenager."

"You mentioned learning Spanish, Detective. Why are you doing that?"

"Our two little girls speak it," he says, voice cracking. His eyes shine with unshed tears. She is surprised by the open display of emotion. "And I use it to communicate with my in-laws."

"Do you regret the language you used many, many years ago as a much younger man?"

"Yes. I regret all of it. I don't even agree with those political views anymore."

"Do you recall what was happening when you made those statements?"

"The September 11 attacks. It's not an excuse, but it was an emotional time."

"Let me ask you bluntly: Do you harbor any bias against Hispanic people?"

"No."

"Did you come to investigate, suspect, and ultimately arrest Mr. Soto for murder because he is Hispanic?"

"No."

"Did you plant any evidence in this case?"

"Absolutely not. Never."

"Did you pressure or manipulate any of the testimony of the independent eyewitnesses who corroborate Mr. Soto's culpability in the murder of Ms. Mora?"

"Not at all."

"What led you to arrest Mr. Soto for murder?"

"The facts. That's it. He was with her—publicly harassing her—the last time she was seen alive. His neighbor recalls the distinct screaming of a woman from inside his cabin hours later, highly unusual for a man who never had a houseguest in three years. Her hair is found in that cabin, although the two were virtually strangers, having met earlier that night. Her bones are hidden at his workplace, where he has access to incinerators, crematories, and tools for dismembering. That's why he was arrested."

The court adjourns until the next morning after his testimony. A few hours remain in the workday, but the emotional energy for a week has been wrung dry.

Sandy doesn't wait for her trial partner and, instead, storms out, leaving the echo of her click-clacking heels behind her. She feels hot tears sprouting, and she has never—not once—cried on the job. Sam, even with lengthier strides that eclipse hers, has to break into a light jog to catch up. His hand on her elbow draws her temporarily short.

"I'm sorry, Sandy."

"Where did that even come from?"

She feels her voice quiver. She refuses to blink to stave off saline vulnerability.

"I think it's still in my personnel file. I was a rookie cop—a couple years into the force—and a bonehead in a dark place. There was a short internal affairs investigation. I was let off with a warning and never heard about it again. I'm sorry. I haven't thought about it since. I had no clue."

"You made me look like a fool, Sterling." She shoves away his hand. "You made me play the but-he-has-a-Hispanic-wife-and-kids card. Do you understand how revolting that is?"

He halts in place. She uses her small hand as a barrier between them. She backs away.

"Do not be confused, Sterling. I defended you because no one—no one—fucks up my case. Be a racist prick at home, but not on the stand in *my* case. Save your apology for Marta. Because I don't want it, and I don't accept it."

He watches her disappear down the escalator.

"Where's my dad, Mom?"

In the darkness of their vehicle, he could not quite discern her reaction. The streetlights on those roads—old, flickering, and dim—failed to illuminate her profile. But her body, sprawled in the front seat though it was, appeared stiff.

"Nowhere you need to be."

She was uncharacteristically quiet. In his younger years, Sam had accepted this nonanswer. But adolescence had instilled in him a recklessness that urged him to push further.

"That isn't enough anymore."

Sam looked at her out of the corner of his eye. It's how he caught sight of the hunk of metal, ensconced in blackness, barreling toward the front passenger side, moments before impact. He slammed on the accelerator. There was a pop, crunch, and screech, so loud they became the only sounds in the world. The Earth spun on its axis: one revolution, two revolutions, three revolutions in a matter of seconds, before the hot, spiraling box in which he sat came to a rest against a palm tree. Sam lost focus. The scene blurred, melting into nothingness.

Light and color reentered his eyeline. He threw his shoulder up against his driver's-side door. It shrieked open, bottom corner clawing at cement. He lurched forward on shaky footing. Soreness gripped his muscles. He stumbled out onto the street.

And for one beautifully tranquil moment, as he staggered down an empty, darkened street in a vacuum of noise, he was the only living soul in the universe.

Two male hands sandwiched him, one flat against his chest, the other on his back. The man was yelling—*that* Sam could see—but he could not hear what. The dial tone in his ears drowned out all else. The man's eyes shook with alarm. A stream of blood fell from his temple. White powder caked his nostrils.

Sam snapped back into his muted surroundings. He flipped around, stared at a heap until he recognized it as his mangled car, and ran toward it. Using a shattered window as a reference point, he distinguished the outline of the passenger door. Drops of viscous red and leaking gas dripped from its bottom corner. He summoned all of his remaining strength and pulled on twisted steel that would not budge. The hands reemerged, this time shoving him back and away from the leaking coffin. Sam was now yelling. He depleted his voice raw until sirens replaced it.

The vehicle had to be pried apart with fire and brimstone. The body was removed and blanketed. Sam watched while seated on the curb. He heard next to nothing of what adults directed to him. He said nothing in reply, handing them his wallet for identification and explaining little else. They came to suspect that Sam was deaf.

Two officers holding down the perimeter droned on in mindless conversation in heavy accents near him.

"Did you see the driver try to run off when units arrived? That man was stoned out of his mind. Had to be gunning it. It sent that car spinning. He has no license, either. No papers. Just a passport. El Salvador, Guatemala—some place near there. That illegal just killed that lady."

07 | DOUBT

Hurry up and wait. That characterized the crux of jury service. There was a lot of shuffling in and out of the courtroom. A lot of shielded conversations and blocked testimony, as if there were some big, critical secret everyone but the all-important seven could know.

"So, we can't tell them this kid killed three other people before this, right?" juror number eleven—an early not-guilty vote—imagined the judge saying in one of those muffled sidebar conferences. He chuckled to himself at the thought.

The other jurors turned to him curiously, but interest faded just as fast.

Mostly, it was a lot of sitting. Hours of active listening followed by hours of hushed stillness with six strangers. Number eleven's tailbone was sore. He walked all day for a living. He sprung from his chair, sending its legs screeching under him, and ambled over to a coffee table set up in a corner.

As he poured himself a cup, he felt a presence nearby. He had not heard juror number sixteen get up and follow him.

His steps were light, as if he walked on his toes. He stood uncomfortably close, killing any reasonable amount of personal space between them.

"Can I pour you a cup?" eleven said.

"You *may*," sixteen answered.

Eleven was unsure whether his emphasis was meant as a grammatical correction or just a symptom of his eccentricity.

"Black," sixteen said. Eleven smirked. "I'll take it black, please."

Eleven laughed.

"Yes, you will." He had no intention of pouring him cream or sugar.

Eleven handed him the cup. Sixteen downed half of it in a gulp, grimaced, and wiped his upper lip on his forearm.

"Cold," he said.

"Isn't that what's trendy nowadays with your generation? Iced coffee?"

"I don't usually drink it, actually. This *may* or *may* not be my first cup."

Eleven grinned.

"How old are you, son?"

"Twenty."

"And chosen for the jury. Unlucky for you. I don't think they often pick kids your age."

Sixteen shrugged. That apathy had come to typify his overall attitude. He had said next to nothing in the group's initial discussions. Eleven found that intriguing, given that the identity of the second not-guilty was still unknown to him.

He lowered his voice: "You're a Latino, right?" A noun. Not an adjective.

Sixteen nodded. "Cuban," he corrected.

"Don't you feel a little uncomfortable as a minority? Like

you need to be extra skeptical? Make sure all the i's are dotted and the t's crossed before letting 'the man' take another one of us down?"

Sixteen paused, appearing to dwell on the inquiry. But eleven noticed fairly quickly—like nothing he had ever before seen—the inactivity behind his eyes. It was as if he were *performing* how a human might act if he were mulling over a thought. He waited the appropriate amount of time, but the wheels just weren't turning. He wasn't blinking.

He shrugged again.

"He's probably guilty," sixteen said, finally. "If the police arrest you, you're probably guilty, right?"

Clifton Robinson pressed his pencil against the paper, shading in the shapes. He sat hunched over, elbows and slender forearms flat against his desk, feet dangling over his seat and two inches above the ground. His pencil scratched loudly as it rolled along the smooth loose-leaf surface in the otherwise noiseless room.

"Mr. Robinson," the woman at the helm declared. "This isn't art class."

The boy didn't look up. He continued coloring.

"Perhaps you can try your hand at answering my question, Mr. Robinson," she coaxed again, softer this time, abruptly switching from negative to positive reinforcement as if a hippy-dippy teaching aphorism she had read somewhere had flashed in her mind.

Nothing.

"The Space Race, Mr. Robinson? Which nations did it involve?"

"Ain't no man been on the moon," he responded instead.

The uneasy laughter of children ensued.

"I watched it myself, Cliff. I was just about your age," she said. "Didn't your parents watch it on TV? Maybe an older sibling?"

"My pops told me it was all a hoax. A fancy Hollywood director filmed it on a fancy Hollywood soundstage."

Heartier laughter commingled with gasps left his teacher's face blanched, lips pursed, and hands up on her hips.

"No, Cliff. That isn't right." It drowned in the crowd's commotion.

"And that AIDS was created by white folk to wipe out the blacks and the gays," he added.

The thunderous slamming of a wooden bar—the hall pass—against his desk squelched the upheaval.

"Why don't you tell the principal all about your father's theories?"

Cliff reluctantly hopped off of his chair and walked out, hall pass in hand and backpack strapped to his shoulders. But first, he handed his teacher his doodle: two rockets blasting off into the atmosphere toward a cratered circle in the sky. One had the label U.S.A. slapped on it; the other, a sickle and U.S.S.R. That answer—however creatively, unorthodoxly, and delayed it came—was insufficient to salve his insubordination. He knew she'd rather do away with him than deal with him.

He followed the glare of fluorescent lighting gleaming off the hallway floor, forming a moving trail for him. His spotless sneakers squawked as he walked. He leaned into the ground to exaggerate the noise, sending it reverberating down his path. He drew up short beneath a cracked overhead beam—vacillating between light and darkness—and peered to the right, at the door to the boys' bathroom: obscured in shadows, stifling human sounds, and secreting sweet-smelling smoke.

Cliff diverted course, swung open the door, and entered.

The haze hit his nostrils and eyes before melting away in patches, revealing eight dark brown eyes of varying height, all taller than the intruder, all turned suspiciously his way. Then emerged eight pouty lips of varying thickness and pinkness, four noses of aggressive size, four chins dressed in scraggly hairs visible only to their owners, and four short cuts with immaculately taped hairlines.

The council of black boys stood in a circle, enveloped in smoke and mirrors. As soon as Cliff's skin color poked through the mist, the alert in their reddened, heavily lidded eyes receded, and he became just another inanimate object in the backdrop.

The smog gripped Cliff's lungs, contracting them for a brief second, before relaxing them to the point they dissembled and flew away. He floated over to the ring of boys, standing just behind a break in the chain, petitioning silently to enter orbit.

"Give Tiny a hit," the leader ordered: marble-mouthed, tattooed forehead—a cross at dead center, between the eyes, and fancy lettering that Cliff didn't have the time to read—and skin so light his black peers would label it red. He called him Tiny, not because it constituted any prevailing nickname, but because the underdeveloped thirteen-year-old remained deeply ensconced at the shallow end of the puberty bell curve. These boys were demonstrably older.

Dutifully, the one nearest to him handed over the joint. Cliff, whose eyes already watered and whose feet hovered inches above the ground, expertly inhaled, having done so two or three times in his life thus far, and soared farther up that room.

Like a puppet, he felt his bones disjoint from one another and collapse, only to droop and be held up by taut strings. It must have been noticeable and immediate, because the cloying smile Red flashed him was comical—near cartoonish—and Cliff's unfocused eyes fixated on how white, straight-set, and toothy the boy's winsome grin had been. Red converted into a leering skeleton with high cheekbones, an angular face, and two gaping holes for sockets where eyes should have been. It was frightening, but it made Cliff chuckle.

The boys shared between them another intoxicant: a glossy magazine featuring close-up, hardcore pictorials of naked black women. Dark, dark skin and lots of natural hair, as if it were both intentionally prurient and political. They exchanged no words regarding the material, declining to acknowledge the pent-up tension of their teenage libidos, which they jointly ratcheted up without release.

Cliff had heard rumors that some boys, supposedly straight, would at times jerk off together in a circle, never touching.

"That's some white-boy shit," he recalled saying.

Red stroked the butt of the gun protruding from his waistband.

"You live in my hood, Tiny?" Red's mumbling cut through the fog.

"Chocolate City. Goulds. In the Villas."

Red nodded approvingly.

"We hang out on the corner of 113 and 216, if you're ever around."

Suddenly, his body glided out from the clouds, out of that room, out of that school—seemingly powered not by his legs but by an unseen force, yanking him away—and into the sun, on hot pavement in the middle of an unbusy road. His skin baked. He didn't perceive a second figure beside him until the gnat got directly in his face: hot breath on his skin, rough hands wrenching at his collar, and shrill voice hollering in his ear.

"Where are you going? What are you doing?"

That gnat was Sully, his best friend, wearing his physical education uniform of short shorts and a white tee, liberally emitting sweat and adolescent body odor. Jean Pierre Sullivan was a mixed-race kid whose Irish American father left his

Haitian American mother before Sully could form a single lasting memory of him.

"See? A man is a man is a man," friends told his mother at the time. "The white ones ain't no better than the black ones."

These women raised sons without even the slightest awareness that they, too, would someday become men, and they, too, could overhear their entrenched low expectations of fatherhood.

John Sullivan had won Daphne Francois over, in part, by deploying an age-old pejorative analogy as flirtation.

"You know, they say the Irish are the blacks of Europe."

He had cleverly censored the more colorful version of that aphorism.

Daphne found it charming. Plus, he was tall, if not exactly handsome; he spoke a little French; and Supreme Court Justice Earl Warren had, along with eight other white men, recently decided that whites and blacks could marry. Not that John was looking for that sort of commitment. The two shared their ancestors' devout adherence to Catholicism and, similarly, an aversion to both contraception and abortion. In short order, their boy entered the world, pinker than Daphne imagined was possible. But he was, nonetheless, marked down as black on his birth certificate.

"A white woman can give birth to a black baby, but a black woman cannot give birth to a white baby," the nurse confidently explained to her. A year later, John was gone.

Twelve years after that, the frilly brown tendrils atop Sully's head shook frenetically as he shook Cliff.

"I saw you walk out of school. You buggin' or something?"

Their eyes met. Recognition, but no less alarm, infiltrated Sully's irises.

"You're high as fuck, Cliff. Your moms is gonna flip. Follow me."

Sully led Cliff in the direction of his home but specifically to the opposite corner of the Villas from where he stayed. Hundreds of units made up the public housing complex. His mother didn't work, not outside of the home at least. She collected disability checks from the government instead. And she wouldn't take kindly to seeing Cliff home early from school and in that state. Sully laid him out in front of his own apartment, using two plastic chairs—one for his head, the other for his feet—as a makeshift bed. He tracked down his older half brother, Mackenson Francois, himself of school age but no longer attending, per a mutual agreement with administration officials.

"What did he smoke?" Mack asked, opening his patient's eyes with his fingers, as if the answer were written in the whites.

"Weed," Cliff answered for himself.

"This ain't no weed trip, partner," Mack said. "Unless it was laced with something else. Keep him hydrated. He'll come down from it eventually."

Sully endured by his side, wringing out a wet cloth in Cliff's mouth to drink, then dabbing his forehead with the same damp rag. His younger half sister, Lovelie Francois, lit a few candles at the base of the chairs once she arrived home from school, dangling a rosary above Cliff as she prayed. Sully routinely teased him about the nascent crush she harbored for the older boy.

"No voodoo shit," Cliff grumbled.

"It's Christian, asshole," Sully replied.

"I don't believe in that shit, either."

Sunlight dwindled, as did Cliff's pupils. Gradually, as the boy's position transitioned from supine to leaning against the armrests to sitting up spine-straight in a single chair, he began to regain his normal disposition. Sully sat beside him in the second chair. The porch lights dispensing dull radiance flipped on automatically. The grass of the ill-maintained communal yards darkened, blending into the black. The streets became dotted with orange spotlights from above. And the former object of the Russians' and Americans' aspiration hung full in the sky, drenching this world in its refracted light.

A song of bullets—shots in the dark—rifted the night. Like a lightning bolt heard before being seen, their thunderous arrival froze time. There were exactly eight tiny earthquakes: a family of three, followed by a string of five. *Boom* isn't right. The sound was more a crackle than an explosion. Not far off from the sound of a whip breaking the skin of the shooter's once-enslaved ancestors. *Crack. Crack. Crack.* Pause. *Crack. Crack. Crack. Crack. Crack.* The clink of ejected casings striking concrete supplied a melodic echo to the discordant firing. Cliff and Sully had heard this symphony before. But even had they not, it was unmistakable.

The first man in history to ever face gunfire must have known exactly then—on sound alone—the danger it portended.

Instinct took over. Sully sought cover inside his home. Cliff ran outward, into the night, onto the grass, in the direction of his own home.

In the bustle, he had not properly tracked the geography of the explosions. The aftermath unfolded before him like a panoramic scene from a movie, just feet from him. He halted sharply before stumbling onto the scene of the crime.

His mind chopped the sight into fragments. It could not safely process it all at once. Spilt blood: redder than red, untarnished and pure. A baseball cap with a stiff-straight bill, worn to the side. Light splashed onto a snarled face. A hand clutched a chrome gun held down by his side. A cross painted onto a cluttered forehead.

The rest of the gaps filled themselves. His body was sent reeling. Minutes later, he could not have accurately named the route he took home. He merely appeared at his door, pounding his fists onto its surface violently.

He had a key tucked away in his pocket. But he doubted he

could summon the dexterity needed to maintain his grip on the thing and steadily enter it into the slot. He also needed human contact, even more than shelter. His thrashing would faster secure the former, even if it delayed the latter. His overwrought heart posed a more immediate threat than the danger he had left behind.

His mother met the theatrics of the moment: swinging open the door, scooping her child in her arms, and shuttering her home in one swift, sweeping motion.

The two said nothing. They merely rocked. And she cried.

A knock came at the door about an hour later. It was an antiseptic knock. A safe knock. A white, adult knock. Ms. Robinson was cooking supper in the kitchen. Cliff—sprawled out on the living room floor, still catching his breath and gathering his wits—answered the call.

The white adult on the other side of the door wore a khaki uniform, a buzz cut, a badge around his neck, a gun strapped to his side, a vest, and black boots. He was civilian police, but—given his trappings and the lingering peril in the area—he might as well have been walking into a war zone. As the police force increasingly militarized, the question became: Were they reflecting a more violent world, or was the world merely meeting the elevated expectations of battle-ready officers?

The officer did not speak at first, eyes scanning the boy and peering briefly behind him, pondering whether to address the adolescent or bypass him for an authority figure. He chose to engage him.

"Good evening, son. Have you heard or seen anything unusual tonight? Gunfire or anything like that?"

A wide-eyed Cliff remained mute. The officer took his reticence as a positive sign. The many tight lips he had faced that evening came paired with vociferous head swinging and slammed doors.

He flipped a photo folded in four out of his back pocket and held it out to the boy.

"Maybe involving this man? He goes by Redbone."

Having gone from seeing that face in person to recognizing it in an investigator's photo just one hour later was a jarring experience. The speed marveled him. The officer noticed. He smiled and took a step forward, preparing to make his way in for further questioning.

Until a shadow from behind Cliff darkened the doorway.

"We can't help you, sir," said Ms. Robinson. "We saw nothing. We heard nothing. We've been indoors all night."

There was the gamut of emotion—from puzzlement to disappointment to resignation—before rescinding his boot.

"I understand, ma'am," he replied.

On the other side of her shut door, she schooled her black son.

"Nothing gets done, Cliff. They won't help none," she said. "They don't live here. They go home to their safe, white neighborhoods. We have to live here. We don't have no choice. They can't protect us. They won't protect us. And they won't do nothing but put us in greater danger. You can't afford to stick your neck out for nobody. You hear me, boy? They is not your friends, the police. You mind your business and survive. That's what you do. You focus on surviving."

Cliff nodded in agreement. The words of his mama squelched whatever moral quandary had begun to form within him. He didn't give it a second thought. And if anyone ever talked about that night—the case, the fate of the victim—he simply walked away. He didn't want to know.

Mr. Clifton Robinson, juror number eleven, tapped the sides of his paper cup. He smiled at juror number sixteen in a way that indicated small talk was over. He returned to the discomfort of his seat. He flipped open his notepad, past his street-level sketch, to the latest page where he had written down two words and a punctuation mark: *police bias?* The bored jurors seated around him caught sight of the movement and diverted their attention his way.

The sight and scent of recently spilled blood—heavy, metallic, and crisp—flooded his mind after decades of suppressing the memory.

Without looking at them, Mr. Robinson spoke up, in a voice that was strong but solemn: "I just want y'all to know that I'm beginning to change my mind. I'm leaning guilty."

"State: Call your next witness."

"The State calls Julia Chambers to the stand."

A petite woman with straw-blonde hair pulled back into a ponytail and hazel eyes, drowning in dark cargo pants far too big for her frame, strolls into the courtroom and up to the witness chair. On the back of her cream-colored T-shirt are the bolded words: CRIME SCENE. She has a youthful, round face and, when she smiles at the jury, she reveals a row of metal braces.

Sandy has delegated her questioning to Nate.

"Put the two of us gals up there, and it's girl talk about sex, semen, and condoms straight out of the pages of *Seventeen* magazine. I don't think so," Sandy had explained. "We need a man if they're going to take any of it seriously."

"You're sexist," Nate joked.

"I'm a winner. You can chastise me after a guilty verdict. Better yet: I make seventy-seven cents to your dollar. *You* can't tell me anything."

Trial is a regressive art. In prioritizing ends over means, it is neither aspirational nor transformational, but instead appeals to human nature's basest, most reflexive instincts.

Nate stands up in a slackened bound, pushing up from his

knees in a single motion. He slides his chair against the carpet and deliberately, soundlessly, and slowly moves his towering, heavyset body to the lectern, his notepad clutched in his sweaty pink hand. He clears his throat, double taps the wood in front of him, and leans into the microphone.

"Good morning, Detective Chambers."

"Good morning, sir."

"Where do you work?"

"Miami-Dade Police Department."

"What do you do for them?"

"I am a crime scene detective."

"What does that mean?"

"I collect, preserve, and impound evidence at crime scenes—anything from gun casings to debris—and I dust for fingerprints and swab items for DNA so that, later, analysts at the crime lab might test them."

"Were you called out to a shack and its surrounding area on Orwell's Berry Farm in Homestead about two years ago for precisely that purpose?"

"I was."

"What did you do first?"

"I spoke with Detective Sam Sterling upon my arrival. He gave me a rundown of the known facts up until that point. He told me what he wanted done. After that, I entered the space and got to work."

"Did you take any photographs?"

"I did."

"Permission to publish what has already been admitted into evidence as State's Seventy-One through Seventy-Five." He addresses the judge. She nods offhandedly.

Nate collects the five color pictures—reproduced on standard-sized sheets of paper—and hands them, one by one, to the farthest jury member, to be passed down once they have inspected them. The five images present different angles and perspectives of that room, but they do not diverge substantially from one another. The room is too small to tell anything but one story. And that's the point of the redundancy: to paint the eccentricity of these cramped, barren quarters as Unabomber-adjacent. Photographs can only convey so much. The prosecution wants the jury to feel and smell the severe misanthropy leaping from these two-dimensional pages. After all, a murderer—they claim—lived there.

"This space, as you call it—what is it?"

"It's a single room. Very small. Can't be over three hundred square feet. It's all wood, even the furniture inside. Not a lot of furniture to begin with. A bed. A table. A basic kitchen, taking up half the width of one of the walls. That's it. No bathroom. There's an outhouse a few hundred feet away with modern plumbing. There's just one narrow window."

"What's the first thing of note that strikes you?"

"The bed," she answers immediately. "It had no sheets. The room looked lived in: a glass of water on the table; nightclothes and hangers tossed on the floor. But the bed was just a mattress on a metal frame."

Nate flashes the jury a picture. The grayed mattress has spheres of lint clinging to its surface, a tag visibly protruding from its seams, and no headboard. Other than a yellowing film, ostensibly from old age, it is not stained.

"What size?" Nate asks.

"A twin."

Nate wants to stress that Gabriel, a recluse of twenty-eight years, appears not to have proper accommodations for romantic partners.

"Did you find bedsheets anywhere inside?"

"No."

"Did you next photograph any one item in particular?"

"Detective Sterling had directed me to a box of condoms by the foot of the bed."

"These?" Nate hands her a photo of the box.

"Yes."

"You took this picture?"

"I did. In fact, you can see my gloved hand in the picture."

"Do you know why you documented these condoms in particular?"

"Well, I am overinclusive in my picture-taking. It was relatively early in the investigation in terms of now having an actual suspect after twenty-seven days. We don't quite know what will and what won't end up being significant at that point. In terms of the condoms, they were interesting in two respects. For one, they were unopened. It was a particularly unhandled and crisp box of condoms in mint condition. That isn't noteworthy if they were purchased recently. But, secondly, the box had been expired for approximately three years. They had been bought, and never used, many years ago."

"Did you come across any stains?"

"I found a stain that piqued my interest, yes. It was on top of the table. The table is a sort of a wooden bench, almost like one you'd find outside, at a park: a picnic table of old mahogany wood. Real wood, with creases in it, with imperfections. I found it while processing the laptop computer, which was sitting on top of the table. Within inches was a circular stain, whitish gray, that had some volume, some texture—as if whatever liquid it had been had hardened and congealed before being wiped off."

"Did you suspect it of being anything?"

"Well, to be clear, I don't test anything. I swab it—and, in this case, we actually sawed off a piece of the wood—to get it to professionals who analyze the substance. But, from my experience, including handling hundreds of crime scenes at this point with any number of liquids present, it looked like a semen stain to me."

"How thorough was your rundown of the room that first night?"

"We do our best. I took hundreds of photographs. I looked at the walls and the floors with my naked eye, trying to find any clues. But the room was messy. And the lighting was meager."

"How is the room lit?"

"A single, low-watt bulb hanging nakedly from the center of the ceiling. It was a dark, dark room. Hard to see. It was late at night that first search."

"How many times did you go back to conduct another walkthrough?"

"Twice more. The second time, I returned in the daylight. Collected more items, like clothing, and really tried to strip the room bare of its contents. But the window is small and translucent only to a degree. The glass is thick and dirty. Even with the front door wide open, visibility wasn't ideal. So I returned a third time, at night but carrying high-beam, military-grade flashlights for inspecting the crevices in the wood and the like. That's when we spotted the hairs."

"When you say 'we,' to whom are you referring?"

"Detective Sterling. He's the one who found the hairs. But I was right there, in the room, behind him. As we were inspecting different walls, he hollered and waved me over. There, clinging to a nail, by the doorframe, were two long, brown strands of hair."

"Is this a photograph of where it was found?"

Nate hands her the image.

"Yes. I took this, in fact, seconds after Detective Sterling alerted me to them. This pointer finger in the picture is actually mine. It was an incredible find."

"What did you do with those strands?"

"I immediately collected them for testing. Sealed them off in a box. Took them to the property room."

"Is this the same box in which you impounded those hairs?"

Nate hands her a small, white box sealed in red evidence tape. She reads her markings on the outside—her name, her badge number, the date, and the police case number—and nods.

"This is it."

"From the time they were discovered until you impounded them in this box, did they remain in your care, custody, and control?"

"Yes, that's right."

"The State seeks to move this item, marked 1-T for identification, into evidence and publish it with the jury."

The judge pokes her head up, sweeping her eyes over to the defense table. Not a stir.

"Hearing no objection, it will be admitted."

Nate slices into the red tape with the end of one scissor, parts the box from its top, and walks its contents ceremoniously before the jury. Members have to stand and peer over into it to make out the two thin strands lying against a white cotton bottom.

"Did you look for fingerprints in that room, Detective Chambers?"

"I did."

"Did you find any?"

"I did not."

"Did that surprise you?"

"No. As I mentioned before, the room and most of its contents were made out of wood. And not smooth wood, but rough, jagged, splintered wood. That's not a surface conducive to fingerprints. The natural oils on your hand pressing up against surfaces: That's what creates fingerprint evidence. And some surfaces are better than others at absorbing and preserving those oils. I could tell right away: Nothing of evidentiary value could be drawn from that wood. There was some glass inside, which is a great surface for fingerprints, but I didn't find anything of *value* there, either. I found a few smudges that *might* have been produced by touch, but for a fingerprint to be of value—for an analyst to later try to compare it against the fingerprint standard of a person—the ridges of the print need to be clearly reproduced on the glass. Smudges won't cut it."

"So, is it safe to say the victim's fingerprints were not found inside the room?"

"Right."

"But is it *also* safe to say the defendant's fingerprints were not found inside the room, despite him having lived there for three years?"

"That's right. No fingerprints at all were found. For anyone. At least by me."

"Did you look for DNA in that room, Detective Chambers?"

"I did."

"Did you find any?"

"Well, the two items that we've already discussed, since both hair and what I presumed to be dried semen contain DNA."

"Of course, Detective. My bad," Nate apologizes. Stifled chuckles spread in the gallery at this overly formal white man deploying slang in a professional setting. Nate's neck, but nothing above it, turns blotchy. "I meant touch DNA. If you don't leave behind a legible imprint of your finger, can you still, nonetheless, leave behind DNA from that touch?"

"You can, but again, that sweat, which is what leaves behind the DNA, needs a surface that can soak it up and preserve it. And it needs to be voluminous enough to be picked up by our cotton swabs for testing. This type of heavy wood isn't good for that. But we were able to find hallmark receptors of DNA like hair and bodily fluids. I was far more optimistic about finding those than I was touch DNA, given the materials we were working with."

"Did you look for the murder weapon?"

"Of course. It didn't take long to determine it wasn't in that room. But there was so much surrounding land and undergrowth where a weapon might be hidden. So I directed K9 officers to lead their dogs across the entire property in search of anything."

"Are those dogs infallible in finding all types of weapons that are purposely hidden?"

Detective Chambers displays a nervous, metal-glistening smile. Nate cocks his head to the side at her pregnant pause as one of those canines might, encountering a puzzling situation or noise.

"I don't know what 'infallible' means."

The widespread laughter, this time, is hearty and vibratory. Nate does not so much as grin as he plows forward.

"Are those dogs *perfect* at finding any and all types of weapons?"

Much of the audience and some within the jury miss his rephrasing of the question.

"Oh, no. They are trained specifically to detect firearms. Some look for metal. A few are looking for remains. But something like, let's say, a wooden bat would not trigger a signal from a gun dog or a metal dog. And, of course, if an item is buried deep in the ground, particularly a relatively small item like a bat, a dog might not signal."

"Did the defendant's neighbor, Mr. Rivas, appear at any point?"

"Yes. That first night we searched. In fact, it was while I was directing the K9 officers to fan out with their dogs that he came up to me. I figured he wanted a rundown of what was happening on the property. I was going to show him the warrant that covered all of the farm, but it became clear to me that he had pertinent information he wanted to share."

"Did you understand what he was trying to tell you?"

"No. I don't speak Spanish, so I didn't let him get very far. I can't even tell you what small bits I picked up. I could just tell it was important. So I flagged down Detective Sterling, who was the lead investigator and who I knew spoke some Spanish."

"What about the defendant's car? Given that the victim's remains were found away at the defendant's workplace, did you try to process his vehicle for forensic evidence?"

"Do you mean his truck? Because his truck was long gone. We knew by then, after speaking with his coworkers, that he had just bought himself a new car: a two-door sedan. Tiny car. Exact opposite of the truck he had been driving on the night of the victim's disappearance. He sold that thing—without a title, without any paperwork—to the owner of a junkyard somewhere in central Florida four days after the victim's disappearance."

"I have one final question, Detective, because I am sure defense counsel will ask you: Did you search and were you able to find any blood whatsoever in the defendant's home?"

It is an odd note on which to end. Attorneys bury the weaknesses of their cases in the middle. They always end strong. A bat bludgeoning—without a trace of blood—is not a good fact.

"I did search. I found none."

Nate begins his walk to his seat. At the edge of the table, just as he was beginning to round its corner, he draws short.

"Oh, one last thing," he says, feigning forgetfulness with a snap of his fingers. "Did you find any evidence of the use of chemicals in the home?"

Detective Chambers meets his aw-shucks sensibility with a moroseness that sends a chill through the nippy courtroom.

"Bleach. Lots and lots of bleach. Poured everywhere."

"No further questions."

Nate's steps are noticeably gleeful as he returns to counsel's table.

Sandy whispers in admiring amazement: "What was that?"

"*That*," he says, "was the Nate Parker show."

"Cross-examination," the judge announces.

Jordan doesn't stir. Instead, the woman seated beside him rises for the first time.

"She speaks!" Sandy whispers to her partner.

Ms. Sofia Peralta wears her heels thin and sky-high and her jet-black hair straight and down to her buttocks. She is distractingly attractive, ostentatiously so: caramel skin, firm calves poking out from a tight pencil skirt, long lashes, and expertly applied makeup that is both natural and busy. She speaks with a hint of an accent—sounding as if she rolls all of her *r*'s, in both English and Spanish—and when asked where she is from, she responds always with the full: "Caracas, Venezuela." She looks far too young to sit on a murder trial. And, at twenty-five, she is just one year out from law school.

By choosing her, Jordan drew chatter from within his own office and from opposing counsel across the street.

"He chose *Miss Venezuela* because he wants everyone—including the jury—to wonder if the two of them are sleeping together," Sandy speculated, the most popular theory.

Not one person, however, alleged an actual affair; it was widely known that Jordan adored his wife, a rather nondescript blonde woman, and that he would never cheat on her. He copped to many vices, but adultery wasn't one of them. In fact, he maintained his exceptional physique almost exclusively to impress other men, not women, whose opinions, in general, he didn't seem to hold in high regard.

The good-looking duo made an impression whenever they entered the courtroom. Like refracting mirrors set up to face one another, their gorgeousness multiplied exponentially.

"Every morning, it looks like they came directly from CrossFit," a colleague once remarked.

"The only thing more typically Jordan would have been to choose someone far uglier, so as not to distract from his own beauty," Sandy had replied.

This would be Sofia's first time speaking after more than a week of trial. The jury sits on the edge of their seats, eager to meet a new character in the drama. Unlike the prosecution, the defense had clearly calculated that such sexually charged testimony was better dealt woman to woman. They want to discredit Detective Chambers, not elevate her.

"Detective Chambers, you've been working as a crime scene investigator for eight years, is that correct?"

Sofia's *ch* sounds are soft, like in *Chicago*.

"Yes."

"So you've processed hundreds upon hundreds of scenes?"

"Been involved in some manner or another in hundreds of scenes. Maybe even a thousand by this point."

"And you've swabbed hundreds of, again maybe a thousand, surfaces for the later testing of DNA?"

"Yes."

"And yet, in this case—with three hundred square feet of surface area—you collected not one swab for DNA testing?"

"As I said to the prosecutor, the cabin was made up predominantly of a wood not conducive to absorbing touch DNA. There was, additionally, not an obvious location to swab for it. I cannot swab every inch of a room—the walls, the floors, the ceiling—especially when none of those places are likely to be touched, bare-handed or -footed, by an occupant."

"There's a metal handle to the front door, isn't there?"

"Well, um, can I see a picture of it to check?"

"Of course!" Sofia flips through a stack of photographs and hands her one. "This isn't a trick question. Take your time."

Detective Chambers takes a moment to study the photograph.

"It appears so, yes."

"And that is an area likely to be touched by an occupant, right?"

"Sure."

"And there's a metal chain hanging from the room's only light source?"

"Yes."

"And that is an area likely to be touched by an occupant, right?"

"Sure."

"And there were silverware, and plates, and glasses, right?"

"Yes."

"And those are likely to be touched by an occupant, right?"

"By the homeowner, probably. Sure."

"Or by a guest who is offered a glass of water after a long night of drinking?"

"It's possible."

"And yet, you swabbed none of those surfaces—those non-wood surfaces—for DNA, is that correct?"

"No."

"No, you did? Or no, you didn't?"

"No, I didn't."

"You mentioned you did happen to see smudges on glass surfaces inside the cabin?"

"A few, yes."

"Do you remember if they were on the window or on the glasses for drinking?"

"I can't recall."

"You were trained in the academy, weren't you?"

"Yes."

"And you received separate and focused training for becoming a crime scene investigator, right?"

"Yes."

"And they train you to document every important thing in your police report, right?"

"Things that are important, yes."

"Because when you're testifying—sometimes many years later—it helps to write it all down?"

"Yes."

"And you consider yourself a thorough crime scene investigator, don't you?"

"I like to think I am."

"But nowhere in your report did you indicate where—or even that you had—found smudges, right?"

"Objection! Improper negative impeachment," says Nate.

"Overruled."

"You may answer, Detective."

"Can I see my report?"

"Of course!" Sofia hands her the report. Detective Chambers moves her lips as she reads silently. The courtroom waits awkwardly as the minutes collect.

"It isn't there," she finally concedes.

"And although a smudge is not valuable for fingerprint analysis, it is created, in part, by sweat, making it potentially valuable DNA evidence?"

"Maybe. If there's enough."

"But that's a determination for a DNA analyst to make, right? You didn't even make an effort, did you, Detective?"

"Ma'am," she begins, caustically, "we found two very DNA-rich sources in that apartment. Hair strands—long and straight—that did not appear to belong to the defendant, as well as apparent semen. It placed the victim in that cabin. Any additional DNA evidence found—even from the victim—would not have added anything. It just wasn't necessary. We already know she was there."

"Answer my question, Detective," Sofia insists, with no hint of Jordan's passive-aggressive sweetness or charm. "Finding other sources of the victim's DNA would help prove that those hair strands weren't planted, right?"

"Nothing was planted, ma'am."

The answers, at this point, are immaterial. Sofia is having a one-sided conversation, all for the purpose of sowing doubt in the minds of the jurors.

"And, certainly, the victim's DNA on a drinking glass might tell us she was there voluntarily, and not forcibly, as the government is suggesting?"

"DNA won't tell us that." Detective Chambers's elfin face creases. She is losing her cool.

"Detective, are you telling this jury that DNA on the door handle—indicating she herself opened the front door—or on the rim of a drinking glass—indicating she drank from it—would tell us *absolutely* nothing about what happened inside that room and whether it was more or less likely that it was consensual?"

"Objection! Speculation."

"Overruled."

"I don't know. I don't know," the detective stammers. "Those are questions better left for the lead detective. I don't speculate. I don't develop theories. I just collect evidence."

"But I am asking *you*, Detective. Wouldn't that information be helpful?"

"Objection! Asked and answered."

"Sustained."

"Ultimately, Detective, we do not know whether Melina's DNA is on that handle, or on that chain, or on that drinking glass, do we?"

"No."

"And that's because *you* chose not to swab those pieces of evidence?"

"I guess. I wasn't directed to do so."

"But you did choose to photograph a box of unused, unopened condoms?"

"So?"

"I ask you the questions, Detective. Not the other way around."

Sofia's face maintains its elegant composure, despite the venom spouting from her tongue.

"You found the presence of condoms in the apartment of a young single man notable enough to photograph?"

"Long-expired condoms, yes."

"You, in fact, counted each condom to ensure none were missing?"

"Yes."

"You didn't dust that box for fingerprints or swab it for DNA, did you?"

"No."

"You found the presence of dried semen in the apartment of a young, single man notable enough to process for DNA?"

"The medical examiner had preliminarily evaluated the bones found at the morgue by that point, so we suspected sexual foul play. And I was right. The semen came back belonging not just to the defendant but containing trace female DNA."

Sofia is visibly put off. Detective Chambers is not a DNA analyst, and she cannot testify to the results of an analysis she heard secondhand.

"Objection, Your Honor," she protests. "Lack of personal knowledge. And hearsay."

The judge peers over at counsel, silent and puzzled. Sandy rests her face in her hands out of embarrassment.

"You're objecting to your own question, counselor?" the judge finally responds, far more sharply than she intends.

Heat rises to Sofia's skin. She opens her mouth, but no sounds emerge.

Jordan stands and barks from behind: "We move to strike the witness's answer as nonresponsive."

"That's better," the judge concedes, nonetheless rolling her eyes in dramatic fashion. "But you opened the door. The cat's out of the proverbial bag. Go on, counsel."

Sofia pauses, swallows loudly enough that the microphones pick up the sound, and then she reengages, undeterred.

"The trace female DNA you mention, it was not matched to the victim in this case, Melina Mora?"

"Not enough was found to include or exclude her. All that could be confirmed was that it was female."

"We have no idea how that mixture of DNA occurred, correct?"

"Correct."

"For all we know, that was touch DNA previously left on the wood, before the semen landed on top of it?"

"I have no idea."

"But you might have had more of an idea if you hadn't refused to swab the rest of the bench for DNA?"

"Again, ma'am, I didn't refuse."

"That semen stain was found just a few inches from my client's laptop computer, correct?"

"Yes."

"Just a few inches from his laptop computer that had a large amount of gay pornography on it?"

"I wouldn't know. I didn't search it myself."

"You said you were the first officer to speak to Mr. Rivas?"

"I saw him first. We didn't understand each other much, so I wouldn't say we spoke."

"And, after that, he spoke to Detective Sterling. Alone?"

"Yes."

"So he alone knows what Mr. Rivas first said?"

"Him and, shortly thereafter, the interpreter."

"The same man who found two brown strands of hair against a brown backdrop on the third time searching that room?"

"Yes. I was there for that. He called me over immediately after he found them."

"You combed that room for blood?"

"Yes."

"You found not one drop of Melina's blood in that room, correct?"

"Correct."

"You, in fact, found not one drop of anyone's blood in that room, correct?"

"Correct. But we did find quite a lot of bleach."

"Let's talk about that, Detective. It's common to clean wood with bleach, isn't it?"

"I don't know how common it is. I know it'd be hard to sleep in there—on the fumes alone—if that much bleach were poured in that room at once."

"Well, you have no idea when bleach was poured in that room, correct?"

"That's right."

"And you certainly didn't smell fresh bleach on any of the days you searched the cabin?"

"I didn't."

"You, in fact, have no idea whether the evidence of bleach you found came all in one pour or over several months or years of cleaning?"

"I don't."

"And bleach can be used not only to clean wood but to treat it, and stain it, and disinfect it?"

"I'm not aware of its multiple uses. I am aware that it can remove stains, like blood."

"You found not one drop of blood on the bed, correct?"

"I already said that. Nowhere in the room."

"And you found no bedsheets?"

"Right."

"But you have no idea whether that bed ever had sheets?"

"I would assume so, if someone used it for sleeping."

"Other than your assumptions," Sofia hisses, lingering on the *s* like a rattled serpent, "you do not know whether that bed ever had linens on it to begin with?"

"I don't know that."

"You found not one drop of blood from the front door to where my client's vehicle would theoretically be parked on the night in question?"

"No."

"And, in fact, some of the dogs called to the scene are trained to detect remains, isn't that right?"

"Yes."

"And they don't just detect remains that are still present. They have the ability to detect where remains used to be, at some previous time, correct?"

"If it's still fresh, yes."

"And they did not alert—not one single time—on any part of the Orwell property?"

"It had been twenty-seven days," she dissents instead.

"Is that a yes, Detective? The dogs alerted not one single time?"

"Correct."

"And a wooden bat—while neither a firearm nor metal— if used to kill, would have remains on it that the dogs could detect?"

"It could. Or it could be cleaned. It could be buried."

"You mentioned that you knew my client had sold his truck to a junkyard in central Florida, right?"

"Yes."

"How many trips to central Florida did you take to try to find and process that truck, Detective?"

Tight-lipped and arms crossed, the witness sulks in silence. Sandy looks up, fearing the detective will remain mute out of sheer defiance.

"None," she finally says.

"On the route from Orwell's Berry Farm to the morgue, you take the Homestead Extension of the Florida Turnpike, right?"

"Not necessarily. You can take local roads."

"The straightest shot is the Florida Turnpike, isn't it, Detective? If you're trying to make good time, right?"

"Yes."

"And on the Florida Turnpike, there are tolls?"

"Yes."

"Tolls without attendants but with overhead cameras, right?"

"Yes."

"Cameras that would pick up the contents of a flatbed truck if it were passing underneath?"

"Objection! Speculation."

"Overruled. You may answer, Detective."

"Can you repeat the question?"

"Do the cameras hanging overhead on the Florida Turnpike have the capacity to pick up the contents of a flatbed truck if that truck were passing underneath?"

"Yes."

"Tell me, Detective, how much video from the Florida Department of Transportation did you review in this case?"

"None."

"But you had plenty of time to individually count a box of condoms."

Sofia does not wait for a reply. It's not really a question. She whips around—mane of hair twirling emphatically behind her, collecting her papers from the podium in one noisy swoop as the bangles on her wrist slam against the wood—and returns to her seat, adding, "No further questions" as she went.

Jordan whispers in her ear. She laughs flamboyantly. In between them is Gabriel, blank-eyed, immobile, and not privy to the professional congratulations his lawyers share.

Most, if not all, within the room have largely forgotten he is even there.

08 | WHERE THE DEAD BODIES GO

The sky at daybreak was on fire as the winter morning dipped to a cool 64 degrees. The doors to the city's oldest bar swung open, coughing up a man shielding a spark in his hands that he promptly pressed against the unforgiving end of a tobacco cylinder. By the empty roadside, he stretched his bones—chest out, elbow bent, fingers to his lips, sucking in smoke that he held protractedly long within him—until he crumpled into himself, taking a seat on the curb.

He laid his palms facedown behind him, kissing concrete, and rolled his head back, watching upside down the turquoise wall in the foreground.

A second man exited the tavern doors in a twitchy hurry. He teetered on the edge of the sidewalk, looking up and down the empty street.

"Can I bum a cig?" he asked, nostrils tickled by smoke, eyes adrift, failing to turn even momentarily to the man he addressed.

The first man picked his head up, turning the world upright.

He dug into his shirt pocket, extended a cigarette, and offered a light. His counterpart pulled in close, bringing his lips within inches of the stranger's own in abrupt intimacy. After the ember multiplied by two, he receded and puffed in rapid, chimneylike succession.

"Late night?" the puffer asked. Haggard and half-eyed, he telegraphed his own exploits with his inquiry.

"Early morning."

He stood back and stared admiringly at the man who walks into a bar first thing in the morning. He wanted to know his name.

"I'm Vlad," the puffer offered first.

"Lee."

They shook hands. Lee's was colder than the temperature warranted.

Vlad scanned the expanse of the street, snapping his vacillating head, leaving plumes of gray in both directions.

"Waiting for something?" Lee asked.

"A ride. You?"

"Death."

"That's self-defeating," Vlad snorted.

"Not my own."

Vlad strained to open his half-lidded gaze and pay closer attention to the macabre man beside him. He wore Chuck Taylors and wrinkled green scrubs underneath a denim jacket. Specks of gray shaded his temples. He wore a mustache from the previous decade.

"You a doctor?" Vlad intuited from the garb.

"That's what the degree on my wall says."

"I've never heard of a doctor who smokes."

"I'm not that kind of doctor."

Lee's pants pocket shook and resounded. He removed his pager. It displayed an address.

"Got to go," he announced, mashing his cigarette into the sidewalk. "I'll give you a ride."

"Aren't you short on time, Doc?"

"I've got eternity."

As his rubber soles soundlessly hit the concrete walkway leading to a suburban home, Lee slapped black gloves on his hands. He thrust open the front door and led himself inside, following the commotion toward the largest room in the back of the house. A sea of policemen parted as he approached.

At the bed, he found the shell of a man—Hispanic, mid- to late twenties, hirsute, and of medium build—shirtless and in underwear, limbs strewn, mouth agape, eyes shut, and black hair in a tousle, matted down by blood that cast a weblike pattern on his pillowcase. Lee picked up the Polaroid camera hanging from his neck and began snapping pictures of the body.

A tall man in shirtsleeves with an air of authority spoke with him as he photographed. He introduced himself as a sergeant, but his actual name was muffled by the flash of the camera.

"Wife says he came home late last night—very drunk—and crawled into bed. It was dark, and she didn't notice the bleeding. Thought maybe the wetness was slobber. He was breathing and snoring into the night, but he didn't wake up in the morning."

Lee stripped the body of its only article of clothing and continued to photograph. The officer winced, averting his eyes from the body's brazen nakedness. The doctor scanned and then flung around the dead man's heavy limbs. Finding nothing, he bent the neck forward, feeling for the source of the blood on the back of the head. He photographed the probable wound.

"Can you rule out foul play?"

The doctor found the question odd. He had found the officer's squeamish impulses odd. Bodies were commonly disrobed at the scene.

"It doesn't work that way," Lee said. "I mean, I can say—

probably off the bat—that he didn't sustain the wound here, in bed. There's no spray pattern on the walls, on the sheets. The wound is flat against the pillow. That's consistent with what his wife says. But I know next to nothing about what kind of wound it is. How long ago he sustained it. Whether it's a laceration or blunt force trauma. I'll need to shave his head, peel back his face, crack open his skull, and do a full workup to rule much of anything out."

The doctor was intentionally using crass language to measure the officer's reaction, which was to wrinkle his nose, as if he had encountered a foul smell.

"You work homicides, Sergeant?"

"Narcotics," he corrected.

"Huh."

Lee chewed the inside of his cheek. He dug into his pocket, pulled out a miniature flashlight, casually flipped open the dead man's eyelids with his fingers, and shined the light directly into the eyeballs.

"Now that makes sense."

"What does, Doctor?"

"His pupils are the size of fucking saucers," Lee scoffed. "Cocaine, likely. And he's probably Colombian."

The officer tut-tutted with surprising bluster. His cheeks turned maroon.

"I am myself Colombian, Doctor. What does that tell you?"

Lee smiled, impressed by the vocal challenge.

"From the circumstances, absolutely *nothing*. My trade is forensic pathology, Sergeant. The science part—the *pathology*—is precise. But the *forensic* part is not. That's where I look at the circumstances and roughly, imperfectly, even indelicately draw conclusions. I deal in probabilities. Stereotypes aren't destiny in life or in my line of work, but they are helpful. It's not too much of a leap, is it, Sergeant? A young, Latin man: uncircumcised, so not born here; eyes dilated as all hell; and dead in a nice home, now crawling with narcotics detectives, in a nice neighborhood in *this* city in *these* times?"

The officer's lips formed an unresponsive straight line.

"Lighten up, Sergeant," Lee said convivially, slapping the bigger man on the back. "There's a massive picture of Carlos Valderrama—the Colombian soccer star—on his wall. Often, there's little to no guesswork involved."

Lee backpedaled out of the room.

"What happens now?"

"My crew transports the body to my office, where I do that science stuff I was talking about. And next time, when I'm done and ready to rule things out, send a homicide detective to come see me."

Outside, Lee stumbled as he dipped below yellow caution tape, catching himself before running into a little girl that stood as tall as his waist, with long hair, long lashes wet with tears, and chipped, rose-painted nails. He gave an awkward and curt nod before darting off to his hearse.

Three days later, a knock interrupted the doctor at his desk, as he sat engrossed in paperwork. The man who entered was just short of average height, boasting broad shoulders and tanned skin, wearing a high-and-tight haircut and soft shoes. His cologne greeted Lee before his extended hand.

"Dr. Musgrave?"

"Yes, sir. Just Lee, please."

"Lee, I'm Reynaldo Lozano with the Drug Enforcement Administration. Just Rey, please."

"To what do I owe the pleasure, Rey?"

"I'm here on the case of Melvin Mora."

Rey sat himself in the chair opposite the middle-aged doctor's desk, uninvited. Lee pondered briefly before snapping his fingers.

"That's the young father found dead in his bed, right? So,

DEA, huh? This must be serious. I thought I told them to send me a homicide detective."

Rey threw up his hands, before revealing a perfect set of teeth that gleamed in the office's lackluster light.

"Twelve years of homicide investigation, at your service."

"In DC?"

"Oh, no, sir. I'm a local boy. Born and bred in Hialeah. That's twelve years with the county. I'm technically still on the payroll. Just on loan with the feds for a task force of indeterminate time."

"A task force relating to the city's drug cartels?"

"I'm afraid the answer to that is classified, Lee."

"Of course," Lee nodded. "What is it about Mr. Mora that brings you here?"

"I understand you worked on his autopsy."

"I did."

"I understand you are working on his report."

"I am."

"Have you come to a conclusion about the manner of death?"

"Now, *I'm* afraid, Rey, that the answer to *that* is classified. It not being finalized and all."

Rey sat in his amusement momentarily, enormous fingers interlaced in front of his face. His eyes twinkled.

"To answer your question: *Yes*, I work on a task force aimed at combating Miami's drug cartels."

He offered the chip blindly, willing to wager against the risk that, if Lee weren't a transactional man, it might not induce a payout.

"I haven't settled on a manner of death just yet," Lee offered. "It's a toss-up between accident and homicide."

Rey was pleased. Not necessarily by the answer. Rather, he had just learned that Lee was not a moral absolutist, and that was a good first step for his purposes.

"What evidence is there of homicide? He was drunk, wasn't he?"

"He was at a point-one-eight blood alcohol level. That's high, but not astronomical. Judging by his liver, he was a prodigious drinker. Alcohol wouldn't affect him as much as it does others. You want him stumbling drunk, I imagine? I don't see that. And you don't want cocaine in his system, I imagine? But it was."

"And yet, why homicide? Why not accidental?"

"The force of the blow. It fractured the skull. Not enough to knock him out cold. So it wouldn't be an object too heavy, like a metal bat. But it had velocity. He loses his balance walking and strikes concrete at *that* speed? His limbs just give out underneath him? No survival instinct? A complete failure to use his hands or ass to brace himself in some way? I don't think so."

"Maybe he trips?"

"Drunks stumble forward. But there's no trauma on the front of him whatsoever. Falls clean backward, like a cartoon character slipping on a banana peel? It might be a fall. Don't get me wrong. But even if it's contact with the ground that does him in, I can't rule out that he was pushed."

"But it was the concussion that killed him, yes?"

"The cause of death is definitely concussion or, in my language, traumatic brain injury."

"So, where does that leave you on manner of death?"

"Indeterminate, likely."

"But 'indeterminate' doesn't squelch curiosity, or investigation, or follow-up inquiry. It doesn't put out the fire. If anything, it stokes it."

"My analysis isn't impacted by political considerations, as I'm sure you're already aware."

Rey stood up, approached the desk, and collected in his hands the weighty triangular prism serving as the doctor's nameplate, complete with his italicized title beneath it.

"Word is that you're up for a promotion. You're due to become the chief medical examiner, right?"

"You mean to imply that it'd be better for my career if I were to manipulate my results—"

"Not manipulate, Lee," Rey interrupted. "Just resolve a genuine toss-up—*your* words—in the direction that will save lives."

"But you do know that the county medical examiner isn't an elected position? I don't need political support."

"It's not elected, but to be effective, you'll need law enforcement on your side."

"You call it resolving a genuine toss-up favorably. What would you have done had you walked into this office and heard that I definitively concluded it was a homicide, with no ambiguity?"

"I would have turned right back around and walked out of your office."

"I doubt it."

"Then both you and I should be relieved that isn't the case. That I'm not in the position of having to ask you to do something so drastic."

"How does this save lives? Why care so much about the death of a dealer or junkie, whoever this man was?"

Rey reclaimed his seat. He searched the doctor's eyes for discretion. Lee had already shown that he put a premium on information. It was the last bit of bargaining power the agent had left.

"He was neither. He was a confidential informant. Team U.S.A., as we like to say. Working for the good guys. An embed in the Colombian cartels that were running roughshod over this city. Helped us make a lot of arrests over the last few years. Really weaken the gangs while maintaining his cover. No one knew about his involvement. Not even his wife."

"Sounds like *someone* knew," Lee muttered. "You know, he was *definitely* high on the night of his passing, Rey."

"That's not surprising to me. That's why we use confidential informants, Lee. They aren't officers. They can engage in behavior us cops can't. Earn the trust of their targets. Avoid suspicion. He had familial ties that proved invaluable to us. And when he first began, he was a very young man, a teenager with two kids, who wanted to succeed in this country for his budding family."

"You want me to rule this man's death accidental, although you're telling me it was in all actuality a hit?"

"I don't know that for sure, Lee," he countered. "If it was intentional, it was a low-level hit. An aftereffect of the dying gangs. A shot in the dark, really. A move of desperation to see if it would blow up in precisely the way I am now trying to prevent."

"And what happens if I let it blow up?"

"At best, we throw a good man and his legacy under the bus. We make Melvin the fall guy: a drug trafficker and gang member operating at the highest levels of the cartels, and his twin girl and boy forever lose the pristine memory of their father. At worst—and this is what I fear is likelier with the media and local police snooping around—it would out a lot of good men and women, like Melvin, who worked in the trenches over the last decade, and it would endanger their lives and those of their families. Might boost the number of bodies passing through this office for autopsy."

Lee sighed deeply, draining his lungs of air. He ruffled his hair. He fingered his mustache.

"The subject had evidence of subarachnoid hemorrhage on the occipital lobe, likely the result of blunt force trauma from a precipitous and unexpected fall," Lee droned, as if dictating to an invisible stenographer. "Elevated levels of alcohol in his system massively slowed his reaction time and coordination, and it numbed the pain so as to mask the severity of the head injury. The drowsiness that accompanied the trauma mimicked the sluggishness of early onset veisalgia. The lack of defensive wounds anywhere on the body corroborates no struggle, no foul play. The subject, although coherent before sleeping, did not report any foul play. The manner of death is therefore, given no additional information, ruled accidental at this time."

Rey shot up from his seat so fast it made him dizzy. He collected himself for a few seconds, before extending his hand for a quick shake. As a drug cop, he knew that no one lingered in the seconds after a clandestine transaction.

"Your country thanks you, Lee."

Rey recoiled at the cold touch. Lee grinned.

"Low body temperature," he explained.

"You're *cold-blooded* and your name has the word *grave* in it?" Rey asked incredulously.

"Sometimes, our destinies are determined at birth."

"My name means 'king' in Spanish, so I like that."

"What, if anything, does 'Mora' mean?"

"Blackberry, I think."

Lee shrugged. "Sometimes a name is just a name."

At the door, Rey made a parting request.

"Is it possible, Lee, to erase mention of the cocaine in your report? It would just make everything *cleaner*."

"In for a penny, in for a pound, Rey."

Dr. Leon Musgrave never married. He sired no children. He preferred quiet. Dead bodies told stories without speaking a word. That appealed to him. His single father and caregiver had been boorish. Lee heard his every movement throughout their home growing up. The shattered glass, the late-night trysts, the staggering in the dark, the punches to the wall, the cursing and slurring—all became the soundtrack to his childhood. He got his license the day he turned sixteen primarily as a means of fleeing the noise. He saved his earnings, allowance, and holiday gift money to purchase from a sympathetic neighbor a beat-up Studebaker Land Cruiser with terrible mileage, and Lee piled on more. He would drive for hours on end: nowhere and everywhere.

No seat belts installed in those times. No Miami congestion. Just open air.

He had his first drink at the then-legal age of eighteen. He had smelled alcohol regularly before—in every *I love you* his father managed to muster only several beers in—but he had never tasted it. Cigarettes he had smoked since junior high school. But alcohol he had intentionally not touched. The thought made his stomach turn.

But a girl on a first date persuaded him.

He fell in love at first sip. It tasted heavenly. His dopamine spiked. It warmed his chilled insides. It didn't take long that same evening to lose interest in the girl—in women in general. Alcohol was enough.

His addictive habit was not extraordinary for the times. His physiology just responded differently. But that was all internal. It couldn't be outwardly seen. Even as he became expert on those internal processes, cognitive dissonance served as a failsafe defense mechanism. Poking hundreds of livers felled by cirrhosis did nothing to spook him. He understood that his compulsion was an outright disease, impervious to logic and self-reflection.

Society changed around him. But he never caught up.

Rey wore sweats and sneakers as he approached the flashing lights of police cruisers. A patrolman barked at the shadowy figure, hand reflexively flying to his holstered weapon. Rey flipped open his badge to cut off the histrionics.

"Lieutenant Lozano," he snapped simply.

The twentysomething man shrank.

"Yes, Lieutenant," he uttered weakly.

"Who's the primary officer?"

"Jay Weinger, sir." He pointed at the second patrol car immediately in front of him.

"You're backup?"

"Yes, sir."

"Stand down, Officer," he ordered, bass down to a growl. "This isn't a homicide scene, son. It's a misdemeanor."

"Excuse me?"

"You're relieved, Officer," he reiterated, marching up to the taller man in a show of force. "What part of 'get back on the road' don't you understand?"

The younger man swallowed hard, suppressing any vestige of testosterone-fueled rebellion within. Civil society bent the rules of nature dramatically. In other circumstances, he might not have been so agreeable.

"Yes, sir." He got in his car, flipped off his lights, and sped off.

Rey met Officer Weinger at his window, badge open at eye level. He asked him to step out. No introduction. Officer Weinger was a relatively scrawny man by police standards, with a boyish haircut that extended in ungainly wisps over his fore-head. He spoke with an exaggerated, meticulous elocution.

"Lieutenant, it's peculiar to see you here. You come from home?"

Rey ignored the question.

"What do we have here, Jay?"

Officer Weinger's already pale complexion blanched at the informality.

"Suspected drunk driver, sir."

"What was the basis for the stop?"

"No seat belt, sir."

"You pulled him over for riding without his seat belt fastened?"

"Yes, sir."

Rey smiled. Some say seat-belt traffic stops target certain populations in certain neighborhoods. Not a white man like the driver. Not a posh neighborhood like this one. Rey was both impressed and worried by his colleague's indiscriminate application of the law. It meant Officer Weinger's ethics were not transactional.

"Good job, Jay."

Officer Weinger nodded uneasily, unsure whether the compliment was meant sarcastically. It wasn't.

"And then?"

"And then, he stunk of alcohol. There are empty beer cans on the car floor visible from the outside."

"You get his license?"

"Yes, sir."

"You recognize the name?"

"No, sir."

"And is that it, Jay? No reckless driving pattern?"

"I didn't follow him long before pulling him over."

"It's not illegal to drink and drive, right?"

"No, it's not. It's illegal above a certain limit, sir. So I asked him to step out so I can administer roadside sobriety tests. But he refused. He insisted I call a friend of his in the department. Someone named Rey Lozano. Is that you, sir?"

The men locked eyes in perpetuity. Rey wasn't smiling anymore. He again swept past the inquiry. Officer Weinger had his answer already anyway.

"I'm taking over this investigation, Jay. Is that understood?"

"Of course."

Obeying the chain of command is by the book, too.

"Am I to draft a report of my involvement, sir?"

"That won't be necessary."

Officer Weinger nodded and started toward his patrol car.

"Hang tight for a second," Rey advised, before approaching the civilian's car, a worn and rust-laden relic, parked a few feet in front of them.

Upon perceiving a new presence at his window, and one with a familiarly pungent fragrance, Lee spoke first.

"Good morning, Rey."

"Where are you headed, Lee?"

"Nowhere. Everywhere. Just driving."

"Drunk?"

"Hardly. It's like water to me now. I'm an alcoholic, Rey. It doesn't affect me. You won't catch me swerving. Not a single swerve."

"No seat belt?"

"Your eagle-eyed colleague caught that? Don't wear them. Never have. It's my right."

"It's actually not."

"I know what blunt force trauma in a car crash does to the organs. I've felt them bruised and battered in my own two hands. I am taking a knowing and highly educated risk."

"It's a Tuesday at nine in the morning, for Chrissake! What happens when I'm not around to bail you out, Lee? You prepared to lose it all?"

"I died a long time ago. I'm just waiting for my body to realize it and catch up. The liver regenerates—did you know that? It's the only organ that can do that. It's like I'm stuck in purgatory. No matter the abuse, it never seems to be enough. But our fates are intertwined, aren't they, Rey? So you won't let mine falter. You'll continue saving me in an effort to save yourself."

Rey slapped the roof of the car.

"Head home, Lee. Officer Weinger will trail you."

"State: Call your next witness."

"The State calls Dr. Leon Musgrave to the stand."

The man who enters has the look and walk of an ancient. He is slow to the stand. His hair is pure white and thin. His skin sags from his bones. His jowls shake. His spine is curved. His finger-nails are long and yellowed. He whistles faintly through his dentures. He has only recently—despite a lifelong career in han-dling bodies—earned himself the nickname "Doctor Death."

Sandy asks that he introduce himself to the jury. She runs through his qualifications with unhurried precision. She wields his advanced age to her benefit.

"Rumor is that you'll be retiring this year?"

"That's the plan. But, again, I've been saying that for a decade now."

"Congratulations."

The testimony of the medical examiner is typically uncontro-versial. The dead are dead. The State worries that the clinical mechanics come off as dry, boring a half-listening jury and converting a soul into just a body. She will, therefore, usually plod through it methodically, being careful not to linger. The defense worries that the gore does little else than remind jurors of life's impermanence, stoking sympathy. That attorney will, therefore, usually stand only to announce that he is sitting back down, without asking a single question on cross-examination. But this case is different. Dr. Musgrave has two tightrope perspectives to share—one, as the employer of the purported killer, and two, as the finder of rather generous conclusions drawn from the decedent's paltry remains—each with its own precarious pitfalls.

"Doctor," says Sandy, "I'd like to direct your attention to the morning of December 10, two years ago. Did something distressing come across your desk?"

"Yes. An employee comment card."

"What are those?"

"As the chief medical examiner, I not only do everything an

associate medical examiner does—in terms of autopsying bodies and responding to crime scenes—but I am the lead administrator for the office. I instituted a system long ago for employees to make suggestions on how to improve office life and morale: slipping anonymous comment cards into a box set up outside my office. I read them myself, usually first thing in the morning. Coffee in the break room, hand sanitizer in the bathrooms— things like that. But this one was very different."

"How so?"

"I can't recall the verbiage exactly, but it implied there might be a body out of place in the shed."

"The shed?"

"My apologies. It's where we house the incinerators out back. We call it the shed."

Sandy picks up a plastic sleeve from the clerk, with a three-by-five-inch card within. She approaches the witness.

"I'm showing you what's already been admitted, by stipulation of the parties, into evidence as State's Thirty-One. Do you recognize it?"

"Yes. This is it. The card I was talking about."

"What does it say, Doctor?"

"It reads: 'A body that doesn't belong was brought to the shed.'"

"What did you do?"

"I thought at first that maybe one of our bodies had been misplaced. So I took stock. I personally laid eyes on the location of all of the recorded bodies we had on-site. And all were accounted for. It appeared that whatever body this involved had come from the outside. I then called police."

"What happened when they arrived?"

"The office was put on lockdown. No one could leave. No one could enter—other than law enforcement, of course. Officers searched the shed."

"Did they need a warrant to do that?"

"No. I gave them full consent."

"You didn't search yourself before calling police?"

"No."

"You didn't try yourself to determine who wrote the comment?"

"No. Once it became apparent that this note, if true, did not refer to an internal misplacement, I wanted to get the police involved. Leave it to the professionals. I'm a doctor. Not an investigator."

"Did anything turn up during the search?"

"No bodies, no. So I told police that within the incinerators are drawers for bones. That they should look there."

"Do bones not burn away during cremation?"

"No. Not at the heat used for cremation. They're pretty durable. Fragments remain. Those fragments are pounded into ash afterward. In fact, that's what's commonly inside of urns. The ash is from pulverized bones, not from the cremation process itself."

"Were bone fragments found inside of those drawers?"

"Yes."

"Was that odd?"

"No. We aren't a private crematory. We're a government agency. We don't use the incinerators for bodies that are claimed. If we did, we might empty out the drawers after each cremation to collect the bones and convert them into ash for the family. The shed is for bodies that have no place to go. Mostly homeless decedents. Those without families. On rare occasions, bodies that cannot be identified. So we allow the bones to collect—to pile up—until the drawers get full and are subsequently emptied."

"So, how could police tell if any of those bones raised suspicion?"

"They couldn't. I can't either. Not by eyeballing them. But a DNA analyst can. Apparently, there was only a single unsolved missing person report in all of the county at the time. Well, only a single *recent* one. There have been many unsolved cold cases over the years. So police transported the bones to the forensics lab and had analysts prioritize seeing whether any of them matched the DNA of that missing person."

"Did they?"

"Yes. Not all, of course. Some were tied back to our recent cremations on record. But of those fragments that did not correspond to any of our records, all of them belonged to the woman who had gone missing a month before."

"What was the name of that woman?"

"Melina Mora."

"Once the identity of those bones was confirmed, what did police ask you to do?"

"Give them a list of names of the people who had access—or, at least, the *most* access—to the shed."

"Did you do that?"

"Yes."

"How did you come up with that list?"

"Well, how I saw it, the employees at the office can be divided into four major groups. The administrative staff, like the secretaries and receptionists, really would have no business back there. That's true of the doctors as well. The janitorial staff does regularly enter the shed. But what's true of all three of those groups is that none of them know how to work the incinerators. Only the body handlers do. I gave police those names."

"How many names did you turn over?"

"Four. I think we had four on staff at the time. Maybe five. Four or five."

"What did police do with those people?"

"They interviewed them separately."

"Did any of those people jump out at you as the type of person who might be involved in a disappearance?"

"Objection! Speculation."

Without looking up, the judge mulls it over for a noticeable stretch of seconds.

"Sustained. Rephrase the question."

"Did any of those people jump out at you as particularly suspicious?"

"Same objection!"

"This time it's overruled."

Dr. Musgrave does not speak at first, contemplating how to put it delicately. A coworker's words, in the days after the arrest, sprung to the front of his mind: *You know how every office has that kid we all jokingly say is the likeliest to come to work with an AK-47 and shoot us all up? He was ours.*

"I didn't know Gabriel Soto well. We didn't interact often. But it's my understanding that he was widely seen as a bit odd. A loner. Very quiet. He was among the names I gave to police."

"Did any of those people have greater access to the incinerators than the others did?"

"Well, yes. Gabriel was charged with locking up the shed at close of business every day. He had exclusive possession of the key. He had the most seniority, so he was in charge of assigning their shifts and scheduling the cremations. A person probably couldn't successfully execute an impromptu cremation without him knowing about it."

"Do you see that man in the courtroom today?"

"I do."

"Can you point him out and identify him by an article of clothing he's wearing?"

"It's that young man in the navy blue suit," he says, crooked finger pointed and quivering in the air. "That's Gabriel Soto, the man in charge of the shed."

"At some point, Doctor, did you conduct the autopsy of the little that was left of the victim?"

"I did."

"Why did you undertake it yourself?"

"Because of the sensitivity and urgency of the matter. I have the most experience in the office. It's my name on the side of the building."

"Was this autopsy conducted under the most ideal of circumstances?"

"Absolutely not. I analyze bodies. This was a loose assortment of bones. Bones that had potentially sustained damage in the cremation process. I didn't anticipate that I would discern anything of value, really."

"And, had you not discerned anything of value, would you have simply said so?"

"Of course. I am a man of science. I find what I find. If it's nothing, it's nothing."

"In this case, were you able to discern anything of value?"

"I am able to tell you—based on the condition of particular bones—what the kind of damage they sustained might be consistent with."

"Did you find any bones corresponding to the victim's head?"

"Yes, several. The skull, while disassembled, had been largely preserved. In a single place—its left flank, in particular—it was severely fractured. The right side did not feature any dramatic fissure whatsoever. It was not disintegration or deterioration. It was a rather deliberate, targeted trauma."

"Is that consistent with blunt force trauma to the head?"

"It is."

"What is blunt force?"

"The striking of the body with an object, typically flattened, like a bat, and not perforating, like a knife."

"Would the trauma you assessed in Ms. Mora's skull be fatal?"

"If she were alive—as in, if the trauma occurred to her skull while it was still attached to her body—then, yes, a blow of that power can be fatal."

"Did you find any bones corresponding to the victim's pelvis?"

"Yes. In fact, those were the only two segments of her body more or less intact: the skull and the pelvis. There was nothing of value I could discern from the remaining collection of bones."

"What did you find with regard to her pelvis?"

"Symmetrical hairline fractures on both ends—left and right—of the upper pelvis."

"Is that unusual for a healthy woman in her late twenties?"

"Not unheard of, but—barring any degenerative bone diseases—it's seen more commonly in elderly populations."

"Is that evidence consistent with sexual battery?"

"Objection! Speculation and lack of personal knowledge. The doctor can't possibly testify to that from a broken hip."

"Your Honor, Dr. Musgrave is the expert here. Not Mr. Whipple." Sandy squeezes in just enough to respond without being accused of arguing too extensively in front of the jury.

"Overruled. Answer only if you know, Doctor."

He clears his throat. Every word is cushioned by seconds of silence, punctuated by reticent periods. They are islands unto themselves, as if separately they invoke less shocking power than all together.

"Given the symmetry, the hairline fractures in the pelvis can be consistent—and have previously been seen—with sustained, aggressive, and violent sexual intercourse, whether consensual or not. As to consent, the bones do not speak."

"Is there any scientific or anatomical reason that these two sets of bones would be conserved over the others?"

"No," he answers, before his eyes blink wildly in bewilderment. "They stood in stark contrast to the remaining bones, which were rendered indecipherable quite expertly. That these were the two areas with extensive trauma—it's almost like the person wanted to get caught, to have the story of her death easily told."

Sandy spins around, announcing her intention to sit down on that poignant point, just as Jordan shoots up from his seat in a start. Their words crash loudly into one another as they move in such an abrupt flurry, creating chaos in the otherwise still, antiseptic courtroom.

"No further questions."

"Objection! Speculation."

"Sustained."

"Move to strike," Jordan whines.

"Granted," the judge rules laconically. "Ladies and gentlemen of the jury, you are to disregard the last answer given."

Sandy is satisfied. Bells cannot be unrung.

"Cross-examination."

Jordan is in a huff. He is thrown off-kilter. He likes to begin sweet and get progressively more combative. But his blood pressure has spiked, his skin is flushed, and he is entrenched in fight-or-flight mode. He grips the side of the podium to gain composure. He smiles through gritted teeth.

"Let's begin where you ended with the *government*, Doctor."

Emphasis on the word "government." Only in front of juries do defense attorneys refer to the State as the government. Everyone hates the government.

"You cannot say *when* the trauma to the skull occurred?"

"No. I can say that someone doesn't walk around with a fractured skull like that. So it had to be at the time of death or afterward."

"Right. I'm asking about the *afterward* part of that answer. Because you have no idea what was the actual cause of death for Ms. Mora, correct?"

"That is correct."

"In fact, the official cause of death in this case is undetermined."

"Yes."

"That's because all the trauma you observed could have occurred far after her death—in the handling of the bones, in the process of pulverizing the remains?"

"It could have."

"In fact, just as consistent with blunt force trauma with a bat to the head, what you observed is consistent with the skull, detached from the body and in someone's hands, falling onto the ground."

"That would be more a shattering than a deliberate targeting, as I described, but no, I cannot rule that out."

"It certainly would be consistent with the impact caused by whatever tool your office uses to pulverize bones?"

"Yes, it could be consistent."

"And you also cannot say *when* the trauma to the pelvis occurred?"

"Well, it's quite symmetrical as to the two ends of the pelvis, so they're likely to have occurred simultaneously. That makes the theories of an accidental dropping or the pulverizing of two sides, assumedly one after the other, less probable."

"But I am now more referring to *before* her death. These hairline fractures aren't fatal, right?"

"No, they're not."

"So you cannot say when in her life the victim sustained those fractures?"

"I would expect them to heal over time. So, if she sustained them while alive, it can't be too long before her death."

"But it can certainly be weeks and perhaps a few months before her death?"

"It can be, yes."

"And lots of things can explain what are essentially slight tears in the victim's hips?"

"A number of things are consistent with that injury."

"Because, in essence, what we're talking about here is weight that is sharply and for an extended period of time pressed up or dropped onto the hips of the victim?"

"Something like that."

"Nothing about it specifically favors sexual intercourse over any other strenuous activity?"

"Just the location."

"And—just as you noted—absolutely nothing anatomically or scientifically favors sexual intercourse that is *against* someone's will?"

"You cannot tell that."

"Because some people consent to and enjoy rough sex, right, Doctor?"

Dr. Musgrave pauses. As a human in the world, he knows the answer, but as a doctor, he does not wish to overstep the bounds of his expertise.

"I am not a sex therapist, sir. I can tell you that the sexual preferences of people cannot be determined from their bones," he replies clinically.

"Fair enough, Doctor. I'll take it," Jordan concedes with a chuckle. The gallery laughs along with him.

"In the end, you cannot tell this jury with certainty that Ms. Mora died from blunt force trauma to the head?"

"Forensic pathology does not deal in certainties. I am able to evaluate whether the evidence is consistent with certain scenarios. Death by blunt force trauma is *consistent* with the evidence."

"Is that a no, Doctor?"

"I was not present for Ms. Mora's death. I cannot testify with unequivocal certainty as to how it happened, no."

"And, in the end, you cannot tell this jury with certainty that Ms. Mora was raped—before her death, after her death, or even ever in her life?"

This time, Dr. Musgrave skips the linguistic evasion.

"No."

"But what you *are* able to tell this jury today, those findings regarding what is and what is not consistent, those have drawn a fair amount of scrutiny in your field?"

"Objection! Inferential hearsay."

"Overruled."

"You may answer, Doctor."

"I conducted the autopsy. No other professional should form a medical opinion unless they had the opportunity to analyze the bones themselves. That is a universally accepted rule in my field."

"But you have faced criticism for conducting an autopsy with a few scattered bones and no body?"

"Objection! Hearsay, Your Honor."

"Overruled."

Dr. Musgrave lingers in thought. His eyes twinkle mischievously.

"Other people in the field who face limitations in their own abilities are understandably unable to grasp or understand how others can do what they cannot."

Snickers from spectators disrupt the stillness.

"You're quite confident in yourself, Doctor?"

"I've been doing this a long time."

"And in that time, you've faced persistent criticism for maintaining an inappropriately cozy relationship with the police?"

Sandy finds that the question, like the others, calls for inadmissible hearsay, but she's been shot down twice now. It isn't worth the repeated dressing-down by the judge before the jury.

"I have faced just as much criticism from law enforcement

when my findings don't go their way. If both sides find something to complain about, then I must be doing something right."

"In one particular case, you cleared correctional officers in the county jail of wrongdoing in the case of a mentally ill inmate who died in their custody after a scalding hot-water shower?"

"Objection!" Sandy does not have to explain. The judge immediately agrees.

"Sustained."

Dr. Musgrave is noticeably piqued. He wants to defend himself. He had not *cleared* anyone—that isn't his job—but he had found, and created a public firestorm in so doing, that the inmate's death had not resulted from the hot water, despite apparent skin slippage. The suggestion is enough to influence the jury, without giving him the opportunity to clarify.

"Move to strike," Sandy requests, defeated.

"Granted. Ladies and gentlemen of the jury, you are to disregard the last question."

"You actually have a professional connection to the Mora family, isn't that right, Doctor?"

"Two decades ago, I autopsied the body of Melvin Mora, the victim's father."

"You were able at that time to provide the family with answers as to his mysterious death?"

"Somewhat. Only what the body told me."

"But you had a full body that time, correct?"

"Yes."

"And twenty-seven days had not passed between death and your autopsy in that case, as it did here?"

"It had not."

"And yet you wanted badly—just like you had twenty years ago—to provide the Mora family with answers in *this* case, even with remarkably incomplete data?"

"My desire was nothing other than finding out the truth, and only when I am able. Nothing else affects my work."

"You, in fact, hired Mr. Soto?"

"He was hired by my staff, yes."

"Well, before hiring, you conduct a final interview with anyone who would be given that level of access to sensitive areas in your office?"

"I do, yes."

"So you, personally, conducted an interview with Mr. Soto before he was hired?"

"Yes."

"And despite what you call being suspiciously quiet, you found him to be trustworthy, responsible, and impressive enough to hire him for such a sensitive job?"

Lee had drawn the blinds to his office. The lights were dimmed. His eyes needed shielding from the brightness. His temples throbbed. His stomach churned. He chugged alternatingly from an oversized bottle of water and a thermos filled with coffee, spiked with Irish whiskey. He peered down at the papers in his hands, but the lines blurred and danced together. He had not slept the night before.

The young man across from him—stocky but soft-bodied, curly-haired, and clear-faced—just sat and stared.

"You want a cup of coffee, son?"

"I don't drink it."

Lee nodded. He clicked his tongue out of tedium.

"I apologize for the lighting. My eyes feel sensitive this morning."

"I don't mind it."

"That's good. There's a lot of darkness here. A lot of quiet, too."

"I was hoping for that. I prefer it."

Lee grinned.

"Me too, son."

Lee tested out the claim. The young man merely watched, but not really. His eyes were open, but Lee couldn't quite see the browns of his eyes. Lee leaned against his chair, head back, eyes swung upward and shut, until the pounding in his head receded.

Dr. Musgrave doesn't answer Jordan right away.

"Did you hear the question, Doctor?"

"Yes," he replies, snapping out of the self-induced trance. "I hired him because he was qualified, and no, nothing struck me as troubling about him."

"If anything, Doctor, the ability to work in absolute silence and alone is a baseline requirement for workers in a morgue?"

"It isn't a catacomb or anything, but your point is well taken."

"And in the three years he worked for you, he had a stellar administrative record?"

"I do not believe he was ever written up, no."

"He had such a good record that he was promoted to being a sort of lead worker among the body handlers?"

"It comes with seniority."

"Part of that seniority involves being in possession of the key to the shed, is that right?"

"Yes."

"But it's not like others didn't know where Mr. Soto kept the key?"

"I'm not sure. I imagine he had it at his desk."

"There's even a second copy of that key, right?"

"Just one other copy."

"And who possesses that copy, sir?"

"I do."

"The sheds out back are outside of the building?"

"Yes."

"So, they're susceptible to being broken into at night?"

"You'd have to scale a very tall fence."

"It's possible, Doctor?"

"Yes, it's possible," he says, but adds: "For someone else to have noticed the misplaced body, however—another colleague, I mean—it must have happened during the day."

"Well, you have continuously recording video inside your facility, including cameras facing the sheds, don't you?"

"Yes."

"And, after reviewing the footage, you found nothing out of the ordinary in it?"

"It isn't high definition. It has no audio. And the transport of bodies, usually covered from head to toe, is a daily occurrence. Given all of that, no, I didn't find anything extraordinary on the footage."

"I'm glad you mentioned the writer of the commentary card. Because to this day, no one has confessed to writing it?"

"Not that I know of."

"So someone is still, to this day, lying and hiding his or her knowledge of how those remains got there?"

"I can't tell you that. I don't know."

"You haven't conducted your own investigation into who wrote the anonymous note?"

"I have not. As I've said, I'm not an investigator."

"You haven't asked your employees to write out the words on the note in their own handwriting as a means of comparison?"

Dr. Musgrave scoffs.

"No."

"You haven't fired or disciplined a single employee as a result of this anonymous note?"

"Other than Mr. Soto, no."

The acerbity of his response inspires electric whoops in the audience. Jordan powers through them.

"There are other ways for a professional in your office to dispose of a body, aside from cremation, right, Doctor?"

"Yes."

"Other ways that—if you're interested in getting rid of any trace of a body—are far superior, yes?"

"It depends."

"Well, alkaline baths are known to entirely dissolve a body, aren't they?"

"Yes."

"Mr. Soto, as an employee in your facility, certainly had access to the materials necessary for an alkaline bath, right?"

"Yes."

"And he certainly knew *how* to dissolve a body in an alkaline bath?"

"Yes."

"And, as you mentioned, he certainly knew how to pulverize bones into ash instead of leaving them there to be discovered?"

"Yes."

Jordan flips his last page and closes the manila folder that is lying atop the podium. He has reached the end of his cross-examination, and he is mentally gearing up for the crescendo.

"Ultimately, Doctor, you wanted answers in this case—"

"Only the answers supported by the evidence."

"—and you stretched the limits of professional ethics to find those answers—"

"I did no such thing."

"—because you are worried that if someone isn't held responsible—like my client—that you will be held civilly liable for allowing an outside body to make its way into your facility undetected and having your equipment used and your anonymous staff participate in hiding her remains?"

"That's preposterous."

"Should you not have conflicted off of the case at the very

least, Doctor, and allowed another county's medical examiner to review the remains, given that your office was a literal crime scene in this matter and your staff witnesses to that crime?"

Dr. Musgrave stammers. His eyes widen. To that, he has no good answer. He remains mum, but Jordan's question isn't rhetorical.

"That was a question, Doctor," continues Jordan.

"Perhaps."

"No further questions."

Sandy has no additional questions on redirect. She has wrung all she can out of this witness. When Dr. Musgrave passes by the tables for prosecution and defense, both Sandy and Jordan catch a brief whiff of alcohol in his wake, but neither is certain if it's a nip of liquor secreting from his sweaty pores or merely the ethanol of an old man's aftershave.

09 | THE EXORCISM OF WHITE GUILT

Little Arnie Weiss charged out from the school doors and into the high afternoon sun in a blitz of energy. He darted from concrete to grass, tossing his sprawled body faceup on the lawn, coating his sweaty skin in dirt, loose blades, and dew. The combination itched his skin, already reddened by the baking heat. As his heart pounded in his ears and his bird chest swelled and fell in a tortured loop, he watched clouds plod along indolently across a canvas sky.

Arnie was always first out.

The exodus then proceeded in waves. The black kids emerged next. Followed by the white kids. Followed by the Latinos. It wasn't clear why. None of it was orchestrated. Much like their parents, who siloed themselves in Miami communities highly segregated by race, the children disassembled by color. For a school that was—by design, by its placement—a third white, a third black, and a third Latino, the racial fault line telegraphed a failed social experiment.

Arnie, a high-achieving but popular student, traversed those labels. He attended temple and the bar and bat mitzvahs of older kids on the weekends, like the rest of the Jews, but during school hours, he clung to the side of Jerome Walker, a short, bespectacled black boy who was always reading. In the spill-out, the concrete open space where students congregated in the lunch hour, Arnie followed Jerome daily into the heart of the black region or—as the school's adults called it, outside of students' earshot—Kiddie Harlem.

On this day, Jerome exited and found Arnie in his customary grassy spot. He extended a tiny hand downward, clasping his friend's palm and helping pull him up.

New faces were lined up along the sidewalk that hugged the length of the school. A nearby junior high school, nestled in a black neighborhood, had opened its doors for the first time that day. Some of those students had walked there, some had bicycled or skateboarded over, to wait for their younger siblings at dismissal and escort them home. Most of them were boys.

As a ripple of white children crashed against the row of older black students on wheels, Miss Lorna O'Shea—tall, brunette, and fair-skinned—began to direct her flock away in a tempered frenzy.

"This way, children," she ordered, ushering them behind a fence, into a literal pen. The black children reunited with their families. The white children awaiting their parents watched through a chain-link fence.

Arnie and Jerome watched as well from a few paces back. Neither could process what they had witnessed. They were too young. But their reaction was innate and reflexive. Jerome's eyeballs burned. His heart raced. His shoulders sagged. His head hung low.

Arnie noticed.

He marched up to Miss O'Shea and tugged on her skirt. She peered down.

The words lurched forward from his throat impulsively,

parroting a phrase his mother had frequently leveled at him when he was acting up.

"Do better."

Miss O'Shea recoiled physically at the admonishment— bordering on haunting from such young lips—but said nothing as Arnie walked away.

She later recounted the story to a colleague.

"Those kids were significantly older. I just didn't want the ages intermixing," she huffed. "For a Jew, that boy sure has a well-developed savior complex."

Arnie grew tall and lanky but impressively self-possessed, with an endearing sense of humor that radiated from mischievous light-emerald eyes. But conversing with him was taxing. His mind processed information too quickly for his speech to keep up. He was welcomed by many, but he inevitably overstayed that welcome every time. His mother might have had him treated for attention deficit disorder, had she believed such an ailment actually existed and was not merely a means to label— and stifle—brilliant children.

As he matured, it wasn't altogether clear where his personal life ended and his politics began. For a period—before Jerome convinced him to get rid of them—he wore cornrow braids under his yarmulke. He hadn't worn the skullcap otherwise, only during this short phase, almost as if he anticipated using it as a shield to ward off criticism of white appropriation by stressing his claim to minority status. Arnie founded and led the student organization protesting apartheid in South Africa. It failed to recruit a single black member, outside of Jerome of course. His first girlfriend, and the only one of her color since, was black. He would go on to mention her with surprising regularity, even decades later. (Jerome, for his part, did not date in high school, and not by choice. He was too late of a bloomer to draw black female attention, and white and

Hispanic girls simply did not see the black kid as an option. It wasn't that he was rated lowly by them. He wasn't rated at all, as if he belonged to an altogether separate species incompatible with theirs.)

Arnie's outsized personality drove him to intermittent excess. He was first to drink. First to experiment with drugs. First to try his hand at sex. But he was highly functional. He pioneered into uncharted territory but, once he had discovered it, he didn't stay all that long. He merely wanted to experience it all.

"*De todo, un poco,*" a Cuban friend of his called it. Of everything, a little bit. He liked that. His was a full life.

As Arnie and Jerome prepared to graduate high school, the two earned their class's top honors. By a mere fraction of a point, Jerome became valedictorian, the first black one in the school's history. Arnie was salutatorian. That meant the former gave a speech at the ceremony. The latter did not.

Their peers found the close friends' adjacent class ranks comical.

"They're a real-life Riggs and Murtaugh," they teased.

Everyone had always assumed that Arnie would place first. He was far more vocal. His intelligence and studiousness had been on full display. Jerome was a quiet force. The news engendered widespread surprise that no one dared vocalize in mixed company.

Arnie found the order of their fortunes preferable.

"I'm glad you're first in the class. I'm glad you're giving the speech," he told his friend. "It's high time something like this happened. In fact, had I been valedictorian, I would have refused the title and given you the speech anyway."

Jerome didn't mention it, and Arnie was not perceptive enough to detect it, but the backhanded offer deeply hurt his feelings. It deflated the importance of the accomplishment.

Jerome ultimately gave a roaring, heart-over-head oration. He summoned a preacher's drawl that boomed out from his small frame. It drew a standing ovation—and tears from Arnie.

Arnie went off to a good college, which he completed in half the usual time, and an even better law school out of state. He, as always, did well there. In organizations and journals, he inevitably voted for minority candidates for positions of power. He did this regardless of their qualifications. He published an opinion editorial in favor of reparations for descendants of slavery. His first vote for president was for Jesse Jackson.

As a new lawyer, he joined a big law firm in Miami, making substantial income and deploying his considerable talents to help moneyed corporations squabble over their riches with other moneyed corporations. This move dashed the expectations of those who knew him and had assumed he would practice in the public interest. Self-billed high-minded contemporaries called it "selling out."

Arnie grew defensive.

"That phrase is anti-Semitic," he groused.

He availed himself of opportunities to volunteer for pro bono work within the firm. One such case involved defending a first-time offender for felony possession of marijuana. He met the client at arraignment, only minutes before her first appearance before the judge. The young black woman briefed him about the police stop and search of her car, interrupted not infrequently by the fussing of two children circling her and a third squirming in her arms.

The broad strokes of her account read problematic to him. The officers' actions weren't particularly egregious, but Arnie doubted they were strictly constitutional.

"We should fight this," he proposed to her. "And not just in criminal court. Sue the police department in civil court. Start in state court. Explore federal court. We might have a potential

Section 1983 claim. Get some money for you and your family, given the harassment these officers put you through."

His client stared at him glassy-eyed. She asked a single question.

"Do I have to come back for that?"

Arnie spoke to the prosecutor as the latter unloaded eight boxes of files in a fluster at the front of the courtroom in the seconds before the judge took the bench. The hurried young man was only half listening. As always, Arnie discharged a whirlwind of words that rendered his audience dizzy. The man was uncharacteristically short in reply.

"I'm offering a withhold of adjudication and one day of probation."

"You're offering a plea?"

"Yes, a plea."

"A plea when her constitutional rights were violated?"

"A plea that ends the case today without a day in jail or making her a convicted felon."

"That offer is rejected."

"You want to convey that to your client?"

"I am authorized to represent her wishes, counsel. Thank you."

The judge—balding, red-faced, with expensive, pointy footwear—emerged from a side entrance and strode in long bounds toward his raised perch. Everyone stood for him. He called the client's case early in the calendar. Her meandering, circuitous route to the podium included herding her wayward children. His Honor wished her a good morning, but it was Mr. Weiss who spoke after the prosecutor announced the charge.

"Arnold Weiss on behalf of the defendant. We plead not guilty, demand discovery, and ask for a jury trial."

"What's your offer, State?"

"Withhold and a day."

"We aren't accepting that, Your Honor. I doubt the stop in this case was legal. We're exploring all of our options, including civil remedies."

Not a line on the judge's face moved. The lack of reaction expressed even more contempt than open ridicule would have. He swung his eyes decidedly past the attorney and spoke beyond him. The defendant wrangled her children with a single, belligerent arm.

"Ma'am, you understand that, should you go to trial, you're facing five years in state prison?"

"What? I don't want trial. I want to go home."

"You understand the offer from the State sends you home today, never to return again."

"That's what I want."

"That would be against advice of counsel," Arnie interjected.

His Honor bore into Arnie with quiet consternation. No one stirred in the otherwise overflowing courtroom. The power of his gaze was deafening.

"Noted," he boomed sarcastically, before facilitating the plea deal. Minutes later, the matter was done, the woman and her brood left, but Mr. Weiss was held back momentarily by the judge.

"In this courtroom, counsel, people are treated as autonomous, free-thinking individuals," he lectured while on the record still. "We listen to them. Their priorities. Their wishes. That woman wanted to go on with her apparently busy life. Not to be condescended to. Not to be used in a cause not her own."

Arnie dug his teeth into his bottom lip. He tasted copper, before stalking out without a word in redress.

Big law, as his field was informally termed, was known for hard work and even harder partying. That left little time for sleep. Associates were known to work eighteen-hour days and head off at the end of a marathon shift, not to bed but to the nightclub. Too much money was being earned not to spend it. That lifestyle pushed the body to its natural limit. Fortunately, another natural supplement popular at the time helped with that: cocaine.

After a particularly lucrative settlement, the partners on the case invited all of the associates with a hand in it to celebrate. That is, all of the associates minus the undesirables: the wedded women, the teetotalers, and the devout. Arnie, the last to leave any social function, naturally made the cut. Never mind that his role in the case's resolution amounted to little more than document review. The outing was admittedly self-congratulatory, but only tangentially related to the work, and more broadly a public exhibition of the excess and spoils of their stations in life.

The revelers spent the evening inside of a hot, dark, and loud beachside nightclub owned by affluent Latin Americans. The music was foreign. The area was roped off. The service was bottle. Arnie indulged: in complimentary alcohol; in dances with dolled-up, monolingual women overstaying their visas; in gift bumps of blow from generous colleagues. He outlasted his peers.

He found himself in the orange glow of dim bathroom lighting, dick in his hand, although long done urinating; forehead against cold, tiled wall; and begging the attendant for drugs. Almost in a whisper, the young Hispanic man standing in front of a cache of gum, mints, cigarettes, and colognes rejected his entreaties, hand left floating in air offering him instead a paper towel for wiping his hands.

Eventually, the man wrapped an arm around Arnie's shoulders and led him away from the urinal, providing him support as he zipped up.

Arnie pulled a wad of bills from his pocket totaling over

two hundred dollars. Gathering the man's hands in his, he transferred the cash without regard to its amount.

"An eighth, please. Keep the change. You've earned it, spending your nights here in everyone else's shit. An honest working-class man like yourself. It isn't right."

The shock cut through the man's muted protestations.

"An eight ball? It's five in the morning, sir. All of that is for you?"

"It's not for now. I'm going home. Just restocking."

The reluctant dealer's eyes—two brown simmering pools of condemnation—ordered him away, along with his words.

"Go home."

Arnie grinned.

"Come on, amigo."

Half of the attendant's face convulsed in a near-imperceptible twitch. He stuffed the bills in his pants pocket. Indelicately, he flipped open the left flank of his vest and from within its pocket pulled out a sandwich bag of white rocks. He tossed it to Arnie as if it were a beanbag.

"Thank you . . ." Arnie faltered, eyes focused with tunnel vision on the name tag pinned to the man's shirt pocket. " . . . Melvin."

The attendant remained tight-lipped.

Arnie stepped out onto humid air and sidewalk seconds later. Two men pulled up on either side of him—muscles, greasy hair, and tattoos—as he walked. Neither spoke for an entire block.

"You two look like cops," Arnie finally joked.

"We are."

Arnie eyed his feet. One step. Two steps. And he was off. In a fluid motion, he cut east across the sidewalk: toward the street, in the direction of the ocean. His bulky guards were caught back on their heels. Arnie made it to asphalt before there was a pop and screech. It was the sound of metal bumper hitting bone and

231

the aggressive application of brakes, followed by the pungent odor of burnt rubber. His limbs spilled onto the ground. A cursing taxicab driver stepped down from his vehicle in a flurry, only to wordlessly drive off in equal hurry once the undercover officers flashed their badges and motioned for him to leave.

Arnie sprung up like an inflatable pin at a bowling alley, assisted by the flood of adrenaline and cocaine in his system. He took one additional step in his attempt at fleeing, but the weight on his ailing bones summarily killed that plan.

The officers at his side asked exactly two questions.

"Do you need medical attention?"

Arnie rebuffed the suggestion.

And "May we search you?"

Their hands were in his pockets before he answered.

"Aren't you already doing that?"

"No, we're not," one said, contrary to fact.

Once found, the bag of drugs was slipped into one of their pockets. They then led him to their car—unmarked, with tinted windows—and placed him in the back seat. No handcuffs.

On the drive, they asked him for his identifying information. He obliged.

Arnie was uncharacteristically speechless. He thought of disbarment. The prospect disquieted him. But, also, he was extremely high. An ironically upbeat '90s hit struck a discordant note on the blaring radio. It only added to his disorientation.

The car didn't pull up to the station. In fact, had Arnie had his wits about him, he might have noticed they had long ago left the island of Miami Beach. Instead, the bright, antiseptic lights of his high-rise apartment driveway snapped him out of his stupor. The officer placed the car in park and waited. It took him embarrassingly long to realize they meant for him to get out and go home.

"You have a problem, man. Get yourself some help."

That was one's departing quip.

The other, as he massaged the bag of crack: "Or stop messing with this cheap shit. It's for niggers."

Arnie had a foot outside of the car by then. He stopped short and looked back. Even in his fog, he contemplated saying something. With a stern look, his merciful redeemer seemingly dared him to do so. Arnie weighed the strength of his convictions against the enjoyment of privilege. He chose the latter.

He went home without another word.

Mr. Arnold Weiss, juror number seventeen, sat with one long leg crossed over the other, left hand pensively fingering his chin and simultaneously clenching a yellow pencil, right hand holding a crisply folded newspaper within inches of his eyeballs. He had been singularly focused on the crossword for hours, having folded the paper so its masthead prominently featured the *New York Times* to the others.

Juror number six, seated to his right, leaned over to him.

"How many letters?" she asked.

"Huh?"

"You've been muttering the same clue over and over for a long time now. You're saying, 'what she wants, what she really, really wants,' right? How many letters?"

"Nine."

"Zigazigah."

"Excuse me."

"The answer is *zigazigah*. I even know how to spell it, I think: Z-I-G-A..." She paused, miming letters into the air with her finger. "...Z-I-G-A-H. I own the CD. Stared at that lyric book while belting out the song in my bedroom hundreds of times. Famous girl group. I love the nineties."

He pressed lead into paper, filling in the letters in a plodding manner.

ROBIN PEGUERO

"It works," he exclaimed. "Guess I'm a generation too late. Or maybe I was just really high at the time."

Number six's eyes widened in silent discomfiture.

"Sorry. That was weird," he apologized.

She shook her head in polite disagreement.

"Speaking of our generations, you're very young. I take it this is all new to you?" he asked.

He was the type of person, at nearly every age, to exaggerate his seniority.

"Yes. It's all very interesting but also stressful."

"It can be, yes. It's not new or stressful to me. I'm a lawyer—"

"Yes, I know."

"—so I'm used to it."

He chuckled at her intervening retort.

"I'm also horribly verbose. Begin repeating myself and everything. Gift of gab, my mom used to say. Both my blessing and my curse," he explained. "What'd you think of the last witness? The old one. I wonder if you youngsters take geezers like that seriously."

"I respect my elders," she replied, somewhat hotly. "And I take experience like that very seriously."

"You got to have a healthy dose of distrust, you know?" he lectured. "Whenever an institution, the status quo, tells you this is how it is because it's always been that way, you got to question it. You got to scrutinize it."

Her nose wrinkled and she sat up straighter in reaction.

"I don't think I agree with that."

"You'll grow more jaded with time. You a Republican?"

The invasive question unnerved her.

"I don't think you're supposed to ask that."

"I'm sorry. I just don't think I've met a Republican so young. It's fascinating. How old are you again?"

"Nineteen."

She had been speaking with Mr. Weiss, but she had rarely,

if at all, turned to look at him during their conversation. Her body and legs were directed decidedly forward. He had pivoted her way every so often, but she appeared to be staring blankly at nothing in particular: a spot on the wall or the carpeted floor.

When she turned into him next—clutching his right arm and staring into his eyes—it was a dramatic development.

"Do you think they would let me call my *boyfriend*? I wouldn't want him worrying about me."

She said it loudly, so others could overhear, and she underscored the word "boyfriend" so pointedly that it took precedence over all the others.

Mr. Weiss intuited the correct intention but, at first, not its intended target. His face flushed crimson at what he perceived to be an unsubtle attempt at warding off his attentions. As a self-labeled feminist—he very proudly did not once tip his preference in an abortion conversation with a formerly pregnant ex-girlfriend, albeit very difficult for him—he was mortified that she had misinterpreted his interest as romantic.

He reconsidered after noting that the girl had not loosened her grip on his arm and, for someone purportedly put off by him, maintained unusually penetrating eye contact with him. Only then did he feel the glare from across the table.

He swung his eyeline in that direction but, as soon as he did, juror number sixteen looked conspicuously away. He had been staring at her.

Mr. Weiss smiled. Rescuer was a role he relished openly.

"Yes, I'm sure they will," he said, performatively, enunciating every syllable with purpose.

She smiled back, released his arm, and relaxed anew in her seat.

"He's a big guy, your boyfriend?" Mr. Weiss added.

"Yes, actually."

"I figured," he said with a wink, before returning to his puzzle.

Mr. Weiss was ultimately not persuadable. His initial vote of not guilty was likely written in stone. It would have been a life accomplishment—and another self-aggrandizing story to tell— to say he stood in the way of a conviction. And if solitarily, all the better. But it turned out that he was the alternate juror. He would be let go before deliberations began in earnest, and he would not vote.

It was a disappointment. There was nothing he disliked more than being told he had no say.

10 | DARLA, DWAYNE, AND JACK

W e're adjourned."

She hops out of her elevated swivel chair in a start. As her heels sink into dingy, decades-old carpet, she carefully descends the three steps that separate her from the plebeians. Gary—tall, dull, doughy, and prematurely balding—races over to offer her a hand, as always. She ignores it, as always. She exits stage left, out of a side door, leaving a room of people standing. Obliged farewells trail her. One, two, and three swift strides down the hallway, and she's inside her chambers, just past the desk of her assistant, who has been jolted awake by the diminutive woman's footfall.

"Go home, Sheila. Tell Gary, too."

She swings shut her office door, pressing her body weight needlessly against it, as if it helped to further shut out the world on the other side.

The Honorable Darla Tackett zips off her robe, kicks off her shoes—barefoot, she is all of five foot two—pours herself bourbon, no rocks, and slouches into her chair.

Her hand floats over to the computer mouse. A scene on a video screen is frozen: a sterile, white room; a long, rectangular table; a man, whose dark curls are plastered by sweat against his forehead, sits on one end; the backs of two broad-shouldered interrogators are visible across from him.

She clicks the play button. The scene comes alive.

"I'm not here to bullshit you, son. That's not how I operate. I lay all my cards on the table," Detective Sterling offers.

"Alright, sir," Gabriel answers.

"We already know you were with her that night."

"Who?"

"The same girl we've been talking about for the last few hours, son. The dead girl. Melina. It will all go a lot smoother if you don't play dumb."

"That's the first time you mention her name, sir. I don't know a Melina."

"That's a lie, son. I don't interview someone unless I already know everything they know. I'm just giving you a chance to save yourself."

"Why is that a lie, sir?"

"Because we have the footage. Of you and her. That night."

"Where, sir?"

"You know where. The Saloon. Off U.S. 1."

"I've never been there, sir. That's impossible. Can't be me, sir."

"You've already been identified by people who know you. Clean shot of your face entering the bar. They're loaded up with cameras, son."

"Can I see it?"

"What?"

"The footage."

"Son. I don't think you understand what's happening here. You're in big trouble. But I'm trying to help you. Once I show you the evidence, it's over. I can't help you anymore. But if you help yourself, if you tell the truth, I can tell the state attorney to go easy on you. Do you know who I just called during our last break? I spoke directly with the state attorney. She's telling me to arrest you already. Take you straight to jail. But I won't do that until I give you a chance to explain yourself. They give the chair to everyone in Florida—you know that, right? I want to hear your side of the story. Allow you to clear your name."

Nothing but video static spans several seconds.

"But I didn't kill her. I didn't kill anyone."

The second interrogator, Detective Silas Acosta, silent until then, shifts in his chair. His melodic voice is a sharp contrast to the combative one before.

"You know, that's the first bit of truth you've told us, Gabriel. Thank you. I believe you. I know you didn't kill her."

The suspect's eyes, otherwise downcast, flit up curiously at the change of heart.

"But you were with her. Tell us about that. You took her back to your place? She led you on? Didn't let you go as far as she at first wanted? Women are like that, man. We're all men here. We've all been there."

The suspect is unresponsive.

"Pussy is pussy, man. Sometimes you got to cum, and she just needs a little push, a little convincing. Is that all you did, Gabriel? Give her a little push?"

A thunderous knock jerks Her Honor out of it. She staggers to rapidly pause the video and keep the obscenities from floating out past the shut door.

"Do you need anything, ma'am?" Gary shouts from the other side.

"No, Gary! I'm fine. Go home," she answers, in a far more aggravated tone than she intends.

She swallows half of the content of her glass—bringing tears to her eyes—and she clicks play again.

"Am I allowed to speak to my mom?"

"You're a grown man, son. You're not a minor. You can speak to your mother once we're done here."

"You don't want your mom to hear this sort of stuff, Gabriel."

"Am I allowed to speak with my lawyer?"

The interrogators look meaningfully at one another. Their bodies become noticeably tense. The veneer momentarily melts. The silence stretches.

"We read you your rights, Gabriel. Don't you remember them?"

The suspect nods.

"Why would you want to do that now? You're telling us you've got nothing to hide, right?"

"I'm not hiding anything."

"Good. Good. Good. Then you'll get to go home. Just tell us everything, and you'll get to go home."

"Do you promise?"

"I can't promise you anything, Gabriel, but I can promise I will listen to you. And I promise I will do everything in my power to help you. If you cooperate, I will vouch for you to the state attorney."

"But I don't know a Melina."

"Alright. Alright. You didn't know her. But you were with her that night, right? At that bar. Just be honest about that, Gabriel."

The suspect's eyes burn in his sockets with an intensity that underscored what he says next.

"She told me her name was Catalina."

The interrogators stumble over their words.

"That's good, son . . ."

"Tell us what else she told you."

"I think I want to speak to my lawyer," the suspect says in a small voice. Then, more forcefully: "No. I *know* I want to speak to my lawyer. And my mom, too."

Not another word is said. Without even as much as an acknowledgment, the interrogators walk out.

Her Honor presses pause, sighs, and gulps down the rest of her bourbon.

Darla had a habit of guzzling her drinks in long swigs. Very cold or very hot did not much matter. In one, or in two, or in maybe just three, her drinks were gone. Brain freezes and burning the roof of her mouth, respectively, were frequent occurrences. It drew both perverted teasing in young adolescence and plaudits in college, where speedy drinking was a virtue.

"Darla Down-the-Hatch-ett!" one inebriated peer dubbed her.

From grade school, Darla was remarkably self-aware. She knew precisely who she was, and never changed. She was a constant. She exclusively wore skirts, never pants. She had worn the exact same haircut—a straight, jaw-length black bob—since she was eight years old. Forty years later, she was instantly recognizable by classmates who had not seen her in just as long.

"You look the same, Darla," they would marvel, and naturally, she loved the sentiment.

She was immaculately organized. In school and beyond, she kept her binders tabbed and color-coded. Pink was always featured prominently in the color scheme. She was easily spotted walking down school halls: hair swinging by her ears, oversized binder pressed up against her chest under crossed arms, and short but shapely legs poking out from an above-the-knee hemline.

Her level of meticulousness carried over into her romantic relationships. It was well known that Darla strictly adhered to a timetable of progressing intimacy with her boyfriends. The first kiss did not occur until the second date, groping not until the eighth date, and so on. Her life plan was plotted out to the finest detail, including meeting and marrying her husband at law school, taking up criminal defense thereafter, and finally, ascending to the bench.

Those plans were dashed when her law school sweetheart, after three years of serious dating, dumped her just weeks before graduation. She was heartbroken but not derailed. She merely excised marriage from her plans—now unsure what benefit she thought having a husband would confer to begin with—and marched forward.

Darla grew up in a doctrinaire liberal household. It never occurred to her to become a prosecutor and jail human beings. She naturally gravitated to defense work. But it had to be private, not public defense. She needed the money to one day launch her judicial campaign.

Correctional officers at the jail—familiar with her pink-infused binder from her frequent trips to meet with clients—began to openly refer to her by a newly released movie.

"Legally *Brunette*!" they would shout at her, with a chuckle.

Conflicted—both flattered and bothered, and then doubly bothered that her kneejerk reaction was feeling flattery—Darla did little but smile and decline to indulge the moniker with a reply.

That same year, she sat behind a tall pile of thin manila folders, one per inmate in a factory line of defendants seeking representation. In a session akin to speed dating, one by one they sat across from her and—in a high-stakes elevator pitch—evaluated whether her counsel was a good fit.

"Dwayne Williams," the guard introduced flatly, leading a young black man—handsome but wearing uncombed tufts of puffy hair—into the room. The door locked behind him, leaving Dwayne alone with Darla. She kept her eyes on the opened folder in front of her.

"Armed robbery of an elderly woman, seventy-two years old,

of her purse that contained nothing but butterscotch candy, blood-pressure medication, and tissue paper."

"That's how you're going to start?" Dwayne asked in disbelief.

"That's how the State is going to start. That's the first impression the jury will get of you," Darla replied matter-of-factly.

"She had a gun in her face. She's old. She's white. It was dark. She didn't see me."

"Good. That's a start. But an independent witness saw you. You two weren't alone on that street. That woman—much younger, no gun in her face, tied to no one—identified you."

"She identified me in cuffs. A black man next to a thousand police cars and flashing lights. Looking a mess after being roughed up by police."

"Because you ran from them. We call that consciousness of guilt. You had her purse on you. You tossed it as you ran. They arrested you blocks from the robbery."

"Over an hour later. Why stick around the crime scene so long? Police planted the purse on me. Or I found it on the ground after the real thief took all of the valuables out of it."

"I like that. Thinking of alternative defenses," she mused. "Who's going to testify to all of that?"

"Me."

"I don't think so. You're a convicted felon. Five times in three short years since you turned eighteen. You testify, they hear all of that, and you're done."

"Aren't you supposed to be on my side, miss?"

She pursed her lips.

"I am on the side of keeping another twenty-one-year-old black kid from a life sentence. You're smart—"

"Thank you," Dwayne interjected hotly, as if it were a swear word.

"—so you're aware that you're facing life. The State is offering you five years followed by probation. You've been up the road before, right, Mr. Williams?"

"Up the road?"

"Prison, Mr. Williams. You've been to prison before."

"Never no five years."

"What's five years? You'll get out in four. You'll still be a very young man."

"That's easy for you to say, miss. I go back to prison one more time, and life's over for me. I'll be in and out for the rest of my life. And, where I live, I ain't making it on probation."

"So move. Maybe you'll make it. Maybe you won't. But if you're sentenced to life, there are no maybes. You will leave prison in a body bag. And, given your youth, God willing, that will be a very, very long time from now. I'll be long gone."

"There's a chance I walk."

"Yes, Mr. Williams. There is a chance you win, and you get to go home that very night. And, at your age, I'm sure that seems like a fair risk. But when you get to my age, you begin to realize that risks are just not worth it. Like that purse. It just wasn't worth it. Cut your losses, Mr. Williams. That's my advice. Save yourself. Take the deal."

"Fuck that, miss."

Her eyes watered under sudden emotion. She nodded and chugged her water.

"Then I wish you well, Mr. Williams. You have a good judge. He'll give you a fair trial. And your current attorneys, the public defenders, are hardworking and very talented. They will fight for you—just like you want them to."

"You mean a public *pretender*? You won't represent me, miss? My trial's in a week."

"I can't, sir. I need to sleep at night. I won't be a part of you throwing your life away."

His family had not accrued the necessary funds anyway. Her

decision had already been made before he had even sat down. Her pocketbook and her heart blissfully agreed.

The whole interaction lasted just five minutes. He was taken away, and another defendant was rotated in. Just as easily as they had entered her consciousness, his face and name were forgotten amid the deluge of caged would-be clients.

That night, Darla wore her customary cocktail dress, pearls, and pink lipstick to a fundraiser for a judge seeking reelection, being held at a crowded, cheap hotel conference room. She ordered a single flute of champagne for the night at the ersatz bar set up in the corner: a linen sheet atop a counter offering one brand of domestic beer and a red, a white, and a sparkling wine option. She didn't bring the glass's rim once to her lips. It was a mere prop. If she drank in her normal manner, she would be too many drinks deep by night's end. Networking primarily, and driving home secondarily, compelled a clear head. Instead, she clutched the glass in her deadened hand until the bubbles therein expired.

Many of the practitioners who regularly appeared before the judge were present. Most were men. All were white. The re-election host committee boasted a long list of names, upwards of fifty. In fact, the eponymous Law Offices of Darla Tackett, Esq.—and its lone attorney—was one of them. No one outside of those fifty names was actually in attendance anyway. It was a party thrown for the benefit of the throwers, an entirely legal, transparent laundering of campaign funds. The money just needed to be spent somewhere. The judge was in no real danger of losing reelection. In Miami, as long as no opponent with a Hispanic surname entered the race, incumbents were safe.

It was tough for the petite Darla to see over the swarm of men.

Once in full swing, the festivities featured otherwise professional men descending into their primal states.

White, bloated faces turned red. Bodily smells—a consequence of lowered inhibition and copious carbonated alcohol—wafted by without public acknowledgment. Shouted vulgarities replaced polite conversation. Darla grinned and bore it.

Too many male hands grabbed greedily at her shoulders, at her bare arms, at the small of her back, in exaggerated gestures to get by her in the congested room. She visibly leapt out of her skin each time but withheld all reproach.

That is, until a man's errant two hands encircled her waist. She slapped him away.

"Just getting by," he explained in a high pitch, the two transgressing hands now raised in the air in innocence.

Darla spun to face him: gray-haired, over ten years her senior, with a receding hairline and his shirt slovenly half-tucked into his pants.

"You wouldn't place your hands there if you were *just getting by* a man, would you?"

"If he were pretty, sure."

Her face contorted in disgust as an involuntary, disapproving growl fled from her lips. He bent down to whisper to her within earshot.

"And you wouldn't protest if a man more like *him* had been the one getting by, would you?" he countered, pointing toward a young, objectively handsome man across the room.

She met his inquiry with an eye roll before returning to her interrupted conversation.

Throughout the night, she maintained eyesight on the event's honoree, awaiting the opportune moment—like a game of Double Dutch in grade school—when she could make her stealthy approach. At a later hour, when others had faded away, Darla persisted and, with her solitary glass in hand, approached His Honor.

"Judge Grunwald," she greeted, planting a Miami kiss on his cheek.

"Please, Darla. It's Jack off the bench."

"How's your girl?"

"Off at college, sadly. But she's just minutes away at the alma mater. Trying my best not to smother her and call every fifteen minutes."

She laughed—a little too hard.

"When are you going to be joining me on the bench, Darla?"

"Oh, I don't see that happening," she said with a wave of her hand, visibly overrun with delight. "The governor's a Republican. I'll never make it out of the nominating committee."

"So, run. Can't wait on Florida to elect a Democratic governor. It'll snow on South Beach before that happens."

"You really think so, Jack? I don't have a donor base like you do."

Jack lifted a long, strong finger to quell her protestations.

"Let me introduce you to someone: Gene! Gene! Come over."

Jack was wildly gesticulating at a figure behind Darla. As she turned to watch him approach, panic swelled within, sending her heart racing. It was the groper. His eyes fell upon her—transitioning from dawning familiarity to smug satisfaction—and he extended his hand straight out in overstated formality.

"I don't think we've been formally introduced: Eugene Aldridge."

"Darla Tackett."

"Gene is one of South Florida's top bundlers," Jack gloated, slapping a hand on Gene's back. "He's a New York guy originally. Taps all of the deepest pockets and largest coffers. Darla is a good one. She's thinking of throwing her hat into the ring. We need more smart women like her on the bench."

"Yes," said Gene, nodding in agreement.

"Why don't you two get acquainted? I need to continue making my rounds."

He left them then: Gene in a permanent grin and Darla smirking.

"You know, I'm all for more women in leadership."

"Is that right?"

"That *is* right. And I think you'd look great in a black robe."

"There it is," she said.

"Forgive me, Darla. Forgive all of us men. We're idiots. Easily distracted. Preoccupied with vulgarities. Ill-tempered. It's why there needs to be a lot fewer people who look like me up there and a lot more people who look like you. Nature made us stronger and taller—and it's skewed the ideal order of things for thousands of years—but it's wrong, and we're only now beginning to figure that out and rectify it."

He spoke with such earnestness that it knocked Darla back on her heels.

"I'd like to help you make that happen. There's nothing I need other than a Jack Grunwald endorsement. You in?"

She raised her glass to her lips and sent the champagne to the back of her throat in one.

"Whoa," Gene softly muttered.

"I don't even know where we would start."

"Leave that to me. Let's discuss it all over dinner one night this week..."

Darla snorted loudly.

"...I mean, coffee. Let's just get some coffee one morning this week."

"Alright. Next Tuesday."

"Next Tuesday it is. We launch the Darla Tackett for Circuit Court campaign," he said, a devilish twinkle in his eye. Her heart thrummed pleasurably in her chest. "For now, how about I get you another drink? You know, to replace the single one you've had a mortal grip on all night?"

For the first time during their conversation, she smiled.

*   *   *

Her Honor slams shut her laptop computer, scoots into her slippers, flips the light switch, and exits from her office. Once outside, she yelps.

"Gary!" she shrieks. "You scared me. I told you to go home."

Gary—having sunk into the seat of his chair—awakes in mid-snore.

"You ready to go home, ma'am?"

She sighs.

"Yes, Gary. Thank you."

"Will Mr. Aldridge be home waiting for you?"

"Yes, Gary. Gene's already home."

"Good. Good, good, good."

The two begin their walk out of the courthouse.

"This isn't a safe part of town, ma'am. You can't leave this late at night by yourself." Then: "Have you decided what to do about the defendant's admission, ma'am?"

"I think so," she says, nearly breathlessly. She has not yet said it aloud. "I'm sticking to my original decision. I'm suppressing it. It won't be coming into evidence."

"Won't that draw scrutiny, ma'am?"

"Yes. Yes, it will."

"But isn't next year an election year, ma'am?"

That, she leaves unanswered.

Sandy is nervously shuffling papers at the podium. The noisy stack features dozens of court opinions, fifty percent of them marked by highlighter yellow, and large, scrawling notes written in shorthand and spanning several pages. Jordan, at the podium beside her, has no papers.

"A woman needs to be twice as prepared as any man, Sandy," she recalls her father, Judge Grunwald, intoning on several occasions. "Your biggest obstacles in life will be mediocre men. They will get twice as far with half as much talent."

Jordan is stretching his hamstrings by lunging in place. She peers at him queerly.

"Yesterday was leg day," he explains.

His grin suggests that he is leaning into the stereotype, perfectly aware that his self-parody is so intentional and second nature that it has circled back to earnestness.

Her Honor enters unannounced from the side of the court-room in her quickened gait. The crowd are drawn to their feet as an organic hush falls over them.

A senior female prosecutor in the gallery turns and whispers to another gleefully in singsong: "Short robe! Short robe!" It is what she calls the judge, who is known for wearing her robe unusually short at the knee.

Judge Darla Tackett signals for the court reporter to switch on the recording system and begins without delay.

"Please be seated. May the record reflect that counsel for both sides are present, as is the defendant, Mr. Soto, and that we are conducting the following hearing outside the presence of the jurors. Ms. Grunwald, this is your motion for reconsideration. You may begin with argument."

"Thank you, Your Honor. I understand this court ruled pretrial that it would suppress the defendant's admission that he did, in fact, interact with the victim on the night of her murder. You did so without prejudice. The State asked Your Honor to reserve your ruling, at least in part, until it heard the argument the defense put forward throughout the trial. As expected, defense counsel—in its opening statement, in its cross-examination of witnesses—has inaccurately represented that the defendant never saw the victim that night, contrary to his own admission. We argue to Your Honor that the defense has now opened the door. Even if the confession cannot come in as substantive evidence because it was obtained in violation of his constitutional rights, it can still come in as impeachment. Through his counsel, the defendant has essentially testified, and we ought to be allowed to bring in his statement to impeach the assertion that he was not with her that night."

Jordan cuts in, crashing the beginning of his sentence into the end of hers.

"We contest that representation. Mr. Soto said he interacted with a young lady named Catalina—not the victim, Melina Mora."

Sandy's eyes roll to the back of her head.

"The detectives had spent a good hour discussing just one girl. They had shown him countless photographs of just one girl. The victim's good friend, Catalina Rosenberg, was nowhere near that bar that night. It's clear that the defendant admitted that the 'dead girl'—Melina, the same one in the pictures shown to him—had given him the fake name of Catalina. Ultimately, *why* he said that is argument meant for the jury to hear."

"On that point, I agree with Ms. Grunwald, Mr. Whipple," Her Honor intercedes. "You will undoubtedly put a different spin on the confession than the State will. And that's just fine. That's allowed. You will argue your respective sides to the jury. But certainly I shouldn't be asked to make a value judgment regarding the weight of the confession. Questions of weight go to the jury. We're discussing admissibility today."

"Respectfully, Your Honor, the State *is* asking you to make a value judgment regarding its meaning. For it to be impeachment, it needs to be a contradiction. It is not. We can absolutely argue in good faith that Mr. Soto never met up with Ms. Mora that night. His statement to police regarding a young lady named Catalina does not contradict that. We can't have opened the door when our argument is internally consistent with that statement."

"I understand," Her Honor concedes, "but that's not where this issue will be decided for me. There's an argument to be made that the two are inconsistent. That's enough for me to consider the State's request. The real concern, it seems to me, is whether a statement that is not voluntarily and freely made should be allowed in anyway, when the defendant has not explicitly taken the stand and lied."

"We agree, Your Honor, that that is remarkably concerning," Jordan begins in dramatic tenor. "What the State is attempting to do here is a travesty. Trying to bootstrap in a statement obtained in violation of Mr. Soto's constitutional rights merely because his counsel has dared to make arguments in his defense? It's unheard of. The officers in this case interrogated my client two times—a little over an hour apiece and over the course of six hours total, late into the night and early morning. They lied. They made him promises. They were vulgar. And they denied him his right to counsel and to speak with his family. It's no wonder he said whatever he could to get them off his back."

"That's a little theatrical, don't you think, Mr. Whipple? Most of the things you mention aren't constitutional violations. No adult defendant has the constitutional right to speak with his mama."

Roaring laughter sweeps the gallery. Her Honor reddens. A judge not driven by ego recoils at the thought of becoming the story. The media in the courtroom pounce on any colorful side commentary from the judge, who ostensibly sits as the stone-faced arbiter on the bench. The moment will undoubtedly draw some ink in the newspapers.

"It is instructive, perhaps, to examine how close of a constitutional question the police tactics were in this case," Sandy begins again, taking advantage of the comedic lull to insert herself. "The police fully and appropriately read the defendant his Miranda rights. There is no question that he waived them knowingly, intelligently, and voluntarily. He was not handcuffed. He was given plenty of water, fed with plenty of fast food, and allowed plenty of bathroom breaks. He was interviewed just shy of two hours total. Not depriving him of any sleep. Not over the course of days. Yes, the officers lied to him. They do not have any footage of him. They do not have an identification at that point. And they told him that they did. But that isn't even a close call. The current state of the law is that officers can unequivocally lie to a defendant regarding the strength of their case."

"Deception is entirely constitutional," Her Honor interjects in support, nodding along strenuously.

The refrain concerns Sandy. The court is comfortable in boosting these minor points because she is ultimately going to side against her. She is losing the war.

"The detectives are not making any explicit promises. Detective Acosta even says, 'I cannot promise you anything.' It is perfectly legitimate to tell a defendant that cooperation may help him. That it might procure him a better deal. That it might stave off the death penalty. Those are all truths."

"Those are *lies*," Jordan says with an incredulous chuckle. "We all know the system. Defendants are better off not speaking. It never helps to confess. He is dangling a fabricated phone conversation with the state attorney as a carrot, while using the specter of the death penalty as a stick."

"And, as we all agree, lying is a perfectly accepted police tactic," Her Honor says, sounding frustrated. "The defendant is not being promised anything. The detectives are coaxing him into speaking. That is allowed."

"And the vulgarity, Your Honor, is completely irrelevant," Sandy continues. "Detective Acosta will explain to the jury in his testimony that he often says things he doesn't personally believe in order to relate to the defendant. He is trying to build a rapport with an alleged rapist."

Sandy instinctively swivels to the audience and finds Detective Acosta seated in its midst.

Sandy met Silas Acosta very late one night at nearly four in the morning beside two dead bodies entangled in each other's arms in their no-longer-quite-*living* room in Hialeah. It was Sandy's first week on homicide duty as a novice murder prosecutor. She had fielded the call from Silas while in bed, registering only every third word as she sought to fully wake up. The only important string of words, for now, was the address. It was the seventh call that week, all after hours. She was exhausted. She pumped herself full of coffee, threw on nominally comfortable but semiprofessional clothes (she was still too new to wear sweats to crime scenes), and drove toward death on largely ghosted streets.

Silas was a middle-aged Cuban man: artificially tan, biceps like tennis balls—one of them adorned with a tattoo of the American flag—bursting underneath tight sleeves, and a gregarious manner—even that early in the morning—that he conveyed through spasmodic gesticulation and inadvertent spitting. He appeared tickled by the mere sight of this young woman lawyer. His handshake was no less aggressive than the ones he extended to men. Perhaps more.

He led her into the dwelling—a single-room efficiency, built as an addition to the back of a much larger home—but she was not prepared. She had retained very little from their earlier conversation. The gore caught her off guard. She nearly lost her footing.

The pair of decedents was elderly. The woman was pummeled with bullet holes up and down her meager frame. She was bathed in blood. The man was curled up beside her, as if he were the big spoon in an eternal cuddling session. His clothes were not as blood-soaked as hers. He sported a single, bloody hole in his forehead. There was a single gun near his hand, lying peacefully on top of her immobile body.

Silas seemed to catch her unsettled reaction. In response to his grin, she tempered it completely, holding still her quivering insides so forcefully that her abdomen grew sore. As a sign of strength, she crouched to get a better view of the faces of death.

"It's a Cuban divorce," Silas said.

She stared at him in confusion.

"Murder-suicide. We still need to analyze the forensics. Take formal statements from the neighbors. But it looks like he shot her several times. Then he tucked himself next to her and shot himself in the head. We call that a Cuban divorce."

She could not help but shudder in silent outrage.

She recalled him getting a phone call afterward. On his phone screen flashed an image: ample, naked breasts, not attached to a head (that was visible, anyway). She saw it. He saw that she had seen it. He only grinned that perpetual grin of his. No other acknowledgment than that.

Sandy looks away from Detective Acosta just as their eyes lock.

"The detectives do everything they're supposed to. Nothing prohibited. Nothing untoward. To call this a blatant disregard for his constitutional rights is absurd," she continues.

"Agreed, Ms. Grunwald. And this court has already ruled that the State may admit every part of the statement, up until Mr. Soto asks whether he can speak with his attorney. Not his mother. That is irrelevant. But those are the magic words, Ms. Grunwald, 'Am I allowed to speak with my lawyer?'"

"But they do the right thing, Your Honor. They remind him that he has already heard his rights. Those rights include the right to speak with your lawyer. They answer his question. They do not mislead him by claiming that he cannot. The law certainly does not require them to reread him his Miranda rights repeatedly over the course of an interview. Once is enough."

"This is not a clear-cut constitutional violation, that is right. I made that clear when I announced my initial ruling before trial. I do not fault the officers for their reaction. He does not unequivocally ask for an attorney. He appears to know how to do so, as he does ask for an attorney—without reservation—not a minute later. The detectives certainly could have just said, 'Yes, you're allowed to speak to your attorney.' That would have been the correct answer. But their answer was not per se incorrect. They reminded him in general, but not specifically, that he had already been informed of his rights. And he nods, as if to agree that he does remember them. But I must nevertheless look at the totality of the circumstances in deciding whether Mr. Soto freely and voluntarily continued speaking with police past that critical question of his. From his perspective—looking at the circumstances—does he of his own will choose to share with the officers that he interacted with the victim that night, after nearly two hours of denying it? And does he do so ultimately influenced by the fact that he is unclear about whether he can stop the interrogation immediately and speak to an attorney? It's a close call."

"And if I may, Your Honor, before you rule," Sandy slips in, feeling the weight of an inevitable loss crashing speedily on top of her. "It is precisely because it is a close call—in conjunction with the fact that the defense has opened the door by making arguments inconsistent with his very testimony—that its admission is compelled. The exclusionary rule is meant to deter officers from constitutionally suspect behavior. We do not have that in this case. Officers are not expected to *dissuade* a defendant from speaking. We expect them fully to try and persuade defendants to talk, as long, of course, as they have advised him of his rights. They did that. They reminded him that those rights still apply. The defendant chose to keep speaking. As you say, he knew exactly how to stop the conversation when he really wanted it over. And the officers stopped it immediately upon that request. And now, the defense—having moved to suppress his admission—wants to disingenuously argue to the jury that he was never with her that night. They do so knowing that that is contradicted by their client's own words. It's close enough to come in on its own, but after hearing their defense, it must be admitted to dispel the misleading impression left with the jury that he has always denied seeing Melina that night."

"But that I cannot do, Ms. Grunwald."

It is a declarative statement. It is time for the judge to rule. Sandy has lost.

"I cannot say that the defendant's statement was involuntarily or unfreely given, but only just a little. I cannot say that his admission was obtained in violation of his constitutional rights, but only just a little. That is like being only a little pregnant. 'Only just a little' means it still must be excluded. And the defendant has not testified and lied. His counsel has given an opening statement, which is not evidence. They have asked the witnesses questions, which is not evidence. Only their answers are evidence. They have not opened the door to allow in a statement that was—however well-intentioned—still obtained without the free and voluntary consent of the defendant. The jury will not hear the defendant's admission."

The air inside of Sandy evacuates all in one. Her heart sags. She and Jordan return to their seats. Nate lays an encouraging hand on her shoulder.

"That being decided, State: Will you be calling any more witnesses or presenting any more evidence?"

"No, Your Honor."

11 | TUESDAY

Mr. Earl Thomas solemnly laid his wide palms on the mahogany table. He readjusted himself in his seat, which squeaked its discomfort under his considerable weight. His eyes darted to each of his five colleagues, rendered silent by the poignancy of the moment. The debate and chatter had reached an organic end. All intuited the result.

Mr. Thomas, the foreperson, pointed his wavering finger down the line.

At the female doctor staring at her quivering hands.

"Guilty," said Dr. Laura Hurtado-Perez.

At the round, red-faced, middle-aged man, smiling broadly and nodding.

"Guilty," said Mr. Joseph Cole.

At the beautiful teenage girl with impeccable posture.

"Guilty," said juror number six.

At the awkward, twenty-year-old Cuban man who rarely spoke.

"Guilty," said juror number sixteen.

And, finally, at the black mail carrier who had previously been the sole holdout.

Mr. Clifton Robinson indulged in the longest pause.

But eventually—and with the requisite bass and conviction—he parroted the words of his temporary colleagues: "Guilty."

The chair of Mr. Arnold Weiss, the alternate—and since dismissed—juror number seventeen, sat empty.

Mr. Thomas took a deep breath. He glanced at his wristwatch. Its analog face read 9:59 a.m. Deliberations ended just shy of an hour that Tuesday morning on which they began.

"Then we have our verdict. It's unanimous," he declared.

He straightened the verdict form on the table and picked up his pen. He then, deliberately and raising a finger to signal to the others that they stand by, dropped everything and dug into his pocket. He removed a scratch-off lottery ticket and a quarter. He rubbed the thin edge of alloy George Washington against the paper card.

"You're playing the lotto?" Mr. Robinson asked, in a half chuckle.

"I always do on my birthday," Mr. Thomas answered plainly.

"It's your birthday?" Mr. Cole asked.

Mr. Thomas nodded. He stared down at his now-revealed game of chance.

"I won fifty dollars," he said with self-satisfaction. "September 11 has always been my lucky day."

The group exploded in laughter. Only a very small fraction of that stemmed from the humor of the moment. It was exaggerated. The majority of it flowed from an instinctual need to reduce the tension collecting in their bodies. A guilty verdict always drew a heavy physical reaction. Mr. Thomas had very much intended to introduce the moment of levity. All of them were acutely aware that, on an otherwise pedestrian morning, they had likely relegated a young man to significant prison time. The psychical release was necessary.

The laughter transitioned into the spontaneous singing of "Happy Birthday."

Some of the parties waiting patiently outside of the jury room for a decision, including the man minutes away from being condemned, could hear the revelry. It signaled to them that a verdict was forthcoming.

Mr. Thomas checked the box corresponding to "guilty," and he signed the form. He dated it: 09/11/01. He knocked on the courtroom door. The bailiff responded swiftly.

"We have a verdict," he advised. The bailiff acknowledged him and shut the door to go alert the judge. The jurors flocked to the single bathroom within the jury room for a respite.

Juror number six waited in line. Number sixteen stood behind her.

They stood at similar heights—short for a man, tall for a woman.

"I like your nails," sixteen said. In their days together, he had never before addressed her. That was a relief for her.

Boldly, he reached out to grab her hand and peer down at her fingernails coated in rose pink. She flinched at the touch but didn't immediately withdraw her hand out of embarrassment.

"I'll let you know the brand so you can pick up a bottle for yourself," she teased, casually pulling her hand back into her body.

He grunted, almost as if in pain, but did not blink. He maintained, instead, uncomfortably piercing eye contact. He had eschewed direct eye contact with anyone in all of the hours they had spent together—except with her. With her, he overcorrected.

His reaction time was severely delayed. Seconds later, he began a slow—but embellished—cluck of laughter. Short bursts of chuckles flew out of him like a sputtering car. A chord of panic struck deep within juror number six. Deeper still, she felt herself soften at his social ineptitude. It evoked a feeling of familiarity.

He killed the laughter abruptly, just as suddenly as it had

appeared. He ruffled his fingers through the tendrils of his curly hair.

"That's funny, because I'm a man. I don't wear nail polish."

Despite herself, she smiled at the childlike simplicity of his explanation.

"You Cuban?" he asked, desperate to prolong the interaction with mindless prattle.

"Colombian," she corrected, hands in her own long, black hair.

The bathroom became vacant. She turned to walk inside. His hand shot out in a handshake offering, drawing her to a halt.

"Gabriel Soto," juror number sixteen introduced himself.

She accepted his moist palm.

"Melina Mora," number six replied.

Once the courtroom settled—judge on the bench, defense and prosecution at their respective tables—the jurors were walked in. Mr. Thomas handed the manila envelope containing the verdict form to the bailiff. He, in turn, delivered it unopened to the judge.

"Before I read the verdict," began the Honorable Jack Grunwald in a somber baritone, "I wanted to alert the members of the jury to what has transpired while you were sequestered. Shortly after you entered to deliberate this morning, we were informed that two airplanes were flown into the World Trade Center towers in New York in what is an apparent terrorist attack. I contemplated interrupting your deliberations, which might have led to a mistrial, but I decided instead to have my bailiff monitor your cellular phones—those of you who have one—in case you received an emergency call from relatives in New York or your children's schools for pickup. I would have ended deliberations if it became necessary. I'm glad you have reached a verdict first, and your hard work, as well as that of the attorneys, won't be wasted. I will swiftly read the verdict and get you all out of here to communicate with your families."

Wide eyes and nervous rustling fanned out across the jury box. Before protests emerged, Judge Grunwald opened the envelope.

"Please stand, Mr. Williams," he commanded of the defendant. His attorneys rose with him in solidarity. "In the Circuit Court of the Eleventh Judicial Circuit in and for Miami-Dade County, Florida, in the matter of the State of Florida versus Dwayne Williams: We the jury, on this 11th day of September, 2001, find the defendant, Dwayne Williams, guilty of Armed Robbery, and that the defendant used, carried, or displayed a firearm in the commission of the crime. So say we all, signed Earl Thomas, foreperson."

Mr. Williams did not stir. His attorney laid a performative, comforting hand on his back, massaging it in concentric circles. The twenty-one-year-old stared blankly at the jurors. Dr. Hurtado-Perez, in particular, could not tear her eyes away from him. The quivering spread from her hands to her entire body. Mr. Soto fidgeted his thumbs indolently.

The condemnation was met with no fanfare. No one sat in the gallery watching, not even a single family member of the accused. The world simply did not care, on that day or on any day.

"With that, I want to thank you all for your service. I understand it is difficult to take time out of your busy schedules for this. Other than military service and voting—both of which are optional—jury service is the only way most of us are able to give back to this country what it has so generously given us. We are indebted to you. Now, go be with your families, and may God bless America on what will undoubtedly be a dark day in our history."

All rose as the jurors were escorted out. Outside the courtroom, the invisible strings that bound them severed, leaving them a little lost. The group disassembled—saying their generalized goodbyes—even as they awkwardly headed for the exit in the same direction afterward. The empaneled women, Melina and Laura, walked out side by side until the sun and humid air hit their faces. Laura's joints, in particular, loosened at the warmth.

"He kept staring. It was uncomfortable," Melina muttered.

Laura nodded.

"I know. It scared me. He appeared so angry. It sent chills down my spine," she commiserated.

"No, not the defendant. Him," Melina indicated, pointing across the street to Gabriel, who was standing on a sidewalk, kicking at invisible nothings, waiting on his mother to pick him up.

"Oh, darling. You're a beautiful girl. I'm sure you're used to it by now. Take it as a compliment," said Laura dismissively, literally waving it off with a hand.

Melina masked an indiscernible grimace with a broad smile. The two hugged and parted ways. Melina pulled out her cellular phone, recently purchased from savings she had accrued at her part-time office job. She dialed a number she had not called in some time.

Rocky Sandoval's phone vibrated on the nightstand, spawning a tiny earthquake.

"Hello."

He heard her stunted breathing first. Nothing else. It warmed his insides.

"Are you alright?" Melina asked, without greeting.

"Yes. Still sleeping."

"On a Tuesday?"

He allowed the sting of her judgment to pass before reengaging.

"You're at school?" he asked.

"No."

"What is it, honey?"

"I wanted to see that you're alright."

"What happened in Indonesia today?"

"Turn on the news."

He rolled out of bed and hit power on the remote control. The screen buzzed alive. He didn't have to change the channel. They were all the same. It took too long for the image of burning buildings to process in his sleep-addled brain. The synapses fired at an arrested pace. Once it hit, the remote in his hands dropped to the floor, and he collapsed onto the edge of his bed in a seated position.

"Fuck," he cursed softly, gently, into the receiver.

Then: "Where are you?"

"I'm at the courthouse. Just finished jury duty," she answered, tears threatening to fall from her burning eyes.

"I'll come pick you up."

Lieutenant Reynaldo Lozano stood at the side of the road, yelling at a man in a car many years his senior.

"It's a Tuesday at nine in the morning, for Chrissake! What happens when I'm not around to bail you out, Lee? You prepared to lose it all?"

"I died a long time ago," Dr. Leon Musgrave replied in a dour tone. "I'm just waiting for my body to realize it and catch up. The liver regenerates—did you know that? It's the only organ that can do that. It's like I'm stuck in purgatory. No matter the abuse, it never seems to be enough. But our fates are intertwined, aren't they, Rey? So you won't let mine falter. You'll continue saving me in an effort to save yourself."

Rey lightly slapped the roof of the car, sending it into a noisy rattle.

"Head home, Lee. Officer Weinger will trail you."

Rey disappeared, and Lee waited for the boy cop behind him to enter his cruiser and signal with his headlights that it was time to leave.

Lee left his seat belt unfastened, but he drove exaggeratedly slowly, continually peering into his rearview mirror to gauge Officer Jay Weinger's frustration.

"Serves him right, stopping a senior citizen," Lee mumbled to himself. "I'll show him old-man driving."

He flipped on the dials and buttons of his car radio. He searched for music, but he found only subdued voices. He switched from FM to AM, but the two were largely the same. He ultimately stopped fidgeting with the radio and listened to the news. The country was under attack.

Officer Weinger caught on to the state of affairs shortly thereafter. He flashed his lights once, wailed his siren briefly, and departed in the opposite direction, leaving Lee on his own. He resumed driving at a normal pace, made it home, settled in front of his television, and poured himself another drink.

The bell hanging off the door handle to a downtown coffee shop jingled and sang as Darla Tackett strode inside. She swept off her giant sunglasses and scanned the room, half expecting to find that she had been stood up. But there he was, Gene Aldridge, seated at a table for two, directly facing the doorway, two lidded cups of coffee in cardboard sleeves perched before him. He was beaming.

She flashed a hurried smile, sat down across from him, removed her purse and blazer, and took a long swig from the drink nearest her.

"It's hot!" he warned. She bared her teeth in pain as her gums smarted.

"Bad habit of mine," she explained.

He reached over to grab hold of her cup with both hands and wrapped all ten fingers and palms around the outside.

"Your hands are cold?" she inquired, eyebrow arched.

"Colder than this coffee, certainly. You know that lawsuit a few years back? Third-degree burns from spilt coffee? They brew this stuff at excessive temperatures."

He maintained his snug grip on her drink.

"Thank you."

She placed her idle hands on the table. Other than the drinks, it was empty—no paperwork, no folders, nothing to denote a business meeting over a social call. She smirked to herself. As a woman, she had often been invited out on pretense of business, only to realize half an hour in that her male counterpart had no such designs. He caught sight of her meandering eyes and deflated posture.

Clumsily, he reached down to pick up and open a brief-case hidden behind his seat. From out of the clunky thing—old, pockmarked, and with peeling leather—he produced an application and a Rolodex.

"I picked up the form to officially launch your campaign," he said, insecurely, eyes downcast. "No one else has yet declared. We want to enter early, raise money, and scare off the competition. And, more importantly, this Rolodex contains numbers to all of the big donors in South Florida politics."

"That thing looks like it's from the seventies. You sure those numbers still work? Rotary phones are no longer in existence, you know that, right?"

"You tease now, but watch and be amazed."

He removed a bulky cellular phone from his pocket, dialed a number from a card in his deck, and began to sell, his voice inflected in an exuberant, car-salesman tone.

"Tommy, it's great to hear your voice, buddy. How are the girls? And Janice? Beautiful. So great to hear. I'm calling because I have recently met a young, brilliant, and tenacious lawyer—a woman—running for judge in Miami. She's the real deal. And we've got to get in on this at the ground level, Tommy…"

Darla turned to the paperwork, leaving his histrionics—which turned her cheeks beet red and pained from a broad smile, in spite of herself—as background noise. A commotion outside the shop's ceiling-to-floor window caught her attention next.

A man in all-dark clothing, unshaven and apparently unclean, carried a homemade sign in his hands, and he was yelling, "Repent! The world is ending!" The lettering scrawled in marker read the same way.

Folks on the street appeared hurried as they approached and avoided him, but their bustle continued long after passing.

Gene, who had stopped talking and was instead listening to the voice on the other line somewhat engrossed, had the color drain from his face. He lowered the phone, forgetting even to hang up the call.

"What's happening?" Darla asked.

"A terrorist attack. Two planes crashed into the Twin Towers in New York. Many are dead."

Her hand flew to her mouth agape.

"That's heartbreaking," she responded. But he looked ashen.

"All my family is in New York," he droned. "My daughter works in Manhattan. In the Financial District, just a few blocks from there."

Darla's hand flew impulsively to his, which was laid out on the tabletop. The pressure she applied was reassuring.

"We'll call her, Gene. Make sure she's alright."

"She doesn't own a cell phone."

"Then we'll try her work number. Come. Let's get to a computer."

Slowly, he nodded. Gingerly, she helped him to rise, pack up his belongings, and join the crowds outside in a state of alert and controlled haste.

Samuel Sterling rolled out of bed that morning at the endless ringing of his landline phone in his cramped, messy studio apartment. He was just a couple of hours into his daily sleep. As a midnight officer, in his second year on the force, he kept a purely nocturnal schedule, arriving home in broad daylight and knocking out until late afternoon. He often let the phone ring ad nauseam, if only because the human on the other end of the line would eventually tire and hang up. Sam did not own an answering machine.

But this time, the ringing persisted for several minutes. Ensconced in rapid-eye-movement sleep, Sam's brain began to incorporate the ringing into his dreams. It finally sprung him from his slumber. Either the matter was so urgent that the human on the other side meant to hang on indefinitely to command his attention, or it was not a human at all, and the robot calling would remain on the line interminably long.

It was the latter.

"Hello!" Sam greeted gruffly upon snatching the receiver from the wall.

"Hello. This is a call from the Florida Department of Corrections," a prerecorded voice began. "This call is to alert you that inmate Pablo Miguel Arellano—the defendant in criminal case number F90-1009—was released from custody in the past forty-eight hours. As the victim in the case, you are entitled to notification. For more information, or if you have received this message in error, please visit us on the World Wide Web or call us at our toll-free number..."

The receiver fell out of his hand. As the weight of tears threatened to push out from their ducts, his foggy mind—with the assistance of his sprawling fingers—attempted to do the math.

"Eleven. Eleven. Eleven," he muttered to himself on a loop.

He slumped into a chair in front of his desktop computer. He had his blackout shades drawn, so the only illumination came from his blue screen. There, enveloped in shadows, he kept dual Internet windows open: one featuring the *Miami Herald* and a major story gripping the world, still unfolding, that he had missed while sleeping; the second, a governmental site dedicated to the entry and release dates of state prisoners.

The face of his mother's killer flashed on-screen. He winced. His eyes dragged across the screen to the text alongside. There, in black, was the incarcerative sentence of fifteen years. But beside it, blinking for emphasis, were two new words in red: Early release. The release date read: 09/11/01. No detainer by immigration and customs. No qualification. Just freedom. Four years short.

A recognizable pressure—this time painful—hovered above where his heart pounded. He reflexively reached for his bedside Bible.

He wept.

He was accosted by full-body heaves, deep-belly whimpers, and tremors that left his abdomen aching. The screen blurred through the distorting lens of his tears.

Half an hour passed. He emerged from his sentimental stupor and entered the dark recesses of online message forums. The shared anger brought him comfort.

Sam wiped away drying tears with the back of one hand and began typing frantically. His inner thoughts materialized on-screen beneath two other posts:

by sterling_is_golden (1 post)
11 Sept. 2001, 10:34 a.m.
Romans 13. Deport criminal illegal spics, too.

He would, in the days that followed, send the link to colleagues he assumed were like-minded. After the attacks, there was a freedom in uncouth speech unlike any other time he had experienced. Not everyone agreed. He stayed in bed the rest of that day, but he could not sleep. Cathartic but heartrending, hatred gave him relief but no peace.

The grieving father answered the intern reporter in Spanish.

"We are devastated to have lost our son. Write that."

That was enough for Domenico Santos. He had gotten his quote. He was simultaneously elated and nauseous on the ride back.

He entered the *Miami Herald* building upon his return, a little less overdressed sans tie and in rolled-up sleeves, eager to show off what amounted to an anodyne, throwaway quote destined for the back pages of the Metro section.

But the newsroom was at once abuzz and dreary.

A rotating group of zombie spectators collected at the television sets hanging at the center of the shared space. They did not utter a syllable. Beside them, posted at rows of computers, were fast-talking, fast-typing colleagues on unceasing phone calls. Only their eyes—wet, reddened, and slow-moving—betrayed the mania that informed their every movement. Some ran out and ran in; others moved torpidly across the room with leaden limbs. They were a mass of sheep without a shepherd, in collective disorganization.

Dom sought out his editor, interrupting her as she barked orders at the blathering, fervent typists under her charge. The portly woman could barely maintain her balance, one leg propped up on a chair to give her height over a row of journalists, as if she were the captain of a mid-century vessel directing her crew to steer past choppy waters.

"Go home. Be with family."

He felt again the light-headed rush—the mortification, dread, spiked adrenaline, shame, and shot nerves—that nagged at him at the dead boy's door. He made the choice to lean into it.

He shook his head in defiance.

She recoiled in near offense.

"I'm here to help," he replied in a small voice. Then, summoning a baritone the twenty-year-old rarely deployed: "I want to help."

Swelling pride diluted any offense to her.

"Go to the criminal courthouse. Review today's docket. Our usual beat reporter is occupied at the moment," she explained, hand gesturing dramatically to the stunted chaos around her. "It won't be a story. Just a log. But it'd help. And you want to help."

A slight nod and a tight, straight-line smile, and he took off in a jog. His agita noticeably subsided.

It is a cool December morning when Diana walks into the lobby of a Tampa, Florida, nursing home. She hugs herself as she steps in, from both the chillier-than-usual weather and her overstrung nerves. She withdraws her license from her wallet and hands it to the receptionist.

"Who are you here to see, Ms. Perez?"

"My mother."

The words leave her weakly, in almost a whisper. She cannot bring herself to make a more specific identification. The receptionist does not need one.

"The doctor?" she asks brightly.

"Yes, that's her."

"Laura Hurtado-Perez?"

"It's just Hurtado now."

"Follow me."

The young brown woman who leads her is garrulous and

cheery. It's a demeanor that pairs well with her surroundings. But it stands in sharp contrast with Diana's own muted countenance.

"She's just a joy here. Everyone loves her. We call her simply *doctora*. So sharp. She just walks around with her notes on a clipboard—diagnosing folks, offering advice and treatment. Helps train some of our younger residents. A real presence."

Diana interjects caustically.

"She shouldn't be diagnosing anyone."

The girl's eyes shoot downward. Diana feels instant regret, but she does not say anything. She allows the sting to linger.

"Of course, ma'am."

They do not share in any more conversation.

They reach the door to her mother's room, and the receptionist knocks heartily. The delay unsettles her. The girl tries again, casting Diana a nervous glance. It opens wide finally, and there appears a sixty-six-year-old, shorter, frailer, and tanner version of herself.

Diana is intentionally quiet, divulging nothing.

Laura's eyes travel: from complete unrecognition to vague awareness to surprising dread.

"Hannah?" she asks.

Pain grips Diana's paused heart.

"No, Mother. It's Diana."

A blank stare resets her eyes, which flood now with warmth.

"Of course, *mija*," she says, leaning in for an embrace. "Come in, darling. I've been expecting you."

Mother and daughter are left alone in the patient's quarters.

Laura is in constant motion from the moment Diana enters: folding clothes, boiling water in a kettle, washing and drying cups, setting out snacks that neither ends up touching. The droning of the news in the background accompanies her flighty prattle.

"You should sit, Mother."

"I will do no such thing," she says. "I'm not past my prime, you know. I'm still with it. I can do for myself. I'm doing great with my mental exercises—crosswords, sudoku, logic games. I've always been a good study, you know that. This is no different."

"Yes, Mother. Are you taking your medication?"

"Of course. They won't let me forget it. They come—in the morning, late at night—just to check up on me. It's patronizing."

"You shouldn't be working."

"Working? What are you talking about? I sit around doing nothing but taking classes for geezers and watching television. Bored to death. A potted plant. Just where you and your brother want me."

Laura was darting about so much she could not see the agony that accosts her daughter at the dig.

"The receptionist told me you've been making the rounds, Mother. Doing checkups of your neighbors."

"I see that they tattled on me. It keeps my mind sharp, *mija*, and my hands from being idle. It makes them all happy. It makes me happy."

"Working is what got you in trouble in the first place."

"Working is what is saving me. It gives me purpose."

"It gave you stress. It made you forget about your own well-being. About taking your pills. About giving others the proper pills. What's patronizing is them allowing you to go room to room for show, like you're Patch Adams. They have *real* doctors for that."

"I am a *real* doctor," she replies flippantly.

"Not anymore."

The elder woman stops cold in her tracks. She turns to her daughter and peers deeply into her. Her eyes and hands tremble.

"What use is there in having this disease if you cannot, at the very least, forget the lowest points of your life? Thank you for reminding me, darling."

It is a gut punch. The air is sapped from within Diana. She gasps from breathlessness. The crowing of the kettle cuts through the melancholy. Laura removes it from the stove, pours the water into a teapot, and places it on the counter to cool.

Diana mutters self-flagellating expletives in response to her own cruelty.

"Has Rich visited yet?"

"Your father?"

Diana does not remind her mother that he has passed. Only in death—and her children's adulthood—had the battered woman chosen finally to drop her hyphenate.

"My brother."

"Oh," Laura says. "No. Not yet. He must be terribly busy. New wife and all."

Diana does not doubt it. Her mother would never forget a visit from her beloved son, diseased or not.

"I just can't see her like this," her coward-for-a-brother will tell her when she next asks. "That doesn't make me a bad man, does it, Diana?"

She will leave that question unanswered.

Laura nears her daughter, gathers her hands in her own, and leans in as if she were about to share a secret.

"Would you like me to boil some water and make us tea?"

Diana's eyes shine with grief.

"You already did, Mother. The pot is on the counter."

Laura's face darkens. It's the pity that hurts the most. She nods. She smiles.

"Serve yourself. I need to use the restroom."

"Keep the door slightly open?"

"Yes, *mija*."

Diana turns up the television volume as she proceeds toward the teapot. She only offhandedly pays the newscaster attention.

"...*In Miami, the trial of the Love-Spurned Slayer is coming to a close. Prosecutors have rested the case against Gabriel Soto in the murder of Melina Mora, who had gone missing for weeks until her bones turned up at the morgue in which Mr. Soto worked. The pair were strangers who met on the night of her death, and the two sides dispute whether they were consensually intimate that night or Mr. Soto raped and killed Ms. Mora. The story has enthralled the entire Miami-Dade community, particularly local Cuban Americans and Colombian Americans, and the public is now anxiously waiting to see whether Mr. Soto will testify or present a case at all. If not, his fate gets handed to a jury of six men and women as early as tomorrow morning...*"

Diana looks up from pouring two cups of tea to catch her mother having floated out from the bathroom toward the screen, mouth somewhat open and eyes wide. Still pictures of a pretty young woman and video of a curly-haired man in a boxy suit sitting between his attorneys flash across the screen.

"I know those two," Laura murmurs softly.

"Who?"

"The defendant and the victim in that case. On the news."

"How?"

"I served on a jury with them. Both of them. They weren't strangers. They had met each other. I was there."

"Are you sure you're remembering correctly, Mother?"

"Yes!" she spat out. "I'm not mixing anything up. I recognize them. I know them—the young woman in particular. Melina was her name. Remember when I had jury duty on 9/11? It was with them. Both of them. Over ten years ago."

Diana watches her silently.

"You believe me, don't you?"

Diana's eyes flutter with apprehension. Her mother desperately needs validation. Her body preemptively seems to shrink into itself.

Then, Diana nods.

"Yes, Mother. I do."

"So help me call the Miami authorities. I need to tell someone."

12 | A VERDICT, WITH PREJUDICE

Sandy's left leg, draped over her right, swings wildly as it balances on her knee. Seated beside her, Jordan oscillates between flat-footedness and stretching forward, shifting his weight onto his toes, flexing his calf in an aerobic nervous tick. Nate and Sofia sit on a couch on the periphery of the room, as present as the room's wallpaper. A windswept woman, the Honorable Darla Tackett, strides into her office, rushes an out-of-breath court reporter carrying a stenograph on his wiry shoulders into the room, slams the door, scoots swiftly behind her desk, deflates onto her giant chair, and sighs.

She signals to the reporter that he is not to begin typing.

"I am not mistrying this case," she asserts with a scoff. "Not after the time, money, and public attention spent. No way."

The young attorneys across from her do not so much as breathe.

"Where did this new witness come from?" she demands in a near shriek.

The limp marionettes come to life.

"A woman currently living in Tampa, Florida, saw a news

report," Mr. Whipple begins. "She recognized both the alleged victim—"

"She's dead, counsel," Judge Tackett says. "Drop the 'alleged.'"

Away from the media, off the record, and frustrated, the judge is stripped of all diplomacy. Jordan clears his throat, pauses, corrects himself, and continues warily.

"She recognized both the victim and my client. She served with the two of them on the criminal jury of Dwayne Williams, a five-time convicted felon and violent career criminal found guilty of armed robbery over ten years ago. I have confirmed it with court records. Melina Mora and Gabriel Soto knew each other. What's more, Mr. Williams was released from prison after serving eight years, just a month before the victim was murdered. This evidence is critical to the defense."

Judge Tackett turns to Sandy.

"You didn't know about any of this, Sandy?"

Sandy flinches at the informality.

"Of course not, Your Honor. I would have turned it over if I did."

"And Jordan, you want more time to investigate, I imagine?"

"I do not," Jordan reveals. "I merely want to call the witness to the stand. And introduce the motive and opportunity of an alternate suspect, Mr. Williams."

"And keep the State from investigating the matter? From being able to respond? From finding Mr. Williams, potentially bringing him in, allowing him to clear his name and explain his whereabouts?" Judge Tackett challenges, anticipating the objection.

"Mr. Williams is dead," Jordan says flatly.

He hands a manila folder to the judge containing the man's booking photo and his death certificate. The judge lingers over his picture. A subconscious pang of familiarity grips her heart, but she moves past it, and it fades seconds later. She has seen thousands of young black men in her former life, and she does little to try and retain their memory in her consciousness. Often, she actively tries to forget.

"He was rearrested four months after the murder on grand theft charges. He died in custody after that."

Her eyes swing to Sandy.

"And you?"

"This is all a leap, Your Honor. There's no *there* there. Maybe if the defense investigated the matter. Found something that tied Mr. Williams to the body. To the bar that night. To the general area. We know nothing except that he was a defendant in a long-ago jury trial, and he was not in custody during the murder. He could have been anywhere. This severely prejudices our case. We have no way to respond."

"That was as good a response as any, counsel. 'It's a reach. It's weak. It's speculative doubt. Nothing in the evidence supports it,'" Judge Tackett mimics. "But you can't possibly argue that the defense has zero remedy? This is new information. It is critical information. Am I to allow a jury to convict a man without them knowing it?"

"I am not saying that," Sandy concedes. "But there *is* a remedy. You can grant a mistrial. And we do this again, but fairly: all of the information available to both sides from the start."

"You can't ask for a mistrial," the judge intones. "Double jeopardy would attach."

"I am not asking for a mistrial," Sandy insists, eyes wide in panic. "But if you deny defense the opportunity to call this witness—who has not been listed by them, who has not been deposed, whose account I cannot verify or contest—they will ask for a mistrial. Or you can declare a mistrial on your own, and as long as it's absolutely necessary, no double jeopardy attaches."

"And what if I am wrong? It goes up on appeal. They say it was not at all necessary. That double jeopardy now attaches. You can't try Mr. Soto again. And he is forever discharged from prosecution in this case. Are you willing to take that risk?"

Sandy's chest rises in tortured but hasty breathing. The judge's eyes are expressive, pushing her to trust in her case and her ability to persuade the jury that this last-ditch effort is a red herring. Jordan notices the subtext, but it ultimately helps his cause, so he does not take offense. He does not want more investigation. He wants the alternate theory of a vengeful Mr. Williams to remain muddied. He represents the specter of doubt he needs. A ghost is more compelling than a flesh-and-blood human being anyway.

With a sharp wave of a hand—like an orchestral conductor ushering in a crescendo—Judge Tackett indicates that the court reporter begin transcribing and flip on his pocket tape recorder.

"What unlisted, newly discovered evidence is the defense seeking to introduce?" she asks with her ceremonial inflection.

"The testimony of Dr. Laura Hurtado, who previously served on a jury with Ms. Mora and Mr. Soto, and a correctional officer in the records department, who can attest that Dwayne Williams—the defendant in that case—had been recently let out of custody during the time of the murder," Jordan replies.

"Are you asking for a mistrial to investigate more leads on this individual? To incorporate this alternate theory into your voir dire, your opening, and your cross-examinations of the State's witnesses?" the judge inquires.

"No," Jordan says declaratively.

"And your client will, on the record, agree with you? That he forfeits any more time to fully develop the lead and incorporate it from the beginning of a new trial. And he will do so being made aware that if he asks for one, I will grant him a mistrial.

But that, if he passes on this now, and he is convicted, this will not be a basis for overturning that conviction."

"Yes. I have spoken with him. He will do so."

"Ms. Grunwald, do you object to the introduction of this evidence?"

"I do, Your Honor, for two reasons. One: This is evidence that could have been discovered by the defense with due diligence. Mr. Soto is undoubtedly aware that he previously served with Ms. Mora on a jury. He clearly hid that fact from his counsel or his counsel made a strategic choice—with his client's assent—not to investigate that lead. In the past two years, Mr. Soto had the ability to track down these jurors. To track down Mr. Williams. He chose not to do so. He cannot now, in the eleventh hour, after the State has rested its case, spring this information on the court and opposing counsel and seek its admittance to great prejudice to our case. Two: Evidence regarding alternate suspects is only admissible if there is a legitimate tendency that Mr. Williams committed the crime. This evidence is too remote in time, place, or circumstance—the connection being nearly a decade ago and his location on the night merely anywhere but prison—to be admissible. It is more prejudicial than it is probative."

Judge Tackett nods complimentarily. The effort is impressive but not dispositive.

"If I do find a legitimate tendency, and I decide to admit the testimony on a very limited basis and with an accompanying cautionary instruction to the jury, would the State still argue that manifest necessity requires that I, sua sponte, declare a mistrial? Is the State willing to take the risk that an appellate court ultimately disagrees and discharges Mr. Soto from all charges?"

Sandy swallows her anxiety. The sound is loud enough to register on the audio record.

"No, Your Honor. We ask that you reject the introduction of

this evidence. If you are wrong, an appellate court will overturn the potential conviction, and both sides will get a new trial. But we are not asking that this court find manifest necessity and risk that double jeopardy attaches, no."

Judge Tackett clicks her tongue, an oddly casual gesture in an otherwise tense moment.

"The State will have an opportunity to fully depose the witness before she testifies. Her testimony—and that of the correctional officer—will be very limited. It will come with an accompanying jury instruction. The State will have the opportunity to present a rebuttal case and call any of its witnesses to highlight its argument that nothing in the evidence—from the bar where she was last seen to the morgue where her bones were ultimately found—indicates that Mr. Williams had any involvement.

"And we will move forward. We are in the home stretch. Let's finish this thing."

"Does the defense wish to call any witnesses?"

"The defense calls Dr. Laura Hurtado to the stand."

Heads in the jury pivot curiously to the door, where the bailiff escorts an elderly woman with self-assured eyes and nervous hands into the courtroom. By now, through openings and an army of State witnesses, the jurors figure that they have heard, at least by name, all of the relevant cast of characters. But this name had not been uttered even once. It is startling. The media in the courtroom, even more familiar with the saga and for longer, are equally jolted. They turn their lenses and flares to the woman, sensing a dramatic turn.

Diana Perez walks in behind her mother and sits in a spot saved for her in the front row, directly opposite the witness.

"Good morning, Dr. Hurtado," Jordan greets her, grinning.

"Good morning."

"What do you do for a living?"

"I am retired now. But I spent nearly forty years as a neurosurgeon."

The jurors shift in their seats, sitting up straight and focusing their attention on the credentialed woman. Sandy sighs.

"Do you live here in Miami?"

"Not anymore. I live in Tampa now. But I lived most of my life here, locally, and my children still live here."

"I would like to direct your attention to September 11, 2001. Do you recall that day?"

"Of course. All of us recall that day."

"And what were you doing on that morning?"

"I was serving on a criminal jury with Melina Mora and Gabriel Soto."

There are no gasps. That would require breath, and the spectators had already been holding their breath, hanging on her every word, since Dr. Hurtado was introduced. It is silence that rings in their ears, the soundless pulse that emerges once human chatter dwindles to zero.

"Are you sure of that, ma'am?"

"Objection! Bolstering."

"Sustained."

"Why do you think that, ma'am?"

"It was a pretty notable occasion. I was among them when I first found out about the attacks. We spent a couple of days together, several long hours together. The two of them were the youngest of the group. Very young. So they stood out. I recall conversing with Melina particularly because she was my daughter's age. We were the only women on the panel. I didn't speak with her at all after that. But during those few days, we were somewhat close."

Jordan fishes out a picture of Melina from the mountain of evidence.

"Is this the young lady you are talking about?"

"Yes, that's her," the doctor answers, softening at the sight. "Quite beautiful. Just as she looked when she was nineteen."

"And the young man you are talking about, do you see him in the courtroom?"

The doctor sweeps her eyes across the gallery of people, nearly a hundred crammed into row after row. Alarm flashes in Jordan's eyes. She is looking in the wrong direction. She scans the room deliberately. The cameras begin snapping. The sharks smell chum in the water. Sandy squeezes Nate's arm. A misidentification would be a boon for them. Diana's hand flies over to her mouth, mortified that her mother might be having a public spell of forgetfulness.

Dr. Hurtado sweeps her gaze over to the jurors next, scanning each one methodically. Time passes glacially, painfully. She has not said a word.

Her gaze drifts to the prosecutors' table. And then to the defense, where she stops short—abruptly and decidedly—at Mr. Soto. She lingers there for an eternity.

"There he is. That's him," she finally answers, extending a finger his way.

Jordan releases his death grip from the lectern.

"Did Ms. Mora and Mr. Soto interact while you served on that jury?"

"Oh, I'm sure. You can't really talk about the facts of the case for most of it, so you just make small talk. Get to know each other." The doctor turns charismatically to the jurors as she answers. They nod in agreement, having spent weeks together themselves and intimately aware of the familiarity it breeds. "We didn't have smartphones to distract us in those days."

"Did the interactions between Ms. Mora and Mr. Soto appear pleasant?"

"Oh, yes. I don't recall any of us having any problems. We all got along quite well."

"Did you render a unanimous verdict?"

"Yes."

"What was that verdict?"

"Objection! Relevance. More prejudicial than probative."

"Overruled."

"You may answer, Doctor."

"Our verdict was guilty."

"What was he convicted of?"

"Same objection, Your Honor."

"Sustained."

"Did you have any impression of Dwayne Williams, the defendant in that case, during the reading of the verdict in particular?"

"Just that he was staring at us. It scared me."

"Was he staring at Ms. Mora in that way?"

Dr. Hurtado's eyes wander, lost in thought.

"He kept staring. It was uncomfortable."

"I know. It scared me. He appeared so angry. It sent chills down my spine."

"Yes. I recall that she complained about it, too. He kept looking at her. It made her uncomfortable," says the doctor in a trembling voice.

"No further questions."

The air feels as if it begins to circulate again in the room, and the audience resumes breathing. Jordan crosses paths with Sandy as he sits and she strides forward. The two ignore each other. Diana hugs herself, her posture tense.

A prosecutor builds up and rarely has the opportunity to tear down. It is now Sandy's turn to confront and diminish.

"Cross-examination."

"Thank you, Your Honor. Good morning, Doctor."

"Good morning."

Sandy abandons the lectern and stalks right up to the witness.

The jury is unaccustomed to watching her so closely. It draws their attention away from the witness and to the strong-willed prosecutor with a spine pulled up to an unnaturally straight line. That diversion was exactly her intention. Direct examination is about the witness. Cross-examination is about the lawyer.

"This all happened over ten years ago, correct?"

"Yes."

"And you just recalled this memory for the first time a few days ago, right?"

"Yes. It returned to me when I saw their faces on television."

"And you had not spoken to the woman you believe to be Melina Mora in ten years, correct?"

"That's right."

"And you had not spoken to the man you today identified as Gabriel Soto in ten years, correct?"

"Correct."

"You have no idea whether the two had any interaction— friendly or otherwise—since then, right?"

"Right."

"Ma'am, you reside currently in an assisted-living facility, correct?"

"Yes."

"And you do so because you currently suffer from early onset dementia and Alzheimer's, isn't that right?"

A tightness overruns Diana's chest. The doctor pauses and her eyes shine as the rate of her blinking accelerates.

"I do."

"In fact, you lost your medical license because of it, didn't you?"

"Objection! Relevance."

"Overruled."

"You must answer, ma'am."

"It's Doctor," she corrects.

"Well, not anymore, right, ma'am?"

Dr. Hurtado's jaw trembles in a mix of rage and melancholy. The shine in her eyes threatens to let loose. She is successful at keeping it pent up.

"Yes. I lost my medical license."

"And that was because you were mixing up your patients?"

"Yes."

"And their treatments?"

"Yes."

"And that had severe consequences for some of them?"

"Yes."

"And you started noticing yourself faltering, correct?"

"Slightly, yes."

"And yet, you continued working until your colleagues reported you?"

"I thought it was just age. Slowing down. Getting older."

"And your ailment affects your short-term memory, right?"

"Yes."

"But it also affects your long-term memory, right?"

"Not as much."

"Well, you've been known to forget the identity of your daughter, who you've known for thirty years, right?"

Despite herself, Dr. Hurtado turns and locks eyes with Diana. The daughter involuntarily whimpers softly to herself. The mother apologizes with her gaze.

"Unfortunately, yes. I have before."

"But you are today identifying two people with whom you've spent much, *much* less time than with your daughter?"

"Yes."

"And you're describing an interaction between the two of them that did not involve you?"

"I was in the same room."

"And that could have lasted mere minutes?"

"I don't know how long they talked."

"Over ten years ago?"

"Yes."

"And before you began to lose significant parts of your memory?"

"I guess so."

"You're *guessing* here today, ma'am?"

"No. You're right. The answer is yes."

"Yes, what?"

"Yes, this was all *before* I began losing significant parts of my memory."

"Thank you, ma'am. No further questions."

Sandy sits. She is shaking and upset.

"How do defense attorneys do this? So-called *progressive* people?" she whispers to Nate disgustedly. "Attack well-meaning people? That was awful."

"Redirect."

Jordan rises. He has only one question.

"Why did you reach out to the authorities upon seeing the news report, Dr. Hurtado?"

She mulls over her answer.

"You believe her?"

"I do. It's hard for witnesses to come forward. It's a drain on their time. It's emotionally crippling, particularly during cross-examination. It's scary to accuse someone, anyone, of a crime. To potentially help condemn a man, a scary man, a violent man, a bad *man, as you look him square in the eye. I, for one, can't help but find her brave."*

"I haven't always been brave in my life. I've allowed fear to keep me from doing the right thing. But this is the right thing. I know what I remember. I owe it to Melina's memory to say what I recall. The truth—regardless of whom it helps—is what's most important. This is the truth."

That last sentence she directs at her daughter.

Diana mouths in response: "I believe you."

For five hours, Sandy waits, the pit of her stomach balled into a fist. Nate is beside her, mumbling encouraging aphorisms, but she remains nonresponsive. She pictures the faces of the jurors as she spoke her final words, studying their expressions for tells. Some of them nodded as she spoke, but did so also with the defense, revealing either a tendency to side with whoever is currently speaking or general agreeableness. Some of them glared: at her, at the defendant, at the tedium—who knows? And some of them smiled, unseemly and awkward, as she told a tale of gore, a bludgeoning, and dismemberment.

Six individual opinions, kept in private, is one thing. The social combustibility of those six opinions—dependent upon who speaks first, who speaks loudest, who speaks not at all, who is liked, who is disliked, and the politics that underlie what is being said, and when—is unpredictable. It's left unrecorded and unstudied, a black box by definition, but jury deliberations represent perhaps the clearest window into the social customs of man.

Sandy's phone rings. She answers. She hangs up seconds later.

"We have a verdict."

"Five hours ain't bad," Nate says.

Juries rarely convict a man in mere minutes. Very short deliberations are bad for prosecutors. But the longer it drags, the likelier an acquittal. Very long deliberations reveal tortured, conflict-ridden division. Juries err on the side of acquittal when tensions are high—if only because it's the safer route, and jurors want to go home—or they hang. A reasonable period in between those two extremes, and the State has a fighting chance at victory.

The attorneys, the media, the families, and the morbidly curious pile into the courtroom in muted, funereal fashion.

The bailiff knocks on the jury room's door, opens it, and leads the jurors out for scrutiny. Sandy studies which member was selected as foreperson, the one holding the verdict envelope in his hands. Lore says it's a signal of the impending verdict whether it's a pro-State juror selected as foreperson or not. She scans the eyes of them all to see if they look to the defendant or evade his eyeline. Lore says if they look at him, it's an acquittal; if they avoid him, it's a conviction. She will know soon enough, within minutes, the fate of the case, but she indulges in these talismanic rituals to soothe her nerves, even if just seconds sooner.

"Do we have a verdict?" Judge Tackett asks.

"We do," the foreperson responds.

The bailiff carries the envelope over to the judge. She removes the sheet inside and peers at it thoroughly. She knows the result before everyone else. Her review is painstaking. She smirks. Sandy's heart, already aflutter, deflates. The noise resounds.

"It's legally sufficient," Her Honor announces curtly, before handing the sheet to her clerk. "Please rise, Mr. Soto. Madam clerk, please publish the verdict."

Defense counsel rise alongside Gabriel, both of them with a hand massaging the stranger's back as if they were family.

Sandy sits peripherally to the clerk. She can see the sheet that is being held out in front of her. She can spot a solitary checkmark at the last possible option and nothing more.

"In the Circuit Court of the Eleventh Judicial Circuit in and for Miami-Dade County, Florida, in the matter of the State of Florida versus Gabriel Soto: As to count one, we the jury, on this tenth day of December, 2011, find the defendant, Gabriel Soto, not guilty of First-Degree Murder. As to count two, we the jury find the defendant, Gabriel Soto, not guilty of Sexual Battery. So say we all, signed Matt Stebbins, fore-person."

A simultaneous shriek flees from the dueling mothers: one of relief for Ms. Soto; one of pain for Ms. Mora. Sandy and Nate do not react. They are trained to remain staid.

"Would either side like the jurors to be polled?" Her Honor inquires.

"Yes," Sandy replies in a small voice.

"When I call your name, please tell me if this is your verdict," the clerk commands. One by one, the six rise and ceremoniously confirm the culmination of years of work.

Sandy tunes out the words of thanks the judge bestows upon them. She stands as they exit, but she cannot feel her legs. One of the jurors smiles at Gabriel and wishes him luck as she passes by him. He fails to emote back. Sandy feels only revulsion in response.

"Mr. Soto, the jury having found you not guilty, I adjudicate you not guilty, and you are free to go," the judge declares. "This court is adjourned."

The man has been two years and one second held in captivity and, the very next second, he is free. Correctional officers drop his chains to the floor. They no longer hold any power over him. Decorum comes to an abrupt end as the judge leaves the bench. Reporters flood the aisles, snapping pictures and shouting out questions. Sandy and Nate grab their belongings and sprint to the doors, collecting the mourning Mora family on their way out.

They will have nothing but condolences—certainly no excuses, answers, or justifications—to share with the family. Mostly, the next-of-kin huddle is an assembly of tears and blank stares.

After the last of them leaves and the limelight dwindles, Sandy is left alone, unmoored and listless in an empty hallway. A shadow waiting patiently in the wings emerges. It's Dom, sheepishly approaching her.

"You have a story to write, don't you?" she asks.

"It will get written. Dozens of outlets are writing the same story right now. Mine will be no different. I wanted to check on you first."

"Can we just go home? Together?"

He is momentarily stunned. But he smiles. And he nods. Her fingers reach out to interlace with his. She lays her head on his shoulder. And, connected, they walk out of the now-deserted building in silence.

On the night Melina was killed, Gabriel Soto waited, back against the wall in an unlit alley, trembling in hot, humid November weather. Only cats, whose six-foot-tall shadows splayed hauntingly onto concrete, joined him, peering and purring curiously. He was watching a woman he recognized walk into the bar. Watching and waiting. He had followed her there.

He collected himself and emerged into the neon light after her.

Inside, the blare of bass-filled music made his eardrums vibrate but calmed his recalcitrant heart. The venue was dark, musty, and relatively empty. The wood paneling provided a familiar, comforting scent. He plopped himself on a stool at the bar, picked up a laminated drink menu for The Saloon, and ordered a dark beer. He sat. He watched. He drank.

The woman he recognized walked by him, her considerable beauty piercing through the dimness: straight black hair that fell against her exposed back; breasts full enough to draw attention; tight jeans on shapely legs above heels that made her tower lithely over others. Her confidence drew everyone's eyes to her. They knew who she was and what she deserved the moment she walked in.

She was alone—her choice, obviously. A girl like that did not need to be alone. She made a beeline for the bar and laid her purse on an empty stool. She would not be needing it.

Men, however sparse they were at that early point in the

night, approached her and paid for her drinks. She asked for shots of liquor, dark in color and high in alcohol. She tossed them back expertly.

The men who advanced were charming, on their best behaviors, but a dangerous undercurrent threatened to emerge at just the hint of rejection. Suitors came with a bullet already in the chamber, prepared to discharge a violent "Bitch!" once they realized what part of them already knew: She was unattainable.

That danger was always present. She carried it with her everywhere. From a young age, she learned to be sweet, attentive, and patient with male interest. It was a survival instinct. She did the same that night, politely engaging anyone who asked for her attention, irrespective of her own desires.

Nearing midnight, as the crowd grew, she planted herself on a spot at the bar beside him, waiting for service. Gabriel was overrun with nerves, paralyzed by a fear that another man might realize she was unaccompanied and intercede, but unable to speak himself. He managed to blurt out three words.

"I know you."

In the noisy dark, she flashed him a curious glance, as if she hadn't even noticed he was there.

"We were on a jury together. Long time ago. September 11, actually," he shouted.

She scanned his face. He waited anxiously, dreading that a gleam of familiarity might never wash over her expression.

She would have pretended to remember him even if she didn't. But recollection did flood her senses, along with a nagging negative feeling that she could not name.

"Oh, yeah. You didn't talk much."

He shot his hand out in affected formality.

"Gabriel," he reintroduced himself.

Despite her do-no-harm ethos regarding the opposite sex, she lied to him for the first and last time that night.

"Catalina," she responded, taking his hand.

He knew that was wrong but said nothing.

He held her hand in his a second too long.

"Pink nails still, after all these years. Beautiful."

She visibly relaxed, her hand resting now comfortably in his. It wasn't clammy, as she had anticipated. It was warm, dry, and larger than his frame suggested. It was reassuring.

"You remembered that about me?"

"You're a hard girl to forget."

She smiled at the simple, understated compliment without a hint of flirtation, and sat down on the empty stool next to his.

"Mm-mm-may I get you your next drink?" he stammered.

"You can."

"I *may*."

She chuckled. His social clumsiness was endearing. He was safe.

She ordered her drink. He paid.

"You remind me of my brother."

She meant it as high praise. She loved her brother more than anyone. But he took it as a lack of romantic interest. She sensed his deflation.

"What about you? Siblings?" she pressed on, sorry to have offended him.

"Only child."

"All the focus on you growing up, eh?"

"Unfortunately. Overprotective Cuban parents who meddle too much. Had to get out. Got my own place a few years back. Quiet, small, in the middle of nowhere—just how I like it."

"Wow. You made it out of a Hispanic household unmarried. I'll need some pointers from you."

"Who said I wasn't married?"

Deadpan. Not even a smirk.

"I'm kidding."

Still no hint of a smile. She roared in laughter all on her own.

"You're an odd one, Gabriel."

"I'm sorry."

"No, don't be sorry. Odd's the wrong word. *I'm* sorry. You're interesting. Not boring."

"Your parents strict like mine?"

"My mom? No, not at all. She's a free spirit."

"And your dad?"

She sipped on her drink protractedly.

"He passed away when I was a little girl."

"Oh, I'm sorry. So sorry." It hit him hard. He shifted in his chair. He ran a hand through his curls. He unfastened the top buttons of his shirt, extended out a chain dangling from his neck, and kissed the golden cross at the end of it. He then mimed the sign of the cross. "May he rest in peace."

It was all so sincere, if over the top. Her father's passing made its way frequently into her introductory conversations. Reactions ranged from discomfort to disinterest. Mostly, people assumed enough time had passed that it could be treated nonchalantly. But Gabriel appeared pained at the news. That acute level of empathy was unusual. She appreciated it.

"Thank you."

She laid a palm on top of his hand for a beat. He looked away nervously. With a mischievous smile, she pushed forward, taking two fingers and lightly brushing at the hair poking out from just below his now-revealed sternum. His heart convulsed in his chest. His body nearly shook along with it.

"You're hairy. You don't shave this?"

"Not really. Girls don't like it, huh?"

She shrugged airily.

"Some girls don't. I like it. My father was the same way. I think it's manly."

His eyes danced away from her. They swept past her for only seconds at a time, the light of her sun too bright to stare directly into.

"You're religious?" she asked.

"I try to be."

"That's good. I seek that sort of stuff out. I wish I had more of that in my life. Structure. Discipline. Tradition. Respect for family and authority. Good conservative values."

"Cool. You work?"

She snickered. "Of course I do. I'm twenty-seven years old. Human resources. At a company. Not so fascinating. What about you? What do you do for a living?"

He dislodged the discomfort from his throat with a pointed cough.

"I work in a morgue."

She furrowed her brow in confusion, less at the answer than at its blunt presentation.

"I mean, I work at an office where they do autopsies."

"Better. Now *that's* fascinating. Not creepy. Never again tell a girl you work at a morgue. Never."

It was his turn to chuckle.

"What's that like? Staring into the face of death?"

He maintained steady eye contact this time.

"Peaceful."

She had to look away herself, or he might never have.

"You came here alone?" she asked.

"Yes."

"Why?"

"I could ask you the same thing."

She debated whether to answer with innocuous nonsense or something deeper. She chose truth.

"I'm never really alone. Not sure if you noticed."

"Do you like that?"

"No, not most of the time. I could use some peace now and again. Your turn."

"I'm not good with girls. With people generally. Not sure if *you* noticed."

She took this to be sarcastic. That wasn't his intention. She smiled. He didn't.

"Am I the first person you've spoken with tonight?"

"Yes."

"Well, let's change that."

She swallowed what remained of her drink in a gulp. His, too, after realizing he would leave it there unfinished. She pulled on his arm, leading him away. He stumbled on his chair. She held on to him in the crowd. The spot where her hand touched him turned red. She steered him outside onto the bar's patio, where the loud chatter of a standing throng of people overrode the music floating from inside.

"Let's stage a breakup," she suggested giddily.

"What?"

"We're going to pretend to break up. Me and you."

"You and I. Why?"

"It draws attention to you. It's intrigue. It's a conversation starter. Plus, it would mean we'd have fucked before. It should increase your social value."

She shoved him, hard, with both hands on his chest. Strands of her loose hair got caught on his buttons. He stood back, less as a result of the force and more out of instinct.

"Come at me again," she insisted loudly, too low to be heard but unmistakably aggressive for show. "Not violently. We don't want anyone to think you'd hurt me. Pursue me—but apologetically."

She walked off, only a few feet away. He obliged and followed.

"Close, Gabriel. Get close to me," she shouted over the music and crowd.

He leaned in. She performed: stomping her feet, spinning and giving him her back, gesticulating wildly with her hands. It didn't last long. Gabriel mostly reacted blankly, engaging in stiff choreography as she barked out orders.

"Now reel them in, just as you did me. Enjoy your night, sweetie," was her farewell, before she planted a quick kiss on his cheek.

And then it was done. She was gone.

Jordan ensnares Gabriel in a celebratory man hug: the one that starts as a handshake and folds into a mutual pat on the back, leaving their interlocking hands—and enough room for Jesus—between their chests. Jordan is smiling, but his hand on the shorter man's back is forceful.

"Go give your family hugs and rejoice in this moment. But I want to see you in five minutes in the side hallway. I want to talk to you about something, just the two of us."

Jordan briefly kisses his wife in the gallery and marches to the courtroom clerk. He picks up something off the pile of evidence, along with a notepad lying on the defense table, and exits out a side door to the narrow hallway. Gabriel takes longer than five minutes, but he eventually joins his former counsel.

Jordan has his hands on his hips. There's an anxious energy emanating from him that is out of character.

He plays with the plastic sleeve in his hands.

"'A body that doesn't belong was brought to the shed,'" he reads softly off a card therein, in almost a whisper. "You wrote this, bro."

Gabriel just blinks in response.

Louder: "You wrote this, bro."

299

Jordan slaps the notepad, filled with pages of Gabriel's trial notes, onto his chest.

"It's your handwriting. I recognized it up there immediately. In the middle of my cross. While staring down at that comment card. You wrote this."

Gabriel purses his lips inward, in showy—almost mocking—deep thought.

"So?"

Jordan notices something in his client's eyes—a confidence, a self-awareness, a mischief—that he has never seen from him before. It chills the usually self-assured lawyer.

Gabriel leans it. He slaps the notepad back onto Jordan's chest, adding a slight shove, stronger than Jordan expected. And he lowers the grit in his voice several octaves. His eyes—darkened, heavy-lidded, wild—stay pinned to Jordan.

"You made it clear what you did and did not want to know," Gabriel nearly growls. "This was a performance, right? Your word, not mine. The show is over now. You played your part. I played mine. Congratulations on the win, counsel.

"And no one can take that away from you, right? As I understand it, I could run out of here and yell at the top of my lungs that I killed that girl, and it wouldn't matter. Double jeopardy, right, counsel? I am forever innocent. Thank you for your hard work in setting me free."

Jordan is tight-lipped. His chest rises and falls at an accelerated pace. The muscles in his body are stiff.

"Are we done here, *bro*?"

Gabriel doesn't wait for an answer. He wipes away all traces of defiance and rolls his eyes upward, resetting them to their lost, blank, and confused default, and he reenters the courtroom to join his waiting family.

That night, Jordan receives text after text of congratulations. He misses them. He leaves his phone on the couch while he spends the night in the bathroom, vomiting. His wife doesn't understand what's wrong. Food poisoning, he explains.

"Catalina" had been right. A new girl approached him—stumbled into him, really—shortly after their staged fight.

She was way younger, not even of legal drinking age, but her legs bent like a fawn's, wilting under the weight of inebriation. Her hands on his shoulders sent a subtle sexual charge through him that was surprising but welcome.

"What time is it?" she managed to ask through lilting, slurred words.

"Too early for you to be this drunk."

He tried his hand at a coquettish grin. His smile was crooked. She didn't find the tease charming. The color drained from her face.

"What the *fuck* is wrong with you?"

He pulled back sharply, as if struck in the face. His cheeks reacted accordingly, marked red by the fire in his veins. Her tottering steadied suddenly, and she pulled her voice into sharp, sober focus.

"You a creep or something?"

His heart sprinted into a horrified jog. Gabriel disengaged from the tangle, backing away in a stagger, hands up in a defensive posture. She pursued him.

"Stop."

"No way that pretty girl was with you. Creep."

"Stop."

She was a braying mule, slogging through her words, heavy tongue crashing up against her teeth.

"Do you think all these people know what a sad little shit you are? Let's ask them!"

She twirled full circle, mouth widening at a slow clip, arms spread and lifted toward the surrounding audience as if she had an announcement. Gabriel took one deliberate step toward her.

"Look, everyone!"

"Stop!" he belted out.

He whipped back his closed fist in a fell swoop that generated great momentum and power, aiming the forthcoming swing at the side of her turned head.

A man intervened before the blow.

"What the fuck are you doing, man? Were you about to hit that girl?"

Gabriel backed away, running past a wall of people and into the bar. He posted up in a darkened corner by himself. He sat. He watched. He drank. Hours passed.

The night grew long, the crowd thinned, and the beautiful girl, "Catalina," remained a firework in the midst of it all: dancing, laughing, singing. Her hangers-on did not last long. Other singles coupled up or called it a night, alone. She kept on.

Nearing last call, a favorite song of hers came on.

She turned gratefully to the disc jockey.

"Finally! The Spice Girls! You played it."

She scanned the increasingly empty room for a companion. She came to a full stop at Gabriel. Manically, she pulled him up onto the dance floor. Inebriated now, Gabriel complied. For two minutes and fifty-two seconds, she pranced and pirouetted around him—a tornado of limbs, extended touch, and giggling. Gabriel was game: moving in sync, keeping his faithful gaze on her. By the end, his tiring dance partner had her arms crossed around his shoulders—easy to accomplish at their commensurate heights—and she leaned into him. He supported her weight easily.

It was she who kissed him. She did it more out of muscle memory than anything else. It felt like a compulsory, inevitable next step.

She was drunk, so the moment wasn't too clear in her mind. But the feeling that it was not bad and, surprisingly, even pleasant did push through. There was a tenderness she seldom felt in the advances of sex-addled men—at least not that late into the night, not that many drinks in.

She recalled something she had told a girlfriend of hers, a lamentation after a series of one-night stands with traditionally virile types: "I wish I could find a big, strong man, but with the sensibilities of a boy inside."

Gabriel was not exactly the former. But he was close enough.

She parted from him with a serendipitous plan in mind.

"I think I'd like to go home with you tonight."

His double take was cartoonish.

"It's late," she explained. "I can't go home now. I'd have to call a cab, fight everyone else closing out the bar for one. You drive here?"

"I have my truck with me."

"You're drunk?"

"Yes. But I'll take the back roads. We'll be safe."

"Your place nearby?"

He shook his head no. "In Homestead."

She pulled away.

"'Quiet. Small. In the middle of nowhere.' Right, I remember now."

She raised a single finger and pulled out her phone.

"Give me a moment."

She walked closer to the front doors for better reception. She dialed a number she had not called in some time. It was late, but she expected him to answer. He always answered. And he would have come for her. She wouldn't have needed to even ask. He would have heard it in her voice.

But she reached his voicemail. She didn't leave a message. She hung up.

Gabriel was in the same spot she had left him. No questions. No attempts at persuasion. Just steeped in childlike jitters.

"Take me home with you."

"OK."

"You ever done that before?"

"No."

"Good. Even better."

It was a long ride to his home, and he drove slowly, carefully, judiciously, avoiding main streets. He didn't speak. She pressed her head up against the glass, nearly sobering up in the lag and lull. She arrived to a dead-quiet farm drenched in darkness and a small, sidelined shack.

"You weren't kidding," she said.

A fright gripped her suddenly, but it was too late to do anything about it now. Instead, she summoned her courage. After all, he was a boy. He would respond more favorably to discipline than vulnerability.

At the entrance, her heel stepped awkwardly into the marsh, knocking her off-balance. She stumbled and her temple struck the doorframe. He didn't turn around to check on her. His mind was elsewhere. He appeared preoccupied.

He flipped on the light. She was repelled by what she saw.

"It's quite minimalist in here. Better we have sex in the dark."

The frankness of the statement rattled him. Hives formed on his pale neck.

He killed the light. By moonlight, he straightened out his sheets, methodically and silently making his bed. His guest stood by, stripping down to her underwear. She crawled beneath the covers. He joined her. The two sat parallel, arms at their sides.

"We need a condom," she instructed.

She felt him hem and haw in the dark. He didn't move. But in the piercing quiet, she heard the gears in his head neurotically turning.

"Pass me my purse," she said dryly, more irritated now. She dug around and produced one.

The sex between them was workmanlike. At first, his body responded ably. The sight of her nude was overstimulating. But soon he grew nervous, the rhythm was off, and his arousal dwindled. It was his first time. After a while, he was just done, growing enervated and dehydrated. He finished without finishing. He lacked the good sense to simulate a crescendo. Not even a whimper. He merely rolled over and slapped off his condom noisily into his hands, signaling it was over.

She shot up in bed, with a spring of energy that astounded him, and now standing, she yanked on the string dangling from the ceiling's light bulb. Metal and glass clanked with vehement force.

"Let me see that condom."

Another demand. She wrenched it from his languid hand. She inspected it to find nothing inside.

She rarely lost her temper. It was one of the things people liked most about her. But a perceived assault on her vanity— her ability to sexually fulfill a man, from which, despite herself, she drew her self-worth—struck her to the core.

"What the *fuck* is wrong with you?" she shrieked.

He leapt out of bed, backing away to a corner yet inches from her in that cramped room, and placed his hands over his ears.

"I get that you're a freak! But what made you incapable of being a man? What made you so *broken*?"

He moved swiftly but soundlessly. His footsteps were notoriously soft. He wrapped his fingers around the thin end of the wooden bat leaning against the wall. He lifted it into the air. It floated up effortlessly. He wound it back.

Gabriel swung the bat, gently lobbing the ball forward off its tee mere inches.

ROBIN PEGUERO

"No, son!" his father bellowed, approaching him indignantly.
"Why are you always so soft? Choke up on that bat."

Gabriel pouted.

"Don't start, Gabriel. I can't stand to look at you when you
whine. You don't like being teased by your friends? Then don't
give them a reason to tease you. Be a fucking man."

He was always cursing at him. Cursing and yelling. Or
he said nothing to him at all. Sports were the only way
the two meaningfully interacted. The father preferred it that
way.

He lurched toward him. His hulking shadow eclipsed the
slender boy.

He reset the ball on its tee. The veins of his muscled forearm
bulged. He returned to his spot several yards away.

"Don't disappoint me this time. Bottle up your feelings.
Launch the ball instead."

He lifted the bat into the air. He wound it back. He poured
everything into his swing—the unshed tears, the anger, the
self-reproach—and sent the ball flying.

It produced a grotesque popping sound.

The shrieking ceased. Quiet resumed. The type of quiet that
filled up space.

He sat on his wooden bench. He brought himself to climax.

He stared at the discarded condom in the corner for several
minutes. Sex had been the reason he took her home. He needed
that motive gone.

He opened his laptop. He began to download pornography
unfamiliar to him—dozens of tabs, site after site, video after
video. All of them gay. He didn't even play them. They were of
no interest to him whatsoever. He just modified the metadata.
He just hid them, but not perfectly. They couldn't be discovered
too early. Lies can be refuted with time.

He knew he was better at this than any government analyst. Years on the dark web had prepared him for this moment.

He wrapped his victim in his sheets. He dragged her to his truck. He was sobbing. He had to pause to wipe away the tears and snot. He agreed with his father: He had always been soft. But he was also grieving. He loved her. She had been his first. He had not stopped thinking of her for eight years. The urge had become too strong. He had to track her down. No other girl had come home with him before. But she saw him for him. He would never forget that.

He had to dispose of her body. There was no way around that. But it pained him that she might be missing forever. That she would never be properly buried, properly mourned. That no one would know what happened to her. She deserved more than that. In the weeks that followed, it wouldn't even occur to him to buy new sheets—he punished himself by sleeping on the lumpy bare mattress. Maybe when things died down, he'd find a way to let them know. He'd save a piece of her. He'd lead them to her. His love.

Jordan had asked Gabriel, "You're accused of raping and killing a—Lord forgive me—quite hot piece of ass, and you neglect to tell me that you're gay?"

Gabriel had told him the truth.

"I'm not."

Sandy Grunwald, in a pewter-blue pantsuit and matching heels, climbs a pair of steps onto the compact dais. Domenico Santos is beside her with a hand outstretched—his left, displaying a wedding band—to help guide her up. He is in a muted gray blazer, no tie, and wearing a button on his lapel. It reads simply, "Sandy!" A cadre of supporters below them—small but vocal, and packed shoulder to shoulder in the boxy space—hold signs with the same exclamation in seafoam green. One of them raises a makeshift sign that reads, "A woman's place is in the House (and Senate)."

Dom steps up to the microphone. Sandy steps back.

"Good afternoon, Miami! Buenos días, Miami!" A cheer sweeps through the swarm at the sound of the native tongue. "My name is Dom Santos. I have the pleasure today of introducing my wife—a lawyer, mother, and tough-as-nails homicide prosecutor—Sandy Grunwald-Santos."

The crowd roars. A sea of signs flaps furiously.

Sandy hadn't fought the hyphenate, much to her husband's surprise. She welcomed it. He had figured his fiercely independent, feminist wife would retain her last name, particularly one as politically potent as that belonging to her legal giant of a father.

"There's no way a politician from Miami can get anywhere without a Hispanic last name," she had explained cynically. "It's a no-brainer."

Being partner to Sandy Grunwald meant perennially excusing crass statements just like that.

"For the length of her professional career, Sandy has sought to keep this community safe by keeping violent criminals off the streets. She has sat with the families of the slain, comforted them, and led them through a complicated and at times frustrating justice system. She has advocated for their loved ones— and won, time and time again. She has been there for us, and now she needs us to be there for her. Can we count on you to do that? Are we ready to roll up our sleeves and put in the work for Sandy?"

Dom pauses for the applause break. He is met with an orgiastic affirmative response.

"She has done all this while recognizing and striving to change from within the system's cruelest inequities: racial disparities that jail brown and black folk disproportionally, out-of-control drug mandatory minimums, private prisons more interested in their bottom line than humane conditions, and cash bond requirements that keep nonviolent offenders in custody simply because they're poor. Make no mistake: If we send Sandy to Washington, we send a progressive champion with the prosecutorial bona fides to get stuff done. Florida has sent only one woman to the U.S. Senate in our history. Let's make sure Sandy's the second. And this time: She'll be a Democrat!"

The partisans trill delightedly. Dom turns and flashes Sandy a smile. The atmosphere is electric.

"So, without further ado, I present to you your next U.S. senator from the great state of Florida. Sandy!"

The couple exchange a kiss.

"Go get 'em," Dom whispers in her ear.

She plants her palms facedown on the lectern. She basks in the adoration. She waves at no one in particular. She gives herself enough time to calm her rebel heart.

ACKNOWLEDGMENTS

Ever since I first learned to grip a pen, I've been writing. As a boy at recess, I sat off to the side with a spiral notebook on my lap, scribbling stories. For my birthdays, I'd draft a script and corral my friends into acting it out and filming it on a camcorder. In high school, I put out weekly chapters featuring my closest friends as the characters. At graduation, I wrote and delivered my first speech. My family and friends indulged me along the way—cultivating my passion, lending a sympathetic ear—and I am indebted to them.

My parents, Moises and Patricia Peguero, came to this country separately as young adults, not knowing the language. They met and served in the U.S. Army, worked blue-collar jobs, and provided for my sister and me. I thank them for their generosity and care. My sister, Kristhy Peguero Pollack, has always stood by me as my best friend, confidante, and counselor. Simply put, I am here—I am *anywhere*—because of her. I do this all to make you proud, Kris. My brother-in-law, Brad Pollack, is a well of encouragement and advice, and my beloved nephews, Brooks and Walker Pollack, light up my life and make my heart swell. To my friends who have known me since we were kids—Kathy Rodriguez, Luis Serpa, and, of course, Christina Millares, who sweetly devoured my high school chapters with zeal—you all are saints for sticking by me, even past those years of teenage angst! I've been fortunate to make solid, strong, and joyful friendships that mean everything to me, with lovely people like Amanda Bosquez and Adam Rankin, Salvador Perez, Robert Fuentes, Angie Mancillas, Erika Rubino, Yasser Navarrete, Amanda Daniels and West Holden, Nadia Haye, Leah McGuckin, Wally Hernandez, Barbara Barreno, David Gomez, Brandon Mordue, Georgina Sanchez, and Rosana Quezada. Thanks for choosing me.

Educators convinced me to take my talent seriously. Thanks go to my high school English teacher, Nell Miller, for seeing something special in me while keeping me grounded, writing a simple "Try Again" on one of my first papers, and to my high school history teacher, Rick Stamper, for fostering pride in my writing. In law school, my criminal law professor, Dan Kahan, and his insights on motivated cognition shaped how I viewed juries as a trial lawyer and how I treated them in this book.

I've spent countless hours reading, writing, editing, proofing, dummying, and debating process within the various publications on which I've served. I thank my colleagues who likewise got their hands inky alongside me. From the growing pains of high school journalism in the *Gator Times*, to the summer I spent crisscrossing Broward County for human-interest stories for the *Miami Herald*. From the editors of the *Harvard Crimson*—you all intimidated the hell out of me; thanks, Margaret Ho, for being my saving grace—to the editors of the *Harvard Law Review*, where I felt I came more into my own. I grew as a person through it all. Two other organizations lifted me up: First, the Harvard Defenders was my crown jewel, a remarkable opportunity to provide indigent defense, fellowship with like-minded people, and burnish my leadership skills. Thanks to all of you who let me do it, put your confidence in me, and don't now hate me for having become a prosecutor! Special thanks go to John Salsberg for his suave mentorship and Hannah Scoville for her steadfast support. Second, Eliot House—in particular, Gail O'Keefe and Doug Melton—granted me a do-over where I could rewrite my history with the college, mentor inhibited students just like me, and stop worrying and just love the bomb that is Harvard. Becoming a resident tutor meant the world to me. Thank you to my students for that gift. Colleagues like Brandon Tilley, Timnah Baker, and Liz Maynes-Aminzade watched out for me. I appreciate you, friends.

Professionally, I've been guided by whip-smart and magnanimous people. Congressman Charlie Rangel gave me my start fresh out of school at twenty-one years old. A good man with a larger-than-life personality, he insisted that only I perform his Google searches because he both misunderstood how easy it was to do and thought I had some special skill in doing it. Working for him, beside role models like Emile Milne and George Dalley, was an honor. I am grateful to Senator Amy Klobuchar for next bringing me into the fold of her Senate staff. Both the congressman and senator were former prosecutors and progressives who commanded credibility in talking about criminal justice reform, and I learned a great deal from them.

Prosecution can be a trying profession, particularly when dealing with incredibly tragic loss of life. I got through it with a little help of my friends. Supervisors like Kathleen Hoague, who always had my back, and Lara Penn, who took me on my first murder trial as a fledgling prosecutor, were invaluable. Thank you to the attorneys I supervised and came to adore: Gabriela Alfaro, my successor; Alexandria Lewis; Michael Sartoian; Yaneth Baez; and every junior attorney who passed through my division. You are family to me. I had the good fortune of appearing before some good, fair, and even-keeled judges, like Miguel de la O, among others. And it was all thanks to Katherine Fernandez Rundle, who hired me and entrusted me with important and interesting cases, including, most recently, the prosecution of police officers for excessive use of force.

I am a novice to book publishing, but many have held my hand and helped me navigate this foreign terrain. Melanie Tortoroli was an early advocate and friend who helped me get my sea legs when I first undertook this project. I am also here in no small part due to my agent, Michael Nardullo, who plucked me and my manuscript from a sea of query letters and dared to see potential. It was his faith in me and what I produced that started this whole thing. And it was my editor, Wes Miller, who was so enthusiastic from the start—I recall how thrilling it was to read his one-word review upon finishing my manuscript: "Wow"—and lent me this incredible opportunity. Thank you, gentlemen, for allowing my lifelong dream to come to fruition.

Thank you to the readers. Time is limited, and to think you spent any of it with me and my imagination unfurled in these pages is humbling. I am blessed beyond measure.

ABOUT THE AUTHOR

Robin Peguero spent seven years storytelling to juries for a living, most recently as a homicide prosecutor in Miami. An Afro-Latino and the son of immigrants, he graduated from Harvard College and Harvard Law School. He has written for the *Miami Herald*, the *Harvard Crimson*, and the *Harvard Law Review*, and he served as a press spokesman in the U.S. House and as a speechwriter in the U.S. Senate before becoming a lawyer. He is currently a U.S. House investigative counsel working on domestic terrorism.